Rough Ride on a High Horse

Jessie Irene Fernandes

iUniverse, Inc.
Bloomington

Rough Ride on a High Horse

This is a work of fiction. All of the characters, names, incidents, organizations, and dialogue in this novel are either the products of the author's imagination or are used fictitiously.

iUniverse books may be ordered through booksellers or by contacting:

iUniverse
1663 Liberty Drive
Bloomington, IN 47403
www.iuniverse.com
1-800-Authors (1-800-288-4677)

ISBN: 978-1-4502-7681-8 (pbk)
ISBN: 978-1-4502-7682-5 (ebk)

Printed in the United States of America

iUniverse rev. date: 1/20/2011

Acknowledgements

To Brian Anderson, Meredith Fane, Fred
Jessett, Mark Knoke, Joyce O'Keefe,
Roger Schwarz and Diane Spahr — thank you
for your patience through four
revisions of this novel. Thanks also to Dr. Julia
M. Stroud, psychologist and editor,
and Barbara DuVourUlrich, who corrected all my plooks.
Fellow writers Dee Barnes, Ward Harris, Larry Kerson,
Daphne Pilon and Jette Townsend who inspire me.

My thanks to you all for enriching my days, each in your unique way.

'Thanks for the Memories'

To my parents: Lt. Col. C.J. & Evelyn Muncie,
my siblings: Alice (Susie) Lawrence, Jean
McNamara and Robert C. Muncie.

Chapter 1

Why was I racked with guilt over something I wasn't guilty of? What can I do to exorcise the ghosts of the past so I can live free in the bliss of the present? I have come to believe that fear of the past ferments the sweet wine of my friendship with Hugh into acidic vinegar.

Those were my thoughts, when I awoke about two in the morning. I was happy, lying naked beside Hugh, my late husband Billy's younger brother, until I remembered that it was now the third anniversary of Billy's death.

Beside Hugh, in the dark of night, I enjoyed the gentle quietness that filled the room. A May breeze puffed at the curtains in the open window. Cooler now than earlier, it didn't call for more than the sheet which lay haphazardly over our bodies. I looked at Hugh, sprawled on more than his half of the bed, and smiled that he relaxed as completely as Cleo the Cat. She had spread herself lengthwise at the bottom, her head half hanging off.

I gazed at the ceiling, awash with conflicting feelings of pleasant debauchery, contentment and nostalgia for our long gone youth. Life had been simpler then. Or is it only that at sixty-three, I'm not so sure I know what I want?

Last year, Hugh and I had launched this fling on the premise of it being friendship with privileges, but no complications. We were both consenting, unattached adults and lonely. I guess I was intrigued a bit at defying convention during a life of conformity.

After almost two years of widowhood, at the New Millennium, I had felt it appropriate when Hugh suggested that we become lovers. I didn't feel guilty about that. It was time for me to enjoy the freedom of a new life. I had been happy ever since — except for the recent intrusion of the memory of Billy's terrible death. This happened most often when Hugh and I were together. Last night my happiness was shaken by ambivalence about the nature of our friendship.

Tonight, I tried in vain to escape the memory of the afternoon that I found Billy near death by pressing my face against the back of Hugh's neck and breathing his unique scent. But the memory persisted.

The pungent smell of newly turned earth. Across the field, Peg hangs clothes. I wave. She waves back. I spot Billy's John Deere Ripper.

His red flannel shirt on the ground. Running, calling his name, I fall to my knees, grit grinds into them. His eyes, intensely blue against the pallor of his face. His hands icy as I clutch them. His lips curve in a smile. He whispers my name.

"Minty, love ..."

"Billy!" I scream. Blood soaks the ground, jeans torn, his legs pinned by the teeth of the ripper. "I'll get help–"

"No." His hand clutches mine. "Stay ... Stay, love." Each word a gasp. His grip slackens, a weak smile, a gurgle. His eyes fade. The awful silence ...

Even then, I shuddered as the dreadful wail of anguish, which raked my throat raw, echoed again in my mind. The horror of witnessing his death, so much blood, the appalling feeling of helplessness, guilt and terror still chilled me. Only vaguely could I remember the aftermath; my indifference to the commotion of activity that followed. I was absorbed in the numbness of disbelief for months.

Why *now* was all the emotional turmoil of the past churning through my brain? The image of Billy's death hadn't dimmed nor had the ravages of aftermath diminished.

Too troubled to sleep, I eased out of bed and went to stand in front of the open window, letting the clean breeze of night cool my skin and calm my soul. Diligently, I masked the memory with a counter-irritant: reviewing my marriage.

Billy and I had been married nearly forty years when I first learned of his faithlessness five years earlier. What I had considered our 'happy marriage' had been a delusion. For years, apparently, Billy had been indulging in a series of infidelities. I don't know how I endured the humiliation of my ignorance, as I speculated on which of our friends had known the truth before I did.

When I discovered Billy's betrayal, I had ordered him from my bed. I was stricken equally by his fecklessness and the mortification of my naiveté. Nevertheless, I faced the community with my head held high. Even the ritual ceremony, the gathering of mourners, failed to alleviate my searing embarrassment and shame. The funeral had been for me a masquerade of condolences. As they embraced me, kissed my cheek or shook my hand, I wondered which mourners had known of Billy's adultery before I did? Wearing my mask of sorrow, I had expressed appreciation for their words.

Later, secure only in the affection of my dearest friends, with Hugh, Philabelle, Lynn and Sarah, could I acknowledge my unhappiness.

At the time of his death, Billy had been retired from his law practice less than a year.

"I'll have time to raise goats," he had said, enthusiastically, when he brought home Edna, a young female pygmy goat. "We can make our own cheese, maybe enough to sell."

At the time, I had asked myself 'And will I be making the cheese?'

As I gazed out at the field where he died, I wondered why I hadn't divorced him when I first learned of his philandering and gotten it over with. Instead, although I booted him out of our bed, I had let him sleep in the small back bedroom.

It was still a mystery — as was the question of why – whenever I reflected on my love affair with Hugh, Billy's death came to mind like an unwanted ghost? Witnessing his death had changed nothing. The scar from his cheating still hurt as sharply as my recollection of that ghastly scene. My damaged self-image was confirmed with each anniversary.

Soothed by the quiet night air, as silently and as gently as possible, I slid back into bed, easing the sheet and a cotton blanket over Hugh and myself. Still asleep, Hugh shifted. I put my arm around him, pulled myself closer, needing his palpable body to keep me in the present. Sometimes the degree of affection that I felt for Hugh worried me. I didn't want to get too emotionally dependant on him. I was ten years older than he and, in addition, if a husband of almost fifty years found a woman unattractive, how long would that delightful fancy last? In view of all that, I knew positively that I wanted our relationship to stay just as it was – the pleasure of friendship enhanced by good sex. I had had enough of love and romance with my faithless husband.

The Whitman brothers, Billy and Hugh, had remarkably different personalities. Hugh bore a physical resemblance to Billy as both were tall, with sturdy physiques and dark hair. But instead of Billy's intense blue Whitman eyes, Hugh's were a warm hazel. Billy was Hollywood handsome. Hugh's nose was not quite straight, his mouth a bit wider. The effect was less plastic than Billy's looks - more rugged.

Billy had been an educated and competent attorney. Socially, he had acted the role of the traditional gentleman of antebellum days. But with his peers he was just another brash, hard drinking, good ol' boy, who roared at scatological jokes and bragged about female conquests. I must have been an idiot to believe that he would change when we married.

Hugh didn't make that kind of social splash, but he was far from ordinary. A *true* southern gentleman, with a quick and dry sense of humor, he was also a staunch friend, compassionate and insightful; qualities that earned him respect and admiration as Whitman's senior physician. The same attributes had earned my deep esteem. Sharing a sense of silliness, and secure in our mutual affection, Hugh and I could disagree without damage to our companionship. Our times together enriched our lives.

It was Hugh who had healed my troubled soul the first year of my widowhood. Thanks to his patience and support, I learned to enjoy the freedom to live life on my terms instead of Billy's. Consequentially, I valued my independence.

I inched closer to Hugh in bed. Drawing strength and comfort from his presence, I pushed the past from my mind and reflected back to the previous evening.

May nights were warm enough to sit out on the side screened porch. Last night, I'd gone Greek for dinner: made mousaka, a tomato and cucumber salad with feta cheese, ripe olives, oil and vinegar. In the spirit of the Mediterranean, the dress I chose had a wide neckline and full skirt, which flattered my five foot nine frame. Since the increase of salt over pepper in my hair had dulled the original highlights, I pulled it back into a neat chignon and added distracting earrings.

The two of us had drunk an entire bottle of that strange Retsina. A bit tiddly, we teased each other with the lightheartedness of high school kids.

"I surely spoil easy," Hugh had said as we shared the chaise lounge after dinner. "Feasting on mousaka and Greek wine," he refilled my glass and handed it to me. "...and thou beside me, swinging in the wilderness."

"We're not swingers, Hugh. We're middle-aged lovers." At least he was middle-aged. I sipped the wine and swished it around my mouth. "How do you suppose they get that tangy flavor – like diluted turpentine?"

"The barrels it's stored in produce the flavor of retsin — hence, retsinated wine," he spoke with authority and lifted his glass to sample it.

"You're so smart. What is retsin?"

"Beats me!" he grinned, leaned his face close to mine and leered, "Why don't we run away from home and live out of backpacks on the beaches of Greece, like the college kids."

"Maybe because we're not college kids any longer?" I laughed.

"Killjoy! I think it's a good idea. I could quit shaving and you wouldn't have to wear a bra."

"Haven't I told you that I don't kiss men with beards? All those whiskers are full of germs." I half closed my eyes in what I hoped was a seductive look, and added, "But going braless sounds comfortable." I winced at the thought of the beginning droop of my breasts.

Hugh sat up and fumbled at the front of my dress, "I'll be happy to help you remove..."

"No, no. It's gotten too chilly out here," I protested and huddled against him.

"Let's go inside, then." He moved to extricate himself from our tangle on the narrow lounge.

In the living room Hugh settled on the couch with his feet up on a hassock. He pulled me down so I lay half across his lap. I was content, anticipating a romantic night together, except I was sorry that he was leaving in the morning for a week. A not uncommon moment of quiet happiness was shattered when Hugh spoke.

"Let's get married, shug."

Surprised, I jerked away from him, almost slipping off his lap, and exclaimed, "You're kidding, aren't you?" I felt a jolt of fright, a jab of pain – as if he'd hit me. Marriage violated everything we had promised each other. And scared the living daylights out of me.

"No, I've been thinking about this for quite awhile and it's time." With a finger, he teased strands of hair out of my chignon, which was Step-One in the art of foreplay. But I pushed his hand away, unwilling to let him renege on our compact.

I shifted my whole body around to frown at him. Compounding my alarm and my now disheveled hairdo, my dress twisted and bunched up. Hugh grinned as I struggled to maintain the appearance of modesty. I felt like a fool, because, under the circumstances, modesty was artifice in a liberated woman. There was, however, a significant issue at stake: the subject of marriage that, surprisingly, precipitated all the horror of Billy's death. Frantically, I shoved that dark cloud away and focused on Hugh.

"But we agreed when we ..." I tried to put it delicately and without sounding vexed, "... when we embarked on this liaison, we *agreed* that 'Once bitten, twice shy'. Friendship with privileges. We *agreed*, Hugh." My heart was beating unnaturally fast.

Hugh, drat him, slid his other arm around me. "Yeah, we did. But that was more than a year ago." He nuzzled my neck. "Your home-cooking works ..."

I pushed myself away, "Now wait just a darn minute." He was stronger than I was and held me, despite my halfhearted resistance. "I don't remember that 'my home cooking' was part of the deal. 'Lovers' is the word you used, not 'cook'." Lovers worked for me, but I didn't want to *fall in love* with a man ten years younger, and marriage suggested love. That raised the probability of being hurt again.

"Yeah, and the sex is great, isn't it?" He half closed his eyes and caressed my cheek, sliding his hand down my neck and further. This was Step Two that stoked the desire which had been smoldering in my breast all evening.

I was too liberated a woman to invoke the Virginia Rules for Polite Rejection of a Gentleman's Advances, so I sat up straight and said, primly, "Stop diddling with me, Hugh. We agreed that we both wanted to avoid a second disastrous marriage." His proposal had aroused an unfamiliar fear that constricted my heart. Aware that a medical conference was taking him away for a week, I struggled to keep my tone light and said, "I'm not ready to risk marriage yet."

I had loved Billy unconditionally. I believed that he loved me, only to discover that he loved a lot of other women, many younger and, I suppose, more attractive than me. Friendship and sex, absolutely. Affection even, but not love again.

Hugh cuddled me against his chest and brushed his lips against my cheek. "Minty, darlin', *I'm* not Billy and *you're* not Sheila. Marriage for us would be different. You and I have been friends since …" he turned on that twitchy smile that annoyed as much as endeared him to me. "I can't remember a time when you weren't an essential part of my life."

Hugh was right; we had grown up as close as family. I considered Hugh like Cole, another kid brother. During the winter, while our father performed his State Department duties around the world, our mother, Cole, Lynn and I had lived in the small town of Whitman, where everybody knew everybody else. We loved becoming best friends with the Whitmans and the two families were together often.

"That's true." I nodded. "But Cole deserted us for California. When he was here for Billy's funeral, I suppose he suggested that you keep an eye on me. Is that why you were so supportive?"

I felt Hugh smile against my now bare shoulder and he said, "No. He knew I'd had the hots for you and pointed out that now I had a chance to marry you."

My years with Billy had taught me that the old 'til death do us part' oath apparently diminished the passion that coerces young folks into a legal commitment. A promise that surely blinded us to each other's flaws – weaknesses that ultimately tarnished the magic.

Still expecting a sensuous frolic upstairs, I murmured, "But we had an agreement, Hugh."

He continued his silky stroking and fondling, which affected my heartbeat despite my pretending otherwise. Neither of us doubted where this fooling around would lead: straight upstairs to my bedroom as usual.

*   *   *

Dosing against the still sleeping Hugh, I understood his desire for marriage. By nature faithful, caring and a bit conventional, I guess, Hugh honored the vows of matrimony. Those qualities were significantly different from Billy and one of the many things about Hugh that attracted me.

Cautiously, I turned on my back and opened my eyes in the dark, asking myself why I felt so reluctant to marry him. The year and a half since Hugh and I had become lovers had been among the happiest of my life. I thought first of the good sex. That confession amused me, probably considered by society as too scandalous and inappropriate for a sixty-three year old woman. But deep inside, I knew my affection was more profound than mere sex. I felt an emotional link with Hugh —a bond, but not *bound* — as I had felt with his brother.

Billy had controlled our lives and I had willingly played the designated role of submissive southern wife and mother. Life with Hugh felt freer. I had no need to play a role with him. A chill of fear ran up my back. I *was* afraid that that lovely freedom would crumble and take away with it the delicate link with Hugh.

Dawn and his departure would come too soon. I pushed apprehension to the back of my mind, turned and inched closer to Hugh, drawing security from his strength, his dependability.

Nothing he had said or done at dinner prepared me to consider marriage. What was he thinking of last night to urge a change in our relationship? And how ironic that he chose this anniversary to do it. Ignoring that urge to make my point, I captured his hand and clung to it.

Chapter 2

The next morning Cleo the Cat landed on the bed with a thump, followed by Buck's big paw weighing down the mattress. Alone again in bed, I opened my eyes to a day bursting with summer sunshine.

"Ugh, dog breath." I reached out an arm to scratch the scraggly dark strands on Buck's head. Half standard French poodle and half heaven-only-knows, Buck's fur showed the stigmata of a mix: instead of curls, his coat resembled a poor permanent. He looked like a mutt, but, more important than appearance, he had inherited his mother's intelligence, sense of humor and loving nature.

Meanwhile, Cleo walked up my body to mark my face with a damp nose. My other hand stroked her silken fur. "Now if only you two could feed yourselves and give Edna fresh water and hay."

Then I remembered that yesterday Lee, our vet, had reminded me for the umpteenth time that pygmy goats needed company. "You'd enjoy a kid. They're more entertaining than a mature one," he had said, "and Edna's behavior indicates that she's lonely for her own kind."

I didn't know the first thing about goat care, but I knew that Lee was right. When anybody, even Buck or Cleo, came in sight, Edna raced over to the fence, butting it as if she had horns and bleating ferociously. So goat shopping was on the agenda for Friday morning.

Duty called, so I sighed and pushed myself out of bed. As I pulled on a robe and hustled down stairs to feed my greedy animals, the fact of this anniversary weighed me down, almost as much as the memory of Hugh's proposal. The prospect of playing bridge with the girls that afternoon seemed a daunting chore, unless I could improve my mood.

I fed Buck, Cleo, Edna and myself and went upstairs to dress to go out. My mouth was full of toothpaste froth when the phone rang. Wiping it off with one hand, I snatched it up.

"Oh Minty." I scarcely recognized Philabelle's voice. My sister-in-law, usually composed, her voice soft and melodious, now sounded like a fishwife — pitched high enough to hurt the ears as she rattled on so fast I could hardly understand her.

"I'm very disturbed! Morton says the town's going to tear down the Manse and build condominiums or stores." She paused and I heard her take a deep breath. "I told him I didn't want to sell and he threatened me. Said he'd take it by empirical demand or something."

I took advantage when she paused again to interrupt. "Whoa, now, Philabelle. Let's discuss this calmly."

With her petite, slender frame and feathery white hair, Philabelle appeared to be as delicate as an antique lace fan. Over the years, however, I had observed that, in her position as senior Whitman, she might bend with the wind like a willow, but she didn't break easily. Even Billy had listened when his older sister spoke. So I was surprised that she let Morton Trueblood discommode her that much. Election as Chairman of the Town Council had apparently gone to his head.

"Tell me just what he said, hon."

I heard her draw in a breath before she said, "Uh huh." Her voice still sharp with emotion, she repeated that, in his position as chairman, he said the city wanted to buy the Manse to make way for progress and, apparently, threatened to use the lever of eminent domain.

With Hugh gone to the conference this week, I'd handle it. I'd faced Morton down before on other issues.

"You know how Morton likes to throw his weight around, Philabelle. It's part of his delusion of Truebloods being one of the First Families of Virginia. This is just another of his cockamamy ideas. Hugh's at the medical convention this week and, since we ladies will be at your place for bridge this afternoon, why don't we hash it over with Lynn and Sarah." After their father's death, Billy and Hugh had quit-claimed the Manse to Philabelle. Now she was sole owner, but I tried to help her as much as I could.

"Do you think so? I'm sorry I got so upset. It's one of the nuisances of old age that we stress easily." Philabelle sounded calmer, but far from her usual aplomb.

"We'll work it out, but let's see what Lynn and Sarah think. If necessary, I'll speak to Morton myself."

"Oh thank you, Minty dear. The mere idea of the Manse being destroyed is devastating."

"Don't worry, Philabelle. Among all of us, we'll set Morton Trueblood back on his heels."

I heard her sigh deeply, presumably relieved.

She drew a deep breath before continuing, "When did Hugh leave?" Her voice dropped down a decibel or two, to just about normal.

"About four this morning. He'll call later today."

She paused and I visualized her smile. Then she changed the subject. "Minty dear, I'm happy that your friendship with Hugh is blossoming so nicely."

I couldn't restrain a laugh at that. "Our friendship 'blossoming'? Oh, Philabelle, I do love you. You're a treasure." I wondered how many in Whitman knew the extent of that 'blossoming' by now. Not that it would be openly discussed. That was not the way of our people – discrete exchange of eye contact and concern for someone's welfare substituted for gossip in Whitman. That was why I hadn't known about Billy until Carmen Schultz blatantly announced it to me on the church steps one Sunday.

I hadn't liked the Schultz's since then. They were new to Whitman and not really one of us. Carmen had mentioned that she'd like to join the Fourth Committee, but I ignored her hint.

Anyway, once I recognized the advantages of freedom, I enjoyed defying convention. Hugh and I had been very discrete. My farm had made it easy.

Philabelle continued, "I'd feel more secure if I knew that someone in the family, you and Hugh, for instance — or even one of the grandchildren: your Jesse or Hugh's Smith — would move into the Manse after I go into an old folks home." She sounded wistful, which was difficult to refute.

"Oh come on, Philabelle. You're only seventy-three. It'll be years before you're eligible for an old folks home," I said.

Although her approval of my relationship with Hugh touched me, at the same time, it annoyed me. I hadn't let Philabelle feel that, however, because it was natural for her to assume romance. Pure carnal sex, even leavened with a solid friendship, might offend her. Besides, my annoyance originated not at her assumption. Its source, I knew, was my rejection of developing feelings for Hugh deeper than friendship. In a way, I did love Hugh, the way I loved Philabelle, my friend Sarah and even my contentious sister Lynn. That was the way I wanted to keep it. Therefore, I didn't mention Hugh's proposal. I exhaled all those fears and wished that I felt as confident about dealing with Hugh's proposal as I did with handling the Morton Trueblood situation.

When Philabelle apparently felt reassured enough to ask about my three children, I answered, "The latest is that William Hamilton Whitman the

Third has been promoted to partner in his *prestigious* law firm. He's very pleased with himself, of course."

"And well he should be. I've always thought that, being the oldest child, he developed a sense of responsibility quite young." Philabelle always saw the best in people.

Although William embodied many of the social customs and manners of wellborn southerners, he didn't hold with the Re-enactors who still talk of people 'who don't know their place'. Many turn a blind eye to the fact that their ancestors were *not* landowners, but merely po' white trash. Election time seemed to inflame their unfortunate indignation.

I agreed about William's sense of responsibility , but asked, "That may be so, but what made him so pompous?" As evidenced by his use of his entire name for his signature.

"He may have inherited it from my father," she paused and added, "I've always believed Billy's indiscretions were a form of rebellion against Papa's rigidity."

Indiscretions, I thought. That was a euphemism for his randy behavior. Struck by either guilt or grief, I couldn't answer. Billy did everything in excess. It was that passion that made him such a successful advocate for his clients. It was that passion that enticed me into our marriage — and, in the end, destroyed it.

After we hung up, I dressed. Ready to go, I let Buck out for a visit to the pasture. A mischievous boy, he woofed at Edna before I pulled him away. Edna balked at going near him and bleated loudly in protest. I scolded Buck and he pretended shame, then I mollified poor Edna with a bit of coddling scratching plus a handful of sweet hay. Ironically, Buck headed to the very field Billy had been clearing the day he died.

That reminder of Billy's big plans for a cheese industry plunged me back to the day of his death – images still sharp enough to ache. The pain didn't end just because the marriage did, especially on an anniversary day.

If I'd been the crying kind, I would have shed a tear or two, but not in self pity. Learning of Billy's infidelities, followed so closely by his terrible death, tarnished what had been unequivocally happy memories of our marriage. That loss deprived me of forty years of my life and, at that point, nothing else mattered very much. I had Hugh to thank that my children and my friends were once again a joy to me. He was an important factor in putting life in perspective for me.

Startling me back to the present, Buck returned and we went inside.

More immediately troubling than the past, however, was how to cope tactfully with Hugh's proposal. I *loved* my life just the way it was. I was not prepared to surrender it lightly.

*   *   *

Later, I was about to leave when the phone rang. Almost tripping over the dog and cat, I grabbed it, and said, "Hello?"

"Mom, I'm so glad you're home." It was my daughter Rachel – remembering her father's death, probably. "Can I bring the kids and stay with you for awhile?"

Struck by tension in her voice, I asked, "What's wrong?" A new disaster for me to deal with?

"Nothing," she said. "Everything's fine, perfectly normal."

Only a disaster or a sick child could push her father's death out of her mind and raise her voice to that shrill tone.

"Is there a special reason to come down now?" I added hastily, "Not that you need a reason other than the pleasure of a visit."

"I just want to … eh, bring the children down." Her pause belied the excuse.

I decided getting the details could wait, so I asked, "Just you and the kids? Howard not coming?"

"No. He's busy with an important case. Can I come today? I'm almost ready to leave the house now, Mom."

The urgency in her voice confirmed my apprehension. Oh crumbs. "I have bridge this afternoon, hon." I wasn't prepared for company, even my daughter.

Rachel interrupted my thoughts saying, "We wouldn't get there until after dinnertime anyway."

"Well. Sure, come today then." I wondered about the urgency. The kids could go goat shopping with me tomorrow."

The fact that Howard was not coming disturbed me, but a phone call was not the time to ask questions. Rachel and Howard had very different personalities, but I'd always considered them happy. Well, I'd find out when she arrived.

I supposed I was not a particularly good mother, but I'd had reservations about her marriage. Not their compatibility, but more about their decision to have two children in less than three years; 'before we get too old' they'd said. Rachel was a very bright young woman. She graduated from Princeton and Harvard Law and loved practicing in the same firm as Howard. Now she was a thirty-seven year old mother stuck at home with two preschool youngsters, one barely out of diapers. I knew that feeling.

Some great thinker, probably a woman, said, 'Once a mother, always a mother'. With all three kids adults and out on their own, I had believed my mothering days over. Ha!

"You can't live your children's lives," I muttered to Buck and Cleo. But I couldn't refuse my daughter's plea for help, so I tried not to consider this an intrusion into my already unsettled state over Hugh's proposal.

Of all my friends, he'd been the most understanding of my emotional turmoil after Billy's death. Hugh had experienced the same demoralizing state when Sheila divorced him and during the custody battle over Smith, who was only ten at the time.

What Hugh and I both had wanted was a monogamous relationship without the complication of marriage. His apparent change of mind added to my own ambivalent feelings about him and purely scared the tar out of me.

Chapter 3

Approaching the Manse that afternoon, I looked at Philabelle's home differently. Since the early 1800s, it had been called the Whitman Manse by everybody since what Billy had called The War of Northern Aggression. Some still retained delusions of the mythical grandeur of antebellum society, ignoring the existence of slavery and a flourishing middle class. My husband had possessed a slightly skewed sense of humor and used it ironically.

The reconstructed Manse derived architecturally from both Georgian and Victorian styles; a bastard architectural structure, I thought. A deep porch behind white columns incorporated an octagonal turret on the north side and a porte-cochere with a side entry on the south. Every time I drove in past the old oak tree, however, a sense of the structure's past and its place in Southern History gave me goose bumps. Our respect for the good manners and values of Whitman heritage was one thing Billy and I had shared and encouraged in our children.

I, probably more than Billy because of my northern college education, deplored the hypocrisy with which descendants of wealthy plantation owners define those days. Not that they were bad people, but too often they ignored their ancestors' dependence on those 'in trade' and 'in service'. They still displayed an unattractive sense of entitlement.

On this anniversary, however, thoughts of Billy filled me with the galloping glooms, but, like a true Southerner, I forced them deep down in the recesses of my mind. I didn't want to dump my mood on the others, especially Philabelle. She was not only my sister-in-law, but the dearest of my three best friends. My younger sister, Lynnetta Burgess Elliot, my friend, Sarah Levin, Philabelle and I made up a foursome.

The bridge game had been on our agenda how many years? Since my kids grew up and left home, at least fifteen.

Although the Whitman and the Burgess families resided here in antebellum days, my sister Lynn, brother Cole, our mother and I really spent only the school years from September through June. Each summer, we had joined our father in whatever country the State Department assigned him. It was not until the 1950s that my family had moved permanently to my mother's family farm in Whitman — where Billy and I lived after my father died — my home now.

My friend Sarah and her husband, Mel, had moved down from New York nearly twenty years earlier when his father assigned him management of the New Emporium branch in New Kent. Sarah and I had been roommates for four years of college and formed a solid friendship during that seminal phase of our lives. Her natural good nature and New York pragmatism had quickly endeared her to Philabelle and Lynn. Now, although Mel, as CEO, traveled a good deal, they were established residents of Whitman.

When I got to the Manse, Sarah's car was already parked in the side drive. As Lynn drove in, I waved at her. Philabelle had set the luncheon table on the inside sun porch. I waited for Lynn, who was the most truly beautiful woman I personally knew. Petite, making me looking taller than I, but womanly, blonde — with dewy blue eyes like our mother plus ten years younger than I am.

She and our brother Cole got the good looks in the family. I resembled my father, which was not a bad thing, but next to the deer-like Lynn, I sometimes felt like a Jersey cow.

Today, she was a princess in a flowery voile dress with a swingy skirt. If I didn't love her, I might hate her.

"Just come from Florrie's Wash and Wave, have you?" I called, playfully.

"No," she snapped. "I'm just naturally gorgeous and sick of being envied." The spite in her voice surprised me, because usually she was as sweet natured as she was good-looking.

I suspected that Lynn's life hadn't been as much fun as blondes are reputed to have. She messed around with a variety of men. Some were good candidates for long-term alliances, I thought. Others were nothing but randy goats. I had pointed that out to her more than once, reminding her that I had set an example of a successful marriage. Unfortunately, that had annoyed her.

She had not appreciated my concern and justified her behavior by pointing out that "women should claim equal rights in sexual patterns as well as equal pay in the work force."

I didn't pursue the issue any further at the time. To everybody's surprise, shortly after that incident, she had married Elliott, a man much older than she. I suspect it wasn't the romance of the century. Even now, as a rich widow, how merry was she really? Or maybe my own doldrums had colored my perspective.

As we devoured exquisite currant pecan scones and homemade jam, Philabelle repeated her tale of Morton Trueblood's designs on the Whitman Manse.

"I wouldn't fret about it, Philabelle," Lynn said. "He's an asshole."

"Why, Lynn, I'm surprised at your language." Philabelle shook her head at my sister.

"He may be all that, but he had the moxie to recruit that Washington developer to build the Creek Woods Retirement Residence – and that's not schlock," Sarah said, taking a bite of scone.

With an air of indifference, Lynn shrugged, "I suppose." Not at her most vivacious obviously.

Although Lynn always exuded elegance, lately I had detected an unusual brittle edge to her voice. Not for the first time, I noticed this air of indifference plus a new judgmental attitude. This disturbed me, but neither Sarah nor Philabelle had commented, so perhaps I was imagining things.

These three women and I had shared our ups and downs, laughed and cried together. Heaven knows, I nearly drowned them with my tears over Billy's treachery. I doubt that there were four females, so dissimilar in personality, size and shape that were as close as we four. Sarah, who complained of being a bit zaftig, still had thick dark hair and gypsy eyes. Of course, Lynn had always been the beauty of the family; I was tall, wholesome looking and smart. Philabelle, still very feminine, had fluffy, snowy white hair, while mine had more salt than pepper and was not quite straight as straw.

Philabelle and Lynn fancied playing the role of Southern belles. Sarah, a product of Brooklyn, and I, like my cosmopolitan father, were more sophisticated. All of this was on the surface. 'Mary O'Grady and the Colonel's Lady are sisters Under the skin,' I remembered.

Lynn and I were widows and Sarah claimed that she might as well be because Mel traveled so much. As I finished my scone, I glanced at Philabelle, a maiden lady, but not unacquainted with romance. During my period of being mired in the 'slough of despond', she had confided her sad love story to me. Perhaps the sense of aloneness bound the four of us together.

After we had thoroughly demolished the tasty fruits of Philabelle's kitchen, we discussed and then dismissed Morton's threat regarding the Manse. I'd clue in Hugh when he got home for his opinion.

Sarah wiped her lips on a napkin, "Hey, gals. Are we going to play bridge here or just continue noshing?"

We decided on bridge and, over our hostess' protest, the three of us cleared the table. Settled and ready, we played several hands. Philabelle and I won the first two games. I shuffled and handed the cards to Sarah to deal. Delighted at having a powerhouse in spades, after Philabelle passed, I bid two spades, over Sarah's two hearts. I was eager for some fancy finessing.

"Minty obviously wants to go to game," Lynn sighed as she looked at her cards. "So we might as well throw in our hands."

"No," I exclaimed. Despite my hand and, depending on how the rest of the trump fell, there was a chance that I might go bust. And we were vulnerable.

"If you want game, you'll get it as usual." Lynn tossed her cards face up on the table defiantly.

"Shoot, Lynn! I wanted to play this hand. You talk as if I always get what I want."

"Well, you do," she snapped.

The suggestion of anger in her voice surprised me. "What'd I do to get your bloomers in a twist?" I made light of her comment.

Aiming those big blue eyes at me, Lynn said, her voice scornful, "You don't seem to remember that today is the third anniversary of Billy's death." Even a scowl didn't mar her beauty.

My mouth fell open with surprise. I sat speechless as she continued.

"You wanted Billy. You married him and then turned your back when he needed you most." Lynn's tone was definitely hostile.

"Wait just a minute, girl. Billy's the one who turned his back on me with his ever-lasting cheating. He slept with every woman in town. Except you three, of course. For which I'm grateful." I squelched my annoyance and looked at my cards.

Sarah's and Philabelle's heads swiveled as if watching a tennis game.

Then Lynn almost sneered at me. "Don't be *too* grateful. He quit sleeping with others when I asked him to." She took a breath, smirked at me and said, "You took him away from me once, Araminta Burgess Whitman, but he dumped all the others when I beckoned him with a finger!"

As if I'd been struck in the stomach, I gulped with nausea, reliving that Sunday morning after the church service when Carmen Schultz had slapped me with her malicious revelation. A terrible way to learn of my husband's infidelities.

In the silence, I was conscious that Sarah was looking down at the cards splashed across the table. I heard Philabelle's quiet words, "Hush, Lynn, don't ..."

"I'm just so sorry if I upset y'all," Lynn snarled at Philabelle, and then glared at me, a flush spreading up her neck. "But I can't stand your indifference..."

"Indifference?" When I'd made such an effort to not mention my grief. "You know how deeply hurt I ..." Pink now flushed her face as she interrupted.

"But you didn't waste any time taking up with Hugh, did you? And today you haven't said one word about Billy." Lynn's voice cracked.

"Hugh's my friend – our friend. We've always been ..." I was astonished at her attitude.

"He hovered around you at the funeral like a dog in heat and you ..." She was outright crying now, tears like glitter ran down her porcelain cheeks.

I scarcely remembered the funeral and had tried to forget the day that I found Billy dying in the meadow. Lynn's attack, her lovely face redolent with grief, revived all my pain and humiliation. In a white hot flash, I realized the significance of her words: 'he quit sleeping with the *others* when I wiggled ...'

"*You* were sleeping with Billy?" I jumped up so fast the chair fell over. Stunned dumb by this double betrayal, I stood breathless, with my mouth hanging open, then managed to say, "All the sympathy you oozed while I wept my heart out over that man ...!"

Lynn sobbed and Sarah fiddled with the cards. Philabelle, hands folded in her lap, watched Lynn and me, alarm plain on her face.

When I could speak again, I heard myself screech, *"And all that time you were sleeping with my husband?"*

Lynn rose, both hands on the table, so we stood face to face and leaned close. "You said you didn't care. I didn't sleep with Billy until you discarded him." Her face crumpled, as she wailed like a wounded child and plopped back in the chair.

"I never *discarded* him," I roared, in full fury now.

"You did, too." Breathing in gusts between sobs, she stuttered, "You said you didn't care anymore."

I thrust my face at her, "You're a slut, Lynnetta Burgess Elliot! *Good lord!* You and Billy Whitman both betrayed me — my own sister and my husband!"

With a howl, Lynn shot up and yelled, "I don't have to stand here while you ...you ... blaspheme me." With a swirl of her flowery skirt, she stormed out of the room.

Philabelle and Sarah, like a pair of statues, didn't blink while we heard

18

the screened door slam. Nor move as the roar of Lynn's Mercedes faded when it spit gravel through the porte-cochere and down the drive.

I inhaled deeply several times, in a vain attempt to regain my composure, and said, "Y'all were there when Carmen Schultz mocked me about Billy's infidelities." Later, I had laid open my mortification at my naiveté before them, counting on their loyalty, their compassion. If one of *them* had been that vulnerable, I would have warned them and saved them from humiliation. Desperate for their support, I looked from one to the other, longing for a hint of sympathy, if not shame at having exposed me to public embarrassment. "And now with Lynn …" Feeling doubly betrayed, I reminded them, "You know how I wept like a child, baring my broken heart before you, but I never said I didn't care, did I?" The silence stretched.

Without meeting my eyes, Philabelle nodded vigorously, lips pressed together, obviously upset.

Sarah, as usual, spoke bluntly, "Yeah, you *did*, Minty." Her face showed reluctance. "You clearly said you 'didn't give a good goddamn who Billy slept with anymore as long as he never got in your bed again'."

Chapter 4

I left Philabelle's in a fury that lasted the entire five miles to my own home. Neither of them had offered me a morsel of comfort.

Sarah had said, "Lynn was a klutz to sleep with Billy, but she obviously believed that you wouldn't care."

I stared at her in utter disbelief. "How could I not care?"

Philabelle, ever the peace maker, said, "It was inconsiderate of Lynn, but ..."

"Inconsiderate?" I sputtered. "How about Lynn's treachery? And now from you – my best friends."

Philabelle reached for my hand and said soothingly, "I appreciate your pain, dear, but it was unkind of you to call her a slut."

"Unkind? She *is* a slut!" I jerked my hand away, stung, my throat tight. I raised my voice, something I'd never done before with my sister-in-law.

As if she hadn't heard my angry retort, she continued her gentle rebuke, "Therefore, as the elder, it behooves you to take the initiative in making amends to Lynn."

"Philabelle, she slept around with I don't know how many men." I couldn't believe these *friends*. "She could have at least left my husband alone."

Philabelle licked her lips and looked away from me before she said, quietly, "I think it likely that it was a combination of my brother failing to leave Lynn alone and her long time affection for him."

Sarah, who had stood silent during this exchange, added, "Lynn's floundering, Minty. Go on! Be a mensch, forgive her and Billy. Get on with your own life."

"Well! Thanks a lot for your support." I pushed myself and my wounded feelings out of the chair to go home. My smoldering anger was overlaid with righteous indignation, my mood seesawing from rage to feeling abandoned.

A pity I had been too shocked to tell them off properly.

✳ ✳ ✳

As I turned into the drive of my farm house and parked in back, I heard Edna bleating and the reality of Billy's absence struck. After that dreadful revelation of his tom-catting, I had hated him. All that suppressed anger surged up at the sight of the lovely farmhouse that had been our home for forty years. I couldn't bear to enter it now filled as I was with thoughts of revenge for what Billy and Lynn had done to me.

The intensity of my anger frightened me. Gripped by an explosion of murderous rage, I pounded my fists on the steering wheel as if I could stab and tear at it, the palms of my hands, red and tender. They'd be bruised by tomorrow, I realized. The ache in my jaw forced me to unclench my teeth as I sat seething for a few minutes.

I got out of the car, but too inflamed to stand still, I strode toward the back pasture. The mid-afternoon sun beat on my shoulders as I crossed the field. Left to nature for three years, it was filled with goldenrod, ragwort and briars, which scratched my bare legs. Seeds and twigs pushed through my sandals as I plunged ahead.

As I approached the spot where Billy had died, despite the heat, I shuddered suddenly with fear. Momentum carried me till I stood on *that* spot.

I saw the crushed foliage. I smelled the odors of newly mown grass, mixed with blood.

I squeezed my hands into fists as if physical pain could override emotion, could quell the urge to destroy …

Reaching for relief, I closed my eyes, but the ghastly vision, the nauseating odor overwhelmed my balance. I gagged, re-orienting myself to the familiar and innocent looking pasture in which my feet were planted. I felt compelled to stand where Billy died, a need to challenge his intrusion into my relationship with Hugh.

I heard myself shout, "You're *dead,* Billy. Get out of my life." Dizzy and exhausted with rage, I fell to my knees.

As I knelt alone, the field around me shimmered and tilted. A nightmarish sense of unreality enveloped me. I hugged myself, frozen to silence, held on to consciousness, until I was able to struggled upright, feeling faint.

Summoning my strength, I shouted, "Leave me alone, Billy."

A dark mist eddied and swirled in front of me and a voice whispered, "Minty ... Minty ..."

Sweating with fear, I mouthed, "I don't believe in ghosts."

As if from within an echo chamber, Billy's voice breathed, "Minty ..."

I heard my voice yell, "Go away, Billy. Go away!"

Oh, God! I turned to run back toward home. Scrambling through the foliage that dragged at my legs, I tripped and fell with my face in the weeds. Sobbing, I pushed them away with my hand, brushing against Buck's wet nose. I heard his familiar 'woof' of concern. I pulled against the sturdy dog, hauled myself up and stood, panting and trembling.

Barely able to speak, I stammered, "Oh, Buck." I twined my fingers in the scraggly curls at the back of his neck for security. My finger grasping his collar, I let Buck guide me home.

As we approached my farmhouse, I felt my fear began melting away. My hand still gripping Buck's fur, we hurried homeward, until I could hear Cleo yowling from the kitchen window, welcoming me back to sanity.

Panting, I collapsed on the steps of the stoop, wiped the sweat off my face and shook my head in equal parts of disbelief, fear and remnants of anger.

Good old Buck, with his usual animal instinct, sat on the step below me and rested his head in my lap. I purely disliked attributing this episode to unbridled imagination. I assured myself that I did not believe in ghosts.

Sorrow overwhelmed me, I yielded to tears and let them wash down my face. I pressed my fingers against my forehead until the pounding ceased. Buck rose, pushed his face closer and began to lick my cheek. Holding his face between my hands, I rested my cheek against the shaggy fur on his head. Finally, with a shaky laugh, I leaned back and let my ragged breathing return to normal.

Self-pity was for the birds, but today had taken its toll. A combination of the anniversary, the shock of Lynn's betrayal and her cruel reference to my relationship with Hugh had cut deeply. All this so soon after the surprise of Hugh's proposal.

The day had left me vulnerable to some psychic phenomenon, I reasoned, most likely an hallucination. Would I ever be free of the vision of Billy's pale, sweaty face, the blood, his voice fading away? His ghost continuing to haunt me? I hadn't caused Billy's death. It wasn't my fault. I hadn't done anything to feel guilty about — so why did I?

Sighing, I rose and greeted Cleo, who sat watching from the kitchen window sill.

"Come on, Buck," I opened the screened door to the back porch and we were home. We trooped into the kitchen. Cleo, too, apparently sensed my mood. Jumping down, she rubbed herself around my legs, purring audibly.

Forcing myself to focus, I refreshed water bowls for my fur friends and poured myself a glass of wine. Then I sat at the table and sipped it. Satisfied, Cleo walked over and jumped into my lap, wet whiskers glistening. Stroking her soft coat helped me relax. Buck joined us. On his haunches, leaning against my thigh, his liquid eyes gleamed with compassion. Thank God for pets!

Back in control after the wine, I convinced myself that the whole episode resulted from my undeserved mistreatment by those dearest to me.

Well, not all my dearest, I remembered with a start. Oh Lordy! Rachel and my grandkids were due in – I checked the clock — an hour or so.

I stomped upstairs to dissipate my irritation by preparing a room for Rachel and the kids. After changing the sheets with unnecessary vigor, I busied myself in cleaning both upstairs bathrooms, put out fresh towels, emptied waste paper baskets. Activity kept my mind off my disloyal sister and friends.

As I worked, I grimaced at Lynn's accusation of my indifference. Ironic, considering the effort I had made to keep my melancholy to myself. Furthermore, her degrading remark about Hugh was unfair and I resented it. That would be hard to forgive.

Finished upstairs, I left that room and stepped over Buck, who snoozed in the hall. Back downstairs, I filled the animals' food bowls, expecting Rachel and the children soon. The children would distract me from my troubles, although, I remembered, Rachel might be bringing some of her own.

'Sufficient unto the day is the evil thereof,' I quoted, forcing myself to stay in the present. Tomorrow I'd check the date of the next town council meeting and settle Morton's hash. Meanwhile, I didn't see Adrienne and Hammie often enough to let adult problems interfere with my enjoyment of them. I'd make tomorrow a fun day for my grandchildren when we went goat-shopping.

∗   ∗   ∗

I was startled out of my doldrums by the ringing of the phone. Heaving myself up, I answered. Happily, it was my youngest son, Jesse.

"I thought you might like to hear my voice today," he said.

"I'm always glad to hear your voice, sweetie." I squelched the urge to ventilate all my anger by describing my day, including the 'visitation', but why cast a blight on his thoughtful effort to cheer me up? Instead, I said, "Your father has been on my mind much of the day. Life goes on, however, and I can't relive the past."

"Of course not, Mom. I'm glad you have Hugh to keep you company," I could hear his smile "… to get you out and have fun with."

"I hope you don't think I've forsaken your father." Aware of my sensitivity about my relationship with Hugh, I focused on playing my maternal role. I didn't mention Lynn's accusation.

"Not at all. I understand being alone, Mom. You know that and how much having Mike means to me."

"I do and I'm happy for you, hon." His voice helped to soothe the feathers ruffled by others as he reminisced about his father. "I have lots of good memories of Dad: the weeks we spent at the lake, playing badminton and croquet, riding," he said.

I was glad to hear that. I never wanted my children to disrespect Billy, but the word 'memories' triggered my recent experience in the field. I shivered as Billy's voice echoed from the nebulous form I had imagined. Suddenly I realized that Jesse had continued talking.

"… parents do," he finished.

"I'm sorry, Jesse, my mind slid back to those days. We were young then, too," I said. It was true. For years I had loved everything about our life: days were exciting with Billy and the nights romantic. My children were beautiful and reasonably well mannered. I had known my life was good, for a long time, until … I took a deep breath, determined to keep my mind on my son. What *he* had to say was more important than dwelling on an hallucination.

"That's okay. I just said that y'all spent lots of time with us as good parents are supposed to do." He paused before he added, "I feel incredibly lucky to have had you and Dad as my parents. Most of the time I didn't mind Rachel. William, even as a kid, was a tight-assed WASP Republican though!"

Hanging on to this time with my son, I managed a laugh and agreed, "Yes." It was hard to keep my own resentment from coloring my voice. My anger at Jesse's father and my sister kept overwhelming my concern for my children. I closed my eyes and visualized William. "Of course, that's how *you* remember him." I tried a chuckle. "*I* knew him as a child and I was proud of him. But, you know, he always made me feel guilty of something – no, inadequate is more precise. Thank God, I outgrew that! I remind myself that he's a successful lawyer and an excellent husband and father."

Just then I remembered what I needed to ask. "Are you and Mike coming down for the Fourth of July?"

"Will William be there?" His tone was impersonal, reminding me that if my son could be impersonal, so could his mother — which worked. Immediately I wondered again why William had turned out so self-righteous?

But it was better than turning out like his father, for sure. Hastily, I answered Jesse, "He'll be invited, but I'll let everyone know that I do not tolerate ungentlemanly behavior or discourtesy in my home. Neither would your father." Billy had his faults, but he was a man of fine breeding. And an attentive father: that was one reason I had let him stay after 'the revelation'.

"I know that." Jesse paused and I heard him exhale. "I know a lot about Dad, Mom. Nobody's perfect."

Neither Rachel nor William had ever mentioned the subject of their father's infidelity. In my dark moments, I believed they had to have known. Now, that wound – that they hadn't shown any concern about what effect it had on me – still ached. They must have known. Jesse, my most sensitive child, had the courage to acknowledge difficult truths, which eased my burden.

I was glad that Jesse and Billy had been close. For that one thing alone, I forgave Billy: he knew about Jesse, respected and loved him as I did. Any disappointment we might have felt was minimal compared to our apprehensions about the prejudice which Jesse might experience in the future.

Secure in the motherly mode now, I was tempted to confide in Jesse about Lynn's betrayal, but that was between Lynn and me. I didn't know whether or not the breech could be healed. Nevertheless, Lynn was Jesse's aunt and he loved her and I didn't want to change that. "Jesse, you didn't say whether or not y'all might join us."

"We're planning to. It would be churlish not to honor a family tradition. Besides, Whitman is the only place I know that still has a celebration that includes the entire town."

"An old southern custom. It's like voting — a privilege that should be valued."

"That's my sentimental Mom. Incidentally, Mike and I've been invited to carry the banner in the Gay and Lesbian parade for the group in Richmond."

My heart beat accelerated with concern and I took a deep breath before I answered, keeping my voice light, "That's quite an honor, isn't it?"

"Yeah, I suppose. It's something we feel we should do."

We chatted a bit longer. Jesse wanted to hear all the latest on his nieces and nephews and any Whitman gossip. Before he hung up he asked, "Do you know if Smith will be with Hugh on the Fourth?" I told him I didn't know, but I'd find out. Jesse and Smith were close enough in age that they played together as kids.

After we hung up, I sat like a stotten bottle on the couch to wait for Rachel. I worried over Jesse's news about the parade, about which I could do nothing. His life style could invite trouble, but I'm grateful that he had Mike.

They were not alone and that was something. As always, our chat had given me the warm fuzzy I needed.

I reflected on how I could fix my daughter's marriage and how to divert Hugh from his proposal without hurting his feelings. Jesse, I suspected, would side with Hugh.

Underlying those issues, however, was my feeling of having been abandoned by my friends. Never before in my life had I felt estranged from my sister as well as from Sarah and Philabelle.

I felt terribly alone.

Chapter 5

The sun set and that curious phenomenon called twilight descended. To me it always felt as if, for a couple of minutes, the earth quit spinning. Sunlight vanished, the breeze paused. I heard sounds so common we're not aware of them, until a hush enveloped me and the day died.

Morosely, I returned to the kitchen at the insistence of my stomach. Reheating leftover mousaka, I set the table and had just finished my dinner when I heard a car stop by the garage. Sure enough, Rachel honked the horn as she parked. I hastily cleared away my dishes and rushed out side.

"Hey, Grandma!" Adrienne, a four year old version of Rachel, dark curls bobbing, raced over to hug me. Hamilton, three and half asleep, stumbled along after her. Although he inherited the Whitman dark curls, his eyes were as blue as Howard's. His smile and disposition promised a strong resemblance to his father. That was a good thing, since Howard was steady in a wind storm where Rachel tended to be gusty.

After the tight hug from Adrienne and a wet kiss from Hammie, I held a hand of each of my grandchildren and we callously left Rachel to bring in the bags. The two children ran the gauntlet of welcome from the animals, squealing with excitement and pleasure.

"Have you had supper yet?" I asked.

"We ate in Howard Johnson's. I had a hamburger and Hammie had waffles," Adrienne said.

"With thirwup," Hammie lisped.

Adrienne shook her head vigorously, curls bobbing wildly. "But we didn't have any dessert. Mommy said no."

"I bet Mommy knew that I had dessert here," I said, loving their smiles. Okay, now let's go potty and then we'll have dessert." I led them into the bathroom downstairs and pulled out the step-stool for them to reach the sink.

"I go by myself now. But Mommy takes Hammie." Adrienne showed signs of being Miss Bossy, which I, as grandmother, found amusing.

"Fine, but don't forget to wash you hands," I said.

My granddaughter 'tsked and mumbled, "I know that."

Hammie and I, with Buck, waited in the hall.

"I thand up now," Hammie said, leaving me confused, until he asked, "Ith Buck a boy dog or a girl dog?"

"He's a boy."

"Does he thand up to wee-wee?"

I had no answer for that and, fortunately, Adrienne came out then, displaying "Clean hands, Grandma."

Rachel brought the bags in and headed upstairs, while I took Hammie in where he demonstrated his skill in 'standing up'. His aim was wobbly and he needed help with the hand washing, but we accomplished both before his mother came back. The remembered joys of mothering little ones — maybe the best part of marriage — washed over me during these mundane routines.

In the kitchen, I sat them at the table, put out cups of custard and a Fig Newton each. When I told them that on Friday we'd drive out to the farm to find a friend for Edna; they were excited about the adventure.

I was pouring glasses of lemonade, when Rachel joined us. My first look at her surprised me so that I had to bite my tongue. In the past, I would have characterized my daughter's appearance as elegant. Today, the words 'neglected', almost 'slovenly' came to mind.

Nevertheless, I greeted her, "Hey, sweetheart, sit down. Would you like something to eat?" I kissed her cheek, ignoring the slightly swollen, pink eyelids. "I understand you had dinner at Ho' Jo's." She nodded and flopped down on the chair I pulled out.

"Thanks for letting me come, Mom." With a sigh, she looked at the children. "Hammie uses a sippy cup instead of a glass. And only half a cup of liquid – before bedtime, you know." She wiggled her eyebrows reminding me of the trying days of potty training. A well prepared grandmother, I produced a sippy cup and then fixed a glass of iced tea for Rachel.

She listened pleasantly, even asked questions, when the children told her about the goat-hunting project.

"While we're gone tomorrow, why don't you contact some of your old school chums. You could benefit from an appointment at Florrie's Wash and Wave, too."

"At Florrie's?" She dismissed that suggestion as if appearance didn't matter.

I glanced at the children; Adrienne was dunking her cookie in her lemonade and Hammie's cheeks were puffed out as his little jaws worked. I caught Rachel's eyes, gestured toward the kids with my head and said, "Reminds me of you and William at that age."

"Except William never made the messes that Hammie makes," she said, a little irritably and moved to tidy up crumbs.

Amused, as Hammie chewed valiantly, I sipped my tea before I commented. "Yes, William was always mature for his age, but you and Jesse got into plenty of mischief. There were not many dull moments when y'all were kids." I caught a swaying motion of Hammie's head, but he jerked up and continued eating.

"Incidentally, Philabelle's looking forward to seeing y'all. I'll stop by with …"

Just then, Hammie's head dropped almost hitting the table, attracting Rachel's attention.

"It's time to get him into bed, if you don't mind." Her face reminded me of pictures of the young Philabelle, except, right now, Rachel's bore the stigmata of unhappiness.

"I'll take them up, if you want," I offered.

Rachel's light mood vanished. Her voice sounded weary as she said, "They expect me to kiss them at bedtime." She didn't smile as she took them upstairs.

Meantime, Buck woofed at the back door and, when I let him in, he begged for a treat. While he gnawed on a bone biscuit, I was aware that, with Rachel and the children here, I had little time to dwell on the wounds that I had just suffered. It helped.

When Rachel rejoined me, I asked, "Would you like something stronger for a night cap?"

Rachel shook her head, "No, more tea's fine."

I topped off her glass and we took our drinks into the living room. I sank into my recliner and Rachel, with Buck beside her, settled on the couch. Cleo jumped up behind Rachel.

Since Rachel's arrival, she had said nothing about her father's death. I assumed that she had forgotten that this was the anniversary. She looked so down-spirited that I didn't remind her. No longer the svelte young woman she was the last time I saw her, her clothes were drab, unbecoming and she needed a haircut badly. This was so uncharacteristic that it increased my concern about what impelled her to 'come home to mother'. A variety of marital problems flipped through my mind, but I suspected that she'd open up now that the children were not here.

Hoping to liven her up again, I asked, "How do Adrienne and Hammie like their new play-room?"

She answered in a voice, which matched her scraggly hair, her ill fitting and dowdy outfit in shades of mud and dead leaves. "They were excited at first, but, they're out doors a lot now that's the weather's nice." Rachel droned on, while Buck, on his haunches, gazed at her like a lovesick puppy.

"The way Adrienne and Hammie reacted to Buck reminded me of the days when y'all were young," I said. "We had some wonderful times as a family. Remember your Dad trying to teach you how to catch a baseball?"

The light glinted off unshed tears in Rachel's eyes as she nodded, obviously touched, but she didn't answer. Now, I thought, it was time for me to lower the boom.

"What inspired this sudden visit, Rachel?" She blinked and opened her mouth, but I continued. "You might as well tell me the whole story. It's pretty obvious that something's wrong."

"Don't hassle me, Mom. I'm just really tired. I'm home schooling Adrienne, which …"

"She's only four years old, for Pete's sake," I blurted out.

"I know, but she's very bright and needs the challenge. She has her own Alpha computer now and Hammie has a Sesame Street keyboard. Research shows that children start learning much earlier than previously thought." Rachel heaved a sigh of exaggerated patience.

"Don't they still need time to be kids? You know, to just *play?*" I asked. Rachel heaved a sigh of exaggerated patience and I saw her lips tighten.

"Well, of *course,* they play," she said coldly. "They take swimming lessons three times a week. Adrienne either has a friend over or she spends an afternoon at one's house twice a week." She recited these activities with considerable sarcasm and continued. "While she's socializing, I read with Hammie or we build something with Legos." Her voice rose several pitches. "He has a fire truck, tricycles, Big Wheels …" Then she started crying.

I produced a box of Kleenex, wondering how I could help. When she sniffed, blew her nose and seemed composed, I gentled my voice and asked, "I'm your mother, Rachel. Level with me. What's troubling you about your life?"

She shrugged and blew her nose and muttered, "Nothing that I should complain about, I suppose."

"There must be something. Have you made friends with any of the other mothers?"

With a sigh worthy of an old woman, Rachel recited, "At the pool, sometimes we talk about the children, compare notes on their progress." She grimaced. "Most of them with kids the age of mine – they're so *young.*" Rachel's voice caught in a sob that she tried to abort.

When she blew her nose, I noticed the ragged fingernails. *This* on a girl who had beautifully cared-for hands! Although I listened the way my mother had listened to me, I noticed the lack of make-up or earrings. My lovely daughter – neatly groomed and gowned — had turned into a drab, unkempt haus frau!

"Is that all y'all talk about? The kids?" I asked and handed her another tissue.

She leaned toward me, eyes staring at mine. "Don't misunderstand me, Mom. I love Adrienne and Hammie. They're good children – very smart. But they're kids." Rachel slumped, eyes unfocused, shoulders rounded as she wadded up the tissues.

"What do you do when you're not with the kids?"

Rachel heaved a sigh from the pit of her soul and, through sniffs, said, "I don't really have any time without them. By the time they're in bed, I'm ready for bed, too."

Detecting a hint of resentment in her voice, I commented, "You and Howard used to have plenty of social activities: cocktail parties, friends over for dinner, backyard barbecues. What do you do with your time together now?"

"What time together? Howard's a partner and works long hours. He even brings work home. He's involved in a couple of intriguing cases – legal challenges." No doubting the envy in her voice now.

Howard's long hours at the office — which I had learned, but ignored with Billy — worried me. I hoped his wife's lack of sex appeal hadn't dulled Howard's interest in her. Never a fashion maven myself, I did know that women couldn't afford to let themselves go, even at my age.

I said, "It sounds like everybody's enjoying life except you, honey. How'd you let that happen?"

Abruptly, my daughter sat up straight, scowling, and snarled at me, "I didn't *let* it happen, *Moth*er!" Buck's head jerked up, alarmed at the anger in her voice. He looked from me to Rachel as she ranted, "I have two small children to care for and it's an exhausting, twenty-four hour a day job."

Humph, I thought: I'd had three children and still found time to play with them, entertain with my husband and give some time to various community activities! Time to act.

31

"What you need is a babysitter two or three afternoons each week, to give ..." I began.

"Babysitters that you can have confidence in don't grow on trees. And they can't provide the intellectual stimulation *my* children need." Despite her anger, her spark of energy pleased me.

"Surely there are good pre-schools in Richmond for Adrienne. Children need time away from their mothers as much as mothers need time away from them. Also you look a mess: your hair, your nails. I'll take you shopping while you're here."

"Mother!" my daughter said, half crying, "Every since I got here, all you've done is criticize me: I need a hair cut, new clothes, the way I'm bringing up my children." Rachel grabbed a Kleenex, wiped hastily at her nose and continued her tirade, "I turned to my mother, hoping for some constructive support. And what do I get? Nothing but abuse."

Surprised that my intentions had been so misunderstood, I ignored her outburst and listened. Her spurt of spirit was exhausted. "I do my best with the kids and don't have time for Howard, to shop..." she wailed, "I know I'm failing ... at everything." She sagged back on the couch. "But I get so tired." Shaking her head, her wet eyes big with despair, she whispered, "I don't know what to do." She wept.

Rising from the recliner, I joined my stricken daughter on the couch to assume the motherly role. Arms around her, I let her cry, handing out tissues as needed, rocking her gently as the sobs diminished and crooning 'There, there, it's all right, sweetie' until, emotion expended, Rachel sat up, blew her nose and dried her eyes.

I rose and, in the kitchen, fixed a whiskey sour. In my absence, Buck had moved and now sat on his haunches by Rachel, paw on her knee. She was scratching his ears and gazed up at me, looking forlorn. "I'd like my kids to have a dog. We always had animals, but I'm afraid I can't cope."

"Sip this and relax, honey." I handed the glass to her. "I'm sorry I haven't been more sympathetic, but first, quit beating up on yourself. You've just forgotten that *you the person* exists." She nodded. I sat across from her and, trying to express my concern, I leaned closer and began, "You need a life of your own. First, you're entitled to have help with the kids. Check with the other mothers, contact local churches and pre-schools for reputable babysitters."

Rachel opened her mouth, but, suspecting that she was too drained to argue, I continued.

"With your organizational skills, you can schedule an activity that will challenge you, take you away from kids several times a week. There must be subjects you've always wanted to explore, hobbies you've wanted to take up, but never gotten around to?"

She had stopped crying. While she wiped her eyes and blew her nose again, I planned my approach. When she appeared more composed, she sipped the whisky sour.

"First," I suggested, "treat yourself to a trip to a spa for a complete makeover. Then check out book clubs, knitting or quilting." I chuckled anticipating her response. "Even that abomination we both deplore: the Daughters of the Confederacy, which you qualify for through the Whitman family."

This brought her first tentative smile. "Oh, Mom, not them. I'd really like something physically active." She gestured with her hands. "I feel stale, dull and, you're right, I do need a challenge." She gulped her drink and her face regained some color.

I was encouraged to see her relax and look pleased, as she mulled over options. I nodded, but didn't intrude. After a few minutes, she sat up straighter and said, "There *are* things that I've missed" Hands clasped in her lap, she gazed into distance for a minute. Then she met my eyes and said, "You know what I'd *really* like to do, Mom?" She leaned toward me, forearms on her thighs. "Take tango lessons! I've always longed to dance." She tilted her head a little, grinning with excitement. My mother's heart cheered.

For encouragement, I burbled, "You could take lessons, but something other than tango. How about clogging? All the rage now."

Rachel met my eyes, laughed and said, "I don't know about clogging ..." she yawned and I noticed that her dark eyes looked sleepy. "Excuse me. I'm really tired. You've given me lots of ideas, but I'm ready for bed now." She leaned down to kiss me on the forehead and we said 'goodnight.' Then she went upstairs, leaving me relieved that I had apparently helped her, despite our moments of irritation with each other. I sighed over the universal discord between mothers and daughters.

Chapter 6

As soon as I heard their voices, I crept into the children's room. We let Rachel sleep late. After Adrienne, Hammie and I finished our breakfast, the three of us spent an hour giving Buck and Cleo a run and setting up Edna for the day.

While they were upstairs with Rachel, getting dressed for our adventures, I called Philabelle and apologized for venting my hurt feelings on her. Gracious as always, she forgave me adding an admonition that it was my responsibility, as older sister, to made amends to Lynn.

"She was terribly hurt, Minty. Perhaps you're not aware of your importance to her." Philabelle was always gentle, never more so than when she felt the need to reprove me. "I suspect that you don't recognize her feelings as guilt and her need for your forgiveness."

"She's the one who offended me." I didn't want to take my anger out on Philabelle, so I struggled to modulate my voice. "Why on earth should I forgive *her*?"

"I appreciate the depth of your hurt, my dear. Believe me; I'm not justifying Lynn's action, but you are the elder and wiser. A more compelling reason is that you've had a happy marriage with three children who continue to enhance your life. Lynn hasn't …"

Pushed too hard, I interrupted Philabelle harshly, "Lynn lived the life she chose. Men fluttered around her like bees to a flower. She had plenty of chances for a happy marriage, but she *chose* to mess around." I felt my anger revving up again.

When I stopped to take a breath, Philabelle nodded. "A sign of unhappiness, a search for love."

"She was the family beauty and we all made excuses for her wild behavior. She's never had to work at anything, flunked out of college and now she's a rich merry widow."

"She's far from merry, I'm afraid. Would you exchange your happy marriage …"

"My *happy* marriage turned out to be merely an illusion," I said bitterly. I sighed, but didn't say anything further to Philabelle.

"Billy loved you and you were both happy in your family." I could almost see her smile by the tone of her voice, when she added, "It may appear now to have been an illusion, but your happiness was very real."

I choked back what I felt like saying; if Billy loved me so much why did he need other women? I had never reconciled myself to that anomaly. The answer was, obviously, that I was no longer attractive enough for him. I'd had to live with that conclusion ever since.

Before I could absorb what Philabelle meant about illusion and reality, she continued, "Yes, Lynn has physical beauty, but you've had a more fulfilling life. Not only with your beautiful family, but *you*, as an individual, have achieved a great deal. No one except you had the talent to galvanize the women into raising money for the school library. You rallied the congregations of both churches to work together on social needs. You… "

Too put-out to listen to that recital any longer, I controlled my voice enough to interrupt, "Hon, I think you're trying to sweet talk me into doing something I don't feel required to do." It wasn't easy for me to disagree with my sister-in-law, but I felt justified on this occasion to ask bluntly, "Why doesn't Lynn apologize for seducing my husband?"

Philabelle's voice was filled with affection when she said, "You know I'm not one to stoop to flattery. My point is that you're capable of forgiveness and I know you're generous enough to forgive Lynn as you have Billy, my dear."

Had I forgiven Billy? I wasn't sure about that anymore than I was sure about Hugh's and my feelings for each other. I knew Philabelle didn't do flattery, so I felt chastened. But I wondered why when *I* was the victim? Too fond of her to argue the issue, I made the effort to rise above myself.

Suppressing my anger, I nodded and said, "I value your opinion, Philabelle. As usual, you've given me something to think about …" I hesitated in order to find the words that I wished reflected my feelings, "… about family and compassion."

There! Although I had mended my fences with Philabelle, I had not actually promised to approach Lynn. I shoved aside the issue of whether I had forgiven Billy. Suddenly, tired of that emotional seesaw, I felt like throwing something – not my usual more effective behavior – so I paused to draw a deep breath to subdue my anger.

Fortunately, my conversation with Philabelle was interrupted when Hammie and Adrienne clattered down the stairs and burst into the room.

"What was that?" she asked. Glad of the distraction, I told her.

"I'd love to see them, Minty. If you're going out this morning, could you stop by?"

I drew in a calming breath and concentrated on my grandchildren. "We will," I said and then hung up.

I needed to chat with Rachel before we set out to find a friend for Edna. "While we're gone, why don't you check with your high school chums and stop at Florrie's Wash and Wave?"

She rolled her eyes at me, probably in exasperation. Then she shooed us out the front door saying, "Y'all have a good time and give Aunt Philabelle a hug for me."

*   *   *

Our first stop was at the Manse. Although Adrienne and Hammie saw their Great Aunt Philabelle on holidays, they were a little wary at first. She quickly coaxed away their shyness and, at her suggestion, I left them with her while I ran across Main Street to Clay Marshall's grocery store to order some of Ola's pastries. Also, Clay would know the date of the next town council meeting and I wanted to attend – with Philabelle, if she'd come.

The buildings on the east side of Main were easily a hundred years old, but well maintained and up-dated in a style appropriate to Whitman's early days. My sense of history was aroused when I acknowledged that Marshall's Groceries as one of the oldest, the business, if not the building itself, dated from the War Between the States. The original general store had served all the plantations and farms within a thirty mile radius. In the 1800s, an early Marshall peddler traveled from place to place with a cart loaded with a variety of items. The family story was that a Whitman donated property, the store was built, carrying grain and feed, plus cotton dress goods, ribbons and I don't know what all. Sometime after the War, that Marshall limited its stock to groceries and local produce. I was grateful that, so far, the town of Whitman had managed to escape the expansion of the nation's capitol, of Alexandria and all the suburbs. Urban sprawl was creeping down I-95 in our direction. Most of the residents were delighted that the expressway had by-passed us. Our two blocks of Main Street provided most of our needs and everything else was within reach half an hour by car.

My age group — except those we called 'the colored' in those days — had attended the local public schools, of course. Now there was one elementary and one high school for everybody and we had gotten acquainted with African American residents as friends and neighbors. Well, most of us had broadened our perspective. A few diehards had set up private schools for *their* children, flaunted Confederate flags on occasions and cherished their illusions of being descendants of the wealthy minority. Too many visions from <u>Gone With the Wind</u> and too little <u>Tobacco Road.</u>

The bell on the grocery store door jingled when I opened it. "Hey Clay, how're you?"

Clay had been quarterback on our high school football team and I had had a terrible crush on him back then. That was before Billy, a couple of grades ahead of us, took any notice of me.

"All I need is your charming company to make my day, hon." Clay was in pretty good shape for an ex-athlete and still had a fine head of mostly gray hair. He leaned on the counter, and flashed his killer smile at me. "Why've you been neglecting me? Seems like weeks since I've seen you."

"I was in yesterday, silly." Suspecting that he still had a soft spot for me in his heart, I obligingly giggled at his teasing.

"Seems too long to me. Let's have a Coke."

"Thank you, no. My grandchildren are at Philabelle's and I have to get back. Has Ola made her Friday delivery of fresh pastries?"

"Just brought them in less than an hour ago: chocolate éclairs today."

"I'd like a dozen, please. I'll take them out to the farm," I said and added, "Clay, you always go to town council meetings, don't you? When's the next one scheduled?"

"You going to run for office?" He turned and looked at the calendar on the wall with a view of one of the Hawaiian Islands. "This Thursday night at seven p.m. What's up?"

Briefly I told him about Morton's disturbing call to my sister-in-law about the Manse.

"Now why'd he go bothering Miss Philabelle?" Clay frowned, looking as exasperated as I felt, while he boxed the éclairs for me. "Nothing like that's been brought up at council, so you can put Miss Philabelle's mind at rest. Must be one of Morton's goofy ideas."

Relieved, I asked, "Why would he want to tear down the Manse anyway? It's one of the few Reconstruction homes left in the county. Although it does have a fair piece of frontage on Main Street." I glanced across at the new brick bank building south of the Manse and the office building on the north – both architecturally suitable for Whitman. "It is prime real estate, I suppose."

"Yeah, it is." Clay shrugged and handed me the box. As I turned to leave, I almost stepped on what I thought was a grubby orange mop on the floor.

"What's this thing?" I asked. It jumped and I identified a pair of ears and two golden eyes glaring up at me.

Clay, scowling, came from behind the counter. "That's my new cat, Minty, and I don't appreciate you calling her a 'thing'." He picked up the little critter and tickled it behind the ears.

"Gosh, I'm sorry, but it is sort of – bedraggled, isn't it? Where'd you get it?"

"Found her, out behind the dumpster in back one night. She doesn't look like much now, but wait'll I get her fattened up a bit. She'll be a good little mouser. I can tell."

I had my doubts, but he apparently had taken to her and a good mouser was an asset around groceries. I just agreed and said, "Cheerio, then."

∗   ∗   ∗

As I walked across Main Street to the Manse, I marveled at the relationships in small towns. Sam Warner and Joe Russo had been tackles on our high school team. Even Morton had joined us girls, plus lots of the merchants, teachers and mothers, on the sidelines as we cheered for the Whitman team versus teams from other communities. Ah, pleasant memories of our youth.

At the Manse, I saw the three members of my family out on the front lawn in the sunshine. Bless them, the two small dark heads accompanied the delicate looking white haired Philabelle, who was directing the little ones in picking pink primroses and white daisies – quite a sight.

When Hammie saw me, he toddled over the grass towards me.

"Fwowers, Gwanma." He handed me about five blossoms, their stems seriously scrunched by his sweaty hand. Touched, I accepted the bouquet and added the bunch offered by Adrienne.

"What charming kiddies," Philabelle said. "I understand you're going to find a friend for Edna?" I nodded and she asked, "Time for refreshments first?"

"No, thanks, I do want to let you know, however, that Clay thinks this bit is all a Trueblood fantasy – about buying the Manse, that is. You want to go to the next town meeting, Thursday, with me? Open it up for discussion?"

Philabelle agreed, if I'd do the talking, which I expected to do anyway.

With a promise to visit again, I fastened Adrienne and Hammie in car seats in the back and we headed out to the Warner farm.

That part of Prince Rupert County was still pretty rural. We passed a couple of truck farms and a nursery before we entered the tunnel of oak trees that lined the drive up to the complex. Although not as old as the Whitman Manse, The Oaks was an impressive estate. A rectangular white frame house with several additions of varying ages plus a number of out-buildings. We drove on to the backyard, which contained the barns, a stable and, within sight, multiple sheds and runs for the goats.

"This was Edna's original home," I told the kids. "This is where she was born."

"Does she have sisters or brothers?" Adrienne wanted to know.

"We'll have to ask." I had never given that a thought.

When I parked, Adrienne and Hammie were so wiggly with excitement, it was a struggle to get them out of their car seats. Sam Warner, Sr. came out of the barn to meet us.

Adrienne pulled at my arm and asked in a loud whisper, "Where are the goats?"

"Ah, you came to see the goats, huh?" Sam answered, smiling a greeting. A typical farmer he was lean and sunburned with straw colored hair. Far from being a hayseed, however, he knew all there was to know about raising pygmy goats, add to that his easy smile and frequent laughter. He and his wife, Jean, were former schoolmates and old friends.

I explained our mission and he called Junior, his son and mirror image, to give us a tour, starting first with the out-buildings and fenced in yard where the young and female goats lived. Pregnant and nursing mothers had their own quarters. The billy-goats were isolated across a pasture, which, in addition, housed the mating area. Adrienne had lots of questions, but Hammie started to suck his thumb, so I held his hand and that satisfied him.

Finally, Junior led us to a run which he called a playground. Perches on varying levels, big rocks and boulders provided places for the goats to climb and jump on. Watching the kids' activity was a big hit with Adrienne and Hammie.

While they were amused, I took the box of Ola's pastries into the farm house kitchen and called, "Jean?" As she hurried into the room, a yellow lab preceded her.

"I thought you might like some of Ola's chocolate eclairs." I handed it to her.

"Oh, Minty. You shouldn't have, but …" she grinned and gave me a hug, "… I seldom get to town before Clay's all sold out."

We exchanged news of our children and grandchildren and I asked, "Are you coming into the town meeting Thursday?"

"Sam'll be there, for sure, and Junior," she said, "but sometimes I baby-sit my grand kids so Alice can go in with Junior."

"I've come to the conclusion that we women ought to take a more active part in town business," I said, "so I hope you can make it." Jean agreed and I went back out to find Sam. I needed to discuss the addition of a goat to our menagerie.

A couple of chickens followed me as I walked toward the big barn. Dim and cool inside, I breathed in the familiar essence of farm perfume — hay, dust, sunshine with a hint of animals — and called Sam.

"Back here in my office," he answered and appeared from behind bales of straw which hid the partition and door.

Edna was supposed to be just the first of the herd that Billy had planned. Now I'd grown fond of her, whether I wanted to or not. I explained that I knew very little about raising goats, basically only the feeding and watering of pygmies.

"You'll probably want a female, about five or six months old or a wether. You don't want an intact Billy, do you?"

No, one was enough crossed my witchy mind, but I held my tongue and cringed at the thought. By the embarrassed expression that flitted across Sam's face, I guessed he was thinking the same thing.

Maintaining my poise, I said, "No, I'm not planning to raise a herd. I just need a companion for Edna. Lee says she's lonely. What's a wether?"

Sam gave me a crash course in pygmy goat society and the issues which might arise. Males were routinely castrated, unless intended for breeding, and are called wethers. I agreed that or another little female sounded good.

This decided, I took the opportunity to change the subject. "You come in for the town meetings, don't you, Sam?" He nodded and I continued, "There's a rumor going around that Morton Trueblood wants the town to buy the Manse property and tear it down to build condos or office space or …" I shrugged my shoulders. "Know anything about that?"

"Tear down the Manse?" His head reared back and he frowned before asking, "Why would he want to destroy a town landmark like that?"

"Clay Marshall was surprised, too. I'd be interested in what you think about it."

Sam grimaced. "Hey, you know me. I'm just a plain old dirt farmer. I don't hold much with this urge to keep up with the times. Whitman as it is suits me and Jean just fine. I'll check with her and Junior's wife. See if they've heard anything. I'd hate to see the Manse go the way of the other old homes."

Sam's reaction pleased me and I intended to interview other suitable supporters.

Turning toward Junior and the kids, I called, "Come on, children, we have business to attend to. It's time to pick out a friend for Edna." Hammie took my hand and Junior led us to a small run to which he brought five goats: two does and three wethers.

The breed came in a variety of tones and shades of white, brown and black and these kids were small, recently weaned. While Sam gave me a history of each, Junior turned the five pygmies, as well as Adrienne and Hammie, into the smaller run.

"These are LaManchas, like Edna," Junior told the children.

"Oh, look at the tiny ears," Adrienne cooed as a sable wether nuzzled up to her.

"They're called gopher ears, honey," Junior said.

Adrienne hugged the little kid, of course, and asked, "Can we get this one? She's so sweet."

"This is a boy goat and we call him Claude," Junior told her.

A black doe approached Hammie, who backed up, slightly apprehensive. Apparently eager for her share of petting, the doe butted him gently in the tummy and he plopped down on the ground. His blue eyes wide, he looked up at me, but Junior had him on his feet before he could cry. Then, kneeling down beside the boy, Junior coaxed the black doe back and showed Hammie how to scratch behind her ears and neck.

After a general discussion, Hammie and I deferred to Adrienne's choice and decided on the brown wether, who seemed less aggressive than the black doe. I left the children in the run with Junior and the goats, while I concluded my business with Sam. It would take a couple of days to enlarge Edna's quarters to include a stall for her new friend.

Sam said they'd deliver the wether with an additional supply of feed on Tuesday or Wednesday.

On the way home, Adrienne, Hammie and I dealt with the serious business of the new goat's name. "They named him Claude, because he was the third born that year, like A, B, C in the alphabet." Adrienne lowered her voice as if confiding something secret to Hammie and added, "Daddy goats get real stinky so they have to live way out beyond the pasture."

"I wanna name our goat Rover after The Big Red Dog," Hammie said.

Adrienne said, "You can't give a goat a dog's name. He needs a proper goat name."

They each presented various names, which I found very entertaining, and agreed that Claude was most suitable by the time we arrived at the end of the drive.

I had successfully recruited two men opposed to Morton's scheme and loved every minute with my grandchildren. What a delightful morning it had been. The sight of home, as I drove up, reminded me of Hugh and of Rachel's visit — problems which I would have to resolve.

Chapter 7

That evening, Rachel, Adrienne, Hammie and I enjoyed an elegant dinner at Philabelle's home, the Whitman Manse. The formal dining room had two windows with a view of the gardens in back and two more windows overlooking the driveway. Both sets were almost floor to ceiling and all four windows were shrouded with tied back wine colored velvet drapes with matching fringe. I don't know how old the furniture was: heavy dark oak with carvings down the stout legs ended in lions' heads.

Tonight Philabelle had the table set with multicolored flowers and fern fronds. In a display of past splendor, she used the best family silver including salad, dinner and dessert forks, as well as two teaspoons at each place.

I was proud of Rachel, whose new hairstyle had benefited from Florrie's skill. She appeared more relaxed and at ease.

As we entered and viewed the elaborate dinner service, I said to her, "This is a subtle way to indoctrinate the children in some Whitman family history."

To my delight, she laughed and said, "And that's just what William would do if he were here. The entire conversation would be The Wonderful World of Being a Whitman."

"I know you're teasing, Rachel, but I'm gratified that William honors his heritage so highly," Philabelle said. I held my breath, half expecting Philabelle to ask Rachel if she and Howard would want to take over the Manse.

"You could do worse than follow his example, Rachel," I said, and with a chuckle added, "Both your father and I honored our ancestors, despite the Daughters of the Confederacy."

"This is beautiful, like fairy land," Adrienne sighed with awe as she watched Philabelle light the candles. Even I appreciated their flickering light. It added a touch of cheer to leaven the brooding portraits of Great-great-grandfather Whitman, his wife Jenny, and Great grandfather Whitman and Sophia.

"You really went all out for grandeur, Aunt Philabelle," Rachel said, but she smiled and I knew Philabelle was pleased. Rachel knew that her aunt did not often entertain in this fashion.

The dinner matched the ambience of the décor in elegance. As we ate, Philabelle guided Adrienne through the proper behavior of ladies at dinner parties with too much silverware. Rachel and I exchanged amused glances at the little girl's intent response to Philabelle's instruction. Hammie lost interest quickly and we excused him from the table as soon as he had finished eating. He quickly plumped down on the floor to investigate the lion's feet. While we ladies indulged in a cup of tea, I could hear Hammie talking to them. Ah, the sweetness of a child's imagination! What a pity it diminishes as we grow into the realities of life.

*   *   *

Later that evening Rachel said that, contrary to her expectations, she had enjoyed her visit with her school friends. They expressed envy for her alleged social life in Richmond which we smiled at together.

Rachel sighed and said, "I suppose I should work on that when I get home."

Restraining the offer of suggestions, I asked her how long she planned to stay.

"Probably a few more days, if that's okay, Mom."

"At least stay until Claude arrives, I urged. "The kids would be disappointed not to see him settled in." Rachel agreed. I hoped to end the visit on a happy note.

John Keen, our tenant farmer, who now did handyman jobs for me, had extended Edna's shed and run. I called Sam to deliver Claude on Wednesday morning.

I'd known the Keen family for years, although in the 1930s and '40s they had attended the school for 'The Coloreds'. I shuddered at the memory. By the time we all had children, the schools had been integrated, so my kids attended school with the young Keens.

✳   ✳   ✳

The next day when Sam brought Claude over, the weather was gorgeous. To my surprise, Edna showed real pleasure when the younger and smaller Claude was turned into her run. With amusement, we watched Edna sniff at him and make efforts to groom him.

Sam said, "She's accepted him already, so you don't have to keep them separate."

"Do you suppose Edna thinks he's her baby? Maybe all along she's been longing for motherhood," I speculated. Rachel snorted, but Sam and the Keens, who knew goats, all agreed that was reasonable.

While we were occupied with settling Claude in, I heard the phone ring. I rushed back into the kitchen to answer it.

It was Madge, Clay's wife, calling to remind me that it was time for the committee, of which I'm chairman, to meet and plan the town's Fourth of July celebration. She assured me that Clay would arrange for fireworks. A couple of aging veterans would goad some younger ones into rounding up bands and marchers for the parade. That would have been the entire celebration, were it not for us women.

We, who make up the Fourth of July Committee, organized and prepared the town picnic, which had been a big success. We drafted some of the men to help with the heavy work of transporting tables and chairs. One of the dreaded jobs was soliciting sponsors for the buffet. In the past, Sarah and I had volunteered for that.

Tentatively, Madge and I set Wednesday of the next week after lunch for the committee meeting. Madge said she'd call all the other members. I thanked her sincerely for that plus the reminder and told her that Sarah was in Richmond while her daughter was post-op.

Poor Madge. She had been quite a pretty, fair-haired girl when we were in school, her round face perpetually pleasant even then. After having three children, she had immersed herself in the role of housewife/cook, which took its toll on her figure. She became matronly and, with her Miss Clairol over-enhanced blonde hair, she resembled Miss Piggy, I thought.

It was unfortunate that Madge never expected anything to work as planned and, sure enough, she always found something to pick at. She was the one who noticed that the devil's food cake was lopsided, the potato salad didn't have enough onions or that one of the library volunteers dressed too flashy.

On the other hand, Madge worked hard as a member of the Fourth Committee, the High School Band Parents and also taught in the Methodist Sunday School. Sarah and I often rolled our eyes at each other over Madge's

44

eccentricities, but we wouldn't complain. Madge was too good a worker and we wouldn't hurt her feelings for anything.

Clay and I had had quite a torrid romance going during high school. Then I married Billy and Clay married Madge.

∗   ∗   ∗

After dinner at home on our porch, while Rachel tidied up the kitchen, the children and I settled the goats for the night and walked Buck. Cleo pretended to ignore us as she crept in and out of shrubs and bushes around the property. Later, with the children asleep upstairs, my daughter and I took our postprandial glasses of wine into the living room.

"This has really been a marvelous break for me, Mom." Rachel, relaxing on the couch, certainly looked healthier and happier than when she had arrived. First, she had been to Florrie's Wash and Wave, for a trim, styling, facial and manicure. Later, at the Emporium in New Kent, she had bought a new skirt and blouse, plus earrings to complement the outfit. I had a fun time with my grandchildren at the school playground swings, slides and merry-go-round, while she shopped.

As Rachel sipped her wine, I reached down to stroke Buck's head before he collapsed on the floor and I speculated what Rachel had on her mind now.

"You look lovely tonight – like my young Rachel."

"Well, I'm not a young Rachel any longer." Toying with her rings, she glanced at me, so I smiled and nodded encouragingly.

"Do you feel more rested now?" I asked.

"At the least, it's given me a chance to think about my situation at home." She drank some more wine and licked her lips before she added, "I will say, Mom, you were right. I've let myself devote my life entirely to the children. Now that they're older, I realize that Adrienne, bright as she is, *needs* the challenge of preschool and then kindergarten."

I nodded again, but couldn't keep my mouth shut, "And don't forget to make time for you and Howard, too."

Rachel's smile faded. "Well, I'll do my best, but he hasn't had much free time lately." Her face lost its animation and I regretted adding my two cents.

Undaunted, I put in a whole dollar this time, "One of the essentials for a good marriage is that husband and wife have interests in common and time together alone. Your father and I had wonderful times —."

"Not an especially good example, Mother," she interrupted with a grimace.

I didn't like that, so I reminded her, "He was a wonderful father, Rachel, and we were an exceptionally happy family."

Rachel drank the last of her wine and sat forward. "Yes, he was a wonderful father and I agree: William, Jesse and I had a great childhood," she said carefully and I noted an interesting difference from her previous comment. She stood up. "It's been a really good couple of days and, once again, you've set me on the right track."

Her tone of voice would have let me know how peeved she was at my remarks, even if I hadn't seen her narrowed eyes and tight lips. I rose, too, and she gazed slightly over my head and said, "It's time for me to take the kids. To go home. I have to get started on my new life style. As usual, you seem to know best. Thank you for your hospitality."

The formality of her remark was not lost on me, but I didn't comment, although I felt the sting.

She leaned over and kissed my cheek dutifully. Buck stood up and she patted his head. Then, "I'd better start packing the kids' things. I'll call you and let you know my progress on the preschool, babysitter situation and my own new activities."

When I asked, "Are you really going home tomorrow?" She nodded. "Five minutes ago you seemed to be enjoying yourself. Why not stay a — "

Rachel shook her head and said, "No. I'd better go tomorrow."

"I don't understand why you can't stay longer."

"To tell the truth, Mother, very little I do pleases you. You did give me good advice about the children when I needed it. And I thank you for that. But I feel that my behavior annoys you and ..." she raised her shoulders in obvious exasperation and avoided my eyes.

"Rachel, I don't know what I've done to make you think that. You're my only daughter. I'm proud of you and you've given me two beautiful grand — "

Rachel stood up, interrupting. Her head half turned away and her eyes closed, she murmured, "I shouldn't have said that. You have been a good mother and I appreciate that. It's just that ..." she inhaled, shook her head a little and her tone raised a notch as she said, "I just get tired easily and I'm anxious to get started on looking for nursery schools."

I read her face easily and knew with a mother's certainty that it was *she* who found *me* annoying.

Obviously upset and unwilling to speak honestly, she finally met my eyes and said, "You've given me what I needed from you, Mom." And changed the subject. "You're expecting us for the Fourth as usual, aren't you?" We both nodded. Rachel closed the conversation by saying, "Let me go home, get to work. I hope I'll have good news of accomplishments by the Fourth. Okay?" her smile bright as a light switched on.

I couldn't do anything but let her go. She kissed my cheek again and went upstairs.

✶   ✶   ✶

I sat back in the recliner to rethink our visit. I was half confident that I *had* given her good advice as well as irritated her, but I was annoyed at her comment about her father and I had let her know that. I poured myself another glass of wine to ease my disappointment.

Neither she nor William had ever hinted that they knew of Billy's philandering, but I felt sure that they talked among themselves. Jesse and I had hashed over the issue of human frailty and the strength of love some time ago. Strange that my gay son and I were closer than my more conventional children.

I sat alone with Buck. Cleo snuck into the room, watched me before she jumped into my lap and made herself comfortable.

At least I had solved Edna's problem and some of Rachel's, whether it bugged her or not. I could do nothing to protect Jesse. William hadn't needed much mothering. He had been born mature and stuffy, but not a worry. In fact, it was William to whom I looked for aid and advice regarding the Manse situation.

As I stroked Cleo's warm silky fur, I realized that I was waiting for Hugh's next phone call with a mixture of excitement and anxiety. I was nowhere near solving my own problem.

Chapter 8

On the front porch Thursday morning, warm with their hugs and kisses, I watched Rachel and my grandchildren as they drove away, leaving me again in a house filled with the painful quiet of an empty nest. Rachel had assured me that she was back on track. She certainly looked better. She promised she'd keep in touch and get a new wardrobe. Since the change in my relationship with Hugh, I had become conscious of the need to keep one's appearance attractive.

*   *   *

That evening, before I dressed, I settled Edna and Claude for the night. Claude was much smaller, but he was a pretty cunning little fellow. I told him to be a good boy and, as if he were reassuring me, he nuzzled my hand softly, making what I assume was a form of baby bleat.

For the town council meeting, Philabelle and I had decided to wear whatever 'power' clothes we possessed. I chose a simple blue light-weight pantsuit, short sleeved and tailored, which I had bought the last time I spent a week with my older son and his family. For color, I added my Laurel Birch parrot earrings – a flamboyance which I loved. Taking my own advice, earlier I had visited Florrie to trim the scraggly ends of my hair and gotten a facial. Ready to go, I checked my reflection. I had achieved my intention of simple elegance and dignity.

I parked at the Manse at 6:30 and, with Philabelle, walked over to the meeting. I was surprised to see an extraordinary number of people of mixed ancestry almost filling the seats in the meeting room, including my friends Clay Marshall and the Warner family en masse. Plus the Keens, who waved. There were a number of people we were glad to see and acknowledge. This enthusiastic exchange of greetings was one of the primary joys of small town life.

Town meetings were held on the second floor over Grant's Hardware, which they rented out for various celebrations. Several years ago, we voted to buy folding chairs with padded seats, as opposed to the previous old wooden ones, and new folding tables. The Grant family, who own the building, maintained the area well and provided heat in the winter and fans in the summer. For the various parties, individual sponsors provided appropriate decorations.

At the Town Meetings, the five members and the President sat at tables facing the rows of chairs. Promptly at 7:00 p.m., Morton called the meeting to order. Kevin Kearns, Fire Marshall and Secretary, read the Minutes of the previous meeting, which were accepted.

Morton reminds me of Humpty Dumpty: bald round head, round face, round body and stubby legs supporting it all. Since he retired as Superintendent of Schools, his position on the council had become his *mission*. Standing in front of the crowd, he banged his gavel and began in his most officious voice.

"The first item on the agenda is approval of funds for the Fourth of July Celebration. The Council has appropriated an additional five hundred dollars because of the rising cost of fireworks. Are there any questions or objections before we take a vote?" The vote passed easily and Morton paused before he banged the gavel and said, "The expenditure, therefore, is approved."

"The next item of business, which was tabled at the previous meeting, concerns the issue of the Town's purchase of the building presently at 22 East Main Street, known as the Whitman Manse." Philabelle grabbed my arm, apparently as surprised as I was at this sneaky maneuver!

Over the rustle of whispers in the audience, I heard a man's voice say distinctly, "That wasn't mentioned in the Minutes."

Morton banged the gavel again. I swear the gavel was a phallic symbol of authority to him. "Accordingly, I made an informal overture of purchase to Miss Philabelle Whitman, which was summarily rejected. Representing the Council, I urged Miss Philabelle to reconsider and advised her that it would be on the agenda for tonight's meeting."

Philabelle sprang up and said, "You certainly did *not*, Morton. I had no idea you planned to discuss it tonight." Laughing inwardly, I persuaded her to sit down. "Well, he *didn't!*" She added to me sotto voce.

A grumble rose from the audience and Morton's eyes searched right and left as if looking for support before he continued.

"At this time, it would be appropriate to hear a motion that a formal offer from the Town to purchase the Whitman property be prepared and presented to the owner." He focused on the Chairman for Ways and Means, Cooper Baxter, often referred to as Morton's yes man. Sure enough, Cooper, an Ichabod Crane look-alike, made the motion.

"Do I hear a second?" Morton asked.

"Is it legal for a member of the Council to make a motion?" a man somewhere in the crowd asked. Another voice said, "Shush, we'll discuss that later."

From a few rows behind us, Sam Warner, Sr., stood and raised his voice, "You know, Morton, this business of the town buying the Manse is news to a lot of us who regularly attend these meetings."

Cries of "Yeah!" arose from the audience, plus a shout of "We need more information."

Staunchly holding his position, Sam continued, "For instance: where would money to buy the Manse come from?"

Another vocal rose from the audience. "How about some discussion from the floor?"

A chorus of "Why buy the Manse?" and "That's right!" filled the room. Philabelle squeezed my hand and whispered something I didn't catch, but I smiled at her and nodded.

People were still talking when Morton banged the darned gavel again and called, "Order! Order! This is a town meeting, not an open discussion."

Old Doc Foster, long time member of the council, craned his neck to look at the Chairman. "You're pushing it, Morton. These people *are* the town. We need to hear some discussion from — "

"We can't have everybody in town putting in their two cents worth," Morton interrupted, but a woman with a strong brassy voice, from way in the back, spoke up.

"Some of us voters heard this rumor and it's our *more* than two cents you're talking about. We're entitled to hear what other people think."

Morton wasn't finished, however. "A number of prominent businessmen, including the president of the Security Bank, agree that this is an acquisition that's necessary for the town's growth."

Walter Kress, said CEO of the bank, also a council member, looked at Morton. "You're misquoting me, Morton. What I said was that, *if* the Manse property were on the market, I'd like to buy an adjoining section for a drive-in window. And I agree with Sam: there should be an open discussion of this issue."

I could feel Philabelle trembling with tension beside me and I wondered if it would be necessary, after all, for me to get up and speak on our behalf. Muttering from the crowd rose in volume and Morton banged away and shouted, "Order! I call this meeting to order!"

"Not until representatives from the floor have their say," a man called, followed by cries of "Hear! Hear!" plus clapping and shouts of "Yes."

Philabelle nudged me to stand up and speak. Before I could, Council member E.J. Rossi, an associate of Billy's, caught my eye. He winked and nodded. Taking a deep breath, I raised my hand. Philabelle poked me again and I rose to my feet.

"I have something to say on behalf of the Whitman family." Although I hadn't attended every meeting, I'd spoken before on a number of community issues, but not on a subject so personal to our family. "If the Chairman will recognize me?"

An attentive silence awaited Morton's response, until Doc Foster said, "Morton, recognize Mrs. Billy Whitman so she can speak her piece for the record."

I saw Morton shoot an angry glance at Doc Foster and he mumbled something inaudible before he said, grudgingly, "All right, Mrs. Whitman, but please be brief."

I inhaled twice and began, "Miss Philabelle Whitman has authorized me to confirm her rejection of *any* offer to buy the Manse. It is the only remaining ante-bellum private residence left in Whitman. In the past, the taxpayers of Whitman have approved restoration of several old buildings of architectural interest in order to maintain the atmosphere of our historic past. They have, also, disapproved renovation on the façade of a store-front on Main Street as being too modern and inappropriate. Therefore, I believe it is in best interests of the people of Whitman that the Manse continue to represent those values of our heritage."

My remarks brought more than a murmur of approval, but I also heard comments such as "Bosh!" "Behind the times," "Run-down relic," and other disparaging statements.

Still standing and maintaining my dignity, I added, "On a personal level, I'd like to request that the President of the Council refrain from threatening Miss Philabelle with eminent domain." I sat down to considerable applause as well as another rash of disagreeable 'Boos!'

Over these rumblings, I heard, "Why would the town want to buy the Manse?" I identified it as John Keen's voice.

The hall filled with conversations, some people agreeing with John. Someone clearly asked, "What is eminent domain?" A female acquaintance, sitting behind me, called, "And don't bully Miss Philabelle. The Manse is historical." She reached forward and patted Philabelle's shoulder.

Most distressing, and to my surprise, there were a number of loud and positive protests: people espousing progress or development, denigrating "Old Stick in the Muds" and general disapproval of my comments.

Doc Foster interrupted to repeat John's question, "What on earth would the town do with the Manse anyway?"

A long time Front Street property owner stood and said, "To supplement Doc Foster's question, I'd like to point out that the town has a number of needs much more pressing than the purchase of the Manse, which sounds to me like a waste of money."

The crowd, clearly out of Morton's control, required repeated use of the gavel before his voice could be heard. "Order! Order! I'll close the meeting if the public can't …"

While Morton continued wielding his hammer of authority, the muttering increased. The crowd refused to cease their discussions.

Finally, Clay, who had considerable clout in town, stood up and shouted, "All right, everybody. Let's settle down and not all talk at once." The noise diminished for Clay, who continued, "Mr. President, you never answered the taxpayers' question: how would the town make use of the Manse?"

Morton stood up again and said, "In the interest of progress and for the general good, we need to expand the business area." He punctuated his remarks with frequent hand gestures, which reminded me of a seal flapping its flippers. "If we want Whitman to grow and to provide better facilities for its residents, we have to have more office and merchandising space. We need more employment opportunities and modern housing for those employees to encourage our young people to stay here."

When he stopped for breath, E.J. Rossi leaned forward to look at him. "Does the town really want more traffic, more residents who require more public services requiring more taxes?"

"And more crime and drugs?" A feminine voice from the back added.

Again the audience resounded with both 'yeas' and 'boos.' It was some time before Morton regained control. I sensed that people were getting tired of arguing and failing to accomplish anything. As soon as the crowd quieted down, Al Schultz, an attorney who had lived in Whitman for less than ten years, stood and requested recognition.

I had avoided contact with Schultz and his brassy wife, Carmen, since her public humiliation of me with regard to my husband. I considerate it inappropriate for Schultz, as a newcomer, to insinuate himself into our Town Meetings. Like Clay, I still resened northerners migrating in and trying to act like southerners. Obviously, none of this deterred Schultz, however.

Morton recognized Schultz, who, as if speaking to ignorant peasants, said, "It has been my experience in other small towns that a lack of progress results in a disintegrating community." Morton nodded his head like a child's toy as Schultz continued, "Young people want more public services, better paying jobs and modern houses. Without these amenities, they move out of town and gradually all small businesses go bankrupt, leaving an empty shell of what had appeared to be a flourishing community."

Unlike Morton, Schultz presents a more cosmopolitan appearance. He was taller and trimmer and, to me he had " a mean and hungry look." Or was it "lean and hungry"? Anyway, he spoke well, without dramatics, and had excellent posture. I gave him that. He had more to say: "Moving forward with the times is essential for the town's existence. The purchase of this property on Main Street is the first step in developing busy, prosperous businesses, which is what we all want."

The audience reacted with vigor; disagreements broke out in several areas, making it clear that 'we' didn't 'all want' the same kind of town. Several men stood up, shaking their fists in the air to emphasize their approval or opposition – I couldn't tell pro from con.

In addition to cries of "tear down the old buildings." I heard muttering against "making our town into a city." From my left, a man said, "Use the Manse for office space?" From closer up front: "We need a parking lot more'n all them trees." At the table, Doc Foster shook his head in apparent despair and Cooper Baxter cowered in his chair. Morton was red in the face as he continued to plead for silence.

By now, the meeting had gone almost an hour over its usual time. My bottom was complaining and I noticed others fidgeting in their seats.

Clay, a former Whitman football star, commanded attention, especially from the middle-aged group which dominated in community business. When he rose and yelled, "Shut up!" he got it. "Assuming that Miss Philabelle was willing to sell the Manse, what would the town do with it?"

For a long moment, Morton sat with his mouth hanging open, as if he didn't know the answer. The officious Schultz rose again and asked Morton, "May I answer that?" He turned to face the audience and said, "The Manse would have to be razed ..." The audience moaned. Schultz raised both hands and smiled as if eager to reply. "It is old and a fire trap. Appropriate up-to-code buildings would be constructed. Furthermore, I've learned, through colleagues, that Wal-Mart is looking for space to open stores in this — "

"Oh, hell! We don't want no Wal-Mart in Whitman." A man's voice over-rode Schultz and echoed through the room, prompting a burst of laughter throughout.

Finally, Mayor Lemp, who had been silent, letting Morton run the meeting, rose and said, "In view of the strong opinions concerning the Manse, I suggest that the issue of buying it be tabled until the Council has developed next year's budget. As has been pointed out, several needed improvements are already under consideration: an enlarged fire house, construction of a proper town hall, new heating/air conditioning for the school…"

"And a skateboard park," a young voice shouted, followed by another scattering of laughter.

With a chuckle, the Mayor concluded, "Our tax base will stretch only so far, which is a major consideration and of importance to all of us."

When he sat down, Schultz rose and responded, "A significant factor in favor of purchasing the Manse would be new businesses which would expand the tax base and could provide for those needs."

By then my bottom felt numb despite the padding. A restless muttering by the audience and the rustle of people leaving in small increments suggested that I wasn't the only one. Even council members shifted in their seats and checked their watches.

Morton leaned sideways to apparently take an inaudible poll of the council members. Then, his mouth pursed like a sour pickle, he said, "In consideration of the hour, I'll entertain a motion to adjourn this meeting." It was seconded by several people. Morton had the last word by thanking the Mayor for his input. He banged the gavel a final time, and a mass exodus, still vocalizing with exuberance, was underway, even as Morton declared the meeting adjourned.

While Philabelle and I moved with the crowd towards the door, I heard someone say, "I hope that's the end of it." Although I silently agreed, I doubted it. I was sure that Morton had an agenda of his own. It was the action by Al Schultz, however, which piqued my worry and curiosity. I was heartened by the number of our supporters and surprised at the number of those in favor of demolishing the Manse.

Firmly, I guided Philabelle through the crowd, impeded by those who wanted to greet her, mostly with encouragement. I was positive that the subject would come up again. Next time, however, Hugh would be home and would probably deal with it.

Secretly, however, I had enjoyed speaking my piece: courteous but firm – that was my Southern gentlewomanly style. Maybe Clay was right that I should run for a seat on the council. It would give me more clout, at least.

On the walk back to the Manse, I expected to hear Philabelle's expression of disappointment but was surprised at her vehemence when she stated, "I won't *let* them destroy the Manse." Then she leaned close to my ear and whispered, "I do have a gun at home."

Chapter 9

After the town meeting, I left Philabelle at the Manse and on the drive home mulled over her statement about the gun; was she kidding or serious? I hadn't known she had one and couldn't imagine her using it. An image of my delicate white-haired sister-in-law standing on the porch of the Manse, defending it with violence, almost prompted a laugh. Any amusement, however, turned to worry when I recalled the lines of tension that had bracketed Philabelle's mouth and the narrowed eyes. Billy used to refer to that expression as 'her face of false passivity'.

The first time I heard the expression was about fifteen years earlier before Hugh's wife, Sheila, took their son Smith and returned to Richmond. The four of us had been having dinner at their house. Over dessert, Billy told the story of Philabelle's intransigence in the face of their father's refusal to let her marry the young man of her choice.

At the family dinner table, Billy, about eleven then, had teased Philabelle about marrying her suitor, Jackson Rawlins, and she insisted that he was the only man she would marry.

"You're too young to consider marrying anyone, sweetie," her mother had said.

"I can get married in two years, when I'll be eighteen," Philabelle pointed out.

"Hrump!" her father said. "Certainly not to that Rawlins boy. He's not suitable. You'll marry one of the young men I have in mind for you."

Courteously, Philabelle had responded, "No, I won't. I'll marry Jackson or..."

Mother had gasped, but my father fixed his eyes on Philabelle said firmly, "You'll marry whomever I tell you to, young lady."

I watched as Philabelle's face assumed the Southern Belle expression of false passivity and she said quietly, "If I can't marry Jackson, I won't marry anybody at all."

"You'll do as I tell you, young lady," our father declared and had sent her to her room without finishing supper.

"Philabelle retreated to her room with her dignity intact. That was in 1943, and, like so many young men, Jackson Rawlins enlisted in the Army and Philabelle had kept her word by remaining a maiden lady."

Sheila had asked, "Why didn't she marry Jackson after the war?"

I knew why: he was killed during the Battle of the Bulge. Recalling that story brought to mind my low days after Billy's death.

Philabelle had confided the story of her love for Jackson Rawlins and said, "I've survived that sorrow, Minty, but nothing that happened after his death altered the love Jackson Rawlins and I shared. I made a new different life for myself, as you will."

By then, both Philabelle and I had been crying, but she had wiped her eyes, squeezed my hands and said, "You have the strength and the courage, Minty, to put Billy's death into the past and make a new life for yourself." I had believed her then, but since Hugh's proposal, three days earlier, I was not so sure I had succeeded. Too often Billy, like a ghost, seemed to haunt me.

$$\ast \qquad \ast \qquad \ast$$

It was dark when I parked behind my lovely farm house. Buck and Cleo welcomed me in their unique ways. It was late, so I locked the doors after I came in and put the kettle on for a cup of chamomile tea. Waiting for the water to boil, I munched on a few M & Ms and compared the contradictory characters of my sister-in-law, her flawed older brother, Billy, and the dependable, kind and amusing Hugh. What an integral part of my life they were. Anticipating Hugh's call later, I debated whether to lay this concern about Philabelle's gun on him. My meditations were interrupted by the whistling of the teakettle; it was steeping when the phone rang.

"Have you been out frolicking tonight, shug?" Hugh asked, "I called about half an hour ago and got your answering machine."

The down home sanity of his voice calmed me enough that I drawled, "Why, I couldn't frolic without you, darlin'." Deciding not to tease him, I added, "But I have been busy."

"Anything wrong?" What made him ask that? Sometimes Hugh seemed to read my mind. Very disconcerting.

"Uh uh, everything's fine." Uncomfortable at this evasion, I briefed him on the town meeting, making light of Morton's threat. As far as Philabelle's statement about the gun, I kept mum. I wanted to discuss it and the ramifications of Morton's threat at leisure with Hugh – face to face. Instead I asked about the conference.

"Interesting. I was flattered that some medical recruiters tried to lure me away from Whitman. Doctors are in short supply all over the world, obviously. It was sort of tempting," he said.

"Forget it, Buster! We need you here as much as anybody else," I responded. I couldn't imagine Hugh leaving Whitman.

I balanced the phone on my shoulder while I poured my tea and the phone slipped. I caught it, but Hugh must have heard something.

"What's going on there," he asked.

"I was making myself a cup of chamomile and almost dropped the phone," I said and continued. "Philabelle and I had a talk about all the family treasures in the Manse. There's a whole museum of stuff there, Hugh. She surprised me by talking about when she can no longer manage such a big house. She's obviously been thinking about leaving the Manse."

Conscientious brother that Hugh was, he sounded concerned. "Maybe we ought to start considering the possibility. Start by having someone appraise that stuff. I don't even know how much insurance she has. When I get home, let's go over it with her. See what she has in mind."

I endorsed that, drank some tea and changed the subject. "When do you expect to get back?"

"Late tomorrow afternoon, probably." He lowered his voice to an intimate sexy tone and said, "Just one more night without you, shug."

His voice excited tingles in my unmentionable places and a renewed sense of loneliness enveloped me.

In my best voluptuous voice, I asked, "In time for dinner with me?"

"Are you co … eh, should I pick up Chinese food on the way? That's quick and easy."

I caught his drift, but felt playful. "No, I have plenty of stuff here. Also quick and easy."

I could hear him breathing clear from Atlanta, imaging his lewd thoughts, but I didn't enlarge on the subject. I just grinned into the phone, as fatuous as a teenager. Juvenile, probably, but who cared. Our relationship, especially at my age, was so delightfully unexpected – like being handed a second chance at life. Sharing that lusty mood, we said our goodnights. Both of us anticipated a romantic night tomorrow, I was sure.

*   *   *

After I hung up the phone, too stimulated to sleep, I put my now cold tea in the microwave to reheat, my mind on Hugh and me. With my drink, I sat at the table and relived that propitious New Year's Eve 1999 — almost two years after Billy's death.

Philabelle had insisted that I let Hugh escort me to her dinner party to welcome in the year 2000. Sarah, Mel, Lynn, her husband Randolph , the Marshalls and the Rossies were the only other guests.

Philabelle overrode my protest. "You've been fogged inside yourself for more than six months, Minty. Billy would detest seeing you hibernate like this. It's the end of a millennium and we won't live to see another one."

*She was not to be denied, so I had yielded and, I must admit, it was a grand affair, all of us in formal attire. I had worn a simple taffeta gown with a low back. About eleven o'clock, feeling the least bit tiddly from the champagne, I had persuaded Hugh to take me home. I don't know why I felt so strongly that, when the year ended, I wanted to be in the place that was now **my** home. Maybe, I needed to start the new century celebrating my new independence.*

Whatever! Hugh had obliged and insisted on staying with me at least until midnight.

"I have Buck and Cleo to keep me company," I demurred, but mildly.

Hugh raised his eyebrows in amusement. "They'd have trouble raising a glass to toast in the New Year."

"I've had enough to drink." I flopped down on the couch, kicked off my pumps, red to match the gown which I'd worn to dinner, and stretched my toes.

"Anything wrong with coffee? I'll make it," Hugh asked.

"That's an offer I can't refuse, but use decaf, okay?"

Hugh knew his way around my kitchen so I let him do the work, while I responded to Buck's need for attention. Cleo jumped up to her place on the back of the sofa and I turned on the TV. Scenes of festivities around the world dominated the screen.

When Hugh brought in the coffee, cups and a plate of macaroons he had found, he sat beside me. Comfortable, feet sharing a hassock, we watched TV re-runs of the New Year's arrival in Sydney, Paris and, finally, London.

Feeling the warmth of Hugh's shoulder against mine, the occasional nudge of my foot by his to make a point, I was conscious of his maleness — a trifle discomfiting. We had been friends for years, but awareness of Hugh as a man excited me and I tried to ignore it.

Then it had turned midnight. Buck barked with excitement when Hugh pulled me to my feet as the Times Square ball descended, raised his cup, and said, "Happy New Year and Happy New Millennium, my dear." He put down the cup, encircled me in his arms and kissed me. Not one of those fond cheek kisses, but a full mouth to mouth, no-holds-barred kiss.

I clung to him so I wouldn't disintegrate with the tsunami which engulfed me.

Shaken to the bone, I opened my eyes and looked at him.

His eyebrows were drawn together, lips still parted, as if anxious about my reaction.

I swallowed, stepped back a little, still within the circle of his arms, and managed a nervous smile. "Wow! I didn't expect that."

"Why not?" He ran his hands down my bare upper arms, raising goose bumps. "You're a lovely, passionate woman, Minty. I've wanted to kiss you for a long time."

Handsome in his tux, he grinned at me then, his brown eyes level with mine. I was giddy with conflicting emotions. Hugh was younger than me, – and worse – my brother-in-law, reason insisted. But it had been so long since I'd experienced such a passionate kiss that my body responded despite my brain.

"Hugh," My voice dragged out the 'u' sound, pretending to protest. "We're in-laws, for Pete's sake. We've been friends forever." I trembled, trying to subdue an unwanted desire. Well, almost unwanted. "It seems … inappropriate."

"What's inappropriate about two mature single adults…" he narrowed his eyes, a lascivious smile on those tempting lips, "…enjoying affectionate sex? You can't convince me that you're not lonely and miss being loved." He rubbed my bare back with both hands and I had to restrain myself from purring.

"People will talk," I began.

Hugh laughed out loud. "This from the Queen of Whitman? You haven't paid attention to gossip since you were ten years old and informed the Methodist minister that you had enjoyed mass in the Temple of the Holy Septum in Jerusalem."

My chuckle burst out and I relaxed into his embrace. He was right and I wondered how a lady told a man that he was sexy without demeaning herself.

He moved his lips against my cheek and I felt him smile.

"Are you suggesting that we … eh, have an affair?" I murmured.

"We're consenting adults, shug. It wouldn't be an affair." His whisper tickled my ear.

Back in the present, I sat smiling over my tea – cold again – until Buck nudged me, wanting to go out. My memory of that night had stayed green over the intervening year and a half. Good friends with privileges we had pledged. The reward? None of the complications of marriage; no demands; no commitments to mar the intensity of our ardor.

Lynn's cruel words, at our bridge game, echoed in my head yet again. Hugh had *never* been like a dog in rut. Always a gentle man, he had proved his friendship over the months of my dismal and capricious adjustment to being a widow. Almost numb with shock and grief, I had needed and taken advantage of his support.

As I had adapted to widowhood, since we were both single in a town whose population was limited, Hugh easily fell into the habit of escorting me to social events. I, as simply, had accepted it.

Since then, I had enjoyed every minute of our wanton relationship. God knows how much I wanted to stay friendly lovers. I refused to be seduced into anything more significant. I sneered at the idea of love itself. Although resentful at Hugh's marriage proposal, I admitted to myself that I was afraid. I couldn't surrender my independence, my present happy, uncomplicated life easily.

What itched was *why* I was afraid. Why should I feel guilty, when I was as innocent as a lamb?

Chapter 10

Friday I woke full of high spirits and, cup of coffee in hand, took Buck out for some fresh air and exercise, then fed and opened the run for Edna and Claude. As I worked, I heard Edna bleating protectively and looked out to see Buck sniffing at the fence near Claude. I shooed him off and he ran out toward the pasture.

I heard the phone ring and raced into the kitchen to catch it.

Knowing that I rise early, Philabelle felt free to call. "I'm not nagging, Minty, but you volunteered to help inventory the contents of the Manse and I wondered when?"

I interrupted. "I haven't forgotten, hon. You want me to come this morning?"

"Whenever you're ready. I'll fix a little lunch for us."

"It'll probably be nine thirty or ten before I get there. Is that O.K.?" It was fine with her, so I hastily fixed breakfast for myself, Buck and Cleo. By then Buck wanted in. I opened the door and then hurried upstairs to get ready for the day.

I had continued to occupy the master bedroom after I booted Billy out, but had dissipated a lot of my painful emotion by a complete renovation: repainted, bought a new bed, side tables with good lamps, curtains — the works. With brick red carpet, it felt warm and cheerful. The red might have been an expression of my anger, but gray walls toned it down. For the windows, I chose white scrim curtains and drapes in a wild print of big red flowers, gray green foliage against a white background. Then the bedroom was *mine*.

Now I looked around with admiration, almost embarrassed at my pleasure in anticipating a romantic night ahead. Quickly I changed the sheets, put clean towels in the bathroom and took out a sheer lacey black night gown.

All I needed were fresh flowers for the bedroom to welcome Hugh home. I went out in the garden and picked bunches of pink, lavender and white sweet peas, for their fragrance, plus a couple of purple iris as an accent. There were enough to make two arrangements, one for each of the bedside tables in the bedroom maybe. I was changing into clean clothes to join Philabelle, when Sarah called.

"Are you home already?" I asked, reaching for a Kleenex to wipe sweat off my face and hands.

"No, I'm still in Richmond, but it's about time for the Fourth Committee, so I wanted you to know I'll be home next week as early as I can get away."

I laughed, "You're getting psychic, girl. Madge just called. How's Becky doing?"

"She's fine. She found a woman to help out and with two of us cluttering up the place it's mishegas around here. I'll be glad to get home."

I could almost see her roll her eyes. I'd be glad to have her back. Sarah had always helped me stay grounded.

∗   ∗   ∗

The morning air was still fresh and fragrant with the scent of lilacs mingled with the more pungent smells of country as I drove past farms where animals dominated. In town, Philabelle was waiting and we started our tour on the second floor of the Manse. I made the list as she identified each piece of furniture. In the master bedroom the most imposing piece was the family marital bed, solid walnut, in the old fashioned sleigh style with matching lady's dressing table and the master's chiffonier.

"I love this blue and white wash basin set." I turned the pitcher upside down. "Look, this is Royal Doulton, can you believe that?"

"Not uncommon, Minty. Look under the bed." I laughed when I saw a matching chamber pot — the piece de resistance of the set. Philabelle chuckled and added, "There's several older than this one and, therefore, probably worth more."

"Worth more? Are you thinking in terms of selling these things?" The idea of *selling* family antiques appalled me.

"Ultimately, of course. You and Hugh, and all the grandchildren, will have a chance to pick out items that y'all like." Well, I thought, that's a blessing and generous, too. "But unless you and Hugh decide to marry and take over, what else would I do with them?"

That statement offended me mildly, but all I said was, "When all the family are together over the Fourth would you want each of them to choose a treasure or two for their future?"

"Good idea," Philabelle said.

Sarah, too, had hinted more than once that I should marry Hugh. I wished they'd realize that I was capable of managing my own life. Sarah had described Hugh as "a genuine mensch. A real keeper."

Philabelle placidly moved on to the next bedroom, the furniture lighter, more feminine. A lovely colorful quilt, which picked up the cheerful blue and yellow of the wallpaper, covered the bed.

"This was my room for so long," Philabelle mused, her mind back in her youth, I supposed. She inhaled, looked at me, tilted her head and said, "The boys had to share a room." I knew that amused her.

We returned to the hall and a larger room — the boys' bedroom. Here we followed the same procedure. Obediently I kept the inventory as she described each item, origin when known and an estimated significance: very valuable, quite valuable and 'mensa mensa'. Since neither of us were familiar with the present value of antiques, I agreed.

On the upstairs screened porch, with its wicker furniture – which Philabelle called 'modern' –she said, "When my plans, as well as yours and Hugh's, are more definitive, it might be wise to invite an appraiser to look at some of the furnishings." I was glad she mentioned that as appropriate.

A small room, next to the Master's, she called the nursery. She smoothed her hand gently on the riser of an old crib and lapsed into a pensive state. She gazed into space and, almost in a whisper, spoke of the changes that she had witnessed during her long life. I mentally compared the elaborately carved crib with the unadorned strictly functional one that my grandchildren slept in. Present day furniture was functional, lacking the still charming elaborations of the nineteenth century. The old crib and the carved sleigh bed were visible expressions of the mutations of time.

Philabelle, hands palm up, fingers spread, as if to holding the riches that transfiguration offered, said, "Life goes full circle, Minty. From an amoeba-like sponge, requiring only food, shelter and love, it absorbs all the juices of life. At Hammie's age, the child has achieved his unique personality and plunges eagerly into the stream of life.

"In old age, the process is reversed: the sponge is saturated to the point where the juices of life begin to drip out. Wrinkled and dried out, the individual fades back into an amoeba-like state, requiring only food, shelter and, that significant constant, *love*."

She turned to me, her smile never sweeter and said, "From birth to death, Minty, it's loving and being loved that makes life the full experience it should be." She took my hand in her soft, small boned hand and looked deeply into my eyes. "I believe it was the poet, Auden, who said: 'If love equal cannot be, let the more loving one be me'."

Mesmerized by her blue eyes, this was a spiritual moment, for me – not a common experience. Her voice speaking Auden's word brought tears to my eyes. I remembered her confiding the sorrow of her lost love. A brief period of her life, but I understood how much she had grown from it. We didn't need to say anything more. Our hearts understood each other.

As we started downstairs, I reflected that people sometimes considered my sister-in-law 'simple'. It was true that she often gave the impression of living back in the 'forties' and she still believed people essentially good. Even when they behaved badly, she tended to give them the benefit of the doubt until proven guilty. I found these qualities enormously appealing.

Since Billy's death, Philabelle and I had gotten even closer and I'd often seen wisdom and common sense in her aphorisms.

Part way down the stairs, disturbed by something in my sister-in-law's mood, I stopped and confronted her, "Philabelle, sometimes you talk as if you're planning to leave the Manse soon."

I didn't want my personal desires to influence her, but her attitude worried me, as if she were preparing me for her death. Hugh and I both knew how much she loved the Manse and I understood her desire that one of the family continue in residence. Conscious that I intended to disappoint her dream of Hugh and me marrying, I felt a pang at my selfishness, too. I hoped Philabelle wouldn't push me about that. But there was no way I could read her mind.

She paused on the step below me, turned and patted my hand. "I'm not in a hurry, my dear, but, pushing seventy-three, I value the security of a well-thought-out plan for when that day comes."

I sighed, feeling reprieved.

At the bottom of the stairs, she said, "Let's do the library next. It's a horror. Books so old they're starting to crumble."

She was right. The library was half paneled on the window and adjoining side. The other two were shelves, floor to ceiling, with books of various size and color. Fortunately, they were accessible by a rolling ladder.

"I'd better climb up and you make the list. O.K.?" I said and pulled the ladder to the far left of the bookcases.

Philabelle agreed and we spent an extremely dusty hour on one tier of shelves. I didn't expect Lena's weekly house-cleaning to include every book, but wasn't prepared for dust to be so pervasive. As I removed each one, it created its own little cloud. Part of it was an accumulation of lint, too, I suppose. Thankfully, I didn't encounter any silverfish or living book-worms.

I did find some real treasures, however. As we worked and sneezed, I discovered several old books that intrigued me.

"Philabelle," I said, "here's one." I read out loud, "The Journal of Jacob Trueblood. It's dated 1872, after The War. And another called The History of Prince Rupert County, dated 1875. We're going to need an appraiser for the books, too. A professional rare book person to evaluate these. From its date of publication," I held up a faded maroon leather bound copy of Tales of Huckleberry Finn. "I'm sure this is a first edition. Some of the other old ones must be valuable, too," I said.

"How do you think Morton would react if we showed him this Journal of his ancestor?" Philabelle chuckled. "Having an ancestor in the Whitman family, he might just be interested in saving The Manse, after all."

That gave us a good laugh and she suggested that we break for lunch.

"I'd like to borrow the Journal and the History to browse through, if you wouldn't mind?" I asked.

"Of course." She steadied the ladder while I climbed down, clutching the two books. "You know, Minty, we'll have to survey all the family members to see if someone would want to take over the Manse. I can't bear the thought of it being destroyed like all the other old homes."

"I'm with you, hon, but I know, also, that the property is valuable real estate. That by itself would probably sell for a pretty penny," I said, to prepare her for that eventuality.

A horrified look flitted across her face, but she didn't comment and continued into the kitchen.

Philabelle fixed chicken salad for sandwiches and a pitcher of iced tea while I put out place settings and we sat down to lunch. She said a quick grace and then continued her thoughts, "If no one in the family can be persuaded to live here, do you think anyone would buy the Manse, just for itself? I'd rather *give* it and all the property, too, to the town of Whitman – if the town would guarantee that it would be preserved as an historical landmark. Anything to prevent its destruction." She shook her head and I could see a light glint of moisture in her eyes.

I said, "Let's discuss it with Hugh. I suspect he'll feel the same way we do." I didn't say so, but I knew positively that Billy would have protested tearing down the Manse. I had a mental image of the three sibling standing side by side on the front porch, Philabelle with her gun, Billy with an Uzzi and Hugh – on second thought, I wasn't sure how Hugh felt about the Manse. I'd have to ask him.

*   *   *

It was mid afternoon before I left Philabelle. I planned to set up files on the computer for the Manse inventory and an official appraisal of its contents. Maybe I could check the internet for estimates of the value of old houses and property in the area.

On the drive home, however, I continued to muse on that spiritual moment when Philabelle spoke about her vision of life. So often I felt the need to protect her, to be a buffer between her and the realities of the twenty-first century. Then, without warning, she spouted truths which transcended time and place.

In that instance, her wisdom, followed by her earlier admonition that it was my place, as the elder, to reconcile with Lynn, forced me to reconsider my entitlement to hurt feelings. Lynn's series of casual relationships in the past had both worried and annoyed me. Truly, I hadn't recognized her behavior as expressions of unhappiness. Instead, I had pointed to my marriage as a guide for her. What irony! Now I suspected that she knew about Billy's dalliances long before I did. What a fool she must have thought me — a conclusion which re-inflamed my anger at her.

Chapter 11

That afternoon, I picked up some groceries for the weekend. With Hugh not due home until dinner time, I wanted to prepare it as much as feasible, tidy upstairs and still leave time for a shower and change.

The big issue was what to wear? Comfortable was important, but, for tonight, my goal was to present myself as a mature, irresistible woman.

Come on, Minty, I told myself: be honest. I wanted to look as sexy as possible without overdoing it. At sixty-three that was a problem. I disliked mature women aping teenagers, but I had qualms about how appealing I could look. Mostly, however, I was excited to have Hugh home again.

Meantime, I wanted everything perfect. As I climbed the stairs, I felt relieved that the dull week was over. Hugh's absence for me had tempered the excitement of the town meeting. In addition, I would have liked to air my concern about Rachel's tango project and his take on parenting adult children. I had learned to value his opinions and they often expanded my own views.

Upstairs, the sight of the red carpet gave me a jolt of pleasure. When I pulled the drapes at night, I felt elegant in my own private world.

A slight breeze fluttered the white scrim curtains. Glancing around, I was struck by how Freudian my choice of color had been five years ago. Amusing! First, I kicked Billy out of my bed and transformed my bedroom. Then, following a decent interval after his death, it provided an exciting background for Hugh and me.

Finished in the master bedroom, I checked the time and realized that I could prepare the others for my family on the Fourth. With another armload of sheets and towels, I hastened down the hall to the small one in the back — the one to which I had banished Billy. It was stuffy from being closed up, so I opened a window to air it. The only time I came there was to make the bed for a family visit.

When I pulled off the bedspread, an uneasy feeling caused shivers to run up my back. I had the irrational feeling that someone was watching me. Billy's ghost literally haunting me?

Don't be morbid, I scoffed. It's just stuffy having been closed up.

I tossed the bottom sheet on the bed, smoothed it and flung on the top sheet. A sudden draft chilled me, probably from the open window. A light flannel sheet served as a summer blanket. As I knelt to tuck them in at the bottom, I thought I heard a noise. Leaning against the foot of the bed, I held my breath to listen. Nothing.

Sound carries a distance on still air. Probably it came from the Keene's place. Either I was turning into a nervous Nellie in my old age or I was letting my problems overwhelm me. Feeling dizzy, I sat on the bed, leaned back and closed my eyes for a minute.

Then I heard a voice call, "Minty." Startled, I jerked upright, ears tense, listening.

"Miiinnntttty." It was louder now and sounded like Billy's voice. I told myself firmly: I don't believe in ghosts.

No! My eyes popped open. I shook my head and insisted out loud, "No, Billy's dead and cremated." I took a short breath. "His ashes buried." Quick breath. "In the cemetery. Next to his parents."

That eerie voice again. "I need to talk to you."

I clutched the bedspread to my breast, and looked around at an empty room. Heart racing, I told myself that I must have dozed off, had another nightmare or something. Carefully I stood up and tiptoed to the door, opened it, slipped out, embarrassed, but still disturbed.

I slammed the door shut behind me and leaned my full weight against it, puffing and shaking. Either I fell asleep or I was losing my mind. I *hadn't* been sleeping well. Neither prospect comforted me one iota.

I swallowed several times and, finally, managed to yell, "Buck? Where are you, boy? Come, Buck. Come to Momma."

Blessedly, I heard his claws as he scrambled up the stairs, skidded around the corner and almost ran into me. I knelt down, grabbed his neck with both arms and buried my face in the thick fur by his droopy ears.

More composed, I hurried downstairs into the kitchen, took a bottle of wine from the fridge and slopped a generous six ounces into a glass. Not usually given to drinking alone, I justified it by remembering that I was not usually given to panic either.

For a few minutes, I sat at the kitchen table nursing my drink and breathing slowly. Regaining control, I knew that it would take a while before I could be upstairs alone again. I thought about calling Hugh, but he was in transit. Philabelle? No, too upsetting. Sarah wasn't home.

I reassured myself that these phenomena took place because I was stressed out by my various problems. Reminding myself that to stay focused, I wiped any sticky off the counters. I checked to be sure the kitchen was spotless. Then, with the loyal Buck hovering beside me, I went out to the garden to pick sweet peas and jasmine. I really wanted their fragrance in the house. I knelt down with the clippers in hand and kept looking over my shoulder, reluctant to turn my back on the field where Billy had died.

With a generous bouquet, I opened the back door and urged Buck into the kitchen first. For a minute, I held my breath and listened. Billy's room was directly overhead. Relieved at the silence, I held the flowers to my nose, inhaling their sweetness. Then I arranged them in two vases. I put one on the table, but still not brave enough to go upstairs, I left the other on the bottom step. A glance at the clock said Hugh would be there in about an hour. Nevertheless, I kept Buck close by while I prepared what I could of dinner.

Then I faced a dilemma: my pretty dress with the cool green fern print was on the bed upstairs. As a last resort, I showered quickly in the downstairs bathroom. Feeling cleaner, I sniffed my shirt and skirt, relieved that they didn't smell. Having nothing else downstairs, I put them back on. I had just finished combing my damp hair, when I heard Buck's friendly woof. He leapt up and raced down the hall to welcome Hugh. I followed, feeling reassurance and happiness in equal portions.

Hugh had dropped his bag on the hall floor and patted Buck's head. He stood upright, called out, "Hey, shug!" and swept me into his arms. I pressed myself against him, feeling his slightly scratchy cheek against mine and inhaled his unique Hughness.

Our greetings exchanged, I asked about his trip.

"Tedious and I'm sweaty, hot and hungry." Grinning, he ogled me from head to foot before he took off his jacket, draped it over a chair and undid his tie. "Want to join me in a quick shower upstairs and then …?" he stood, tie in hand, eyebrows doing his Groucho Marx thing and waited for my answer.

Shower sex no longer appealed to me, unfortunately. It required more gymnastics than I was comfortable with.

"How about it, shug?" Hugh asked.

Conscious of the difference in our ages, I hoped he could not read *my* mind, but said, "No, I just got out a few minutes ago." The thought of Billy's ghost flitted through my brain, but I quickly added, "My hair isn't even dry." I ran my fingers through it as if in confirmation.

That was a stupid thing to say, but Hugh seemed okay with that and he picked up his bag, opened it and handed me a box wrapped in navy blue and tied with gold ribbon.

"Oh, Hugh, you're so sweet. You shouldn't have." I mouthed the cliché as I removed the elegant ribbon and paper. A bottle of Very Irristible by Givenchy. "Awww. My favorite." I kissed his cheek. Because it was Hugh's favorite, I had used up my supply, so I was genuinely pleased.

Hugh smiled and said, "Good. I'll go shower and get into something more comfortable." He leered at me and patted me on the bottom before he headed for the hall and the stairs.

"Go ahead," I told him. "I'll bring these." I urged him forward and leaned down to pick up the vase of sweet peas and, peeking down the hall at Billy's room, I followed Hugh into the bedroom.

He had a drawer for his things and room in the closet. He took what he wanted and went into the shower. At last I could change into the feminine dress I had chosen for the evening. I dumped the dirties in the hamper, pulled the light voile over my head and checked its fit. At my dressing table, I fixed my face, added earrings and dabbed on a touch of Very Irresistible. I laughed into the mirror, delighted to hear Hugh's rowdy singing, "Gimme the beat, boys, and free my soul, I wanna hear more of that rock'n roll an'drift away" from the bathroom. Billy had never outgrown The Beer Barrel Polka, I remembered, happy that it was *Hugh* in the shower.

For a minute I wished I had joined him, before I remembered my problem with shower sex: too energetic. It was partly my age, I suppose, but also the worry that I was no longer attractive as a woman — an insecurity for which I blamed my late husband. Whose ghost might still be trapped in the back bedroom, I thought, and shivered.

I dragged the comb through my almost dry hair as if *it*, not my inadequacies, had taken the edge off my pleasure at having Hugh home. Forget Billy, I admonished myself. You don't want to think about that.

On that unhappy note, I sighed, feeling that I had done what I could with my appearance and might as well go downstairs. I was putting the finishing touches on dinner, when Hugh joined me, looking cooler in a pale blue short-sleeved cotton shirt and khaki shorts. His dark hair glistened with moisture, but I resisted the urge to muss up it up. Instead, I reached up in the cupboard for two crystal wine glasses.

I'd made a salad and dessert and carried everything out to the screened porch. Hugh as usual grilled the hamburgers outside. When he brought them in, we settled down to eat. I sat in the swing and he took the wicker lounge. Buck settled on the floor close to the screen and gnawed on his treat. Cleo slept on a cushioned chair.

As we ate, I asked more about the conference.

"It gave me a lot to think about."

"Yeah?" I encouraged him and took a bite of hamburger.

Hugh chuckled, "Yeah. Didn't I tell you that I'm such a renowned physician that I was invited to join the teaching staff at UVA Medical School, as well as turn NGO volunteer, when I retire?" He tasted a forkful of salad, closed his eyes and hummed, "Ummmm!" with approval.

He had told me, but I'd forgotten. "What's an NGO? You're not considering retirement surely."

He shrugged, "Not necessarily. But it's gratifying to realize that there are opportunities for me in the big world outside Whitman. NGOs are non-governmental organizations, like CARE, Mercy Corps, humanitarian groups, which interest me. How'd your visit with Rachel go?"

While we polished off dinner, I gave him a quick synopsis and added, "I told her she needed to arrange some interests for herself." I grimaced. "She mentioned learning to tango."

"Will she? Take tango lessons, I mean. That's one sexy dance." He shook his head and drank some wine. "What about Howard?"

I grinned and said, "Who knows. I've always believed that he has unplumbed depths. Maybe the tango will turn out to be one." Lazily swinging, I wasn't in the mood now to introduce my anxieties.

Conversation was desultory, covering our various families, including Philabelle's future and idle news about town, until Hugh finished his dinner. I stopped the swing while he refilled our wine glasses and asked, "What's for dessert?"

I took the napkin off the plate of brownies and offered it to him.

"What else is new?" he asked and bit into one.

I mentioned that I thought Morton had some scheme with Al Schultz to bring progress to Whitman and added, "I thought we were safe from the demon developers when we avoided becoming a stop on I-95. I don't like all this talk of change. Whitman's just fine the way it is." I dragged my feet to stop the swing again to put my plate on the table and pick up a brownie.

I hadn't thought my anxiety about the Manse and Philabelle showed, but Hugh was a sensitive man and apparently picked it up.

"You can't stop the world from turning, shug. I understand your feeling bad about Philabelle's talk of moving, but she'll decide when it's time."

I nodded and tried to think of anything new that might interest him while I munched on a brownie. He pushed the edge of the swing with his foot to start its cycle again. "Speaking of change, Minty, it's time for us to set a date for our marriage. We've dawdled around long enough."

Oh crumbs! I blinked. Too caught up in my own problems — especially with the appearance of the ghost —I had forgotten about marriage. Desperate to discourage talk about it, I said, "There's no hurry, Hugh, is there?" I moved the swing again and said, "I'd like to get this Manse bit cleared up first. Besides, have you forgotten our agreement was friendship with privileges, not marriage?"

Hugh reached out to hold the swing still and stared up at me. "No, I haven't forgotten, but I didn't count on a change in my feelings. This living half here with you and half back in town no longer suits me. I'd like us to live together."

Panicky, I had stuffed too much brownie in my mouth and couldn't talk.

"What's your objection? You think I'm too difficult to live with?" He tilted his head, questioning, and added, "*I* think we get along together just fine. I don't complain about Cleo joining us in bed and you don't complain that I leave the toilet seat up."

My mouth suddenly dry, I struggled to swallow some gooey brownie. Half nodding to indicate that yes, we got along as friends and half shaking my head that no I liked the status quo at the same time, I gulped. Tears welled up in my eyes. I put my hands over my face. I was not the crying kind and had nothing but contempt for women who used crying to manipulate men. Too much was happening to me too fast and I was having trouble coping.

Hugh, bless his heart, recognized my brownie problem and joined me on the swing. Trying not to laugh, he put an arm around me. "It's O.K., shug. I don't want you to choke. I guess we have time to talk it all out."

Holding me against his chest, he used that tone of voice that reached into the marrow of my bones, into every blood vessel in my body and every electrical connection in my brain.

Why wouldn't he understand how important it was that we go on this way? I couldn't bear the thought of not having Hugh in my life, but, since Billy, I didn't trust *love* and marriage implied that – it *requires* love to endure.

"Our friendship is vitally important to me, Hugh."

We swung gently back and forth in silence. Finally, I suggested, "You could move out here with me." The air around us was still except for some night insects squeaking in the nearby shrubs.

In distress when he didn't answer, I whispered, "Do you hear those bugs?"

Hugh sighed, "Those are mating calls." His arm still held me close as we swung, but in his doctor's voice serious with patience, he said, "Minty, I don't want to stay in Whitman without you as my wife."

*　　　*　　　*

Hugh stayed the night, of course. I loved being in bed with Hugh. He was so different from Billy. Not until recently had I appreciated the sense of security that Hugh exuded. He was not flashy but dependable, fun and a great lover.

As we lay cuddled together, in post-coital bliss, a cooling breeze blew in the curtains. It reminded me of Billy's ghost. Billy was dead, I repeated to myself. With some foreboding, I decided to tell Hugh about it.

I could feel my hand begin to perspire on his bare chest, needing to feel close, and whispered, "Hugh, do you believe in ghosts?"

"Ghosts, like on Hallowe'en?" his drowsy voice told me he'd almost been asleep.

"No, I mean like a dead person coming back to talk to a live person." Aware that I would sound ridiculous. I held my breath.

"I don't know, shug. I hope you're not getting into that paranormal stuff," he murmured and shifted toward me a little. He yawned into my hair, but didn't open his eyes.

"No, I'm not. I just wondered if you, as a scientist, think it's possible that dead people can actually materialize as ghosts?"

Hugh turned his head, more alert now, and I felt him thinking about the concept. "There's a lot in this universe we don't know, Minty," he snorted with chagrin, "that butts me in the face every day at the clinic." He probably had a specific patient in mind.

Hugh raised his head to look at me and added, "The trouble with those zealots is that they play at trying to contact the dead. Their failure compounds their grief." He pulled me close, nuzzled my neck and added, "It's just not healthy, shug, Leave it alone."

"Hmph! Are you implying that I'm weak and vulnerable just because I'm a widow?

Hugh's chest quivered with quiet laughter. "No. You may be vulnerable, but you're far from weak. Are you thinking about Billy? Want to hold a séance, contact him and give him hell?" His amusement irritated me.

How could he get inside my head like that? The words 'I don't want anything to do with Billy' almost burst out. I remembered in time that Billy was Hugh's *brother*, so I made a joke of it.

"No way, but a séance might be fun."

"I'd avoid the womens' group at church, if I were you." He yawned again and snuggled against me, closing the conversation.

He had failed to reassure me. But I still worried about the possibility of a ghost.

Chapter 12

When I woke, Saturday morning, I was alone in my bed: Hugh, Buck and Cleo all absent. As quickly as feasible, I toileted, grabbed a light robe and loped down stairs. When I smelled coffee and bacon, I grinned, reassured that I had not been abandoned.

Hugh was singing "Oh what a beautiful morning" when I joined the three of them in the kitchen. Buck sat on his haunches by Hugh, who was frying bacon; Cleo crouched on top of the fridge, poised to pounce at a propitious moment.

I picked up the song where Hugh left off " …the corn is as high as an elephant's thiiiigh, and the la lala la lala … sky!" By this time, Hugh and I were both laughing — until the toaster pinged.

"Oops," he said and, like a ballet dancer, he swiveled, dropped the toast on a plate and, pirouetted back to the stove to serve the bacon and called, "Good morning, Merry Sunshine" to me all within a fraction of a second.

"You're a good man, Charlie Brown," I caroled back at him and bussed him heartily on the back of the neck. I saw that Buck had already been out, back in and both food bowls filled. "What needs doing?"

"Pour the coffee and we're ready."

While I followed orders, Hugh retrieved the eggs, added the bacon and brought everything to the table. Buck followed the scent of bacon, always courteous but hopeful. Cleo jumped down for her share.

With the sun lighting the room, fragrant with the sweet peas I had picked earlier, we devoured breakfast. Hugh shared bits of bacon and scrambled eggs with both greedy fur critters.

When he noticed my disapproval, he said, "I've seen you do the same thing, shug."

"Yes, but *after* we've finished," I shrugged. "Oh well, I can't complain. You're too good to me." I smiled and patted his hand.

His eyes crinkled with amusement and a grin creased his face. "Have I overwhelmed you with my cooking skill … " His grin turned into an evil smirk. "… or was it my sacrificial offering on the altar of passion last night?"

"Tough to make a choice," I drawled and, to keep from laughing, I ate the last piece of toast loaded with homemade strawberry jam.

Hugh refilled our cups with coffee, sat, smiled into my eyes and said, "It's good to be home, shug." Caught with a mouthful I could only nod vigorously. Then, before I could make a clever comment, he added, "Last night was just a sample of the advantages available on a regular basis to a wife." He grinned lewdly and winked like a dirty old man. "Given any further thought to marriage?"

Unprepared for this sudden reference, I blurted out the best, quick excuse which came to mind, "I've been too busy — you know, with the Manse and Rachel's visit." And, apropos of nothing, I added, "I got a new goat while you were gone."

"Ah." Hugh raised his eyebrows and nodded. "I didn't know you needed a new goat and I'm not fooled by your changing the subject." He drank his coffee and gave Buck and Cleo the final two bits of bacon. Then he looked at me, eyebrows elevated and head tilted, obviously waiting for a response. The appealing expression on his face, reminded me that marriage implied the existence of love and of my present lack of confidence in *love*.

"But we agreed that friendship with privileges was what we wanted and," I pointed out to him again, "no complications."

"Are you afraid that marriage would destroy our friendship?" He looked skeptical for a minute before he said, "You know that friendship is the surest guarantee of a happy marriage."

Unable to think of an adequate response to that, I glanced at the clock and asked, "Isn't Mac expecting you at the Clinic?" I feigned concern, but knew I was being manipulative and I despised manipulative women. But defense required it this time.

He pushed back his chair, picked up my empty plate, stacked it on his, set his mug on the top and took them over to the dishwasher. Buck's woof to go out broke an uneasy silence. Hugh opened the door for him, before coming to sit down facing me again.

"Minty, I'm not trying to stampede you into this, but I don't *understand* why you're so opposed to marriage," Hugh spoke calmly, but seriously enough that I felt compelled to reply intelligently, but could only natter foolishly.

"I'm not *opposed* to marriage per se, but we did agree that neither of us want another," I hesitated at the word 'failure' because neither Hugh nor I had been at fault. It was his wife and Billy who had failed us. Hugh sat studying me and, in consternation, I stammered, "But marriage seems so … so *permanent.*"

Hugh's mouth opened, he squinted and finally stated, "Nothing's *permanent*, Minty. Don't you consider our present relationship as long term?"

"Well …"Alarmed at the prospect of it being finite, I experienced a flashback to the Sunday Carmen told me, and everybody within hearing distance, that I 'should keep Billy at home and out of other women's beds'. I felt again the humiliation of my ignorance and that insecurity that I was no longer attractive to men. I swallowed, aware of the difference in Hugh's age and mine. How long before Hugh noticed that difference? I raised my hand to touch my hair, more salt than pepper.

I was coming unglued and looked at Hugh's face, still troubled, and waiting for my reaction. I fluttered my hands uselessly and finally managed to say, "I just need a little more time to adjust, I guess." Not brilliant, but the best I could do.

"Come on, Minty. You've said that before and I told you that I'm not prepared to spend the rest of my life with us just fooling around. I want you to be my wife." His eyes reflected his determination.

My ire rose at that expression. "We're not *fooling around* like teenagers in the back seat of the car, Hugh. We're free, consenting adults and very discreet."

The silence that followed my outburst was broken when Hugh spoke, "I've said before that a future in Whitman, without our being married, doesn't appeal to me." He rose and walked over to the counter. "Let's clean up this mess." He took the frying pan off the stove and put it in the sink.

As I cleared off the table and put things away, my annoyance faded. I recalled his joke about job offers away from Whitman. That scared me and I said, "I'm sorry, honey. Let me get the Manse and Rachel squared away. Just give me a little more time to clear my head."

I opened the dishwasher and Hugh leaned against the counter beside me, arms crossed on his chest. "How much time are we talking about here? A week? A month? A year?" He was disappointed, obviously, but, at least, Hugh was willing to compromise — which required me to follow suit.

I turned the dishwasher on. Over its rumbling and gurgling, I said, "A month or so, maybe, would, eh …" I licked my lips, feeling at a disadvantage. My only answer for procrastinating was that Billy might be haunting me. Literally.

Buck butted against Hugh, who scratched the dog's head, before he said, "Well, suppose we say four weeks from now – the sixteenth of June? Decision made by July fourth. That allows an interval for further discussion. By then you'll have made up your mind. Does that work for you?"

His patience shamed me and I had to agree. "I guess so. Except July is a busy month. Smith usually comes for his visit and y'all go fishing. I have my family over on the Fourth. Let's get through July first, O.K.?" I hoped I wasn't pushing it too hard.

Hugh shook his head, flung up his hands. "O.K. Smith *is* coming the third week in July. We've been talking about walking part of the Appalachian Trail. So we'll settle it no later than August first?"

Surprised at his agreeing, I asked, "Mac's giving you a whole week off? Can he manage without you?"

"He'll have help. I thought I'd told you about the young family practice man I met at the conference. He's checking out locations in this area and will work with us for awhile this summer. Mac and I both get more of a break." The expression on his face relaxed and he glanced at his watch, and added, "He's looking to join someone as an associate. A New Yorker who thinks small town practice in this area would work for him."

Then Hugh kissed me lightly and left. I was sure, however, that neither one of us felt fully satisfied at the semi-resolution of the marriage problem.

*   *   *

I called Philabelle to distract myself. She agreed that we should finish the inventory. Hugh had offered the use of his video camera, but I didn't want to appear on film and Philabelle said it was too heavy. We'd stick to pencil and paper.

We finished in the library in the morning, me up on the ladder and Philabelle taking notes in her old fashioned Palmer Method handwriting. It was so much easier to read than the modern day scribbling. Or the curlicue calligraphy in the Journal where I hoped to find some historical reference to the Manse.

About 11 o'clock, we took a break for tea and crumpets on the side porch. While Philabelle heated water, I picked a couple of sprigs of mint from her garden. The scent of the locust trees was strong and I inhaled deeply. The trellis was hidden beneath a wild crepe myrtle. A stand of delphiniums added a medley of blues. Nearby platoons of iris rose behind clumps of begonias – a glorious triangle of pinks and lavenders against the lawn.

A pang of regret at the thought of losing the Manse reminded me that I should think of options to selling – in case no one in the family wanted it.

Philabelle called from the side porch and I joined her and asked, "Have you ever thought of opening the Manse as a bed and breakfast, hon?"

She looked at me in astonishment, blinked and stammered, "Oh, Minty, I don't think at seventy-three I'm capable of operating a B and B."

Oh course, she wasn't. What was I thinking? But I had another idea.

"When you do have to leave, maybe it could be turned into a tea shop. Lynn hasn't got much to do and she's good with people. She might be interested in managing it for you."

"A clever thought, Minty, but speaking of Lynn, have you done anything about reconciling with her?"

"Me make the first move? Why should I?" Not this again, I thought, feeling testy.

Quietly, Philabelle put down the Haviland tea cup, which she was using. "Because she needs your *forgiveness*. I'm surprised that you don't appreciate how *fortunate* you've been in life. Especially compared to her life."

"Oh sure," I could hardly believe Philabelle was serious. She seemed determined to make me the villain. That was unfair and maddening. "Lynn's the pretty one, remember? And rich as all git-out, too. What's unfortunate about her life?" It took an effort not to raise my voice, but I controlled my temper at the injustice of putting me at fault.

"But you're the one who enjoyed many happy years of marriage and now you have Hugh. Lynn has had very little love as an adult." Except with my husband, I thought.

Considering the dismal end of my marriage and the betrayal of my love, I almost said 'oh bull puppies', but I didn't like offending Philabelle. I filled my mouth with crumpet and let her reference go.

Meantime, as I chewed, I diverted my irritation by contemplating the splendor that surrounded the Manse. On the far side of the lawn lay what was essentially an arboretum.

To change the subject, I said, "You know, Philabelle, it might be a good idea to have a horticulturist appraise the various plantings in the woods. They have value, too." I washed down the crumpet with a swallow of tea.

"You're right. My father's uncle lived about a mile north of here – long before any of those were built." She gestured toward Main Street. "He's the one who was a landscaper. As the old farms were sold to developers, he collected examples of native and exotic trees. He shared them with my grandparents, who lived in the Manse then. At one time there were several acres of various species."

Quietly, we gazed across the side yard. Both dogwoods and redbuds had dropped their flowers, but a variety of foliage formed an impressive background in shades of green.

"I've always loved the oak trees especially." I pointed at the biggest. "That one shades this whole side of the house. How old is it?"

"I don't know. It's been there all my life." Philabelle gazed at it. "My mother and I sometimes sat under it to play 'having tea with the Queen'. We used my small table and chairs and my miniature porcelain tea set. I still have that, you know." She smiled, reliving the past for a minute.

Then she made a face, turned to me and added, "Oh, Minty, I had hoped that someday you and Hugh would live the Manse with all the family furnishings." I opened my mouth to protest, but she held up a hand. "I know we've been over this before, but it would have been perfect."

For a second, I visualized marriage with Hugh and living in the Manse. Sleep with him in that enormous walnut sleigh bed? In a pig's eye, I said to myself. His threat of leaving Whitman returned like the itch of an insect bite and my heart clenched at the thought of losing him.

I'd already let him become far too important in my life. It would be easy to fall in love with Hugh and marry him while in that crazed state. But I couldn't risk what might happen later.

I switched back to the safe subject of the Manse and said, "Philabelle, if Ola's granddaughter were to come more often to help, couldn't you live here … for five or six more years?" Until she died, I had almost said. I couldn't deal with *that* yet. She was only ten years older than I was. After my mother's death, Philabelle had been not a mother, but an example, an advisor, as well as a friend.

I suspected that I let myself get emotionally dependent on people too often, – another thing I had learned from my experience with Billy.

She interrupted my morbid thought. "The fact is that I've heard appealing things about Creek Woods Residence. Their program is impressive. They offer life services, you know, which is the type of security I want in my old age." She wrinkled her nose at me, "Don't look so disapproving, Minty. Whitman's have good genes. Many of them lived long lives and it's realistic for me to prepare for the inevitable."

We tossed the subject of her age back and forth, agreeing that the wise course was to plan ahead. Philabelle, despite the limitation of living in the Manse all her life, was not isolated. She was a reader and kept in touch with what was going on all over the world. She and Sarah frequently engaged in energetic discussions about politics, the environment and, surprisingly, argued over the results of college football games. Philabelle enjoyed her activities and her independence and she deserved both.

I said, "You know I'll respect your decision, honey. You're certainly capable of managing your affairs. But I want you to know that I'd welcome your company at the farm."

Philabelle was obviously pleased that I would consider her moving in with me and we left the conversation there. I dismissed the thought as unlikely.

My heart was heavy for the rest of the day, imagining not only life without my sister-in-law, but a possible change in my relationship with Hugh. Nothing seemed to be working smoothly.

Chapter 13

The next couple of weeks were busy ones. The appraisers came and went and Sarah and I had coordinated our search for sponsors for the Fourth in the interests of efficiency. Meantime, I wanted to confirm the plans with my children.

Settled at the kitchen table with a glass of iced tea, I called William first and asked whether he and the family would join us for the Fourth.

"Of course, Mother. It's traditional and we wouldn't miss it. Myra and the children would be disappointed if they didn't get to visit you and the family." He paused slightly before asking, "Is Jesse coming?"

I had to bite my tongue before replying. I didn't understand why Rachel and William seem incapable of accepting Jesse as gay. But I didn't let that intrude on my answer. "I'm not sure. He and Mike might have a commitment, but I hope they can make it. The family wouldn't be complete without Jesse and Mike."

I let that sink in before I thanked him for recommending McCormick and Winkler, the appraisers.

"I'm assuming that they did the job satisfactorily?" he asked and I assured him that they had and efficiently. He continued, "Will you let me know, for my file, when Uncle Hugh receives their report?"

"They're sending it to Philabelle, William. Why would they send it to Hugh?" I bristled at his ignoring her authority.

"As the surviving male head of the household, he'd be …"

"Philabelle is the senior member of the family and it's her home that's involved." Amused, I couldn't resist a little dig. "Come on, William. That kind of chauvinism is inappropriate in the twenty-first century."

Over the wire, I heard him inhale and then exhale, "I don't think I'm old fashioned, Mother, but Philabelle is getting on in years …"

With considerable effort, I squelched my impulse to retort to that unpalatable stereotype. Instead, I interrupted, "Actually, the three of us are working as a team. That way it's not a burden on any of us." thus setting the proper example for my son. I, at least, have learned to accept life's disappointments gracefully.

"That's a reasonable approach, but the fact remains that the time is coming, faster than you may wish, that Philabelle won't be able to live in that huge house alone," he concluded.

"William…" I had put off asking because I was afraid of the answer. "How serious is Morton's threat of eminent domain?"

Always deliberate, he paused before he said, "If the town has a definite need for that property, it's more than a threat, Mother. We always have recourse to sue, if there is no adequate argument for necessary use." William apparently heard my groan of dismay. "Did I understand that Morton said a developer had approached him about buying the property?"

"Yes, he did. No, wait a minute. Morton said the town would buy the property for shops, office space," I thought back to remember accurately. "That was Al Schultz – he's a new lawyer in town. I don't know whether you know him. About five years ago, he bought a house, in the neighborhood where Lynn lives. He has an office in town. Also he had some role in the sale of the property for the new retirement home on the Creek. Anyway, he's the one who described how the Manse property would be used and why the town needed to progress. That was the key word: *progress.*"

"What's his name again? I'll check him out. Why would he be speaking in support of Morton? Is he on the town council?"

I told William as much as I knew about Schultz and tried, as best I could, to suppress my prejudice against the man and his garish wife. Surprisingly, William said it sounded odd to him. That made me feel better *and* worse. If our suspicions were justified, more was at stake than I expected. Pompous he might be, but my son William was nobody's fool. Sometimes, he reminded me of Billy's father: a shrewd man, but not your 'hail fellow well met'. I was glad to have William as an advisor and agreed that the situation with the Manse was a complex legal issue.

He concluded by saying, "The Manse, as well as the adjoining property, would fetch quite a desirable price on the market, Mother. I hope you and Aunt Philabelle won't make any hasty decisions."

Pleased that he had taken note of Philabelle's status, I forebore from reminding him that I was not prone to hasty decisions.

My tea long gone, I let Buck out for awhile, stretched and then sat down with the phone again.

Next on my list was Jesse, who, as hoped, accepted my invitation enthusiastically. When I asked him about taking over the Manse, to my surprise, he expressed some interest. "At this moment, I can't see how it would work, but I've always loved the Manse and, if possible, I'd like it to stay in the family. I hope that it will be a good while before Aunt Philabelle feels that she must leave it. It's a big house for one person though."

Enormously cheered by his response, I assured him that Philabelle wasn't retiring to a residence for adults anytime soon.

Those calls taken care of, I checked on Philabelle, who said, "If it's agreeable to you and Hugh, I'd like you both to come to tea. Perhaps this Saturday? Hugh is off work this weekend, I believe. I have ideas which I'd like to discuss with y'all."

That worked fine for me as Hugh and I had planned to spend the weekend together.

*   *   *

Saturday the sky was over-cast, but the temperature stayed hot and humid. Not a day for outdoor fun. Hugh offered to pick me up, but I said I'd drive into Whitman.

Philabelle had set up a tea table in the small lady-parlor between the library and the kitchen. A bow window on the side looked over her perennial garden, which was in full and fragrant bloom. The furniture was typical Victorian with Alice-blue velveteen upholstery, white lace window treatment (as they say now instead of curtains) and a blue and cream Aubusson carpet, which echoed the wall paper design.

Philabelle brought to the twenty-first century the charm and elegance of the early twentieth. In her own style, for the occasion, she used the best Havilland teacups, plates and silver service. She'd made finger sandwiches, some with cream cheese and watercress filling, and miniature croissants with home-made blackberry jam and clotted cream. I realized that I was hungry.

"How graciously you entertain, Philabelle. It's a talent you and my mother shared, but I wasn't receptive to learning." I fingered the fine linen cloth with its hand crocheted trim, which matched the napkins. "These are surely family heirlooms, aren't they?"

"Yes and I hope that some of the young people in the family will value them. I know which of our lady ancestors made several of them. They're getting almost too frail to use, but I've seen small pieces of fine embroidery and crochet framed attractively."

I knew that William's wife, Myra, would treasure anything associated with Whitman history and said so. I marveled that Myra managed to retain her essence of Southern womanly gentility and accept so gracefully the changes of the Civil Rights Movement. So many of the old families secretly clung to the past, while ignoring the injustices. During my meditation, Hugh arrived.

Philabelle poured the tea and said, "Since this is in the nature of a business get-together, I might as well explain right away that I have a plan for the Manse, which I hope you two will find acceptable." She sipped her tea before she began, "While Minty and I were inventorying the library, it occurred to me that the Manse would be an excellent site for a town library. Obviously, many of the books, such as the American Heritage Literature series, would be an adjunct to the school library.

"So, that seed planted in my head, after considerable thought, I conceived the idea of donating the Manse to the town, stipulating, of course, that it would be preserved in perpetuity." Philabelle sat back, head tilted a little, blue eyes beaming, obviously awaiting our reaction.

"Oh, Philabelle, you can't mean to *give* it away." The idea upset me more than I could have anticipated. Surely, we could think of making use of it after Philabelle … I avoided facing the fact of her not living there. "It's been in the family for generations."

"Who in the family wants to assume the responsibility of residing here and/or maintaining it?" She sounded quite reconciled to leaving the only home she had ever lived in. At the same time, I was relieved that she had not put a time limit on her moving out. "All the various families have rejected an offer to live here."

"Nevertheless, there must be some way we can keep it in the family," I protested. "Maybe, turn it into a book store? Or a tea shop?" Both of them looked at me with total incomprehension. "We'd have to find some one to run it, of course."

At their lack of enthusiasm for my suggestions, I made a moue and shrugged. At the same time, Philabelle turned to Hugh for his response. Hugh put down his teacup and wiped his mouth with the napkin. Then he spoke in a tone appropriate as the only male family member, which both amused and irritated me.

"The Manse, including the arboretum, is a saleable property, I believe, and that should be checked out first." His face assumed a thoughtful look and I glanced at Philabelle. We sipped our tea giving him time before he continued, "Much as I regret the Manse leaving the guardianship of a Whitman family descendant, I congratulate you, Philabelle, for devising what I think would an excellent solution – *if* selling is not feasible *and* if the town accepts the conditions of your proposal."

"Oh, Hugh, ...," I started to object at how willingly he'd discard the Manse and my worry surfaced again.

But he continued, "I can't see any other way for the Manse to survive. I'd rather give it to the town than see it leveled by bulldozers." He turned to his sister, "You may not realize that the process of donating a property of this size to a municipality is long and complicated." He stopped to drink some tea, before he continued, "There are new building codes, the issue of taxes, costs of modernizing the structure. As the one who lives here, Philabelle, and knows the house from attic to basement, would you consider it viable as a home?"

Philabelle chuckled in her gentle way, "No, Hugh. Since none of the family want to live here, I conclude that it's not an appropriate home for a twenty-first century family."

I picked up a mini scone, and, tried to be objective, before I asked, "Why not?"

Philabelle smiled, her small hand light on my wrist, "In your heart, Minty, you know that it is an historical landmark, not a home any longer. The heating system is inadequate; the rooms are too small and the ceilings too high; there's only one bathroom and the plumbing's forty years old. The entire floor plan doesn't fit modern tastes. Plus, there're all the accoutrements that have accumulated over the years"

"The only redeeming virtue is that we've maintained the basic structure," Hugh said. "So it is still a financial asset. That's an important factor to consider." He glanced at me and added, "I think William could give y'all helpful advice about selling."

I felt like throwing the Haviland teapot at Hugh and throwing myself at Philabelle's feet and begging her to – I don't know what! Despite her callous words, Philabelle had made it clear earlier, to both Hugh and me, that if I married Hugh, she would give the property to us. Anxious to avoid any hint of 'marriage' right now, I controlled my initial response and said nothing. The Haviland was safe from me! Silently, I agreed that William knew his way around the business world. I could count on his advice.

At least, if the town agreed, the Manse and its arboretum would remain intact for my children and grandchildren, for Hugh's son, Smith, and his children to know and appreciate. Needing to make a final plea, I said, "But so many of our ancestors were born and died in this place, married, loved and, maybe even hated each other here. We still have memories tied to the Manse. It would really hurt to lose it." Silently, I vowed to check the Net for the procedure to have it declared an historical home. That might be our redemption. Even Morton couldn't have it torn down then.

Hugh had the final word on that subject: "There's a time for sentiment, Minty, and a time for practicality. You two have done a brilliant job of the inventory, but the process of donating something of this value is an involved legal process." I took this opportunity to devour my third sandwich. "I repeat: we should enlist William's help and E.J. Rossi, too. If a competent realtor doesn't think it's saleable, there'll be time for the lawyers to draw up a sample proposal for the town to consider."

"Surely, Philabelle and I can draw up a proposal," I said, conscious that essentially I was clinging to the Manse by injecting myself into the project of preservation.

"Are you reluctant to ask William for suggestions?" He turned to his sister, "Have you discussed this with anyone else?"

"No. I wanted you two to consider it first. William is, of course, my first choice for advice." Philabelle looked at me and I could almost read her sweet devious mind: *Minty, dear, if you would marry Hugh and live here, we wouldn't have this problem.* I knew the discussion had ended.

The distress I felt hadn't diminished my appreciation of Philabelle's entertaining style. To ameliorate my emotion and to change the subject, I told her *that* and finished my tea. "I hope you will pass these amenities of gracious living down to your grandnieces and nephews as well as the material things." I behaved like a proper southern lady instead of the termagant I felt like.

"If they will accept them, I'll be glad to," she chuckled, "But I don't see little Hammie being satisfied with finger sandwiches." She picked up a sandwich and turned to Hugh, "He's such a darling little boy. I think he resembles Smith at that age."

"Yeah, they're both blonds. But I remember Smith as being more of a hell raiser than Hammie," Hugh said.

Philabelle rolled her eyes and admonished him, "I wish you'd watch your language, Hugh. Especially when all the youngsters are here for the Fourth."

We discussed plans for the Fourth until it was time for Hugh and me to leave.

*   *   *

Later that afternoon, at aperitif time, Hugh stretched out on the lounge on the side porch with a bowl of whole peanuts in his lap. I sat across from him by the table holding the pitcher of whiskey sours. I relaxed, my feet up beside his on lounge. First we picked holes in Philabelle's plan to save the Manse and agreed to make use of the talents of both William and E.J. Rossi to disentangle the mass of red tape involved. At least Hugh wouldn't oppose Philabelle's plan.

Complacently, I said, "Saving the Manse is going to be my project for the summer." And sipped the cold drink while he shelled peanuts.

"If that's your project for the summer, what about me?" He raised his eyebrows.

"You could give me a hand in recruiting supporters."

"Supporters of what?" he mumbled around a mouthful.

"Preservation of the Manse, of course," I said and added, "The rule of war is that a 'strong offense is the best defense.' My father said that."

"Yeah? Who are you out to offend?" he scoffed, bumping his foot against mine. He didn't seem to be taking this seriously.

"The team of Schultz and Trueblood, of course," I said. My voice sounding frustrated. "I'm sure they have an agenda which includes tearing down the Manse and building one of those glass and steel monstrosities for condos and offices."

"Come on, shug. I can't visualize towers of glass and steel in downtown Whitman."

Hugh chuckled.

"Maybe glass and steel is an exaggeration, but you see my point," I insisted. Peeved at the supercilious expression on his face, I took a gulp of my drink. "They're out to 'bring Whitman into the twenty-first century'. This is the home that you grew up in, Hugh," I said firmly for emphasis. "How many generations of your family lived here?"

"Here." He held out a handful of peanuts. "Lots of generations, but nobody of historical significance. It's not exactly Monticello, hon."

Buck's woof, at that moment, requested entry back into the house. Hugh stood up, brushing shells off his lap. "I'll let him in."

I ate the nuts and when he returned, Buck at his heels, Hugh leaned down close enough to blow in my ear.

"Don't do that when I'm eating. It tickles." I glanced sideways at him, recognizing the overtures to a romantic evening. Usually I play this game eagerly and with some skill. Tonight, however, my goal had been to enlist his support. Distracting Hugh from the subject of matrimony was important, but so was changing his attitude toward the Manse.

"Don't you think that our children and grandchildren deserve to have a voice in the future of the Manse?" I asked.

He flopped down on the chaise again. I shifted a little so I could see his face. Buck, who can scent edibles anywhere on our property, ambled over to stand and stare at me.

"Sit and stay," I said, fumbling in my pocket for a dog treat. Impatiently Buck stepped over to the lounge by Hugh, who had the bowl of peanuts again.

"Here, Buck." He held out a handful, grinning as the dog's big tongue scooped them up.

I reached for my old fashioned glass and said, a bit tartly, "You didn't answer me."

"What? About our children and grandchildren? I don't think they give a damn, Minty." He swept shells off his lap. "and I think you're obsessing about this. Just because Morton thinks modernizing Main Street is a good idea, you're taking off on a crusade to 'Save the Manse' ...." He raised his voice theatrically. " ... to the exclusion of more important issues."

"Don't patronize me, Hugh. You act like you just don't care about what, to many of us, gives Whitman its personality." I hadn't meant to provoke a disagreement. I just wanted his support.

"I'm not patronizing you, but this issue doesn't require immediate resolution. I've endorsed my sister's plan to donate it to the town. I'll support that and help however I can. But I don't want to spend the little time we have together trying to revive a period of southern history that's best put behind us," Hugh said loudly, sat upright, facing me, and placed the bowl on the table.

"Well, don't yell at me," I complained. All I wanted was to avoid any talk of marriage, I thought. I certainly dislike the antebellum fanatics, but I felt strongly that the Manse reminded all of us of the beauty and grace of the past. We should cherish those qualities while we discard the evils of racial discrimination. I sighed in exasperation. He was right about our time to be alone and loving, however, which is where I hoped we were headed.

In a conciliatory tone, Hugh said, "I didn't mean to yell. If I raised my voice too loudly, I apologize." He stood and filled both our glasses emptying the pitcher.

"I'm sorry, Hugh. You're right. Let's forget the Manse. I have shrimp salad and brouchette for dinner."

I rose, too, and for a minute, we stood leaning against each other but not speaking. Buck broke the silence with a woof, obviously asking for more peanuts.

"No, boy," Hugh said, patting the scraggly fur on the dog's head. "You'll ruin your appetite for dinner." Hugh picked up his glass and finished off his drink. Buck gave an agreeable "Rrrfff." And stood ready for what we'd do next.

"Are you getting hungry?" I asked Hugh, aware that we were standing in a mess of shells.

Hugh, always so sensitive to other people's feelings, said, "If you get supper, I'll clean up this mess." I could have kissed him, but he gently urged me towards the kitchen.

Our argument happily over, all three of us headed that way. I began to set the table, while Hugh got broom and dustpan and we went about our chores with the familiarity that characterized our relationship. I retrieved the salad, fixed the brouchette and when Hugh came in he filled the animals' bowls. Our conversation during supper was desultory at first, broken only by the clatter of silver and china.

When he finished eating, Hugh said, "That was an especially satisfying meal, Minty."

"Thank you. I have strawberry and rhubarb pie a la mode for dessert."

"Hadn't we better feed the goats and put them to bed before dessert?" he asked

"Good idea. Maybe there's something worth watching on TV tonight," I answered.

The heat of the day had waned with the sun and it was pleasant outside as we took care of Edna and Claude. Buck visited the pasture and Cleo scouted out the bushes for any critter she could harass. Hugh and I sat on the stoop until the mosquitoes arrived and I called Buck to come back inside.

Dessert devoured, we spent the evening in front of the TV, reading the newspaper and sometimes engaging in amusing repartee. A frequent scenario for us, except that we were more carefully courteous. Other evenings, one of us often made an overture with carnal intent.

After some yawning during the eleven o'clock news, Hugh rose and held out his hand. "Come on, it's gotten late. Let's go to bed."

Upstairs, he said, "Good night, Minty," … kissed me and we lay down holding each other, our minds in separate places, I believed. Dissatisfaction covered us instead of leaves. But unlike Hansel and Gretel, I was afraid that angels weren't guarding us.

*   *   *

Sunday morning, I let him sleep in while I went to church. Appearing there regularly was the best antidote to gossip in Whitman. After that, the day was ours. We took Buck for a walk out at the lake, where we chatted with a number of friends and watched the dog play in the water with some children.

Hugh had an early Monday morning clinic and didn't stay that night. As I locked up and prepared for bed, the fact that Hugh hadn't mentioned marriage all Sunday nagged at me. Had he changed his mind? Did I want him to change his mind?

Chapter 14

The Fourth of July Committee was meeting here in the afternoon, so I could not afford time to struggle with the issue of marriage. With an effort, I pushed all that back into the deepest recesses of my mind and focused on preparing for the meeting.

Having cleaned house Tuesday left me free to prepare refreshments at leisure. Brownies, lemon cookies and petit fours were easy and by noon the refreshments were ready.

I enjoyed entertaining, if not as elegantly as my mother and Philabelle, at least using my most refined equipment. As I considered my choices, I remembered that my garden still provided sweet peas, lupine and roses, all pinks, blues and lavender. I had a Minton dessert service in matching colors, and, against the background of a pale green tablecloth and napkins, the flowers and china harmonized perfectly.

The first to arrive were Madge with Philabelle and Janet Rossi. Someone always brought Janet, as E.J. didn't think she should drive. Since the sudden death of their son five years ago, Janet had lost touch with reality. She was quite forgetful and once got lost between Main Street and their house, three blocks away. We were all fond of Janet and, in Whitman, we didn't desert our friends.

Madge took one look at the table and said, "Oh heavens, Minty. You made far too much. The girls will be so busy gobbling up all these goodies, they'll never get down to business."

I mumbled, "We'll see." And I greeted the guests.

The other committee members showed up in a flurry and, aware of Lynn's absence, for some reason my conscience pricked me. It would be childish, if she stayed away to 'punish' me. Nevertheless, her absence took the bloom off the fun of an entertaining meeting.

Despite Madge's misgivings, refreshments in hand, we settled down, called the meeting to order and discussed the assignments. Everyone volunteered to repeat her last year's job. That was one of the nicest things about Whitman; you can count on people pitching in. Within two hours, our business was dispatched efficiently, leaving time for a pleasant social.

I noticed that, despite Madge's worry, most of the refreshments disappeared. Her obsessiveness amused me. I didn't know why, but I did find the odd ways of some of these women diverting.

As they were leaving, I overheard Madge say to Liz Waverly, something about retiring to Florida.

"Did I hear right? Y'all are thinking of leaving Whitman?" I asked.

"If Clay can find a buyer for the store," Madge said.

"Why on earth would you leave here?" I was surprised.

"I've barely been out of the state of Virginia in my whole entire life and I'd like to see more of the world." With a hand under Janet's elbow, Madge continued moving towards the door. "I've never been really happy here… " *Was there any place where Madge would be happy, I wondered?* "… and stayed because Clay insisted that it was a great place to raise children. Well, they're raised now so we can leave."

Madge must have seen the shock on my face, because she stopped and said, "I know I don't complain about it and it's different for you, Minty. Your family's lived here since the dinosaurs, but you've traveled all over the world. I'd like a taste of big city life before I'm too old."

Distressed as well as surprised, I said, "I can't believe Clay would sell the store. It's been in his family for generations."

"That's what I said," Janet, who agrees with whatever anybody else says, nodded her permed grey curls vigorously.

"Well, none of our children or his siblings want to run the store. They're settled in different jobs and scattered all over now anyway. Besides Clay's tired of being a small town grocer."

Madge urged the still nodding Janet out the door.

As a courteous hostess, I held my tongue and thanked each of the women for their willingness to make this another great Fourth.

As I tidied up the refreshments, however, I felt depressed. I couldn't imagine Whitman without Clay and Madge. I thought Clay loved Whitman as much as I did.

Everything seemed to be changing. Even Philabelle with her talk of moving to Creek Woods.

As usual, she had stayed to help me clear up. She also took time to scold me for not yet contacting Lynn.

Feeling put-out, I asked, "Why didn't she come? Madge called her."

"I don't know, dear. She's *retreated* to their beach cottage and didn't say when she'd come back to town." My sister-in-law's blue eyes skewered me, as she added, "Your words at our last bridge game *wounded* her deeply."

Truly miffed and still hurting myself, I kept my voice civil, "I wounded *her*? Philabelle, she slept with my husband."

"Your bluntness is unbecoming, Minty." Her usually pleasant expression changed: the corners of her mouth turned down and her pale eyebrows drew together. "I suggest you give a little thought to the circumstances that led to her indiscretion." She gathered up the tablecloth and napkins to take into the utility room.

Too astonished to reply, I stood like a goose with my mouth hanging open, both hands full of iced tea glasses.

When Philabelle returned, she added, "My hope is that you'll take the initiative towards reconciliation. She is your sister, younger than you, and more vulnerable."

I put the glasses on the counter and turned to face her. "In what way is Lynn more vulnerable, pray tell me? She's been a social butterfly since she turned fourteen and ended up richer than all of us put together. Our family always made allowances for her promiscuity because she was the youngest."

"Vulgarity is quite unladylike, dear." Philabelle shook her head reprovingly. "Have you ever asked yourself *why* she engaged in unsuccessful relationships? Or why she finally married a man as old as her father?" I didn't answer, and Philabelle chided me further. "I'm afraid that you were so absorbed in your h*appy* and fruitful marriage that you failed to observe her *unhappiness*, her loneliness."

Now I had an answer. "I doubt that she had time to be lonely. She always had a man or three at her beck and call. More than once I cautioned her about the character of some of her 'friends.' You must remember the one who turned out to be a drug dealer." I inhaled righteously. "I did what I could to straighten her out, Philabelle. It was a blessing that Elliot was so besotted with her that he married her. His daughters objected, you know." My voice was harsh with anger.

The hurt look on Philabelle's face shamed me. Even though she was pushing too hard, I couldn't bear her distress and reached out to lay my hand on her arm. "I'm sorry, Philabelle. I shouldn't take out my sore feelings on you."

Philabelle relaxed and smiled, "I understand, Minty. You've suffered, too, but you enjoyed many years of love and happiness with three splendid children and, now, Hugh." Philabelle patted my cheek with her soft hand. "Surely, you're generous enough to forgive Lynn. You've always had a resilience she lacks."

My anger diminished somewhat, but I grumbled a bit about Lynn running away to the cottage. Once again, Philabelle had used her mystical ability to make me examine my opinions. So when I drove her back to the Manse, I decided that I might just run over to Plum Point and check on Lynn – as soon as I can fit it in.

Chapter 15

Too restless to sleep well nights lately, after another unsatisfactory evening with Hugh, I turned my brain loose to focus on our relationship. The thought of life without him frightened me, but the thought of marriage was equally scary. What frustrated me most was that I couldn't figure out why, whenever Hugh mentioned the word I relived Billy's death and I cringed.

I must have twitched because Cleo, who slept against my legs, grunted in complaint.

My aversion to marriage was emotional, not intellectual, that I understood. I had been happily married to Billy for over forty years. But the marriage had been shattered, first by knowledge of Billy's cheating and then compounded by his sudden death. During the three year healing period that followed, supported by my friends, Philabelle, Sarah, Lynn and Hugh, I had developed a pleasant sense of self-sufficiency. I had even forgotten the exhilaration of sex, until Hugh and I became lovers.

Coming back to the present with a bump, I snorted, which woke Buck who slept in his bed by my dressing table. He trotted over and nudged me with his head. I sat up and turned on the light. Fondling his dark curls, I looked into his eyes and marveled at the depth of our pets' compassion.

"Buck, I'm a sixty-three year old woman who still doesn't understand her own desires." The concern in Buck's eyes encouraged me to go on. "Hugh is Lynn's age – only fifty-five. Apparently, I was not attractive enough for Billy. How long would Hugh find me attractive? What if he wanted more than I've got to give?"

Stroking Buck's warm head, I knew that, as with Billy, I had assumed Hugh was happy with our relationship. Our companionship had been so comfortable, so durable. I could easily slip into loving him enough to marry him. But that was a formula for grief.

Hugh had ignored my suggestion that he move into the farmhouse with me. There must be some compromise we could make that would satisfy both of us. I heaved a sigh, decided to think about it later and I reached to turn out the light.

"I'm not going to solve my problem tonight, am I, Buck?" I said and shoved him gently. "Go back to your bed, sweetie."

Then, in the dark, in a flighty moment, I said, "Good night, Mrs. Calabash, wherever you are," and snuggled down despite Cleo's soft song of disturbance.

*   *   *

It had been a long and restless night filled with ill-defined dreams of Hugh fading away like Billy's recurring ghost. I reached out to Hugh, but was unable to move my arms. I was glad when dawn gave me permission to get up. The sky, gray with darker clouds scudding northwest, reflected my somber mood. Occupying myself with morning chores, I let Buck and Cleo out and provided for Edna's and Claude's needs for the day.

After breakfast, I called William, who was pleased when I asked him to research rare book dealers and, to my pleasure, expressed concern about Philabelle's health. I briefed him on my recent chat with her and, before we hung up, sent my love to Myra and the boys.

Speaking of Philabelle reminded me of her insistence that I make the first move to reconcile with Lynn. Although I felt strongly that I was the victim here, second thoughts forced me to examine my feelings about Billy's infidelity compared to loyalty to my sister.

Feeling alienated from the kid sister I had cherished for so long offended me. I decided to take Philabelle's advice. As the elder I should set the example, take the initiative in settling our dispute. Also, although I don't attach omen status to dreams, last night's had left me with a sense of insecurity with regard to my relationship with Hugh.

With those concerns in mind I made my decision. Aware that John and Pat Keene were early risers, I called to ask if John would mind the animals.

"I'm driving over to Lynn's place on the river today. I expect to be gone most of the day. Would it be inconvenient for you to let Buck in and out a couple of times?" I asked.

They have a key to my house, and, bless John's heart, he was gracious in helping me out, as usual.

"Be prepared for rain, Minty," he warned. "The radio says a hurricane's left Florida and is headed up the east coast."

Whitman is too far inland for hurricanes to do more than drench us with rain, so I wasn't worried. Nevertheless, I dressed in comfortable beige knit slacks and top and took my yellow slicker, in case I needed it. I fixed a Thermos of tea and a cheese sandwich for later. I put a small tomato in the bag and drove northeast to New Kent Highway.

The weather had changed overnight, so I wasn't surprised that it was cooler. A brisk breeze dropped a light rain before I had turned southeast on Eltham Road toward Slatersville.

Into the slot, I slipped a CD of Joseph Campbell's PBS programs on myth, but it failed to distract me from my ambivalence about Hugh. He filled a place in my life which had been empty too long. Forget it, I admonished myself. You're on a mercy mission to placate your sister's hurt feelings. Philabelle's words floated around on my consciousness like pond scum and I accepted some of the responsibility for precipitating our disagreement. Philabelle was right; as the elder, it behooved me to take the initiative.

I had already made my peace with Philabelle and Sarah before our disagreement could fester. The day after the bridge game, my affection for them overcame my pride and I had called them each to apologize for taking my annoyance out on them.

With some concern about how mad at me Lynn was, I purposely hadn't called her. I suspected that she'd hang up before I could pacify her. She was slower to anger than I was, but slower to forgive, too.

At a junction, the signs reminded me to turn southeast. The rain had become heavier, so I switched the windshield wipers up to full. Nevertheless, the poor visibility made driving more difficult and it was noon by the time I reached Slatersville. I stopped for lunch and a potty break.

Refreshed, I headed now towards Plum Point and the Paumununkey River. The breeze had changed to strong gusts that smacked the side of the car. The storm was fiercer than I had anticipated, but I reminded myself that virtue required perseverance. For the next stretch, I concentrated on driving to counter the increasing wind. The torrent was almost too much for the windshield wipers to clear. I felt as if I were driving underwater, a most unpleasant situation. Having past the point of return, I had no option except to continue. Whether or not my efforts would be rewarded depended upon my sister.

Although I'd taken this route several times, I almost missed the turnoff to the street where Lynn's cottage was located. It was a narrow road, lined with trees and shrubs, now agitated by the wind. There were only three houses, widely spaced, which gave a pleasant sense of privacy in the summer. More like isolation at the moment. I was happy to spot the driveway into Lynn's backyard.

Parking the car, I dragged on my yellow slicker, pulled up the hood and ran to the kitchen door, water splashing up the bottoms of my slacks. I had to bang several times before it opened a crack and Lynn peeked out.

"Oh! It's you!" Her voice was short of welcoming.

"Well, are you going to let me in?" I yelled. The wind jerked my hood off and rain ran up inside my sleeve as I tried to hold it on.

My sister opened the door enough that I squeezed in past her.

"Don't drip on the clean floor," she grunted.

"I'm soaked, Lynn. Where do you want me to drip?"

Lynn hesitated before she said, as if tolerating an imposition, "Give me your raincoat and take off your shoes. You're a mess."

Lynn, the immaculate, had on gray sweat pants that sagged in the seat and a sweat shirt, torn at the neck, but still looked ravishing. *Your outfit's not Versace, for sure.* I thought. I opened the slicker and pushed off my shoes, terribly aware that my hair resembled a wet dog's and my neat slacks were shapeless and discolored by dirty water.

"Stay here," she took my things and left. Clutching myself with my arms to hold in what heat my body retained, I huddled by the kitchen door, dabbed at my wet face with damp tissues and shoved my wet hair back so I could see.

When Lynn returned, I asked, "Could you get me something to wear while my clothes dry? I'm soaked through to the skin."

"You're going to stay that long?" She must have noticed that I was shivering visibly, because she added, "You're bigger than I am. My clothes won't fit."

A definite draft seeped in around the door and I was tempted to comment on the chill indoors as well as out.

Instead, I said, "I don't care about fit. I'm freezing to death here." I tried to keep my voice pleasant, but the wind and the rain were so noisy I had to raise it a bit.

"Okay." My sister turned and left me, cold and wet in the small puddle forming on her clean kitchen floor.

She returned with an extra large navy blue sweat suit, probably her late husband's, which she offered, "Here."

Hastily I pulled off my blouse, pushed down the slacks and stepped out of them.

"You underwear's wet, too," she said, still in that tone of total indifference.

I stripped and she handed me a towel. Grateful and still shaking, I dried myself and snuggled into the dry clothes. With sleeves and legs rolled up, they worked and were warm. Carrying my soggy clothes, I went into the powder room off the hall, wringing out as much water as possible into the sink. Then I hung my clothes in the laundry room.

Back in the kitchen, the noise of the storm sounded much louder than before. When I asked Lynn if she had any socks that were big enough for me, I had to raise my voice over the moan. Only then did I realize that she had put water on to boil. She turned from a cupboard with two mugs in her hand.

"What are you doing here, anyway?" This time she scowled.

"Lynn! I'm your sister. I don't like our …" I gestured with a hand, feeling insecure. "… not being friends. The way we used to be … before the bridge game." I wasn't being very articulate and waggled my head in a random sort of way. "You know. To apologize. Sort of."

She snorted, as she opened the tea canister. I could tell my apology hadn't been very effective and remembered *forgiveness* for her dalliance with my husband was required, not an apology.

In spite of her coldness, I was resolved to make amends and said, "I think I spoke too harshly at bridge the other day." I looked for some response, but she just stared back at me, without any emotion. "I was so surprised when you told me that you and Billy … eh, you know, that I … eh, over-reacted."

The kettle whistled louder than the storm and startled both of us.

"I'll fix tea. We'll take it in the lounge. It's warmer there." She handed me a bottle of Couvoisier brandy, put the teapot and mugs on a tray and I followed her. The lounge, the entire width of the house, had windows on three sides, fronting on a wide deck. Across the room, near the stairway to the second floor, stood a dining table and chairs. Builtin shelves, between the stairs and the door from the hall to the kitchen, held a variety of books and magazines. Mixed in were souvenirs from the river: shells, stones in weird sizes and colors, and a dried giant starfish. On previous visits, I had added occasional bits to the collection.

Putting the tea tray on a low table, Lynn pulled a hand-knitted Afghan from the back of a couch and shoved it at me. "You can wrap up in this."

I did so with pleasure and hunkered down, tucking my cold feet into its soft warmth.

"Thanks. That was thoughtful of you," I said, minding my manners.

Lynn poured the tea and added a dollop of brandy to each mug. I had just lifted mine, when a burst of wind slammed against the house surprising me so I nearly scalded my lips.

"Wow! This is getting to be quite a storm," I said. In a chair nearby, Lynn glanced out the windows.

She said, "It must be the hurricane." I squawked when she added, "I heard on the TV one was headed toward the Chesapeake Bay area." For the first time, her voice carried a note of concern.

"Hurricanes come this far up the river?" Inland they were just windy rainstorms.

Lynn nodded, "Not often." She lifted her mug and I noticed that her hand was trembling.

"Is there a drill for preparing?" I asked. A sudden flurry of rain pelted the windows, sharp enough to break the glass, I thought. I glanced at Lynn, who sat rigid as a poker, but she didn't answer.

The wind had increased in intensity radically since I arrived. It was dark for mid-afternoon, too, and all the trees and shrubs waved wildly. I was amazed at how far the trees bent without breaking. Storms didn't disturb me all that much, but Lynn's big blue eyes reminded me of the scaredy cat she had been as a child.

Although I still resented her cold reception when I arrived, I suppressed that, rose above the pain of her treachery and took the bull by the horns.

"Let's lock all the windows and the doors and pull the drapes closed." I rose and looked out the front window, but, because of the rain, couldn't see the dock or the river – about fifty some feet from the house — and wondered how high it might rise. As I watched, one of those big green plastic garbage cans bounced across the grass along with leaves and branches of various kinds. A lawn chair skidded off Lynn's deck onto the lawn.

I returned to the couch and I felt the teapot. "It's still warm. Want some more?" I asked. Lynn had followed me around, silently locking windows, obviously doing her share. Now she sat on the couch, her hands locked together in her lap. With a pang, I could feel my sister's fear of the storm and sat beside her, forcing myself to stay calm and reassuring.

"Why don't we turn on the radio? Maybe hear a weather report while we finish our tea." I poured more plus a bit of brandy into our cups and sat back. With one hand outside the Afghan holding the cup, I rewrapped myself.

"I'll turn on the TV." Lynn did.

The fortified tea tasted good.

Sitting there side by side, we watched the screen, where the storm on the Bay dominated the news. A newsman, reporting from Newport News, I think, stood in front of a gas station. Drenched, he hunched, back to the wind, holding his microphone, while a sign on a nearby pole whipped madly back and forth. Suddenly, it tore free of its mooring and sailed down the street along with miscellaneous debris.

Lynn refilled our cups from the brandy bottle, while the TV camera panned out to show masses of branches tossed around like confetti and pieces of corrugated tin flying by. The poor reporter could hardly be heard over the din of the storm.

During the hour or so that we watched, our conversation was spotty. My previous visits here had been later in the summer and all I remembered was good weather.

I asked, "Does this happen here every season?"

Lynn answered, "No." She vigorously shook of her head and, except for exclamations of "Oh, look at that", "Unbelievable", we watched in silence.

When a blast of wind, keening like a wounded banshee, battered the side of the house, I gasped, appalled at the violence. Lynn let out a squawk and grabbed my arm.

"Well! That was a blast," I tried to sound amused. Lynn, white faced, didn't respond.

The house shook and rain pelted the windows so hard, I worried that, sooner or later, the glass would break. It didn't, but the hurricane's fury didn't abate either.

I watched the trees toss and bend, fighting to live. I suppose my fear reactivated the anger I felt at Lynn. My emotions swirled like oil on water, sitting with her on the couch, watching her tremble — a frightened child. And I was the older one.

Breathing deeply, I calmed myself and asked, "How long do these things last, do you know?" I tried to keep my voice gentle and firm, but had to speak loud enough to be heard.

Lynn's voice quivered a bit and she shook her head, her voice raised, she said, "I've never seen it like this before."

All the misery of my anger dissipated. Nothing that happened in the past could be changed, I realized— only Lynn and I could change.

With a howl, as if in pain, a gust slammed against the front of the house. Automatically, Lynn cowered against me. I held her hand and made shushing sounds of comfort.

"I guess this is the worst it gets, don't you think?" I lied, but didn't convince myself. When that burst passed, I said, "It'll die down gradually now."

Lynn sat upright again. As if I were an oracle, she stared at me, blue eyes dilated, but nodded like a trustful child. So I added, keeping my voice level, "At least we're warm and dry inside."

She nodded again and forced a thin smile, but looked too scared to speak. Like my sister, I had never experienced anything like that before and didn't like it one bit. Maybe it was the question of our survival that made me need to be sure that we were friends again.

The fury of the wind seemed to lessen and I took the moment of relative quiet to say, "Lynn, I've apologized for my untoward words." She looked down at her clasped hands and nodded her head but didn't answer.

"Come on, Lynn, I'm trying to do a little reconciling here. I said I was sorry." I expected some reaction from her. "Hey. I'd like a little help."

She glanced up at me, frowned, and said in a dismissive tone, "That would make you feel better, wouldn't it?"

"Shoot, Lynn. I thought maybe you'd like to …," I tried to think, despite the noise. "Don't you … Couldn't you say something … to help?"

Lynn turned her head to focus on me and bellowed, "To help what?" The noise of the storm forced us to raise our voices to be heard.

Outside the uproar accelerated, fanning my irritation. But I couldn't let it distract me.

"You might say something… You know, to let me know that you're sorry that… eh." I bawled out the hurtful words, "… that you slept with my husband."

"Oh, I see." She laughed ironically and shook her head vigorously, "You want me to grovel or something?" She hooted her contempt.

The violence of the storm seemed to activate primal emotion. Or was it the need to yell?

"No. I don't want you to grovel," I exhaled and sort of yowled, "I think you might say something like you understand how hurt I felt to learn that you had …" She looked at me with such scorn that I blurted out, "Why *did* you do that to me?"

Lynn pulled away, blue eyes blazing with fire, and shouted at me, "What I *did* was to offer comfort to a man ravaged by remorse. A man who'd been discarded by an indifferent wife whom he adored."

Her words penetrated the bedlam of the storm and I was stunned silent before I could defend myself against the 'indifferent wife' accusation. The dam that had restrained Lynn, however, had busted wide open. She continued in a fishwife voice I never imagined she had.

"When Billy came to me, he cried that he had hurt you. And *you!* How could you reject him so cruelly?"

She pulled away, turning and screamed at me to make herself heard over the din of rain beating against the windows. "You humiliated him. So contemptuous in your superiority!" At last, she stopped to take a breath and dissolved into tears.

The idea that Lynn believed she was helping Billy cope from wounds I had dealt him struck me as funny and I burst into nearly hysterical laughter. The *irony* of Billy feeling remorse while he was sleeping with my own sister, apparently, escaped her. The tears running down her cheeks were not for me! She had no concept of my feelings at learning that my husband had violated our vows. I fought to control myself – a mess of jumbled emotions.

"I am so tired of your being *perfect*," Lynn spat the word. "Always the older sister who knows everything. All I ever heard was that …" she sneered, "… Minty got all the brains in the family. Follow Minty's example. And I was the dumb blonde little sister!" She twisted, her face distorted with rage.

Finally, the camel's back had broken. What possessed me to drive over here, risking my life to make an unwarranted apology to a woman who didn't care one iota that she had seriously wounded me? Still huddled in the Afghan, now in harmony with the yowling wind, I raised my voice to overpower its whining and protested, "*You* were the family beauty and I spent a lot of time trying to help you with homework and to give you the benefit of my experience. But you didn't need any help being May Queen or with the boys, did you? You played the seductive siren with every man, including *my* husband."

She jeered back at me, "*You* call it giving me advice; I call it bossing me around. All you did was sit in judgment on all my mistakes," she yelled to be heard over the banging of something bouncing across the deck just outside the front door.

"Lynn, I never sat in judgment on you or anybody else," I shouted, needing her to realize that my intent had been to *help* her. I wanted to shake her, to make her understand.

As if reflecting the force of our dispute, the strength of the wind escalated again. Something heavy —my car? — rammed into the back of the house, which shook on its foundation.

"Oh Lordy," Lynn cried out, jerking toward me. "The house is going to blow away and we're going to die."

I reached out to put my arms around her. "We're not going to die, Lynn. This can't go on forever," I screeched, hugging her close. "That banshee is still out there." Our favorite name for our enemies as kid. She shrieked something back. I couldn't understand her.

"What?" I hollered, but doubted that she heard me over the increasing volume of banshee cries. My throat felt raw from yelling.

"I'll g… mo …" Lynn's mouth opened and closed. She pulled away and grabbed the empty brandy bottle. She raised it to her lips, indicating that we needed more to drink. She wiggled away from me, rose and staggered towards the kitchen.

To lend support, I mouthed back, "Not without me." I disentangled myself from the Afghan, and struggled to my feet. Clutching each other, we reeled through the hall toward the kitchen.

The eerie screams continued, rising up the scale and howling down and up again. Stifling a vulgar curse, I faced the fact that we might be found dead in the destroyed ruin of Lynn's cottage.

Chapter 16

Not willing to die without a fight, I considered our options. Apparently, the wind was sweeping upriver, across the front of the house, so it seemed reasonable that it might be quieter in the kitchen. Clinging together, we reached the back of the house and I was right; the noise seemed a decibel or two lower.

Shielding my eyes with both hands against the kitchen window, I checked outside for my car. As I feared, light from the window sparkled on water. It was already half-way up the wheels of my old Volvo, which meant that the house was surrounded. Heaven only knew how much deeper it would get. Based on the continued intensity of the wind and rain, my estimate was that it would rise higher.

Our prospects for the future were grimmer than I expected. Mother of pearl, I thought, was this really the end for us?

Aside from pure fright, my strongest feeling was regret. With a pang I thought of Hugh, afraid that I might never see him again. I wished desperately that he were with us.

I forced myself to focus on the present situation. My best option was to distract my sister before I had to deal with outright hysteria, her's and mine both.

From the series of muted banging and smashing sounds, apparently, lawn chairs or garbage cans were still being tossed around. I visualized my car windows busted in, but kept my voice up-beat and, despite the flickering of the light, ignored the possibility of electrical failure.

Although the kitchen was quieter, we still raised our voices, but I could ask more easily, "What we need is something to eat and drink, okay?" If we had to drown, it needn't be on an empty stomach.

"I suppose so— in case the electricity goes out." Lynn turned and stepped toward the refrigerator. "You coming?"

"Sure. What'da we have that's quick and easy?" I joined Lynn and we stood checking out her well-stocked fridge. Fortunately, she seemed calmer with something to do and talking helped. "Hey, here's some cheese." I reached in and took out a package. "Sharp cheddar." I liked a good sharp cheddar. "Do you have crackers?"

As Lynn grabbed an unopened bottle of wine, she said, "There's only red left. I know you like white."

"That's fine. Beggars can't be choosers."

"You may not be all that welcome, Minty, but you're not a beggar in my household." Her face had a woebegone look and she sounded hurt.

Despite my apology, she was still touchy. I said, "I know that, Lynn. I didn't mean anything. You've made me comfortable here." Except for my cold bare feet, which I didn't mention. "And I appreciate it." It felt good to reassure her.

The lights flickered off. I held my breath.

Lynn grunted, "Oh!"

They flashed back on. Her blue eyes were round with apprehension. Sorry that she scared so easily, I reverted to my role as big sister. "Does the electricity go off around here very often?"

She nodded, as if that required serious thought, before she said, "Sometimes."

She's scared stiff, I decided. "You think we ought to prepare for that?" Again she nodded, her mind obviously not in full gear. "Do you have storm lanterns or flashlights?"

She said, "In the laundry. I've never been here in a storm like this before."

"No, I haven't either, but we'll manage."

Meantime, the moaning of the wind was eery, like a thousand old crones keening, and the rain, heavier and steady, battering against the window.

I said I'd go look and she stayed close behind me. Disregarding the pandemonium outside, we went into the laundry room, just off the kitchen.

On the shelves, we found several lanterns but no kerosene or oil for them. There were two flashlights in a drawer; the larger one worked, but the smaller one was dead.

"Elliott always had batteries someplace in here," Lynn said and opened all the drawers while I probed the back corners of the over-head shelves. With something to do, she acted more composed, but she squeaked each time the lights flickered, which happened more frequently.

"What about candles?" I asked, hoping desperately that they wouldn't go out permanently.

Lynn found a box of Christmas candles, but neither of us found any matches. Armed with the large flashlight, we returned to the kitchen, for the cheese and crackers.

I picked up the wine bottle; Lynn set the flashlight on the table and reached for a box of Pepperidge Farm Harvest Wheats in the cupboard.

A sudden burst of wind slammed against the wall, shaking the house and breaking the back window. With a crash, glass spewed all over the floor.

At that moment, we were plunged into darkness.

This time the lights didn't come back on. The tempest ratcheted up another notch, from moan to shriek. Wind and rain swirled in through the broken window along with the noise.

In the dark, Lynn screamed. Clutching the wine bottle and suddenly conscious of my bare feet and the broken glass, I called, "Where are you?"

I could hardly hear her voice when she answered, "Over here."

'Over where?' I wanted to scream. Instead, I yelled, "The flashlight's on the table, but stay away from the window." With one hand, I inched away, toward my right, running my hand along the counters, sliding each foot forward carefully on the wet floor, using my toes to avoid broken glass. A cut foot might do me in.

I bumped into the table and fumbled for the flashlight. I couldn't find it and called again, "Where are you, Lynn?"

Her voice sounded close. "Down here," she answered in a quivery voice.

She was crouched on the floor behind the table, back against the wall. Squatting down beside her, I felt her trembling and knew she was scared petrified. I wasn't too happy myself. In fact, I had an instant vision of being found dead, with my chest crushed by the wine bottle, which I still clutched, my blood mingling with the wine on Lynn's kitchen floor. Oh Hugh, sweetheart, I thought, I am really scared.

The constant din of the storm made it hard to gather my wits. I realized, however, that it was up to me to stay in control. The kitchen wasn't safe; the broken window let in wind and rain. We had to head out the hall, lock the door and hunker down somewhere else.

Giving Lynn the bottle of wine, I stood and felt along the top of the table, relieved, this time, to find the flashlight. I grabbed her hand and led her out of the kitchen and down the hall. I closed the door against the exhausting noise. It didn't have a lock, but we made our way into the more sheltered lounge.

Apparently, the wind had shifted from the front of the house to the back and the living room seemed quiet now in comparison to the kitchen.

By this time, Lynn was whimpering softly.

"We'll be safe in here, hon. It's scary, but we'll be all right." I was lying, of course, but I thought it important to reassure my little sister, to calm her fears the best way I could.

We settled on the couch to catch our breath and I tucked the Afghan over our legs. Although I didn't mention it, I was concerned about staying in any room surrounded by windows, because of the airborne debris. The turbulence outside continued, sometimes rising to a piercing whistle that threatened to rupture our ear-drums. But at least we had the flashlight and a bottle of wine.

Lynn twisted off the cap and offered it to me. I took a good swig and said, "Thanks. That's good," not sure whether she heard me or not.

As she lifted the bottle to her lips, it occurred to me that in tornados a bathroom is the safest room, or so I'd heard. Apparently, the plumbing sort of anchors the tub to the structure. Something to consider.

"I want to check out front," I said and pushed aside the Afghan. Over by the window, I pointed the flashlight outside and fanned it across the lawn — not at all pleased to see it reflect on water already lapping up on the wide deck. Having no idea how high the river might rise, I instinctively reasoned that I needed to get Lynn upstairs.

"Minty?" Lynn called from the couch. I hurried back across the room, planning our next move.

"What?" I asked.

"Nothing. I don't like sitting in the dark." She was huddled in on herself, as if making herself small would help.

"O.K. I need to pee, hon," I said. "Let's go upstairs." Docilely, Lynn, still gripping the bottle, followed the light as I pointed the way, lugging the comforting Afghan. Lynn didn't mention that I could have used the hall powder-room.

She insisted on sticking close to me and, in the dark after all, there was no need for modesty. The room was small with little floor space. I remembered that the tub was an enormous, old-fashioned iron one with lion's claw feet — fortunately wider than most — which gave me an idea.

After I peed, I said, "Let's gather blankets and a pillow and make ourselves comfortable here." The bathroom was totally enclosed with a single small window up high.

"In the tub?" she sounded incredulous.

"Sure. It's the safest place."

Without further comment, Lynn helped me gather a pillow and a couple of quilts, plus the Afghan, with which we lined the tub. Activity seemed to give Lynn courage. Skillfully coping with the open bottle, she got into the tub, with wine intact. I joined her with the flashlight. Thus we maneuvered ourselves, pressed together, to wait out the storm.

"We might as well sit in the dark and save what light we have," I suggested and switched off the flashlight. For a few minutes, we relaxed in our bizarre recliner and listened to the sound effects of the wind, as if we were waiting for a movie to begin. But this was no movie and inaction allowed the terror, which I had stifled, to gush up. I didn't want us to die, dammit!

Notwithstanding our approaching demise, I forced myself to take comfort in the feel of my sister leaning against me. The thought of her being alone in this situation made me shudder emotionally. In a perverted way, I was glad that I'd come. Undefined regrets began to invade my conscience, so I was grateful when Lynn passed the bottle to me.

"As hostess, I'm offering you another drink," she said. I took the bottle and marveled at the amusement in her voice. Despite the somewhat muted, but constant storm noises, her lips close to my ear, I could hear her say, "Think how our mother would disapprove of us southern ladies drinking wine from the bottle."

Encouraged by her finding humor in our situation, I turned my head to reply, "Worse, we're both drinking out of the same bottle."

Reasonably comfortable (even my feet were warm now), suddenly, I felt a bizarre tranquility.

"Do you remember how excited we used to get at Christmas in Whitman?" I giggled and we began to reminisce about our childhood celebrations.

"Oh yeah. We spent weeks preparing. Jaunts into the woods for holly and mistletoe."

"The delicious odor of pine; the secret wrapping and hiding of presents."

"Remember Mom taking us into Richmond to buy gifts for each other and friends?" Lynn said.

"And that big stuffed polar bear outside the fur store? I loved him, but he scared you."

"Pfff!" Lynn actually chuckled. "The best part was the whole the town decorating the big tree for the Christmas Eve lighting and caroling."

"Yeah, it was a genuine extravaganza." My mind flooded with happy memories.

Abruptly, we realized that quiet had descended upon the house.

"The eye," Lynn whispered, as if speaking might precipitate a catastrophe.

"Is it over now?" My heart jumped with relief.

"No. I'm afraid not." Her sigh expressed despair. "There'll just be a break before it all begins again." Our period of deliverance from fear would be limited.

"How long does the eye last?" I asked, feeling as if this were death row.

Lynn shrugged, "I don't know." Now she sounded almost indifferent.

"Oh shoot!" I felt deflated and depressed at the prospect of more, maybe worse. Paradoxically, I was hungry and remembered the cheese and crackers we had left downstairs.

At my suggestion, and bolstered with Dutch courage and wine, we crawled out of our nest. Leaving the half-full bottle on the counter, we stretched our cramped limbs and, with Lynn guiding us by flashlight, we eased our way down to the kitchen. Cautiously, I slide my bare feet through the broken glass to sneak a quick glance out the window. I could hear water against the kitchen steps. I supposed by now it was over the wheels and my car in danger of floating away. Adding to my dismay, a gust of cold rain spattered all over the front of my shirt.

"Where are you?" Lynn called, spotlighting me.

"Don't shine that in my eyes. I need night vision to find the cheese and crackers," I said, peeved at my wet front. "Sorry, honey," I muttered and eased my feet over to where she stood.

Lynn pushed the flashlight into my hand. "Here."

"What?"

"I'm bringing another bottle. We don't need glasses. You'd better bring a knife, too."

"Lynn, I can't carry the food and the flashlight." I handed it back to her. She had only the bottle. "Let's just get back upstairs before the flashlight dies." I headed towards the hall.

Obviously, a bit tiddly, Lynn babbled as she followed me up the stairs, "I rather like the intimacy of drinking out of the same bottle," she giggled. "So wicked and unlady-like."

Somehow, in the confusion, our moods had shifted: I still harbored considerable apprehension, but Lynn sounded almost cheerful. Only living in this quiet moment? Or beyond scared?

Bundled together again in the warmth of the tub, neither Lynn nor I said much. We hacked off pieces of cheese for the crackers and ate. Like the storm, we needed respite for a few minutes. My thoughts, however, immediately returned to Lynn's statement that the cycle would start all over and I wondered if I could cope with any more. Trying to gather my strength via our cocktail fare, I paid attention when Lynn broke the silence.

Apropos of nothing, she said, "I really loved Billy. And I had ever since fifth grade." She paused and intuition plus a mouthful kept me mute. "I dreamed that, when I grew up, he'd marry me and we'd live happily ever after. Billy was very kind. He paid attention to me and, when I told him about the boys, he wanted to beat them up. I wouldn't let him, of course." In the dark, I felt her turn her head to look at me. "I never would have *done* it, Minty, if I hadn't truly believed that you no longer cared that Billy slept around."

"What boys?" I asked, shaken up by that news of 'the boys'.

"Ohhh," Lynn heaved a sigh and added, "Boys in high school. All the men when I got older, but not smarter. Being pretty isn't always fun, Minty. Boys – and men, too – think the only thing we're good for is to grope." The cynicism in her voice made me want to cry. "to 'go all the way'… to 'give out' behind the school gym or in the back seat of the car. So they can brag about it." She paused. "I felt wicked, but thought it was my fault."

"I never knew that, Lynn." I felt angry and guilty, I suppose, and asked, "Why didn't you tell me?"

"It's hard to confide in your competition." A hint of irony balanced the sting of her words. "I don't care very much any more, Minty. I'm nicely drunk."

"Yes. I am, too," I agreed. Deeply distressed, I recalled the series of inappropriate men who had wandered in and out of Lynn's life before her surprise marriage to Elliot. *Now* I remembered what Philabelle had said about Lynn feeling unloved.

Lynn interrupted my musings, repeating, "All my life I loved Billy." She sighed heavily, her voice pensive, as if dreaming out loud. "When I was in sixth grade," she lifted her head to look at me. "He married you. He really loved only you, Minty." She paused and I was speechless. "He reproached himself painfully because he had hurt you. He was grateful that you didn't divorce him, that you let him live with you – even though you denied him the comfort of your bed."

Dumbfounded at my sister's candor, I felt an unpleasant tingle of shame, even as I wondered for the thousandth time: if Billy loved me why did he need all those other women? Then, as if prompted by Lynn's frankness, I questioned why I *had* let him stay, instead of divorcing him. Ironically, I knew that I had enjoyed Billy's continued presence. But was 'enjoy' the *honest* word for my true feelings? Or was it, instead, satisfaction, a sort of punishment for his infidelity, to keep him bound to me?

That was an unpleasant idea, followed by the return vision of his death and that feeling of guilt. Enough of what's done and over with, I reprimanded myself. We were in the midst of a hurricane now. At that moment, when our future was in jeopardy, my sister was my immediate concern. If we survived this storm, I'd find time to make her appreciate how *I* had felt.

As if on cue, I heard a whistle of wind and knew that the storm had returned.

Cuddling against her, to comfort her, I said, "I surely didn't know you felt that way about Billy, honey." Too engrossed in dealing with her sorrow, like a physical pain, I asked, "Why didn't you tell me how you felt?"

I brushed at my eyes. The gusting was constant again and the crescendo of havoc outside made them water.

"Too tough." She offered me the bottle and said, casually, as if numb with misery, "I understood why Billy loved you: your enthusiasm and vitality — more powerful than mere *pretty*."

Holding the bottle, I blurted, "You're way more than pretty, Lynn. You have a sweet, appealing innocence." I scanned back to the happy days of my marriage and I saw that it had taken this calamity for me to understand what Lynn perceived as my indifference. Those had been days of grief and despair for her while I had lived in ignorant bliss.

In my humility, I ignored signs of the storm's vengeance until a terrible crunching sound, as if part of the building were being wrenched apart, shocked me into the present. Lynn gasped and gripped my arm. The fury still raged and we were still in peril.

"Oh, Lynn," I raised my voice, over the renewed howling, "I'm so sorry I didn't understand." I put my arm around her, holding her so that we could not be blown apart.

In the midst of the havoc, Lynn shook her head and patted my hand, which I took as confirmation of our reconciliation. Then she lay her head on my shoulder as if in total trust. Almost teary with a surge of love — regret that it took death for me to accept my own short comings — I closed my eyes and relished the warmth of Lynn beside me.

During our final chapter of chaos, I relived the last moments with Billy and his whispered declaration of love. If only I had been generous enough to allow him to find surcease with Lynn and not behaved so meanly. Now years later, Lynn's grief had burst her restraints at bridge.

With resumed violence, the hurricane had recommenced and too soon the howling and buffeting of wind against the house and the racket of flying debris made it difficult to talk. It also increased my melancholy; I wondered if Hugh was worried about me.

During a period of relative quiet, when the wind was only a high pitched whine, Lynn said, "Men are such cads."

Feeling far away from Hugh, I said, "No, not all of them."

"You're right. Not Billy." She nodded slightly, sounding almost unconcerned.

"Billy was a randy old goat, Lynn, just like those losers I warned you about before you married." The banging and clatter of flying objects increased. I had to shout this time, "I don't understand why you didn't see that in Billy."

A sharp burst of wind shook the house and we cringed together, like babes in the woods, waiting for another lessening of the storms force.

Lynn spoke in my ear. "When Billy died, I thought I'd die, too. Maybe part of me did die." I decided that she hadn't heard what I said about him.

The despair in her voice devastated me. This was my little sister, hurt like this, and I had never noticed. How could I have been so blind? And Billy. I believed that Billy loved me. He should have loved Lynn, too. After his confession, he had thanked me for letting him stay on at the farm. I grimaced in the dark, mystified at his behavior.

Then something big and heavy hit the house, which shuddered, and it sounded like part of the house was being wrenched away – the downstairs deck, I suspected.

In the midst of this life-threatening situation, I regretted my lack of compassion. At least, now I could tell Lynn …

She shifted against me, bellowing over the racket outside, "I don't much like the idea of dying drunk in a bathtub," she pronounced. "It's lacks dignity. And style, Minty."

Quelling an hysterical urge to laugh, I asked, "You want to go out on the sun-porch? At least we could see our fate approaching." At that moment, I forgave her — how could I not?

Getting out of the tub, this time, however, took considerable effort with a great deal of bumping against each other, the toilet and the sink, as neither of us coordinated very well.

"Bring the blankets and the pillow," I said. "I don't want to die cold either." I grabbed the Afghan. A paradoxical feeling of euphoria came over me. If these were our final moments, at least Lynn and I were friends again and I'd make the rest of our time as good as I could!

Our progress, with an open bottle of wine, several quilts, a pillow and the Afghan, was unsteady to say the least. We succeeded, however, in wrenching open the door to the sun-porch over the living room, letting in the loud demons of the wind. Nearly incapable of standing, we made ourselves comfortable on the floor, against the house with pillows behind our backs. Indifferently, we faced the wall of windows, fortunately still intact. And Oh! Sweet miracle, with a bottle of wine and a handful of crackers.

Without let-up, the tempest raged around the house, rattling the windows, tossing anything loose around. A monsoon of rain beat against the glass, accompanied by a variety of moans, howls, and shrieks like a maniac seeking to tear from the earth everything built by man or nature.

After Lynn opened the last bottle of wine, she drank and passed it to me. Then she leaned her head on my shoulder, her arm tucked into mine.

"Are you going to sleep?" I asked.

"Possibly, " she answered.

"Lynn, hon, don't leave me alone."

"Keep me awake, then."

"What do you want me to do? Sing to you?" I said and raised my voice, "Hail, Mary, rollin' down the river, rollin', rollin', rollin' down the river," Then I asked, "What's the next line?"

"For Pete's sake, Minty. It's not Hail, Mary. It's 'Proud Mary' first. Then 'burnin' down the river, burnin', burnin', …" Lynn lifted her head and sang, "But I never saw the good side of the city, 'Til I hitched a ride on a river boat queen."

Unable to hear our voices against the tumult surrounding us, we sang drunkenly together.

My mind, however, recognized the irony of our drowning on a sun-porch. Holding onto my sister, I kept singing, so I wouldn't cry that I'd never see Hugh or my children again.

"'Big wheel keep on turnin', Proud Mary keep on burnin'. Rollin', rollin', rolling down the river.'"

Chapter 17

I awoke the next morning, chilled through, stiff and frightfully hung-over, to hear Lynn caroling cheerfully, "The hurricane's over, Minty. It's a beautiful day and we survived."

My sister's voice cut through my brain like a hot knife. What I thought was the beating of a drum inside my skull, turned out to be the putt-putt of an outboard motorboat.

"We're being rescued, Minty. I think it's Hugh and Clay coming for us," Lynn continued with ear-piercing cries of joy.

"For mercy's sake, please speak quietly," I mumbled and staggered over to where she stood near an open window.

Unfortunately, I was in no condition to admire the blue sky or the sunshine. I did, however, appreciate the warmth of the day and a glimmer of pleasure that we had survived despite part of me hoped to be euthanized.

Lynn stood at the open window and called, "Thank you. Thank you." Her enthusiasm reminded me of my success in mending my fences with her. Lacking the strength to witness whatever destruction the storm had left, I yielded to my primitive need to wrap myself in the Afghan, to close my eyes again and sink into oblivion.

But that was not to be. I felt Lynn's arm lifting me and protested feebly.

"Oh, you're hung-over, aren't you?" This time she modulated her voice with sympathy. "Poor thing. Come on, I'll help you downstairs."

Because my head was twice its normal size and I suspected that it was badly broken, I found her unrestrained bounty distasteful. Nevertheless, I mumbled something in the nature of a plea for silence.

With a persistence I had never before witnessed in my sister, she got me up on my feet and together, we lurched off the sun porch and toward the stairs. Too feeble to express my appreciation for her help, I steadied myself by sliding my hand along the banister.

When we reached the bottom, Lynn said, "Let go of the Afghan, Minty. Leave it here."

I'm afraid that I whimpered and clung to it. Then I heard the wonderful music of Hugh's voice.

"Let her keep it, Lynn. She's cold with dehydration."

I kept my eyes tightly closed against the bright light, held my throbbing head stiff on my neck and fought what I considered a noble battle not to throw up. The surge of fresh air revitalized me enough to quell that urge. I followed Hugh's instructions as he and Lynn maneuvered us over piles of broken lumber and, finally, hauling me into the boat.

Wrapped in blankets and plied with coffee, I huddled against Hugh in the stern, while Lynn — beautiful, un-hungover Lynn — recounted her version of our night. Including our drunkenness, naturally. In my case it was obvious, so I leaned, eyes closed, against Hugh, who kept offering me water.

"You get dehydrated when you're drunk," he repeated, until I obeyed, silently damning all sober people, doctors not excepted.

Once we were settled, Clay started the motor and over the putt-putting, I listened dully to their observations.

"Aw, my poor deck," Lynn muttered, as we abandoned the house. "...half destroyed. It'll take some repair and look at the size of that branch."

The nerves in my brain screamed with every putt putt of the darned engine.

"... broken window... " Clay's voice. "...another one. There may be water damage on this side, Lynn."

"Where?" He must have pointed because she added, "Oh yeah. I'll have it checked out."

She didn't sound concerned so I felt no need to hear about more damage. Still swaddled in Lynn's afghan, I pressed against Hugh, refusing to open my eyes.

"Quite a few shingles are gone, too." I felt the vibration of Hugh's voice and fancied I could feel his heart beat. I let that lull me into unconsciousness.

I don't know how long I dozed, because I don't remember their checking the three other houses for victims. I vaguely felt being trundled out of the boat and into a car, but was not motivated to stay conscious.

When we got back to Whitman, Hugh, bless his generous heart, put me to bed and let me sleep the rest of the morning, leaving Clay to drop Lynn at her house.

*   *   *

About noon, I returned to the land of the living and, after several aspirin and a bowl of chicken noodle soup, felt decent. Decent enough, apparently, that Hugh felt free to alternately complain at my reckless behavior and to minister to what he considered to be my needs.

"I don't see anything outrageous about driving over to check on my sister after a little spat," I defended myself.

"At least you had the sense to tell John where you were going. You owe him, you know. He not only took care of the animals, but he called me when the radio and TV news described the location of the hurricane."

"How high did the river flood?" I thought of my poor old car.

"High enough to break a hundred year record." Hugh was fixing dinner for us and the fragrance reminded me that I was hungry. "After dinner, I'll get Philabelle and she'll stay here tonight. I'm sorry I can't, but Mac's been on call all weekend and took up the slack again today."

Contented, I slept again, thinking like Pippa, "God's in his heaven. All's right with the world."

Sometime later that afternoon, I became aware that I was in my own wonderful bed and badly had to pee.

Following the fragrance of coffee, I went downstairs where Hugh had scrambled eggs and toast. I salivated over the odor of bacon. Marvel of marvels, I could see out of both eyes. Never had Hugh looked so handsome: warm brown eyes, smiling at me. He put his arms around me and I rubbed his chest through the open collar.

"My hero," I said, stroking his stubbly unshaven cheek.

"Sit down, shug. I've fed all your animals and it's your turn now."

As I ate, small bites in respect for my sensitive stomach, Hugh brought me up-to-date on the consequences of the hurricane. Considerable damage had been done further south of the Plum Point area, but no deaths reported. At Lynn's cottage, lots of debris – branches, pieces of wood were scattered around and a garbage can caught in the azaleas. He added that Philabelle, Sarah and Lynn had called to check on my condition. He concluded with the admonition that he didn't appreciate the scare I had given him.

"You make it sound as if I caused the darn storm," I said, feeling defensive because of my now obvious inability to hold my 'likker'. Plus I hadn't combed my hair, was still in a grubby old nightgown with a faded limp cotton bathrobe on top. Certainly not attractive.

Hugh frowned and said, "No, but you surely used poor judgment in driving into a hurricane area unnecessarily."

"Poor judgment to go stay with my sister in spite of what I thought was just a rain storm?" I scoffed. I expected warm fuzzies for my bravery, not criticism. "And don't smile that twitchey smile, Hugh. It's not funny." Misery sharpened my tongue despite my recognition that I was beholden to Hugh as well as Clay.

Hugh was standing leaning back against the counter, arms crossed on his chest. "What smile?"

"That smile when only one corner of your mouth sort of smiles and twitches. It means you're laughing at someone or feeling superior." I disliked the fretful tone of my voice.

"Come on, shug. This isn't worth bickering over." He rose and, before I had a chance to air my peeve, took his dirty dishes over to the dishwasher and reassured me that my car was in fair condition and Lee's garage would call when it was ready.

As Hugh added to the list of their efforts on my behalf, I flushed with embarrassment at my petty need for recognition of my courage. Quickly, I added, "I appreciate you and Clay rescuing us. I do take issue, however, with your categorizing concern for my sister as unnecessary. I consider it a mercy mission."

Obviously Hugh didn't feel chastened. Instead, he put his arms around me again, holding me against his chest. "I don't know what made this a mercy mission, but, shugar, you just scared the bejesus out of me."

I must have been a little weak still, because I leaned into his embrace and my irritation was assuaged as he rubbed my back. Mother of pearl! What a tower of strength and how essential to my life Hugh was, I thought as he drove away a few minutes later.

Over-whelmed with affection for him and, probably because of my weakened condition, I thought that maybe marriage to Hugh was possible.

But only for a minute — before the specter of the aftermath of my marriage to Billy reminded me that I was no longer a naïve young innocent. Damn Billy – the everlasting spook.

I wanted what Hugh and I had right now. Gambling on marriage was too great a risk.

Chapter 18

After Hugh left that afternoon, I returned to the kitchen and stuck the cup of cold coffee in the microwave and pressed 'On'. Apparently, for Buck, the sound of the microwave meant food. He loped into the kitchen at the same time as the telephone rang. I gave him a dog cookie. Not inclined towards casual conversation, I debated answering and let the phone ring four or five times before curiosity kicked in.

My 'hello' must have sounded a bit disgruntled, because my daughter Rachel, who was calling, asked if something was wrong.

"No, dear. Everything's fine. Sorry I sound so cross; it's been a frustrating morning." I stood in the middle of the kitchen with a cup of hot coffee in one hand the phone in the other.

"Did y'all get some of the wind and rain from the hurricane?"

"I was with Lynn at her cottage on the river. We sure did –an entire night of fierce wind and torrents of rain." I wanted to sit down at the table across the room, but the curly phone cord was all tangled around itself.

"So y'all had a bad night. Did Lynn stay there? Was there any damage?"

I sensed a tone of courtesy overlying something she wanted to say, so I played the episode down. "Nothing serious. Lynn came home and she'll call her handy man for repairs on the cottage. But we got no sleep and I still feel testy." She didn't need to know about our drinking binge.

"I'm sorry to hear that, but maybe my good news will cheer you up," she said over a repressed giggle. While I looked around for a place to put the cup, she continued, "I took your advice, Mom. I started dancing classes two weeks ago and it is *so much fun*. You were absolutely right. I did need a new interest and I've found it."

"I'm glad to hear that, sweetie. How does Howard like dancing?"

"He's not going. There's just me and five couples, fellow students. The instructor, Tony, dances with me, but we'll be exchanging partners once we've learned a few basics – to gain confidence, of course." I turned round and round to untangle the cord and slopped hot coffee on my hand while Rachel bubbled on. "After the first four classes, Tony said that I'm a natural and, in no time, I'll be ready for the tango. I'm so excited. My whole outlook on life has sky-rocketed."

I rephrased my question, "Did you *invite* Howard to go with you?" Cleo wound in and out around my legs, adding to my exasperation.

Rachel said, "He's not interested, Mom." Now *she* sounded a petulant.

I leaned over to set the cup back on the counter, but couldn't quite reach. Instead, I listened patiently as my daughter described the routine of coordinating dance classes with Adrienne's pre-school and Hammie's day care. I pulled the cord as far as it would go and managed to get rid of the cup and to force enthusiasm into my voice.

"I'm really glad that it's working out well for you. But you didn't answer my question about Howard: did you *ask* him to go with you?"

I could hear Rachel's heavy sigh over the phone, "He's O.K. with my going and is happy for me. Actually, he said I'm looking prettier."

Her skirting the issue raised my hackles and I said, "Rachel, it's essential for a healthy marriage that husband and wife do things *together*. I told you that before, when you were down here." I stretched as far as I could, trying to reach a chair to sit on.

Her annoyance was obvious in her tone when she responded, "I discussed it thoroughly with Howard and he's not interested, Mom."

"But did you actually tell him you *wanted* him to go with you?"

"Not in so many words," her voice scratched up a notch. "Howard and I understand each other and are capable of making our own choices." I heard a catch in her voice as she continued, "I object to being scolded as if I were a child, Mother."

Even when she was acting like a child, I wondered? With my finger tips, I dragged a chair out from the table to where I could sit in the middle of the room. More comfortable now, I agreed, "I suppose not. So let's change the subject. I hope y'all are planning to come down for the Fourth of July celebration."

"Of course. Isn't everybody coming?" She hesitated. "Jesse, too?"

I was aware of Rachel's affection for her younger brother, but she was still not at ease with his bringing his partner. I answered her unasked question, "If he and Mike don't have another commitment, yes, they'll be here."

After the briefest of pauses, Rachel said staunchly, "Good. We're looking forward to it, of course. The kids still talk about Edna and Claude."

With the resumption of normal conversation, I took the opportunity to relate Morton Trueblood's threat and my project with Philabelle to inventory and have the contents appraised. Rachel was upset at the possibility of the Manse being razed.

"That's what might happen. Philabelle would like to have someone in the family live there." I glanced at my cup on the counter getting cold.

"In the Manse?" she sounded as if I suggested they move to Krybuckistan or wherever.

What did I do that my children expected me to solve all their problems? They all loved the Manse, but nobody wanted the responsibility of maintaining it. Myself included, of course.

Rachel expressed concern over if or when Philabelle couldn't cope with such a big house and our conversation ended agreeably enough. I thanked her for calling and Rachel assured me that she and her family looked forward to the Fourth.

I knew she resented my 'interference'. I regretted that, but felt that I had done my maternal duty in re-enforcing the need for her to strengthen her bond with Howard.

When she had first mentioned the tango, I assumed that Howard would be her partner, not one of those slick young hunks on TV. In *my* opinion, the tango verged on vertical sex and with a man not one's husband? Questionable!

If Rachel's zeal for dancing continued, I worried that her relationship with Tony, plus the time away from Howard, might introduce problems for her.

I'd be glad when Sarah got home. We had raised our daughters together and I needed to tap into her store of Brooklyn pragmatism.

Chapter 19

I'd been looking forward to the fourth of July with excitement. This year it fell on a Wednesday, which made it a bit inconvenient for the working members of the family. Nevertheless, I was glad the Federals hadn't changed *it* to a Monday!.

Rachel and her family arrived about 7:30 Tuesday evening. While she unpacked upstairs, Howard, Adrienne, Hammie and I had fun settling the goats in for the night. Hammie, newly brave, climbed up on one of the benches I'd put out for Claude and tried to persuade the kid to join him. Adrienne helped me fill their trough with fresh water. Howard obviously enjoyed it as much as I did.

"Nothing's more entertaining than watching kids when they're absorbed in their activities," Howard said.

I asked, "Which kids are you referring to?" which gave us a laugh. "My mother would have insisted that only goats have kids."

I liked Howard so much. He was quite ordinary looking: good height with slender build, brown hair. But his intelligence, humor and personality shone through his blue eyes. Hammie had inherited both qualities plus the blue eyes.

I heard Jesse and Mike arrive, so I returned to the house. I sometimes forgot what a handsome couple they made: both tall, but Jesse had Whitman dark hair and Mike was Scandinavian blond.

After our greeting, they joined Howard out back and the newest arrivals drew me to the front door. I welcomed the William Whitman family with warm hugs all around. I suspected that William might introduce the first touch of tension. While Howard, bless his heart, accepted Jesse and Mike as part of the family, William was courteous, but distant. I couldn't remember seeing him in conversation with Mike in the three years he and Jesse had been together.

As William's sons, now thirteen and eleven, rushed to join the group out back, Howard, who had turned the youngsters over to Jesse and Mike, came in to greet the newcomers. Myra and Rachel wanted to watch the kids and we left the men in the kitchen.

I felt fortunate with my grandchildren. Although William's boys were older than Rachel's kids, they cheerfully entertained their young cousins.

Rachel, I was happy to see, was chatty and animated as well as neatly groomed and becomingly dressed. A red and white French sailor shirt and nicely fitted jeans were appropriate. I hoped to have a few minutes with her to check on how her new schedule was working.

I left the two women and walked back to the house. Howard, who was not much taller than Rachel, stood on the top step of the stoop, on eye level with William, who also out-weighed him. With a beer each, they were discussing Philabelle's possible donation of the Manse. I noted that William, slightly near-sighted, wore dark rimmed glasses now. He looked scholarly.

All my family together for the first time since Christmas! Billy would be pleased and so proud. I was both, but since his death, Hugh and Philabelle had taken his place in my heart. I glanced back over my shoulder across the field and wondered whether Billy was hanging around ready to materialize. A vision of the group's reaction amused me, but I shivered at the idea and wished I could dispel this ghost business.

✱   ✱   ✱

The parade downtown started at ten o'clock on the Fourth, followed by the town picnic. There were enough vehicles to accommodate everybody. My car was loaded with buffet equipment, however, so I said I'd drive alone to the ball park.

The parade was wonderful: the high school band marched, colorful and youthful in their red and white uniforms, if not quite in sync musically. The Boy and Girl Scouts, a contingent from the local Sunday Schools and a number of veterans from three wars carried Virginia or USA flags. At the end, the Mayor, with the current Miss Whitman, rode in Doc Foster's ancient Studebaker touring car with the top down.

By the Confederate Memorial, the parade halted, while the Mayor gave the obligatory speech honoring those who had defended the glories of our

Confederate past as well as the United States. The band first played the Star Spangled Banner as we all sang in a different key and almost everybody joined in a rendition of "Dixie". Briefly, I scanned the gathering and, sure enough, someone waved their Confederate flag and gave the obsolete rebel yell. That got little response, fortunately.

Since we Committee members considered ourselves hostesses, we left early and hurried to the ball park to prepare the buffet.

With the help of several men, Lynn had posted direction signs to prevent some of the confusion of past Fourths. As planned, Clay and his troop had six tables ready, while high school boys scattered folding chairs around in shady areas.

I unlocked my car and called Lynn over. She looked dazzling in a blue and white sundress, "Lynn, give me a hand with the table cloths and stuff, please?" I handed them to her.

"I'm not sure we have enough food," Madge Marshall worried, as she checked the boxes of rolls.

Rachel joined Lynn and as quickly as they spread the tablecloths, committee members placed platters of food.

"We want rolls and hot dogs on the table by the grill, okay?" Sarah asked and undertook that task. Hugh, carrying a tubful of ice, skillfully skirted two running boys. I directed him and other people with supplies so that each table had some of everything, two women serving at each.

"Where are the napkins?" Myra asked; I handed her several packages and she hurried away, recruiting a helper back to the buffet. Crowds of people were gathering on the ball field.

As I shooed a curious group of girls away from the tables, a teacher rushed up, "What can I do?"

"Get lines started at each table so we get as many fed as fast as possible," I said, calling a belated "Thanks." My foresight in planning multiple feeding stations proved successful, limiting the confusion that had marred past Fourths. Many of the local women automatically handled crowd control — proof that too many cooks don't necessarily spoil the broth.

While I was congratulating myself on how smoothly the picnic was running, one of my elderly lady friends, Mildred Thrasher, pushed up her walker to join me. I filled her glass with lemonade and asked how life was treating her.

"Better than I have a right to expect," she chuckled. "It's a blessing to me to be able to celebrate my eighty-eighth Fourth of July."

"You wear your years well, Mildred." I wondered how I'd make out at eighty-eight. "Did you get some of Ola's chocolate cake? It's wickedly good." Although Mildred was some years younger than my mother, they had been friends and conspirators against the traditionalists in the Methodist Church. I had always liked Mildred; she had a happy and realistic approach to life.

"You bet! I eat dessert first now and my veggies last." Her laughter sounded like music. I carried her lemonade over to the table where she sat with several ancient ladies. I visited with them until Marge Marshall came to ask me something about the high school band. That taken care of, with nothing to do, I gazed around.

Despite the controlled confusion that ruled the field, I loved the whole thing. The traditions of the Fourth inspired sentimentality and the size of the crowd filled me with hope for our future. So many people to talk with, children who had grown over the year, band music until the musicians were served, balloons tied to young wrists, the odors of hot dogs, hamburgers and beer! What wasn't to love?

Feeling a bit peckish, I needed a break. I fixed myself a hot dog with pickle relish and ketchup and retreated to the sidelines to eat. I didn't see Schultz until he sidled up to me from behind.

"Your celebration's a big success, Minty. You must be proud," he said.

He knew that I disliked both him and his brazen wife. Nevertheless, he persisted in pretended friendship. I thought it presumptuous of him to call me Minty, but that was being picky. Only my mother's admonition to always speak civilly kept me from telling him just how repugnant I found his presence.

"It's not *my* celebration, and, to *us,* it's a fitting remembrance of this Holiday." I chomped down on my hot dog so I obviously couldn't engage in idle chitchat. A mouthful also prevented me from condemning his lack of reverence for the significance of the celebration.

He leaned closer and had the gall to put his hand on my bare forearm, which I resented. "Ah, but you're the spark plug who gets things done in Whitman. You know, Minty, if you worked *with* me instead of *against* me on this Manse project, we'd both profit." He raised his eyebrows and stared intently at me in a way which made my skin crawl. "Otherwise, the fight could get rough. Think about it, girly."

I'd taken a step back and continued chewing, but gave him 'the finger' with my eyes. When he realized that I wasn't going to answer, he grinned at me with malices, daring me to say something offensive.

My appetite gone, I tossed the remains of the hot dog in the trash, left him and walked back to the tables. Then I washed away the taste of the encounter with a glass of lemonade. I refused to let Al Schultz's crass words spoil the day for me. He wasn't worth making a scene over.

Chapter 20

That afternoon, following the buffet, the crowd dispersed and the Whitman clan separated into several groups. Jesse and Mike went to the Manse with Philabelle. The rest returned to my farm, including Hugh, his son Smith, and Lynn. Rachel put her exhausted youngsters down for a 'happy nappy'. Smith volunteered to take the boys out to swim again, Myra went upstairs with Rachel. I served beer, iced tea and Coke on the shady side of the porch for the rest of us.

William, Lynn, Hugh and Howard, I was pleased to note, were discussing the tenuous situation with Manse and, this time, I muscled in.

"How much is the Manse worth on the Market, do you think?" Howard asked.

"The Manse by itself? Very little, I surmise," Hugh said.

Howard' eyebrows rose. "Really? It looks in good condition. Interesting architecture."

"We have maintained it, but it would require expensive renovation to meet code. The value lies in the land itself," Hugh grimaced. "Philabelle will probably ask each of you whether you'd be interested in …"

"I already have," I interrupted. "I'm hoping that there's some historical association with the Manse. Regardless, it's important for the community to keep it in the family."

"But is that practical?" William asked. "Desirable, but who would actually want to live there?"

"What's wrong with living in Whitman?" My voice may have been a bit shrill; Hugh glanced at me with *that* look.

"Nothing at all, Mother, except we all have homes and careers in Richmond or Alexandria." William's effort to placate me was not successful. "That's prime real estate for business, but not residential."

For a minute, I wanted to slap my son, but I restrained myself. Fortunately, Howard spoke up.

"I'm not connected by blood, of course, but I understand the family value involved." As usual Howard took the long view. "If the town actually wants to buy the Manse, that ..."

"They don't want the house," I insisted. "They want to tear it down for new condominiums or office buildings, Howard. That's what hurts me and Philabelle, too. She'd rather give it away with assurance that it wouldn't be razed."

William scowled, "That's an enormously valuable piece of real estate to *give* away." He turned to Hugh, "The property itself would bring a considerable sum, don't you agree?"

"In a way, yes," Hugh shrugged, "But, unless one of the grandchildren wants it, I don't see a more viable solution. Philabelle certainly can't continue to live there alone much longer." Hugh's indifference to its fate disappointed me deeply.

Lynn, who had been silent, said, "I'm by way of being an outsider in this discussion, too, but I wonder whether taking a vote among the grandchildren would help?"

That was not a feasible course, I thought, and persisted, "The Manse is a symbol of the entire personality of Whitman — the last residence of its kind. Destroying it would bad manners to force confrontation at an occasion of celebration, so I laughed in fake levity. I kept to myself the theory of a conspiracy to demolish the Manse and somehow cheat Philabelle in the bargain.

Rachel and Myra had joined everyone on the porch, a few minutes earlier. Sitting a few feet away, they were comparing changes in their children since the previous Fourth. Lynn stayed close to the cluster of men, while I moved to a chaise near Rachel and Myra. I was anxious to put my case before them, still believing in the power of women to persuade men.

During a lapse in their dialogue, I said, "You are aware of the situation with the Manse, aren't you?" They both nodded, but Myra spoke first.

"It would be wrong to let the town destroy it. I'd like to see it kept in the family, of course, but it's important to the town history." Her response warmed my heart. "Surely, Aunt Philabelle isn't in a hurry to leave her home, is she?"

"No," I said, "but that time is coming and she wants to resolve the fate of the Manse in advance of relocating. You know she suggested that she donate it to Whitman to be used as a library, among other things?" I looked at Rachel, anxious for her opinion and wondered silently if Myra and William had already discussed it.

"Don't look at me, Mom," Rachel said. "I agree with Myra about keeping it in the family, but I can't imagine any of us living there. It's a mausoleum," she scoffed. "I suppose the property is valuable, but who would want to buy it as a home?"

The conversation diverged then onto the topic of the antiques and their value, but I more or less quit listening. Myra would follow William's lead, I felt sure, and Rachel regarded its value primarily as saleable property. I hadn't had a chance to talk to Howard, but, knowing him, he would absolve himself of any claim on the family decision.

*   *   *

Draped comfortably on the chaise, I must have dozed off. When I woke, Rachel and Myra had gone somewhere, as had the men. I was alone on the porch. I stretched, checked the time – four thirty. We were due at Philabelle's for dinner at seven. I wanted to change and rose to go upstairs.

As I passed the living room, I noticed Hugh and Lynn sitting on the couch deep in conversation. Curiosity nibbled at me while I changed. What were they talking about so seriously? It seemed unlikely that the Manse was their subject.

As I showered, I fretted over how Hugh could dismiss its significance so casually. For Lynn to presume a familial interest, would be not only out of line, but inappropriate. Her uncharacteristic concern grated on my nerves. While I was picking through my closet for something cool but proper for dinner at the Manse, I was vexed that so many of the townspeople failed to appreciate the historical value of the Manse, especially those who flaunted the Confederate flag. If they dismissed the symbolism of the Manse, nothing would prevent wholesale development from taking over. I frowned: that would happen only over my dead body.

*   *   *

Dinner at the Manse was a grand affair and I was pleased to see that the young adults were impressed by the elegance of their great aunt's hospitality as well as the grandeur of family portraits watching over their descendants and their treasures. Myra and Rachel, I knew, had gone to the Manse early to help Philabelle. They were good women, those two.

Even Adrienne and Hammie stayed awake for the fire works. Clay planned to set them off over the ball park, when it got dark, about 9:30. The bleachers were packed and an over flow of people had brought lawn chairs and blankets to spread around. It was a grand display for a town this size and the applause that followed confirmed the crowd's enjoyment.

By the end of the celebration, Hammie was asleep in Howard's arms and Adrienne so drowsy that she held Rachels's hand and stumbled along. Everybody agreed it had been a splendid celebration. Jesse and Mike escorted Philabelle home and the William Whitmans, who had reservations at the Old Oak Motel, said goodnight.

I had driven Philabelle to the ball field and asked Lynn, "You want a ride home with me?"

"No thanks. Hugh's taking me home," she replied curtly. My surprise must have showed, because she added, "He's not hand-cuffed to you, sister dear."

Despite a jolt of chagrin, I managed a laugh. I certainly hadn't planned for Hugh to go home with me that night. I had no intention of flaunting our relationship in the faces of my children. I had hoped, however, for a few minutes with him alone to talk about the Schultz encounter. I'd have to wait for a more auspicious moment. Seeing him with Lynn again left me uneasy.

Chapter 21

Sunshine and bird song woke me at six the next morning. While everyone else slumbered, I let Buck out and made coffee. As soon as it was ready, I took a mug and, with a Danish and Cleo, sat on the back stoop steps to inhale the fragrance of farm life. Sitting alone, my eyes gazed idly across the landscape, half expecting Billy's apparition to actually appear. When Buck returned, I thrust away my morbid thoughts and with Buck, we went inside to prepare breakfast for my family.

While I set the table in the dining room, my mind was still on Billy. I realized that nothing I could have done would have changed his death. It had been Billy's choice to fix a pasture for the goats. A dutiful wife, I had acquiesced. Unbidden, the question of my response to Hugh's proposal surfaced. I stood with a handful of silverware. My reluctance to marry him bewildered me. I had confidence in our mutual affection, despite the age difference. He was incapable of lying or cheating. Definitely, excellent husband material.

Still feeling glum, I was glad to hear the phone ring and answered with a cheerful, "Hello?"

"It's me -- Hugh," he sounded sick. "Sorry to disturb you so early, but I wanted you to hear this first. There was a small fire at the Manse last night." I gasped. "Everybody's fine, so you don't need to worry." I collapsed on a chair as if shoved. "The back porch and part of the kitchen are damaged."

I babbled with panic, "A fire? Oh no." My hands were sweaty and I could hardly breathe with the shock.

"Clay got everyone out safe, before —"

"I'll come right — ," I began.

"No! There's nothing you can do here. It's not as bad as it sounds, Minty. Not even much smoke damage inside. Clay said the wind was blowing east, away from the house, fortunately. So it spread onto the grass instead of inside."

"Mother of pearl! I'm speechless. Philabelle can stay with me until it's safe. Is the Manse badly damaged?" I babbled.

"One thing at a time. Lynn heard the fire engines and came over in the middle of the night. Philabelle – who's surprisingly calm under the circumstances – is staying with her right now. I offered Jesse and Mike shelter, but they opted to stay on in the Manse."

"But …" I was frustrated, but strove for composure. Hugh wouldn't deceive me.

"Don't worry. The firemen checked out the entire house and said it's safe."

Hugh was always so in control. I guess you get that way being a doctor. I had a thousand questions, but couldn't think straight. Meantime, Rachel had come down and checked the fridge to start breakfast for the children. She looked at me with raised eyebrows, mouthing questions.

"What can I do, Hugh? I can't just …"

"You can take care of your family and call Lynn, but not until about 10 o'clock. It was after two this morning before they left the scene, so I expect they were still too stimulated to sleep right away. Meantime, everything's under control. We'll see y'all at your barbecue tonight anyway, right?"

In the rush of anxiety, I'd forgotten, so I assured him that we were looking forward to it and we hung up. I stood gathering my wits for a moment. Something sounded not quite right. How could the Manse catch fire in the middle of the night?

By then, Rachel was demanding answers and Howard had brought down the kids. Eager to see Edna and Claude, they dragged Howard outside while I briefed Rachel.

"Are we still going to have the barbecue?" she asked.

I nodded and said, "Hugh says there's nothing we can do for them and we have everything ready. Meantime, I need a second cuppa. Can I fix you sausage or eggs?"

Rachel had found the orange juice. "No, thanks, Mom, I'll have one of those Danish, if that's okay. I'm not big on breakfast," she said and sat at the table.

Within the next hour, the Junior Whitmans arrived and kept me busy. I passed on word of the fire. Later Jesse and Mike stopped by to add details.

"The Manse is a mess at the moment, but a small mess, Mom." Jesse, like

Hugh, had the knack of reassurance. "Aunt Philabelle's something else. As soon as the firemen arrived and doused the flames, she began making plans to call for an estimate of the damage."

Questions were repeated and answered. There was an unpleasant moment, however, after Jesse and Mike asked William's boys if they wanted to go swimming. The boys were thrilled and I got towels out of the downstairs bathroom for them.

I was still in the hall when I heard William say, I presumed to Myra, "I wish you'd consult me before you tell the boys they can go off again with those men."

I couldn't hear her reply. Towels in hands I went into the front hall. The boys rushed pell-mell down the stairs.

"Take these with you," I said and, with a hasty 'thanks', they grabbed the towels on the run.

Myra followed them out the front door. Already annoyed at William's lack of interaction with Jesse or Mike, I grabbed his arm.

"What's with you and Jesse and Mike? You act like they're undesirable companions for the boys."

Apparently, I'd surprised him; he almost stuttered when he said, "You know what they are, Mom. I just feel it's not a good influence."

"Jesse's your *brother*, William, and he and Mike are not pedophiles. Also, I object to your denying the boys time with their uncles."

"Mike is not an uncle," he grunted at me.

"He would be if the State of Virginia weren't so bigoted."

To give him credit, William looked chastened. Nevertheless, I added, "I won't tolerate that sort of talk in my house."

William exhaled with obvious exasperation, "I didn't say they were *that*. It's not —."

"You're afraid, aren't you? As if it were contagious."

"It is in the sense that it puts ideas in their heads," William fought back.

"Poppy cock! This is your brother you're disparaging," I repeated. Then, my annoyance assuaged, added, "You're too big a man to harbor such anxieties, William."

"And I wonder sometimes if you're not too trusting, Mother."

Fortunately, Rachel came down the stairs, ending the discussion.

*   *   *

By 6:30 that evening, everybody had arrived. Hugh had brought Lynn, Philabelle and his son, Smith. Hugh joined Howard and William, who were manning the grill out back. Myra, Rachel, Philabelle and I prepared tables on the screened porch – our antidote to summer evening mosquitoes.

Jesse, Mike and the boys returned all dressed in shorts and shirts, with neatly combed and still damp hair. Hammie and Adrienne were watching Sesame Street on TV, while we spread out the serving dishes. The youngsters sat at a small table and the adults had opted for another buffet. Lots of tray tables were scattered over the wrap-around porch.

During dinner, I heard Hugh tell William that the Kevin Kearns, our fire captain, had called an arson team from New Kent to check out the Manse. There was an odor of gasoline, he said. Immediately, I wondered who would want to burn down the Manse. Schultz, I thought, but held my tongue, not wanting to make an issue of arson in front of Philabelle. The men began to discuss fire insurance and I decided to talk to Hugh later.

I'd find a good time to invite Philabelle to stay with me. When I did, Philabelle patted my arm to answer, but Lynn interrupted, "I'm closer and I really enjoy her company."

I didn't much like Lynn's tone of voice, but people were beginning to make their departure, by then, so I didn't comment.

The Junior Whitmans would head out to Williamsburg early the next morning. Jesse and Mike planned to visit Jesse's old high school friends. Lynn had disappeared and I followed Philabelle, Jesse and Mike toward the front.

I kept an eye out for Hugh. I wanted to catch him before he left. To my chagrin, I saw him going down the steps with Lynn. Apparently, he heard us, because he turned and called, "Good party as usual, Minty. Good night all." and waved.

Rachel, Howard and I stood on the porch watching the cars lights twinkle down the drive before we went back inside. With the youngsters tucked in upstairs for the night, I offered Rachel and Howard a nightcap. "Grand Marnier goes down nicely." I retrieved the liqueur glasses.

Howard said, "That would be the perfect end to another wonderful day to remember."

Rachel opted to get ready for their departure the next day. I was disappointed on two counts: that they weren't staying longer and I hadn't had an opportunity to talk privately to my daughter.

"I'll sit for a few minutes," Howard indicated the couch. "I haven't had Grand Marnier in years."

"I guess it's not in style any more," I sat and took a sip, hoping that he might ease my worry. "I've wanted to ask how you feel about Rachel adding more dance classes."

"I think it's good for her. She loves it and, paradoxically, seems to have more energy. She's happier and looks prettier, too."

"Have you considered joining her? It's a lovely activity for husband and wife."

Howard grinned. "I'm afraid I've got two left feet. They're planning an exhibition, a sort of recital, I guess, the end of August. I'll be on the sidelines rooting for her."

That left me no room for objecting. Buck butted my hand with his nose and I fondled the warm soft ears. I was basically a touchy, feely person. Textures of all kinds invited my hands: weirdly, Hugh's unshaven cheeks, silks, velvets, tweeds even wood. Hugh and I were alike in that way. At that moment, I nursed a feeling of being neglected.

In the quiet, Buck's head in my lap warmed my heart. With a sudden chill, I thought that, if the Manse had burned down, there'd be no question of its becoming an historical landmark. That would certainly make it easy for Morton and Schultz to justify buying the property.

Were they capable of arson? I couldn't decide, but I would certainly find out.

Chapter 22

On Friday, restless in the empty house and needing to see the damage to the Manse, I phoned Philabelle at Lynn's. Lynn answered, "She's gone back to the Manse with Jesse and Mike." I grunted, feeling protective of Philabelle, while Lynn continued, "It's perfectly safe and the carpenter came and blocked off the porch temporarily. You don't need to bother about coming into town."

"Isn't she apprehensive about the culprit setting another fire?" I asked.

"What culprit? What are you talking about?" Lynn sounded testy.

"Hugh said they suspect arson. Something about odor of gasoline. That's what I'm talking about, Lynn," I made an effort to curb my annoyance and heard Lynn sigh, with exasperation, I supposed.

"*Suspect* is different from fact. As usual, I think you're being melodramatic. Hugh wouldn't let anybody stay in the Manse if he thought it were dangerous."

That being true, I couldn't dispute it. I felt as if I'd been dismissed, however, and, instead of responding defensively, I said, sweetly, "Thanks, Lynn. I'm coming in to the market anyway and may stop at the Manse to look at the damage."

Although I didn't say that to her, I was sure Morton and Schultz had something to do with the fire. When I picked up a box of pastries, I wanted to run my suspicions by Clay. He was first at the scene and would have the 'true facts'.

He was arranging the display of greeting cards when I opened the door.

"Ah! My favorite girl friend of all time. You've made my day," he almost sang when he saw it was me and held his arms open for a hug.

Clay liked to pretend we were still high school sweethearts and I greeted him with, "Hail, rescuer of Whitman women." He always made me feel good.

We laughed together, before I asked him, "You too busy to talk right now?"

Pretending surprise, he raised his eyebrows and said, "Never, hon. What'd you want to talk about?" He picked up the empty carton and walked behind the counter.

"The fire, of course. I heard that the Fire Chief thinks it was arson. You were the first one there. What do you think?"

His face flushed a blotchy pink, when he turned and stammered, "I … eh, was out for a walk."

"In the middle of the night?" I never figured Clay as a solitary walker. "Madge and I had a disagreement. I needed to get away and cool down, you know how it is." He did look embarrassed.

"Been there and done that!" I snickered. "Back to the subject: who do you think would want to burn down the Manse? Morton comes to mind."

Clay's eyes popped open and he laughed, "Morton? He's too much the old school southern gentleman. Besides, he doesn't have the gumption."

Not so old school that it prevented him from consorting with an outsider like Schultz, I thought. Clay commenced to fold up the cardboard box, leaning down to tuck it on the shelf beneath the counter. Without looking up, he said, "Besides he's from one of the founding families. You've given him a great face-saving device by offering the Manse as a library."

The bell on the door tinkled and E.J. Rossi came in. Clay nodded at him and continued his thought, "That knocks the props out from under his argument. He still may want to buy the property next to it – the treed area – for development though."

"Are y'all talking about the fire?" E. J. asked. Not the handsomest man in town; his ears stuck out from his bald head, fringed like a monk's with faded red hair, but a wonderful friend.

I nodded and explained, "Trying to figure out who would want to burn down the Manse. Morton had already condemned it as a tinder-box and —."

"No, that was Al Schultz and he used the expression 'fire hazard", E.J. interrupted. "Either way it's just an expression. Besides it was an accidental fire of some kind."

"You don't take it seriously? That it was arson?"

"Not until the Arson Squad confirms it. Don't make too much of the word 'possibility', Minty. You don't want to scare Philabelle," E.J. replied.

Hugh had said that and it did worry me. I'd check again in a few days when the report was final. I suspected they were all — Hugh, Clay and E.J. — trying to placate me. For now, I would let them think they had, but I was sure it was arson. Too much of a coincidence and I didn't believe in coincidences.

"How's Janet?" I asked E.J.

He made a moue of discouragement and said, "No worse. I really appreciate your driving her out to visit Ola last week." I raised a hand in dismissal. "You know how much she enjoys it. I took her out again this morning, since Ola's kind enough to invite her."

I nodded and added, "Ah, yes. That's why Ola's late. We women do like to chat and forget to watch the time."

We all laughed at our tolerance of feminine stereotyping. Notwithstanding that, it reminded me about the pastries. "I'll stop by before I go home."

*   *   *

When I returned to the Manse, Philabelle, Jesse, Mike and Lynn were standing outside. I wanted to see the damage, so we all trooped around back. It was nasty looking and smelly. The fumes of wet smoke, burned wood and rubber hung in the air. I could see that most of the porch was destroyed, part of the kitchen was damaged and windows broken. It was a mess, but, although badly scorched, the back wall of the kitchen was intact.

Philabelle, all business, said, "I'll be getting an estimate on the repairs this week. Meantime, I can manage in the kitchen. The stove, fridge and microwave are all available and functioning."

Philabelle's independence was remarkable in a seventy-five year old woman. I was afraid she'd feel threatened, but, obviously, she was doing fine. There are times when ignorance was bliss and I wasn't going to upset her. Let the fire chief and the men do that.

The three of them made a joke of Clay's arousing them and the hustle of the volunteer firemen putting it out.

"We were disheveled, but Lynn, who got here ..." Jesse turned to her. "... about the time the fire truck arrived?" Lynn nodded. "She was dolled up as if for a party."

Lynn slapped at his arm and said, "I was not *dolled* up. Decently clothed is the proper expression."

"It could have been a real disaster," I chided them with my own humor. "Y'all make it sound like you were having fun. A pity that you didn't have any marshmallows to roast."

"Fortunately, Clay spotted it before it did much damage," Philabelle said.

"And the fire department arrived before we had the garden hoses hooked up." Mike laughed, "Jesse and I didn't get a chance to play hero."

I made tsk tsk noises at them. "Are you sure it's safe to live in?"

"Don't worry, Mom. Half the firemen checked the place out — wiring and everything, not just the kitchen, the entire house," Jesse said.

Then, ever the southern hostess, Philabelle suggested that we have something cold to drink. Jesse and Mike had a date with a several old friends and left Philabelle, Lynn and me to our own devices. Since the back entry was closed off, we walked around to the side door. I stayed because I could see that my sister-in-law was delighted to have Lynn and me together.

While Philabelle went to fix tea, our conversation dealt mostly with re-hashing the visit with family and I said the fire was suspicious.

Philabelle returned with a pitcher of iced tea and glasses on a tray. "Suspicious of what, Minty?" She set the tray down.

"Of what caused the fire," I said, intrigued by the possibilities. Philabelle looked skeptical and Lynn's face puckered with contempt. Philabelle served us a glass of tea, garnished with a mint leaf.

"Don't be so melodramatic," Lynn said shaking her head.

I took a sip before I pointed out, "Hugh said there was gasoline smell all around."

Philabelle spoke up, as if offended. "I don't keep gasoline around here."

"Which makes it suspicious," I blurted out, completely forgetting, in my annoyance at their disregard of the severity of arson, that I hadn't wanted to frighten her.

Immediately, Philabelle showed alarm. "You don't believe someone would intend ..."

"Of course not, Philabelle," Lynn spoke quickly, giving me a dirty look.

Wishing I'd kept my mouth shut, I turned to Philabelle, and said, "It's perfectly safe, hon, they just have to follow their protocol if there's anything suspicious." I hoped that Lynn understood that I was deflecting Philabelle's anxiety, when I added, "What I'm looking for are clues to why, all of a sudden, Schultz and Morton want to buy the Manse."

Lynn cooled her hands on her glass, "Don't you think it's a waste of your time – meddling in small town politics?"

"It's not just the politics. It's to save the Manse. It's historic." I tended to come on too strong sometimes, and struggled to contain my irritation at their disregarding the possibility of arson. Tactfully, I changed the direction by adding, "Incidentally, speaking of history: I'm hoping that the Trueblood journal from after The War will reveal some historical plums. Something that warrants the Manse being classified as an Historical Home."

Lynn turned to me, "Have you uncovered any old family scandals?"

Restraining a sigh, I said, "Not yet. Using family names as a guide, however, I've learned that our ancestors were a curious lot." I shook my head and tried to lighten my voice. "Trueblood, Whitman and Marshall families were interwoven before the 1860s. It was almost incestuous." I knew that would intrigue Lynn.

"Minty!" Philabelle looked shocked.

"Don't pay any attention to her," Lynn smiled at Philabelle and patted her arm. "That's one of Minty's attention getting devices." She turned to me, "No evidence of hanky-panky?"

"Nothing yet," I said, knowing that I'd disappoint Lynn. "What I want is something the equivalent of 'George Washington slept here'."

Philabelle, the peace-maker, said, "I expect there were some of both: scandals and history. Maybe Martha Washington slept here. She owned a plantation in New Kent, you know."

Lynn pretended disappointment. "That's Minty's sort of thing, of course."

"Let's wait and see what turns up in the Trueblood journal," Philabelle said.

I shrugged. "Meanwhile, I've made notes on the computer about Trueblood shenanigans. Maybe it'll trigger some memories for you, Philabelle, and conjure up old family stories."

"Off hand, I can't remember anything remarkable, but I'd enjoy reading your notes," Philabelle smiled.

Before we went our separate ways, I reminded them that the second town meeting was coming up and urged them to attend with me. Philabelle, of course, was eager to join me.

"I still think it's silly to get involved in politics," Lynn said and when I opened my mouth to protest, she added, "All right. I'll be there but don't push."

Pleased that I had successfully kept my irritation to myself, I took my suspicions and left.

Chapter 23

On the night of the town meeting, I parked at the Manse. Philabelle and I had agreed that we would wear what we called our 'power' clothes. She wore a navy blue dress, a strand of pearls and she flourished an antique ivory lorgnette with an ebony handle.

"You're the epitome of lady-like dignity, Philabelle. Most impressive," I said. Beside her, I, in my pink linen with white embroidery, felt over-shadowed, which is the way I wanted it. Hugh, with a briefcase containing the copies of our offer, was quite natty in a suit and I felt that we presented an impressive force.

Most of the town seemed to be walking toward the hardware store or already climbing the stairs to the meeting-room. All the windows were open and fans whirled overhead. Two long tables for council members faced the rows of new chairs that filled the room.

I spotted Sarah and Mel first and stopped to greet them.

"There are copies of the town's offer to buy the Manse on the table up front. See the sign?" Sarah handed me some papers.

Mel leaned across her to say, "Don't fall for their stated intentions, Minty. Nowhere do they demonstrate interest in the Manse. It's all about the property."

We scanned the documents before we found seats. The town's 'offer' was primarily a request for approval for the council to approach the owner with an offer to buy the property. It was vague and pretty much asked the town to let the council do what they wanted with no constraints.

Hugh chuckled as he steered Philabelle and me to seats further forward and in the middle. We wanted everybody who attended to hear every word of what we planned to say.

As people trooped in, I kept an eye out for Lynn, who had said she'd join us. Through her work with Elliott she had contacts outside Whitman who could help or hinder our interests. I saw Clay and Madge, the Warners, Sr. and Jr., with wives and the Keens. Even Lee and his wife were there – a first for Isabelle, as I knew they had two small children.

The place filled up quickly, well before all the council members were seated at the table in the front. Word had spread, I supposed, about the offer to buy the Manse. It might be a more contentious issue than I suspected. Philabelle, I knew, avoided confrontation, but my dander was up and I was ready to fight the town.

Over the rustle of the audience, I whispered to Hugh, "Did you bring everything?"

"I'm sure. Are you nervous?" He leaned his shoulder against mine, which I took as reassurance.

I shook my head; "We've got lots of support." I felt excitement stirring within the room and was anxious for Morton to start, but nervous waiting for Lynn.

Finally all the council members were in place and Morton picked up the gavel to call the meeting to order. The secretary read the minutes, which were approved right away.

Still no Lynn. We needed all the influence available and her presence itself would have impact.

Morton rose and announced, "The first item on the agenda is the town's overture to Miss Philabelle Whitman concerning the purchase of the Manse and property, pertinent to the minutes of the previous meeting. Did everybody get a copy of this offer?" A mass of "No's" answered. Morton looked around. People raised their hands and the secretary distributed copies. A murmur began with the front rows and swept back over the crowd as they read the document.

Then, as solemnly as if announcing a death, Morton said, "Let the Minutes show that the Council published an offer to purchase the Whitman property."

The audience responded with shouts of "Boo" and other objections, but more of "Good" and "Hurray", I thought.

A man in the back called, "Some of us haven't had time to read the town's proposal, because it wasn't made public until tonight. Why wasn't there a public notice of some kind?"

Al Schultz presumptuously raised his hand and was recognized before he spoke, "A notice of the proposal was posted in a number of places and copies were available at the Town Registrar's Office." I wondered how Schultz knew that when the rest of us did not.

A muttering of disapproval arose. A strident voice in the back declared this "a clear failure of communication on the part of the council members".

A woman behind us apparently stood up and was recognized. "We need a few minutes to read this before any discussion or vote."

That started as a murmur across the audience which escalated into an increasing hubbub. The noise brought Morton's gavel into play with his cries of "Order. Order." Having gotten the attention of the audience, he called for a motion to take a ten minute break to allow reading of the document.

During the approved pause, I caught bits of various conversations questioning the use of the Manse and someone else thought the brouhaha was wasted energy. Despite the fans whirring softly overhead, the temperature of so many bodies in one room increased incrementally with the discord within the crowd. Groups discussions began softly, but gradually the decibels rose to a roar. Confusion climaxed when someone in the back, shouted, "I make a motion that we impeach the entire council."

Laughter and boos over-powered the general noise, until someone with a basso profundo voice raised the issue of discrimination against the poor, who were always the last to know. This set off a flurry of hoots and hollers. Someone quite near us asked, "What's that got to do with it?"

By this time, the controversy had accelerated to such a volume that no one could hear the pounding of the gavel or Morton's fruitless efforts to call for order. A disagreement between two men became physical. One pushed the other hard enough that he almost fell in a woman's lap. Philabelle leaned close for me to hear her concern about a fight.

"They'll get it under control," I assured her.

Quickly, the town security guard and the Mayor, with the help of several strong men, succeeded in calling a halt to the turmoil and quieted the crowd. Although the ruckus died down, the heat of the evening increased and council members huddled together in conference. Finally, Morton faced the assemblage and announced weakly that he would entertain a motion to postpone discussion on the proposal for two weeks to allow time for everybody to read the town's offer.

I had a momentary pity for the red faced, sweating Morton, who had reached the state of stammering. Kevin tugged at Morton's jacket, and whispered something to him. With a visible sigh, Morton faced us again.

"The council has no other business to present and, if there is no new business from the floor, I'll entertain a motion …"

Hugh poked me in the ribs, but before I could raise my hand, Philabelle rose, staring at Morton through her antique lorgnett, and said, "Mr. Chairman, I have new business, which will be presented by my sister-in-law, Mrs. William Whitman, Senior." Morton, who preferred the title of 'president', grimaced at her down-grading his position.

Morton looked around, as if for help, I thought, and receiving none, said, "I recognize Mrs. William Whitman."

Recovered from the surprise of Philabelle's initiative, I rose, glad for once of my height, and made my announcement, "Miss Philabelle Whitman and the Whitman heirs have authorized me to present the possibility of donating the Manse and a large portion of the surrounding property to the town for use as a public library. Dr Whitman has copies for those interested." I paused to let it sink in and Hugh used the time to deliver a stack of copies to each row, as well as council members. "The building is in good condition and, in addition to it and the real property …"

The commotion of clapping, shouts of "Bravo", "Hurray" that broke out exhilarated me to the extent that I scarcely credited the booing mixed in.

"We need a decent firehouse more than a library," I heard a woman call, despite Morton's application of the gavel.

"And an air conditioned meeting room," someone else added, as if free speech had become contagious. Fortunately, that precipitated more laughter than disagreement. But the commotion rippled throughout the room while poor old Morton banged away with the gavel, shouting, "Order! Order!"

Finally, Clay, well known by everybody in town, stood up and shouted, "Shut up and let Minty finish what she has to say." The crowd quieted down, and I continued.

"The family would stipulate that the Manse be designated an historic site in perpetuity as a representation of the early days of our town. In addition, Miss Philabelle would donate the books in the Whitman Library, some of which are first editions, and include writings of our founding families." I looked Morton squarely in the eye, and said, "Many of the books would be of particular interest to long-time residents. One, that intrigued me, is entitled 'The Journal of Jacob Trueblood' – one of your ancestors, wasn't he, Morton?" I sat down.

Into the pause that followed, Doc Foster, who had been listening to all the random comments, spoke, loudly to be heard, "This is a most generous offer and I make a motion that we accept it without further discussion."

Although whispering among the audience continued, it was relatively quiet. Most were taken by surprise at Philabelle's generosity, I expect. I was curious as to see how Morton would respond.

"A proposal – eh, a donation of that magnitude – would have to be taken under advisement." His cheeks flushed an unbecoming puce. "I'm not sure there is a legal procedure —"

"Poor guy's too worn-out to know what he's talking about," I whispered to Hugh. Philabelle grabbed my hand and held on. I could feel her quivering, I hoped, with the same amusement that I felt.

Al Schultz was recognized and said, "That's true. Obviously, the Manse is an old building and I foresee a lot of problems. For example, there are building codes to be considered, which might require extensive and expensive renovation. That would probably exceed the cost of construction of a new larger building. The town can't continue to live in the past. A new modern building could accommodate a library as well as office space, apartments, condominiums and a new town hall. A prominent developer has expressed an interest in consulting with the Council."

Wait'll I tell William about this was my immediate reaction. My second was awe at Schultz's arrogance.

"What's this developer's name?" I recognized Lynn's voice and Philabelle squeezed my hand.

Boos interspersed with nodding of heads, arguments for and against, which Morton tolerated for another fifteen or twenty minutes. He finally picked up the gavel. At the same time, Henry Samuelson, a long-time and respected businessman, rose and gestured for silence before he spoke in a trembling but authoritative voice, "Mrs. Whitman has a point. I, too, would like to know the name of this developer, Mr. Schultz." A few soft "yes's" and "boos" followed. I suspected that the interest level of the crowd was waning as the temperature in the room increased.

Schultz stood up to respond, "An important detail: Mr. Gustaf Nourikian is the developer. He has offices in Washington, D.C., as well as in Richmond. You may recall that we can thank him for the lovely retirement community Creek Woods Residence. He would be glad, I'm sure, to meet with the council and present his ideas for Whitman's future."

Ah, ha! I thought. Schultz was an associate of the developer and expected to make money somewhere in this deal; he and Morton must be in cahoots with this Nourikian. But we wouldn't take an invasion from strangers lying down.

Mr. Samuelson thanked Schultz and then continued, "In as much as Mrs. Whitman's extraordinary offer has surprised us all, what we need right now is time. On behalf of the taxpayers, I believe that the council should seek a legal opinion and advice to guide them in deciding on the next step. This would give the Whitman family time to prepare a formal statement of intent and for the council to keep all of us up-to-date on further negotiations. Therefore, I make a motion that this issue be tabled for a minimum of three weeks."

Doc Foster seconded Mr. Samuelson's motion and, finally, Morton, with an air of weariness, asked for a motion to close the meeting. That was made and accepted. I was relieved, as the seat was hard despite its padding. Morton whacked the table once more to declare the meeting adjourned.

As folks elbowed their way towards the door, the din of jabbering increased, along with the scrape of chairs being shoved aside. Hugh rose and, with a hand on our elbows, guided Philabelle and me towards one of the two exits. Although I tried to eavesdrop on some of the conversations, I couldn't decipher enough to determine the dominant trend.

In the middle of groups of people moving slowly toward the doors, Hugh, Philabelle and I intercepted Sarah and Mel. They congratulated Philabelle on her community spirit. Clay, with an unusual frown on his face, was running interference for Lynn. The seven of us squeezed out the door and started down the stairs to the outside.

Smoothly, before I could greet my sister, Hugh herded us down the stairs and outside. In front of the hardware store display window, we clustered together like conspirators. Taking grateful breaths of the fresh air, I made another effort to take the temperature of the town, glancing at similar groups of four or five people re-hashing the meeting as they inched down the sidewalk.

*   *   *

Twilight was just darkening the sky and the streetlights cast eerie shadows on the moving crowd. E.J. Rossi agreed to meet us at the Levin's home.

Philabelle said, "How thoughtful, Sarah. It's still early and such a pleasant evening, we can walk the few blocks." And we three women led the way, followed by Hugh, Clay, Mel, E.J. and Lynn. The noise and the crowd thinned out quickly, replaced by the quiet of evening as we trooped around the corner and down Cedar Street. By the second block, we had left downtown behind for the neighborhood where Sarah and Mel lived.

An occasional breeze treated us to the fragrance of jasmine as we passed various front gardens. Houses were set back from the street and, through shrubs and trees, I noticed that people inside were turning on lights. Unconsciously, we had lowered our voices, allowing the sounds of TVs and an occasional dog's bark to float through the air.

A pensive mood took hold of me, as we led the others through the residential area until we reached the Levin's home. Love for this small town filled me, replacing the earlier tension I had felt. Contentious as it had been, the meeting left me hopeful.

Instead of traipsing through the house, we skirted the front porch and opened the gate to the backyard. There, we settled on the deck off the dining room. Sarah and I took orders for drinks.

"I'd prefer iced tea," I told Sarah, who agreed.

In the kitchen, we fixed a tray of beer and glasses for iced tea plus a bowl of mini pretzels. When we took out the refreshments, from their laughter, I could tell our friends had enjoyed, at Morton's expense, the raucous reaction to the issue of the Manse.

"We really need to replace Morton, but I'd be reluctant to deprive him of the status," Hugh said. "He enjoys it so much."

"Until tonight," E. J. added. "He didn't much like opposition."

As their laughter quieted, Mel said seriously, "You know what impresses me most? This was pure democracy in action. We've lived," he gestured toward Sarah," in New York, Philadelphia – a number of places – and, except for small towns in New England, I've never seen anything like this. It truly is government *by we the people*." He shook his head and smiled. "Remarkable."

Philabelle, who sat beside me on a wicker couch, said, "Remarkable, yes, but nothing has been resolved yet." Sarah nodded and murmured in agreement.

"Did you expect it to be resolved tonight?" Clay, looking tired, commented, "We made progress of a sort."

Hugh, across a low table from the me, said, "I was surprised there's so much resistance to a gift of such value."

"It's not the Manse they want," I said, "It's the property. I can't understand the thinking that destroys history in the name of *progress*."

"Whether we like it or not, Minty, Schultz is right. Young people are leaving. Mine already have and yours, too. The town will die if we don't work to keep it alive," Clay said and drank some beer, leaving a bit of foam on his upper lip.

Sarah asked, shaking her head in disapproval, "Why does progress require changing things so radically?"

Mel patted her knee. "Life is a series of changes, love."

"But we don't want to stay living in the middle ages either," Lynn commented. "The Mayor had a point about needing a new firehouse, a library. How do we do that without losing our Southern identify — like the Manse and …?." she stumbled.

Hugh said, "Good question, Lynn." He put his beer on the table. "Development is creeping south from the hub of the federal government. It'll engulf us, too, probably in our life time. But it's our responsibility, as residents of Virginia, to remember our breeding, our culture and pass it on to our children."

All that talk was discouraging to me. Maybe *I* would have to be the instigator of halting the decline by saving the Manse. "That's true. But we don't have to sit back and let development creep all over us," I added.

Clay snorted, "Cotton is no longer king, folks. The South ain't gonna rise again, unless we make it." He gulped some beer. That wasn't what I meant and Hugh was right: we didn't have to let it alter our culture, our heritage of honor, good manners – all that made the South great in its day, but I continued to listen.

"The development's already started. Have you been to New Kent lately? Cheap new buildings going up all over," E.J. said. "Creek Woods Residence, however, is a recommendation for this Nourikian."

Philabelle leaned forward, looking at him and said, "You're right about the Residence, E.J. I've checked it out. It's tastefully done in an architectural style suitable for Whitman. I expect to live there some day." I wished she wouldn't keep harping on that. Planning, yes, but the thought depressed me.

"Oh don't talk like that, Philabelle," Sarah said. She refilled Philabelle's glass and handed it to her. "You're not ready for that." She looked at Lynn, "Can I fill yours?"

Lynn nodded and said softly, "Elliott spoke highly about Nourikian."

Sounding discouraged, Clay, said, "I wonder if we can stop the Damned Yankee carpetbaggers from infiltrating our territory?"

Out of the corner of my eye, I saw the hurt expressions flicker across Mel's face.

"Not all northerners are carpetbaggers, Clay," I pointed out, nodding subtly at Sarah and Mel.

Hastily, Clay stuttered, "Of course, not all … I didn't mean …" A blush rose up his neck to his face.

Hugh said, "I think what Clay refers to those who don't adapt to our …" he chuckled, "sensibilities."

That got a tension-relieving laugh. Clay's comments earlier, however, still annoyed me, but I hoped he'd help me stop them. "I still think Schultz and Morton have something up their sleeves and I'd like to know what it is."

"I'm curious, too, but it's premature to concern ourselves, Minty." E.J. looked at me. "William called me with regard to the complexity of procedures for a gift of real estate to a municipality." He lifted his glass to drink.

"My son William called you, E.J.? Why you?" I wondered, why not me? I was mildly put-out.

E.J. nodded, "It's pretty natural, as his father and I worked together on so many cases. We weren't legal partners, but we had been friends and colleagues." He leaned a forearm on his knee, closer to me. "He's just concerned for Philabelle's interests. There are tax issues, too, and you mentioned getting status as an historic residence: you'd want to apply for that via the State Historic Site Officer."

"It sounds like a much more complicated process than I expected," Hugh said.

"It is, but y'all have the benefit of having a lawyer in the family. This sort of thing is right up William's alley," E.J. said.

I noticed Philabelle delicately hiding a yawn and suggested that it was time to leave. In the bustle of saying our goodbyes, I asked Lynn if she'd like a ride home.

"No thanks," she said, "Hugh's walking me home."

Oh? I thought, but I offered Philabelle my arm and we headed back to the Manse.

E. J.'s comments reflected a side of my son that I sometimes forgot. William might be pompous, but he was smart and honest. Sometimes I needed reminding that my children were adults, capable of lives outside my purview. I don't know why that saddened me, but it did.

It was not yet eleven when we parted. As I drove home, I intended to concentrate on the problem of Schultz and Morton rather than Lynn's smirk. Perversely, my mind kept returning to Lynn. Until tonight, I felt sure that we had out-grown sibling rivalry during the hurricane ordeal.

Chapter 24

The next day was gardening day and as I dead-headed and weeded, I remembered what had been plaguing me since the gathering at Sarah's. Hastily, I tossed the debris in compost, washed my hands and called my sister.

When she answered, I asked her, "Remember at Sarah's the other night? You said that you recognized the name of that developer? Do you know where you heard it?"

"I said Elliott knew him," Lynn said. "What do you want to know for?"

"It's the only clue I have to find out what Schultz and Morton are up to."

Lynn sighed so heavily I could hear it, but she answered, "I remembered that Elliot did some business with him involving Creek Woods." She paused before she added, "They all know each other, contractors, developers and real estate people all over eastern Virginia."

Ah ha, I thought. "Yes! You worked for Elliot before y'all married. Any idea what happened to his records?"

"Humph! His daughters and the lawyers went through them. They found nothing that could disinherit me and dumped the whole mess back on me." Lynn felt put upon, apparently, even though she had plenty of room.

"Are the files identified or something so you could find anything the developer was involved in? It might give us a clue."

Lynn snapped, "The files are adequately identified. Believe it or not,

Minty, I was a competent secretary." She laughed, but without humor. "That's why Elliot married me: free labor."

"That's not why he married you," I scoffed. "He was besotted with your beauty." Too late I remembered our drunken ramblings during the hurricane. Beauty to Lynn was not an advantage, not something to be proud of, so I added, "and your charming personality." Keeping my tone as conciliatory as possible, I continued, "I really would appreciate it, Lynn. If you locate some folders that look pertinent, I'll do the work of reading through them."

"Well," Lynn hesitated before she said, "I suppose I could make time this weekend." Her tone let me know it was an imposition.

I bit back the retort that came to mind. After our hurricane experience, I vowed to be more insightful in dealing with my sister, but it wasn't always easy.

*   *   *

Several days later, Lynn called, "I have three cartons of files which should satisfy your urge to play detective. When can you pick them up?"

Surprised, but pleased, I asked, "I take it they relate to that developer with the Armenian name?"

"What Armenian name?" she sounded puzzled.

"Mc –something-kin."

"I told you before!" With exaggerated patience, she spelled it out, "N O U R I K I A N," How do you know it's Armenian?"

"Names that end in 'ian' are Armenian: Saroyan, Katchaturian."

She made a sound of disgust, "You are such a smart aleck. It gets tedious, you know."

Here we were back on the antagonistic kick again, I thought. At such times my anger at her betrayal flared up and it took will power to douse it. Quietly, I asked, "Is something wrong, Lynn?"

"No, nothing except I spent most of the week in these damned files and still have another drawer to sort."

"With Hugh on call this weekend, I could help you." I hoped that my new approach would work.

"No, thanks anyway, Minty. They're really old ones. A couple of cartons had nothing about Nourikian, so he probably wasn't on the scene," she remarked.

"Oh, Lynn, you're a doll. I really appreciate all your efforts. Can I pick them up today? After lunch?" She agreed.

My 'thanks' was probably a bit extravagant, but at last, I was getting somewhere investigating the devilment behind the scenes. Nobody could discourage me from ultimately revealing whatever sharp dealings the Schultz-Morton duo were planning and in proving that my suspicions were on the mark.

I was excited that now I had two resources and was eager to begin digging into Elliott's files. I believed I'd find what I needed, but that would have to wait a day. I was still struggling with 'The Journal'.

It was a hot sunny July day, and after I worked for two hours, I pulled on a Hawaiian muumuu – the coolest clothing and the wildest colors in my wardrobe – and, with Buck harnessed in beside me, drove into town.

Stopping at Clay's first to restock my cupboard, I released Buck and opened Clay's door with the old fashioned tinkling bell.

"Wow! You are one gorgeous vision in flowers, Minty," Clay greeted me with a big smile and leaned down to scratch Buck's head.

"You are such a sweet man," I said. As usual Clay made me feel good.

He looked up from Buck and made an 'aw shucks, Ma'm' face at me, then asked, "Remember old Cash? She was one sweet bitch."

Cash was a black standard poodle, who had appeared, obviously, pregnant, in town five years ago. She hung around Whitman, scrounging from whomever (especially Clay) would feed her. Finally, my soft hearted-sister-in-law took her to our vet, Lee, who figured that she was eight or nine years old – too old to be having puppies.

Philabelle gave her shelter and Clay named her Cash from the old expression "cash and carry". She was a lovely dog and when her puppies (obviously mixed breed) were born, Billy brought Buck home for us and Clay and Madge adopted one also.

"We have Buck and Penny. What happened to the other two? Do you remember?" I asked Clay and handed him my list.

"Clay, Jr. took the other female and named her Nickles. She's still with them, but they call her Nicky. Lee found a home for the other one. You won't believe what they named her: Dollars." He roared with laughter, "You know, like Delores?"

"I get it. I get it"

"But they call her Doll – or they did, the last I heard." He turned to grab a box of Honey Nut Cheerios off the shelf and put it on the counter. "Incidentally, how's Miss Philabelle managing? Anything I can do to help?"

"Philabelle's remarkable." I held up a finger and told Buck, who was sniffing the shelves, to stay. Then Clay and I continued our conversation about the fire as he went back and forth collecting my groceries for me.

He set a box of spaghetti on the counter and grimaced. "I hope it wasn't the fireworks that set the fire." He shook his head. "The ballpark's blocks away from the Manse."

"I'm sure it wasn't, Clay. Hugh said yesterday that the Fire Chief called in the New Kent Arson Squad … Oh, I already told you that? Getting old, I guess."

"Never, sweetheart. You'll still be young when you're ninety." He leaned against the counter, gazing at me with those blue mesmerizing eyes. Just like back in the days when I had a crush on him.

As if he'd read my thoughts, he said, "Life was good back in high school, wasn't it? You were the prettiest girl in school, Minty, – and the smartest, too."

"Don't leer at me like that, wicked man." I shook my head and checked the fresh baked goods case. "I was not the prettiest by a lot, but those were carefree times, all right." I couldn't protest 'the smartest'. While he continued filling my order, we reminisced about our after prom meetings out at the lake.

"Aside from the ruckus over integration, my primary recollection is of the terrific crush I had on you and how thrilled I was when you asked me for a date," I said. Clay laughed and affection filled my heart. "You boys always tried to get us to go skinny dipping." I clucked as if chiding him, denying our pleasure at their teasing.

"We succeeded, too, more than once." He turned to check my list, added a bottle of Worcestershire sauce to the items on the counter and said, seriously, "Nostalgia deceives us into remembering the past as 'good old days', but they weren't for the 'po' white trash'."

"Yes, they weren't good for everybody, were they?" I had in mind the town's African Americans. For most of us, people – who are friends now – were called 'darkies' or 'coloreds'. "But by golly, in the fifties and sixties the Civil Rights Movement resulted in some wonderful changes. And I'm purely proud that we were part of it."

Clay nodded, but his eyes weren't focused on me. I wondered what unpleasantness had surfaced in his memory and was tempted to ask. Then, I remembered the bitterness with which he'd spoken of 'po' white trash' earlier. "I'm on my way to Lynn's. She has a carton of Elliott's files for me."

"His old business files? What do you want with them?" Clay started bagging my order, totting up each item on the register.

"I want to check out that developer Al Schultz was talking about – Nourikian. He built the Creek Woods Residence and I suspect he has his eye on Whitman as the next place to develop." My voice must have gotten a little edgy, because Clay glanced at me quickly and then concentrated on tallying my account.

Without looking at me, he said, "Sooner or later, progress is coming to

Whitman, Minty, and there's nothing anybody can do about it." He sounded a mite sad, I thought.

"Well, I'm not going to let a big-shot Yankee like that come in and take over our town." He was packing my groceries and I asked, "My account still under my limit?"

Still without meeting my eyes, Clay said, "Sure."

I avoided further discussion, puzzling over his sudden change of mood. Fretting over my impression that something bothered Clay, I started to pick up one of the bags. "Come, boy." I looked down at Buck, who rose, tail wagging.

Abruptly, Clay reached for both bags. "I'll take these out for you."

I hurried to open the door for him and nearly tripped over an orange cat, who raced inside between us. Buck twisted and eyed the critter as she streaked by.

"Buck!" I squealed, "Leave it." Buck was a really good dog and obeyed, but he gave me a look of disappointment.

"Sorry about the cat," Clay muttered and preceded me to my car. I opened the back door and he loaded the bags and, without even a smile, turned to go back in.

Mystified at his behavior, as cheerily as I could, I called, "See yuh, Clay." and drove back to the farm.

＊　　　＊　　　＊

That evening would be the first time Hugh and I would be alone since the Fourth of July and I wanted a quick shower and to change into something fetching.

As I prepared, I reviewed my conversation with Clay. Possibly, Madge was nagging him to leave town, which would account for his mood. Clay had deep roots. He might retire, but leave Whitman?

By the time Hugh arrived, I had fixed vichyssoises, crab salad with avocado, mixed greens, oil and vinegar dressing, some Pepperidge Farm wheat crackers and Gouda cheese. A bottle of chardonnay was chilling in the fridge. At the last minute, because of the heat, we decided on iced tea instead.

At first Hugh seemed quiet, but he tucked into dinner with good appetite, so maybe he had a worrisome patient. He never discussed them with me, of course. Most of our conversation lately revolved around the situation with the Manse. He disagreed that the fire was arson, but conceded that Morton and Schultz had a hidden agenda.

"Schultz is probably the power behind Morton," he said lifting a forkful of crab salad.

I nodded, adding, "Clay said Morton's too much the southern gentleman to set a fire and I can't imagine who else would want to burn down the Manse."

Hugh smacked his lips and said, "Hmmmm, good! Put the idea of arson out of your head, shug. Not likely."

His scoffing at my premise annoyed me, but I really wanted to avoid controversy. Without comment, I pushed my empty soup bowl aside. "Incidentally, Jesse stopped by the other day. He and Mike are convinced the town will snap up the Manse."

Hugh raised his eyebrows but continued to eat. I took a bite of salad. He was right; it was good. For a few minutes, we ate without conversation.

Then Hugh spoke, "Lynn said you'd picked up Elliott's files hoping they'll throw some light on the developer." He cut a few pieces of the cheese, put one on a cracker and handed it to me. "Have you had a chance to go through them yet?"

"No. They're on the schedule for tomorrow. Did you see Lynn again? Is she sick or something?"

"Not really. She's had trouble sleeping. Probably overtired; you inspired her to clear out a lot of Elliot's stuff," he shrugged. "Shoving heavy boxes around. I stopped by to give her a sample of sleeping pills and she invited me for dinner." He handed me another cracker. "Then I stayed to give her a hand with the boxes."

Again silence ruled, except for the clink of the knife against china, the crunch of chewing, with occasional comments on food and drink. Nevertheless, a mosquito of disquiet occupied my mind, which I wouldn't classify as jealousy. Hugh and Lynn had been friends since childhood. Why shouldn't they have dinner together?

We were clearing the table, when Hugh said, "I'm a little worried about Lynn. I asked her what she'd been doing for fun and she said 'nothing'." He picked up the cheese and cracker tray. "What do you want to do with these leftovers?"

"Put them on the counter and I'll take care of them in a minute." I was loading the dishwasher. "Why does that worry you? She's never done much but shop and socialize since Elliott died."

"That's it. She has nothing that she wants to do. As intelligent as she is, she needs something – a goal to work toward," Hugh persisted.

"She's been stagnating since she flunked out of college. Except for her job with Elliott." I wrapped the cheese, put the crackers back in the box and stored them away. "A job which I think he offered because he was attracted to her and she took because it amused her temporarily."

"You seriously underestimate Lynn's capability. She had the files organized, even cross-catalogued by subject. All the boxes are identified on the outside." Hugh's disapproving tone at my remarks was out of line, I thought.

He stood leaning against the counter, not quite frowning, arms crossed on his chest, a familiar pose. "She needs a focus in her life." My mind veered off, distracted by his new interest in my sister. But he continued, "She's been frittering it away and now she needs help. You should talk to her, Minty."

"Huh," I snorted. "Lynn accuses me of being bossy. My daughter Rachel thinks I interfere in her life. *I* should give anybody else advice?" I shook my head, pretty despondent myself at the moment. "Hugh, I drove all the way to Lynn's cottage to be with her during a hurricane. I apologized for my well deserved harsh words and she seemed appeased. Now I am working on my relationship with her. Giving her advice is just not appropriate at this point."

Hugh leaned close to me and put an arm around my shoulders. "Not give her advice, but suggest projects that might interest her, where she could apply her skills." He squeezed me and said, in a deep seductive tone, "You're *very persuasive* when you want to be, shug."

That totally melted the iron in my blood and I cheered up. Maybe that's why an idea popped into my head.

"Whether or not the town accepts the donation of the Manse as a library, we'll want help getting the books ready for an appraiser." My little gray cells were fairly jumping with enthusiasm.

"And Lynn need's a job. Good idea. They'd need cataloguing, too."

I nodded, half thinking about dessert, "There're a couple of things I'd like to discuss with you. First, how do you feel about strawberry shortcake?"

His velvet brown eyes beamed a hearty 'yes' and he asked, "With a wine chaser?"

Quickly he took out a bottle and, delighted at his response, I got out the marinating bowl of fruit and whipped the cream. Hugh cut the biscuits and I dolloped cream on the berries. We took bowls and wine into the living room so we could sit on the couch and put up our feet.

Then I began, "Did I tell you that I found what I'm sure are a couple of first editions which I think the State Library might be interested in? They're in pretty good condition for their age."

"If they are valuable, they'd probably deserve the protection that a professional library could give them. You mentioned the old Trueblood Journal; is it legible?"

"The script uses that fancy 'S' that looks like a capitol 'F'. But I'm deciphering it, hoping for an historical connection." I presumed on Hugh's interest to ask, "How important is the Manse to you, Hugh? A couple of times I thought you didn't much care either way."

He looked at me curiously, "What do you mean? Of course, I don't want to see it razed, but the fact is that, if the town doesn't accept the offer we've made, it'll have to be put up for sale." He shrugged. "Chances are the land is worth more than the Manse."

We had settled on the couch, cuddled together, all cozy and intimate with Cleo dozing on the back and Buck snoring softly on the floor under our legs. Normally, I relished fondling, but my worry about losing the Manse was an itch that I needed to scratch. I wanted to maintain the intimacy, but Hugh's indifference to fighting development, like Clay's, goaded me. I *had* to convince both of them that destruction of the Manse would be the first step toward losing the heritage of Whitman.

Trying to inject a *persuasive* tone in my voice, I said, "Some of our friends are willing to fight tooth and nail against the Mortons and all those who want to turn Whitman into another New Kent. Especially that developer, Nourikian. Doesn't that bother you?"

Hugh inhaled deeply enough to shift me slightly before he said, "Keeping Whitman a small isolated town is a lovely dream, shug. The reality is that urbanism, or whatever you call it, is oozing south from the D.C. area and east from Richmond. Ultimately, it'll be hard to tell when you've left New Kent and entered Whitman, whether we like it not. You heard Clay the other night. All our children are leaving Whitman for better jobs, more ... "

"Not all of them," I interrupted, speaking too quickly and stopped with my mouth open to tell him about Jesse and Mike.

He drew his head back to look at me, "What?"

I closed my mouth and improvised, "There are others ways to keep young people without inviting greedy carpetbaggers like Schultz and Nourikian to turn Whitman into a carbon copy of New Kent."

Hugh looked at me as if I had said something ridiculous. "Schultz and Nourikian, may be outsiders, but they're just enterprising business men, not evil critters bent on destroying Whitman."

"But they want to destroy the Manse, probably tear down all the shops across the street and put up glass and steel monstrosities. I'm convinced that somehow they're involved in the fire."

"Minty, the arson folks have determined that it was an accident. Dooley Markham was there fixing the lawn mower and left gassy, oily rags under the porch for the trash. Don't start obsessing about the fire. Can't you just ..." He sounded cross because we'd had this argument earlier.

"No," I interrupted. "I'm worried that they'll try again. Philabelle's alone there, Hugh. Aren't there motion sensors or something that would alert the police if an intruder ..."

"Yes, there are and if I had the slightest inkling that it had been arson, I'd do something positive to protect her."

"I think I'll get on the net and see if I can find someone who handles these devices." I sometimes wondered if I'm the only one in the family who got things done.

"Minty," Hugh didn't quite snarl at me, but he did 'show his teeth' dog style. "Philabelle is perfectly capable of taking care of herself. She values her independence and, although I know you're concerned for her — let her make her own decisions."

I was irritated enough that I left a couple of spoonfuls of strawberries and cream in the bowl while I silently contemplated what he'd implied. Tactfully, like the gentleman he is, Hugh had just told me to mind my own business. Coming from him, I wondered if I had been getting bossier than was appropriate. But I couldn't stop wanting to help and protect the family members that were so precious to me. I didn't want to lose anyone else. Apparently, I must have exuded pathetic pheromones, because Hugh leaned against me, picked up my hand and rubbed it against his cheek.

"Oh, come on, shug. In your anxiety about Philabelle and the Manse, you're making mountains out of mole hills." Hugh dropped my hand and leaned down to Buck, who had intruded his head between us. Hugh nudged my plate of strawberries and cream toward the sharp-nosed dog.

"Preserving the integrity of the family and the town is hardly a mole hill." I stood up. "I don't understand your indifference to the Manse." I picked up our plates and headed toward the kitchen. Hugh, with the glasses, plus Buck, trailed along behind us.

"And I don't understand your sudden devotion to it." He took his customary stand, leaning back against the counter, arms crossed on his chest.

"Generations of your ancestors lived and died in that house." His obstinacy made the tone of my voice sharper than I intended, "Doesn't that mean anything to you?"

"It means to me that the Manse is old fashioned, drafty, expensive to maintain and to heat. It's a museum, not my home any more."

"You grew up there, Hugh. It must mean *something!*"

"Yes, Minty, it means that I *did* grow up and left the family homestead to seek my fortune." His eyes fastened intently on mine as he said, "I sincerely hope the town will buy it, but not enough to dedicate my life to saving it. There are things more important to me than fighting a loosing battle against change."

I slammed the dishwasher door shut. Curbing my annoyance, I stared back at Hugh. Abruptly, he stepped closer to me, lifting his arms to embrace me, and murmured, "Like you and I alone together. We've got better things to do than argue about a crumbling old ruin."

"Don't leer at me, Hugh. It's not a crumbling old ruin." I pushed both hands against his chest, intent on maintaining my position. "And I don't like being made fun of."

"I'm not making fun of you, shug. I'm trying to make love to you," he whispered and pulled me close.

Despite my determination, my body treacherously responded to his caresses and doused my flickers of irritation as if with a bucket of cold water.

"I hate it when you do this to me," I said into his cheek as he pressed against me.

"I know, but I'll make it up to you, darlin'," he breathed against my lips.

Weakly, I yielded and let myself enjoy our love-making. Later, while Hugh slept soundly, I lay unable to sleep, unable to forget his failure to support my crusade to save Whitman. Turning over, I realized, too, that I was genuinely worried about another fire and vaguely unsettled by Hugh's concern over Lynn. Was he speaking just as a doctor? Oh God! I thought I could not bear it if Hugh followed his brother's example!

Billy! With a shudder, I relived that indescribable combination of grief and guilt. Why did I keep picking at guilt as if it were a hangnail?

Chapter 25

I stopped at Lynn's the next day for the rest of the files. We carted two more boxes out to my car and Lynn said, "Come on in and let's have something cold to drink."

I was delighted, of course, and accepted. Casual in khaki shorts and a sleeveless white cotton shirt, Lynn looked much younger than her fifty years. She had cut her hair short when the weather got hot and it framed her perfectly oval face in gamine chic, emphasizing the Lolita look that men couldn't resist. Hugh was right, however; there were dark circles under the blue eyes and she didn't look happy.

"Let's go out on the sun porch," she said and, with glass in hand I followed her. One of my favorite rooms, it overlooked her garden, which was colorful with California poppies, orange against the shades of blue-to-purple lupine.

"Lynn, I surely appreciate the work you did on the files. I scanned through half a box this morning and found several memos, in Elliott's hand-writing, of phone calls from Schultz. He was offering to work with Nourikian on future projects in Whitman."

Savoring the iced tea, I reflected on Lynn's ability to attract men. I wanted to observe her reaction when I let her know that Hugh confided in *me*. With some trepidation, I baited the bear in her den. "Hugh says y'all had dinner and he helped you sort the newer files."

Lynn nodded and a wicked grin flickered on her face, "Yes, we did."

Ah, I thought. This was going to be a fencing match. Clearly, she hoped to provoke anxiety in me. Shoot! I *did* feel defensive, but being too canny to let her know that, I parried her move by a show of sisterly concern. "Last night Hugh recommended that I take advantage of your organizational skills." A reminder of *my* place in his life as well as recognition of my leadership skills.

Instead of snapping at me, Lynn raised her eyebrows and said, "Did he? It's nice to know that someone gives me credit for something." I don't know what expression crossed my face, but it apparently provoked her to add, "Believe it or not, I enjoyed my secretarial work with Eliott." She added more tea to my glass and changed the subject. "Have you found anything useful in that old Trueblood diary?"

Surprised, yet tickled at her interest, I answered, "Nothing which might help getting the Manse on the Historical Homes Register. Only that Truebloods were related to Whitmans."

"That's ironic. If Morton only knew!" Her eyebrows arched up and her smile — the one that turned everybody on — was genuine. "How?"

"Back in the late 1800s, after the War Between the States, a Trueblood man married a Whitman and a Whitman woman married a Marshall." I grinned at her.

Lynn laughed, "Are you telling me that we're all related by blood – even if the blood is pretty thinned out?" She stopped suddenly, the smile wiped off her face. "What am I laughing about? *I'm* not a Whitman." Her eyes had a left-out-again look, which unsettled me.

"Oh Lynn, honey," I touched her forearm. "You and I are Burgesses and we're a big part of Whitman's history. I expect, as I decipher more, I'll find Burgesses marrying into all the other families." I hadn't spent much time in 'The Journal', considering the search for Schultz's design on the Manse more urgent.

Her face a mask of indifference again, she said, "Well, whatever."

"I'd like to have you and Philabelle out to tea and we'll read it together. I'm anxious to go deeper into the Journal, but the faded old fashioned script is tedious to decipher."

"Philabelle would like that, especially if you find some historical connection."

Although she agreed, she didn't say *she* would like it. On that ambivalent note, I took my leave.

After re-establishing our sibling closeness and mutual confidences during the hurricane, I expected us to resume our friendship. Before Lynn's confession, Philabelle, in her wisdom, had warned me that Lynn was troubled and only now was I sharp enough to spot evidence of it in her mercurial moods. It was hard to tell what went on in her mind.

I left wondering whether we were anywhere near friends again and told myself I wasn't jealous of Hugh's helping her. The mere hint that she had designs in that direction chilled me through and through.

*   *   *

Back at home I intended to spend a couple of hours on my detective work. I was finishing a stand-up lunch when Jesse stopped by.

He said, "We didn't get much time together with all the family here, Mom, and I couldn't go without a one-on-one." He reached down to fondle Buck, who promptly rolled on his back, inviting tummy scratching. Jesse obliged.

"I'm glad to see you, hon. Let's sit in the kitchen. Would you like a cold drink?"

"A beer would be fine," he said. I handed him a bottle and poured myself a glass of iced tea. "Tell me the disagreeable truth: how bad is the damage at the Manse?"

"Dempsey Rudolph came over this morning to survey the area. The porch will have to be replaced. The back wall of the kitchen is badly scorched, two windows and part of the pantry need replacement. Meantime, the kitchen's usable. Mike and I persuaded Philabelle to let us fix dinner last night. But she was up early to make breakfast." He chuckled and took a drink. "Dempsey said his people will start reconstruction Tuesday of next week. Meantime, the temporary boarding will keep any rain out."

I agreed, "Dempsey's a good man." I was comfortable with Philabelle's choice. "This was the first time Mike has stayed at the Manse, wasn't it?"

Jesse nodded, with a grin. "He found it educational. Did you know that Aunt Philabelle still keeps a china pitcher and bowl on a stand and a matching chamber pot under the beds?" We enjoyed a laugh at that.

"There's a set in every bedroom. She says she didn't know where else to put them."

Buck bumped Jesse's elbow with his nose and Jesse did the ear pulling bit that Buck enjoys. Buck made ecstasy noises in the back of his throat.

"Jesse, the last time we talked you hinted that you might be interested in taking over the Manse, if the town doesn't accept it. Were you kidding?"

"In all probability the town will accept it, Mom. They'd be crazy not to. It's a magnanimous gift." He responded, but didn't answer my question

"I'm not counting my chickens before they hatch. But it would be nice to have y'all closer." It seemed too good to be true, keeping the Manse in the family and having Jesse and Mike living there, as well. "Where is Mike this afternoon?"

"He's checking out possibilities for setting up a business in this area," Jesse said, rolling the bottle between his hands, not meeting my eyes.

"Oh? I don't trust that cat ate the canary smile, boyo." Affection for my youngest welled up in me.

"Mom, this is strictly confidential. Mike and I are talking about relocating to this area. We're fed up with the hassle of city life, the traffic." He shook his head, resembling his father when he showed irritation. "As a potter, Mike can throw pots anywhere and his name is known well enough now that clients would come here to buy his work. Did I tell you he has a show scheduled in Philadelphia in October?"

"No. That's exciting. But what about your job? Would Krug give you this territory?" Jesse had majored in business and marketing at the university and had been promoted recently to regional manager for part of western Virginia.

"Probably not. The man that has this territory is doing a good job. You know, we spent some time with Clay's sons? Chuck said that their father tried to "foist the family grocery store on them", in his words. His parents want to retire, apparently."

Involuntarily, I made a tsk of dismay. "I can't imagine anybody but Clay running the store, but …" I remembered the other day how oddly Clay's mood turned from upbeat to somber, when I mentioned Elliott's files. Strange, I thought, but Jesse broke into my musing.

"All this is premature, Mom," he lifted a cautionary finger, "I didn't have a chance to talk to Clay about it. Besides, Mike and I want to consider this move a bit more thoroughly. I like dealing with people. Besides, I'd pick up all the gossip in town."

Jesse, who had never answered my question about taking over the Manse, repeated his cautions not to reveal this to the family yet. Of course, I agreed. He had finished his beer earlier, so now he rose to leave.

I stood inside the screened door and watched my youngest drive off in his dented old VW 'bug'. Apprehension punctured my pleasure and I questioned how some of the towns-people would react to their relationship. Offhand, I couldn't remember the subject of homosexuality turning up in casual conversation — certainly not in the Reverend Clover's sermons.

Also, I felt a pang at the prospect of the Marshalls leaving Whitman – another concern to those already a burden.

With Buck's weight leaning against my leg, I took a deep breath, reached down to diddle the curls on his topknot and said, "Well, my fur friend, I've got enough to take care of in the present. 'Sufficient unto the day is the evil thereof.' Let's get back to work."

*   *   *

Years ago, Billy and I had renovated the small 'lady' parlor next to the living room into an office. Now I had taken over the computer and that was where I kept the boxes of Elliott's files.

Settled at the desk, I pored through letters to Elliott from business associates, copies of his responses, mostly dealing with wills, contracts and various real estate transactions. Over the years, large pieces of property, sections of what had been old family plantations, were sold in small increments.

More and more estates were razed and the property developed into smaller parcels. The original Trueblood mansion was one. I never saw Truebloods living there. I remembered the noble structure as a child, before the several small farm houses rose where once it had stood. Or was it only pictures in my grandparent's album that I had seen?

I sighed at such moments of nostalgia before I realized that it had been a mistake to start with a box with files which dated during WWII and into the fifties – far too old to involve any of my peers. It was dry, dusty tedious work and frustrating. I stood up to stretch and get a cool drink. Buck rose from his nap under the desk and I let him out for a run. Cleo had secluded herself in one of her hidey holes.

I stood with a glass of water gazing out the kitchen window, exercising my arms to loosen up, until Buck scratched at the back door. I let him in and decided that I was tired of sitting bent over old files. The phone being handy, I dialed the Fire Marshall's number. When he answered, I asked point blank, "Hey, Kevin, have you gotten the final report on the Manse arson?"

"You're not still worried about that are you, Minty? I'm sure it was Dooley's oily rags."

"What did the experts say about an accelerant?"

"There was no evidence of anything other than gas and oil. I'm confident it was purely an accidental fire."

"Well, don't get grumpy, Kevin. I'm just checking."

"I am not grumpy and you know it. I'll give you a copy of their report if it will make you feel better," he chuckled like the good-natured man he is. "Don't you believe that, if I thought there was any hint of arson, I'd get the big-wigs down here to double check?"

At that point, I suspected any further insistence on my part would go beyond courtesy. I wasn't totally satisfied and hoped to find evidence of malfeasance in Elliott's files to justify my belief. In my quest to save the Manse, I had two resources: Elliott's files and Jacob's Journal.

Chapter 26

Since I had no commitments for the day, I tackled 'The Journal' before Elliott's files. I had gleaned data on marriages, births and deaths of family members, so I concentrated on searching for visits by historical figures during Reconstruction. Mostly, I struggled through tedious details of crops planted, workers paid and very little social activity. Only the possibility of discovering something of historical value fueled my efforts.

Finally, my eyes tired from the faded script and discolored paper, I put it aside for the day. Still surprised at Howard's lack of concern over Rachel's aspirations, I decided to check with her while I had a break.

I dialed their number. "It's Mom, hon. How's everything with y'all?"

"Everything is just wonderful. Both the kids are happy with their activities and I *live* for my dance classes. You were inspired to suggest them." I hadn't suggested them specifically, but that was beside the point. "Tony, the instructor, is the most marvelous person. He dances like a dream and I'm so lucky to have him as a partner. He says I'm becoming a real Ginger Rogers. I wasn't sure who she was, but Howard says she was part of a great dance team. He's seen them on late night TV."

She must have run out of breath and I said, "Well, I'm so glad it's working well. I only wish Howard was your partner rather than this ... Tony – is it?" Also, her 'living' for dance class disturbed me.

"No way Howard could replace Tony. Not only is a he a dream dancer..." she lowered her voice and her lips must have touched the phone when she added, "Mom, I can't thank you enough for guiding me to this …" I heard her sigh over the phone. "Dancing with Tony has changed my life."

Shocked mute, I gasped with dismay. She seemed to be reverting to adolescent behavior; she had been more mature as a teenager. Frantic, I said, "Oh, Rachel. You sound hypnotized by the joy of dancing, the romantic music." Not to mention that Tony person. Rachel had never been boy crazy. Now she sounded euphoric over dance – totally uncharacteristic for her. Or was it over Tony? My mind fumbled with what to say; afraid that it might be the wrong thing, I let her continue.

I heard her inhale, "I think I must have been born to dance, Mom. Tony says we were made to dance together and I'm hoping he'll ask me to be his partner in the preliminaries for next state competition."

That tore it! I didn't have the guts to accuse her of – what? That was the trouble: I didn't know what. Rachel had already accused me of not trusting her, so I swallowed my suspicions. I couldn't risk totally alienating my daughter; fear or prudence restrained me.

Taking a deep breath, I said, in a light tone, "Rachel, what does Howard think of your zeal for competition?" Too late I remembered his enthusiasm when we had spoken together.

"He's pleased that I'm enjoying myself. What's your objection, Mother?"

"I don't *object*. You just sound infatuated with it, especially the tango. It's such a sensuous dance — it's just not seemly." I paused for her response, but she didn't speak. That was as far as I was prepared to go.

Even so, there was silence before she said, her voice ice cold, "What are you implying? That I shouldn't dance the tango? You consider me so shallow, too immature for a sensuous dance? Or is it my dancing with Tony that you object to?"

Disconcerted by her insight, I couldn't think of an intelligent response before she continued.

"I find it insulting, Mother," she snapped. "I'd hoped that you'd be pleased that I have a purpose, a goal in my life now. That you'd give me credit for some intelligence." Rachel's voice had an edge that raised my hackles.

"Rachel …" I began, but I heard the receiver click as she hung up, leaving me with my mouth hanging open. I held the phone wondering how I could have handled this better. She must have read my fear that she'd fall in love with this Tony. Is that why she thought I considered her shallow and immature, I wondered? I sat dazed that once again she had misunderstood my intention. The buzz alerted me to hang up the phone.

I longed to ask Hugh's advice or Sarah's, but neither were available at that moment.

"Buck?" I called, listening for the click of his claws. "Buck? Where are you, boy?"

He came loping into the kitchen, his eyes asking what I wanted. Holding his face between my hands, I said, "I need the comfort of your presence, old boy." I ran my fingers through the scraggly fur on his head. "I'm afraid my daughter is headed for trouble." I gathered my scattered thoughts. If Tony were sincere about the possibility of competition — I visualized Rachel away from home, from Howard and her children, on tour for weeks. The strain on the marriage! Too upset to sit around worrying, I moved to stand up. But Buck pushed his cheek against my hand and I scratched where he needed it.

"Do you think that maybe Tony says these things to all his women students?" I asked the dog, whose black eyes echoed my concern. "If he doesn't ask her to be his partner: then she'll be bitterly disappointed and hurt by that."

Weary from my work on the Journal, I didn't have the energy to worry longer over Rachel's expectations. I felt overwhelmed by the Manse, my relationship with Hugh, and now Lynn as well. I heaved a sigh and Buck made a sound in response. "You really do understand, don't you?" Tears pushed behind my eyelids and my only comforter was a dog.

Chapter 27

Several days later, I was in the kitchen fixing whiskey sours and a bowl of whole peanuts, when Hugh called from the living room, "Anybody home?"

"In the kitchen," I shouted back, reminding myself to avoid anything controversial. I was pouring our drinks when he kissed me on the back of my neck. Apparently, our earlier disagreement about the Manse had not changed our relationship, which was a relief.

"Are those your famous whiskey sours?" He asked.

I turned and handed him one, we touched glasses and tasted them, maintaining eye contact. He smacked his lips. "Hmmmm. Tasty, but not as tasty as …" he leaned forward and kissed my lips. "Hmmm. Twice as tasty."

I laughed, "You're in a cheerful mood tonight. How about you taking this bowl out on the side porch and I'll bring the pitcher and our drinks."

He led the way and I followed. Hugh pulled the chaise lounge closer to the table, sat down and, after I put down the tray, pulled me down beside him.

"This is a bit crowdy for two, isn't it?" I asked as he handed me a whisky sour.

"That's the way I like it." He had the bowl of peanuts in his lap and began shelling them. He held a handful up to my mouth. I opened and he tipped them in. As I chewed, he continued, "We haven't had that much time together and I've been thinking about the rest of this summer."

Relieved that we had by-passed that subject of the Manse safely, I relaxed and he continued to open the peanuts, dropping the shells on the floor. I heard the click of Buck's paws as he joined us.

"I swear that dog can smell food a mile away," I said and sipped my drink.

Hugh held out his hand with some nuts in it and Buck slurped them up with his big red tongue.

"Anyway," Hugh wiped his hand on his slacks and said, "I won't be able to take a lot of time off," he paused to take a drink while a chill of apprehension ran down my spin. "… partly because I took off a lot last winter and this spring and partly because Lee and his wife want to go visit her family in California."

"That's okay. We had our vacation in February." Good, I thought, that meant no time for a wedding.

"I figure I'll take a couple of three-day weekends and we can go someplace not too far: Virginia Beach? One of the resorts in the Carolina mountains? What do you think?" He continued to shell peanuts, eat some and feed Buck and me. And dropping the shells on the floor, of course.

"That's fine. Three-day weekends work for me." I accepted more peanuts, with a feeling of relief that we'd skirted the marriage issue. "It's easier to arrange sitters for my furry friends for short periods."

"They're as much trouble as a bunch of kids," he said.

I snorted, "No they're not. They don't cause me half the worry that my children do. I still don't know what to do about Rachel's fantasy of a career as a dance contestant." Since I'd been a widow, Hugh and I often compared our parenting experiences. His common sense approach balanced my sometimes too hasty reaction.

"It's not your problem, shug. She and Howard will work it out." Hugh put the nearly empty bowl on the table and shifted position, sliding an arm around my shoulders.

"That's easy to say, Hugh, but I was hoping you'd have something more constructive to suggest." I snuggled against him. "Although I do appreciate your gesture of comfort."

For the next hour, we sat snacking, drinking and teasing each other. I did remember to tell him: "You were right about Lynn's needing something to do. I suggested she help us with the library and she was pleased at the idea."

"I'm right proud of you, sugar." Hugh nuzzled my neck. "You are a most loving and generous soul."

"Nooo," I drawled. "You gave me the idea, darlin'. Remember? You're the doctor who diagnosed the problem. I just filled your prescription."

We were nicely cozy, until Buck put his front feet on the side of the lounge and it almost tipped over.

I was too mellow to do more than say, "Down, Buck."

"He just wants to cuddle with us," Hugh laughed.

"We're crushed together enough without a sixty pound dog crowding in," I objected, although I'd didn't object to the intimacy of my body pressed against his.

Hugh looked over at Buck, "Sorry, boy. Wait'll we get upstairs. There's room in the bed for three of us."

"There is not. Beside Cleo usually squeezes in around our legs," I said, wondering if sex would suggest marriage. I hoped not. A little sex would be good, but no more controversy. "Where do you want to have dinner: here or in the kitchen?" It wouldn't take long to fix. "I'm getting hungry."

"Oh, yeah?" Hugh turned so that I slid down half on top of him. "For what?" He ran a hand down my bare leg. Keeping cool, I tried to ease a bit away from him. He tightened his arm around me.

"How does this sound: gazpacho, garlic bread, home-made blueberry yoghurt, apple pie ala mode for dessert?" Pushing against his chest, I struggled upright, reaching for the floor with my foot.

Hugh flung his other arm across me, held me down and kissed me enthusiastically. I don't know whether it was Buck who bumped the leg of the lounge or whether it was our wrestling around that collapsed the chaise. We slid down to the floor, in a muddle among peanut shells and my whisky sour, which Buck instantly lapped up.

Hugh sprawled over me, one leg pressed so firmly between mine that I identified his gender through the thin voile of my skirt. Half annoyed and half amused, I said to Hugh, "Stop it! This sort of thing is an affront to my dignity as a southern lady." I tried to untangle myself from him, but he lay there laughing at me.

"Thank God your southern lady dignity deserts you in bed!" But he rose, brushed peanut shells off himself and said cheerfully, "I'll clean this up, shug. You go fix dinner."

Giddy with affection, I did just that.

Shortly, he joined me in the kitchen and set the table. In comfortable familiarity, we ate dinner before taking our dessert into the living room in front of the TV. When the news ended, humming with complacency, I took our plates back into the kitchen.

When I returned, Hugh was deep in the newspaper. He looked up, "Hey, shug, I found a new place in the Piedmont area of North Carolina; great for a three day honeymoon."

Stunned, totally unprepared, having thought that we'd moved past that point for the evening, I stopped still. Whatever expression crossed my face, Hugh responded immediately.

"What? Did you think I'd forgotten about our getting married?" He closed the paper roughly and looked up at me, like a disappointed child, which added guilt to my dismay.

Trying to marshal my thoughts, I took the paper from him and folded it neatly before I sat down.

"Well? How about an answer, shug?" Speaking softly, he took my hand and held it against his cheek.

I loved the strength and the gentleness of Hugh's hands. They said so much about his character, but I felt like a fool, overwhelmed with affection, but reluctant to hurt him or to agree. I sat, leaning against him before I spoke, "You surprised me." I looked down at our clasped hands. "I hadn't forgotten, Hugh, but you said you'd give me time."

He dropped my hand to tilt my head up and frowned at me, "How much time do you need, for God's sake?"

I jerked my face away, "Don't yell at me." He hadn't raised his voice, but I played for time to think. It upset me that I had annoyed him.

"I didn't yell, Minty, but … " The corners of his mouth turned down and he sat up, away from me. A picture of disappointment, hands dangling between his knees, shoulders sagging, he said, "I don't understand why you seem opposed to marriage."

Stumbling over words, I managed to say, "It's not that. It's just the wrong time. There's …eh… so much going on." Strangely, his insistence on marriage felt like another betrayal, not the same as Billy's, but we had agreed: *no commitment.* Why couldn't I tell him that? Was I being dishonest?

He glanced at me, softened his voice and sounded really curious, "What's going on that makes it the wrong time?"

I licked my lips and stammered, "Well, Rachel's problem …" He rolled his eyes. "… the trouble with the Manse …" and quickly wished I hadn't mentioned that."

"William's handling the Manse, isn't he?"

"Just the papers — that offer to donate or whatever he calls is. He's not doing anything about Morton or that developer, Nourikian." I didn't want to get into that. My apprehension about Clay's involvement was too tender to touch. My hands began to sweat because my feelings about Clay were as up-setting as Hugh's insistence on discussing marriage.

Impatiently, he rose and walked over to turn off the TV. Clay and I had been best friends for so long — as long as Hugh and I had been. If Clay also betrayed me with Schultz and Morton — I gasped out loud.

Hugh sat down, not close as before, and looked at me. "What?" he asked. His brow was furrowed with concern? Anger?

Caught in a trap of self-induced confusion, I blurted out, "And William's so homophobic! I just don't know what to do with my children anymore." This felt like lying to Hugh.

He gentled the expression on his face and inched closer. "William and Rachel are both adults, married with families. You aren't responsible for them anymore."

Ashamed of myself now, I heaped lie on lie and said, "I know, but I can't just ignore their bad choices, their prejudices." Especially when I was inventing excuses.

"I think your worry about William's attitude toward Jesse is needless. He'll come around and accept Mike. I didn't see any ..." he gestured with a hand, "... evidence of discourtesy when they were all here. It's been my experience with families, where this is a problem, that time smoothes over differences. Acceptance of the situation takes place gradually. Most people accept homosexuality now, but it takes time. Besides ..." Hugh moved closer to hold my hand and I let him think that he had persuaded me. "... you can't control their choices."

In avoiding a discussion of Clay with Hugh, I felt mean-spirited and deceitful — a feeling that I disliked. Honesty, dependability and fairness were qualities that I respected and I applied them in my relationships.

In a consoling tone, Hugh said, "I know how hard it is to let go of your adult children."

I nodded and echoed him, "I know." But I questioned my integrity, feeling dishonest. From the gravity on his face and the forbearance in his voice, I could tell that he was being tolerant. Hugh was like Philabelle in his preference for reason over argument.

"If you insist, Minty, we can postpone discussion of marriage until after the next town meeting?" He shifted his position, leaving a cold space where he had been touching my thigh. "But, please, quit fritzing around and concentrate on our relationship. Your children are capable of resolving their own issues."

I moved around to face him and asked, "Isn't the fact, though, that Schultz and Morton may be conspiring to cheat Philabelle out of the Manse more urgent than whether or not we get married? Are you unhappy in our relationship now?" Unlike Hugh, I failed to keep irritation out of my voice.

Hugh stared at me for a minute, without a hint of humor on his face. "Perhaps it is to you, but I've got to make a commitment to the University or Medical Mission soon." I must have looked surprised — I *was* surprised. "I *told* you over a month ago that I had offers which interested me. I've been waiting for your answer so I can make my decision."

Hugh sounded impatient again and I knew that my procrastination wouldn't buy much more time. That pressure forced me to ask, "You'll leave if I don't marry you? Is that right, Hugh?"

I turned away from him, my foot treading on Buck's tail. He yelped and I leaned down to comfort him, murmuring, "I'm sorry, sweetie. I'm sorry." I felt bloated with anxiety but, fighting back rather than crying, I stared up at Hugh and commented, "This is a subtle type of black mail, isn't it?"

For a minute, a heavy silence filled the room. Hugh stood up and kept his eyes steadily on my face. I felt a moment of panic. Had I gone too far?

Then, taking a deep breath, and exhaling slowly, Hugh said, "Maybe I'd better go before we say something unforgivable."

Chapter 28

The next day, still depressed from the troubling conclusion to my evening with Hugh, I decided to engross myself in Elliott's files marked Schultz/Nourikian. I intended to work until noon and began by emptying the box on my desk. The folders scattered all over, loose sheets fluttering around the room in the breeze from the overhead fan. Buck, who with Cleo had joined me to enjoy the cool, jerked upright, a page covering his face.

Pish tush, I muttered, picking it off and wasted time getting the files in order and back in the carton. Finally I settled down with the files, one at a time on the desk. I scanned the documents, re-filed the first and got out a second folder.

When I reached the fourth folder, I found a memo hand-written by Eliott summarizing a phone call from Schultz; it read:

'Schultz says Nourikian interested investment in Whitman.
To ask property owners on Main Street.'

Apparently, Schultz and Nourikian *were* in cahoots. It was dated April 22 1996 and was a start. I realized that random information wouldn't tell a coherent story. So I sorted the papers by date in order to follow the trail chronologically. In no time, I came across a memo, dated May 4 '96 about another phone call from A.J. Schultz, acting on Nourikian's behalf, I assumed, which read, in part:

'...five of the eight parcels on the east side of Main
owned by one man' ... 'eager to sell for a price.'

Mother of Pearl! That had to be Clay's property. I'd *known* for years that
he owned them, but Schultz's interest shook me to the core. As anxious now to
find evidence that would clear Clay of involvement, as I was to hang Schultz
and Nourikian, I continued scanning documents.

With unsteady hands, I read:

'Others interested. Entire block on the
west owner P. Whitman ...'

Some merchants owned their own lots, but I hadn't heard any rumors
of selling, except for Walter Kress. At the town meeting, he'd said that *if*
Philabelle were selling, he'd be interested in buying a piece of the property.

But Clay eager to sell? Jesse had said Clay wanted to retire and Madge
had confirmed that. Nevertheless, I could not believe he'd get involved in
Schultz's scheme.

Thoroughly upset by this corroboration, I fumbled with papers in the next
file. Most of the letters from Nourikian and copies of Elliott's replies dealt
with Nourikian's purchase and development of the Creek Woods Residence,
during 1993 – 1994. Was Creek Woods only the first step that Nourikian had
in mind? It sounded like that to me.

A letter from Elliott to Nourikian caught my eye. Apparently, Elliott
was planning to retire and unable to work on future projects. Hastily, I re-
filed that folder and picked up a more recent one to hunt for evidence that
incriminated Schultz and Nourikian. Clearly whatever was stirring involved
the Manse.

Giddy with excitement now, as if I were in the middle of a mystery novel,
I picked through this correspondence. I enjoyed the role of detective and was
good at identifying patterns.

A memo, again in Elliott's handwriting, summarized a phone call from
Schultz that asked Elliott to:

'... persuade Miss Philabelle to sell Manse and property.
Entire deal hinges on that. Not interested!'

The possibility of Clay selling out to Schultz and Nourikian made me
flinch. At Sarah's, Clay had opposed destruction of the Manse. I hated the
thought that he, of all people, would deceive me.

Reluctantly, I forced myself to ask the painful question: if Clay was the owner who was eager to sell, what was I going to do about it? Persuade him not to sell? That would be presumptuous. Especially if he refused. Imagining that scene tore up my innards. The fact of the fire, however, left me no choice except to continue investigating.

It was easy to believe that Schultz was so determined to buy up all of Main Street that he'd stoop to burning down the Manse. I supposed he was from some place in the north, where the ethics were looser. Impossible to suspect Clay – but he *had been* the first one on the scene. That thought made me feel sick. I sighed and pressed my hand on my forehead as if I could push the thought away.

Buck, who had been snoozing under the desk, wiggled out, nudging my leg. I glanced at my watch and realized that it was lunch time. Diddling my hand in Buck's topknot was such a sensory tickle, that I said, "You're right, old boy. If I eat lunch, I'd better finish up here and fix something."

As I tucked the documents back into the folder, a half a sheet of paper slipped out:

'Morton/ council — purchase/razing of Manse?
<u>Strongly opposed</u>. Philabelle wouldn't sell.'

That was pretty incriminating motivation, but I needed more. At least Elliott was on our side. I let Buck out and mulled over what I'd learned. Elliott had died a few months later. I shivered and wondered if his ghost ever visited Lynn.

More to the point: why had Schultz and his conspirators waited until now to act? Waiting for Philabelle to move or to die, for God's sake? I understood why Hugh didn't want me to frighten her, but why couldn't he see that the fire was too coincidental to be an accident? Equally disturbing was the possibility that Clay might have colluded with Schultz.

Chapter 29

During lunch, I re-examined the file about the property owners Schultz had contacted. Concern that Clay was entangled stung like a bee. He had been one of my most dependable friends. I couldn't abide the thought of his being disloyal. The fear of another betrayal ignited my anger at Lynn all over again.

While I wrestled with those hateful emotions, Philabelle called, her voice full of excitement or urgency, I wasn't sure which. "You won't believe this, Minty. Morton called to invite me to a luncheon next week to meet that Mr. Nourikian – the big developer, remember? What do you suppose … ?"

"Luncheon with Nourikian? Next week?" I interrupted. "Was I included? No? The gall of the man." I stopped when I heard the harshness in my voice. "I'm sorry I sounded so crabby, Philabelle. Residual annoyance because of something else. About the luncheon: it's still early. Maybe Morton will call me later today."

"I should have asked, but I was so surprised that I just thanked him. Mr Nourikian suggested that we meet in the Plantation Room at Creek Woods Residence." Philabelle's voice quivered, probably because of my earlier indignation.

Apologetically, I regained my composure and said, "Well, don't worry, hon. We'll just wait and see. This certainly is a surprising development, since we're in the middle of preparing our agreement to donate." I sighed, shoving the situation with Clay out of my mind temporarily.

"Indeed it is. I do hope he invites you, too. I'll feel much better having you with me." Philabelle was so tactful. I was relieved that she needed me with her. I snorted a laugh at Morton's machinations and said that it was probably Schultz's idea of a strong offensive tactic. Invited or not, I'd be at that luncheon, I thought to myself, ignoring the disrespect of Nourikian's not including me.

"If he calls me, I'll let you know. Meantime, Philabelle, I've been busy with Elliott's files and the Trueblood Journal. Did you ever hear of a James Lafayette, a free black farmer in New Kent during Reconstruction?" The name meant nothing to her, however.

"Lynn is hoping for some scandal, I suspect." Philabelle's gentle chuckle amused me.

I asked, "Are you free this afternoon? If you are, I'll call Lynn and Sarah. Maybe we can get together today." In their presence, I'd skip any mention of the developments I'd found in Elliott's files. Philabelle was free and after we hung up, I called Sarah.

Exuberant as usual, Sarah said, "I wouldn't miss it for the world. Like reading your personal GWTW. Fun, even though I'd be classified as a carpet-bagger."

"And Lynn as Scarlet O'Hara?" I asked and we both laughed.

When I called Lynn, I passed on Philabelle's big news before I asked if she were free this afternoon.

She sighed before she said, "I'm glad you found something intriguing and I'll bring Philabelle." Then she dismissed me. "I'd better get back now to what I call work."

The dispirited tone of her voice added to my distress, confirming Hugh's concern with a pang. I'd make an effort to cheer Lynn up that afternoon, I decided. All in all, I was pleased with myself for my forbearance. During my youth, my mother often cautioned me that, if I couldn't behave like a lady, at least I must be kind to people. She'd be proud of my patience with Lynn and my worrisome children.

*   *   *

The side porch of my home was shady in the afternoon and I kept my mind off my problems as I set up our tea. I found some of Ola's cream puffs in the freezer and defrosted them. There was always a pitcher of sweet tea in the fridge and I added several cans of Coke for Lynn. She preferred that.

By three, I slipped on a loose-flowing seersucker dress. The muted green looked cool, although I felt uncomfortably warm. Sarah burst in looking like a Hawaiian in a muumuu, all pink orchids, blue hibiscus and green palm fronds.

"Gaudy but cool," she said, fanning out the skirt. I agreed.

Philabelle and Lynn arrived soon after. Philabelle wore a becoming pale blue outfit and Lynn's sundress shouted Paris chic. Flowing white against her skin, it cast a silky sheen of tan on her complexion. My mood lightened as my friends gathered on the porch, adding a rainbow of color.

Beaming with excitement, Philabelle said, "I'm anxious to hear the family stories you've found." She reached down to scratch Buck's head. " Hello, Buck." And added, "I still miss Cash. What a sweet dog she was."

"Buck inherited her disposition, even if he doesn't have her curls." I gestured toward the table. "Let's start with drinks and snacks." I lowered my voice like The Shadow and added, "Then I'll reveal all." A bit of dramatics helped me stay on track.

Without comment, Lynn skirted Buck and Philabelle to pick up a Coke. "Oh, good, cream puffs." She took one and a napkin and settled in one of the lawn chairs with an air of indifference. Ignoring her mood, I led Philabelle to the lounge, pulled over a table and served her a glass of iced tea and a pastry.

Eager to see their reaction, I played the role of entertainer. I picked up the sheaf of notes and began, "Apparently, Jacob Trueblood and Ezra Whitman returned together after the war." I glanced up and announced, "I'll read several direct quotes from the journal, which are self-explanatory:

Married: April 5ᵗʰ 1868 Jenny Leigh Trueblood
to Lt. Ezra Hamilton Whitman, C.A., Retd, by Reverend William
DeGraf, Methodist Circuit Minister.

I wet my whistle with tea and looked at Philabelle. Her blue eyes opened wide, her voice questioning, she said, "A Trueblood married a Whitman after the War Between the States? What a surprise." Then she grinned like a mischievous child. "Oh, my goodness! Morton and I are kissin'kin!" She patted Lynn's knee. "Isn't that rich?"

"I think that'll rattle his case nicely," Lynn smiled at me. "Is that it, Minty?" she asked, clearly disappointed.

"I'd say that's quite a shocker," Sarah piped up. "Of course, as a DamnYankee, I'm a gornisht helfn."

"There's more," and I read from my notes:

Born: February 14ᵗʰ 1869 to Ezra and Jenny Trueblood Whitman,
a son, Jesse Hamilton Whitman.

Born: May 3ʳᵈ 1873, to Ezra and Jenny Whitman,
a daughter, Alice Florence Whitman.

"Ezra Whitman: that would be my great …" Philabelle started to count on her fingers. "How many greats would that be?"

"Start with your father and count back," Sarah almost jiggled with enthusiasm.

Philabelle leaned back, gazed into space thoughtfully and spoke slowly, "My paternal grandfather was William Hamilton Whitman, who married Charlotte LeForte. My father was born in 1915. So grandfather would have been born toward the end of the 1800s, during the 1890s?"

Lynn, relaxing on the chaise, added, "If Jesse was born in 1869, he'd be about thirty somewhere in the 1890s." She nodded. "He'd be your great grandfather. And Ezra would be your great, great grandfather. Jenny Trueblood would be your great, great grandmother."

"And Morton's great, great aunt, I think," Sarah added. "What happened to Alice Florence?"

"I've never heard of her," Philabelle said. "But who was Jenny Trueblood's father?"

"Jacob Trueblood had to be Jenny's father and there must have been a brother to carry on the family name," I said. "Most of this I gleaned from scanning for the Whitman name. My primary mission here was to find some historical reference including the Manse. But I came across these bits and thought y'all would enjoy them." I bit into a cream puff, thinking. The journal dealt mostly with Truebloods. But Jacob had provided considerable detail and I'd gained the impression that he had survived Reconstruction with some success. That's where I came across James LaFayette. My cream puff devoured, I licked my lips and, Buck, who had gazed at me patiently, deserted me for Philabelle, where he sat staring at her hopefully.

Sarah, smiling like an imp, turned to Philabelle. "So you and Morton share a common great, great relative."

"We do," Philabelle answered, ignoring the dog. "I look forward to disconcerting him when I reveal our relationship." Then softy that she was, she tore off a piece of pastry for Buck. I watched as she daintily wiped her fingers on her napkin.

Lynn smiled, having observed without commenting, until she responded to Philabelle. "Wait for the judicious moment to tell him, when it'll have maximum impact."

Apparently, this frivolity had improved her mood, as it had mine. We began inventing situations most propitious for startling Morton with the news.

It apparently inspired a bit of the bawdy in Philabelle. "You know it's possible, in the 1890s, that Jesse was born in the big old sleigh bed in the blue bedroom."

"Maybe the bed deserves a brass plaque commemorating the union of the two families," Lynn suggested.

We all giggled over this, our minds imagining the physical as well as metaphysical union, I suspect. None of us verbalized our naughty fantasies, of course. I was pleased that the Journal amused them plus aroused their curiosity about the lives of our ancestors. To include Lynn, I pointed out that references to our Burgess family most likely appeared in the History of Prince Rupert County that I'd found in Philabelle's library. Personally, I was most intrigued by the mysterious free black landowner.

Finally, we calmed down and I said, "There's more, ladies."

Philabelle, still giggly, said, "I don't know if I can stand any more."

"Me neither. But lay the rest on us," Sarah settled back after refilling our glasses.

Reading the journal refreshed my memory of Virginia history. I was torn between picking up the History of the County, but remembered that I needed to find something to substantiate an historical connection for the Manse. Success there would brighten up the dark summer for me.

"I had hoped for something racier," Lynn commented. "But I suppose a Whitman marrying a peddler's daughter was scandalous."

"There's also documentation of a Marshall son marrying a Whitman sister in 1865. So that's another unseemly mixing of classes," I added.

"Which reminds me that my mother had mentioned a Carrie Trueblood. I wonder where she fits in."

"Maybe you'll find something titillating when you get to the Roaring Twenties," Lynn said hopefully.

"Lynn, there's not going to be any 'twenties' in the Journal. Jacob Trueblood would have died before the twentieth century," I reminded her.

"Oh, shhhoot!" Lynn said and stood up abruptly. I realized that, by pointing out the obvious, I had tread on her sensitive toes again, when she added, "Well, I think it's time for us to leave. How about it, Philabelle?"

Vexed at Lynn for taking offense and at myself for saying too much again, I was relieved when Sarah asked, "Is there anything about the tummel over the Manse?"

"What's a tummell?" Lynn's curiosity kicked in.

"Yiddish for disagreement, related to turmoil, I guess," Sarah answered. Lynn nodded.

"I'm still hoping to find a reference to the Manse during Reconstruction," I said.

"To have it registered as an historical residence?" Philablle asked.

"Absolutely. This stuff is amusing, but not what we need."

"I can't believe they'd even consider tearing it down. Why would they want to do such a thing?" Philabelle, as always, was reluctant to anticipate difficulty.

"I agree!" I said. "That would be criminal."

"You're making too much of this, Minty," Lynn said firmly, her tone dismissing any credibility in my information. "Don't worry, Philabelle. You can find out all the details at the luncheon next week. Then you'll have to keep us posted on the *real* story."

Sarah looked confused until Philabelle explained about Nourikian's invitation. Lynn, still standing, was obviously ready to leave. So Philabelle, always courteous, rose and took my hand.

"I'm very grateful, my dear, for your hard work to save the Manse regardless of the results." Her expression consoled me. "Thank you for an entertaining and enlightening afternoon. I look forward to more interesting history of our ancestors." She made motions toward clearing the table, but I shooed her after a glum looking Lynn and walked them to the front door.

When I returned, Sarah had already stacked the plates.

"You don't have to," I said.

Ignoring me, she carried them into the kitchen, "I know that. You can bring the rest," she cast over her shoulder.

As we loaded the dishwasher, she asked, "Lynn still on your case?" Buck, who had followed us, stood by the door, head turned toward me and his eyes asking to go out.

"Yes," I replied and opened the door. "Sometimes I wonder if I can do anything right in her eyes." My pleasure in our afternoon dissipated, allowing my multiple miseries to resurface again. Secure in Sarah's presence, I let my despair color my voice.

"Aw, she's just a lost girl." Sarah stood with the tea cloth and napkins in her hands, her face lovely with affection. "I miss my sister and brother, but sometimes I'm glad they live in New York and I live in Virginia. Southerners are gentler in their speech, at least."

Touched by her empathy, I could have cried, aware that her shoulder was handy. At the same time, I felt enormously cheered by her steady friendship. Instinct, however, told me that this was not the time to break down. There were too many things that required my attention and I was not one to fail my responsibilities.

Chapter 30

The weather, typical for August, continued hot and humid, like summer's last fling. Hugh's partner, Mac, and his wife were away and Hugh was on call, so we didn't get together. There was no way that we could resolve the stalemate of our relationship that week.

In the spirit of duty and with determination, on the day of Nourikian's luncheon, I prepared to carry out my plan. I still had no idea what reason I'd give for being at the Creek Woods Residence, but would think of something.

I easily found a place in the parking lot, which was to the side of the two-story building. A path through a stand of pine trees led to the porte-cochere and up the steps to a wide front veranda. I turned to admire the view across a gentle slope of lawn, tastefully landscaped which allowed attractive glimpses of the river. Excellent planning, I admitted and, maintaining my composure, I entered the lobby to gaze around inside.

As Philabelle had said, the décor was tasteful, suggestive of Victorian style, but, thankfully, lacked that typical over-abundance of decoration. Rich maroon and a muted royal blue dominated, but the palest yellow walls lightened the entire room, giving it an aura of elegant comfort.

The Plantation dining room also exuded an air of casual refinement and I quickly spotted Morton, Philabelle and a man with frizzy gray hair at a table for four near a window. I assumed a mantle of confidence. As my mother had taught me, I straightened my spine, held my head high and approached their table.

Feigning surprise, I said, "Philabelle, Morton, how nice to see you." I looked at the man I presumed to be Nourikian, met sharp blue eyes and smiled. He rose immediately; taller than me and closer to my age than I'd expected, he returned my smile, revealing dimples, surprising in his lean face.

"I'm Minty Whitman, Philabelle's sister-in-law, and you're...?" I asked.

"Gus Nourikian. Having heard interesting things about you, it's a pleasure to meet you, Mrs. Whitman." His voice, nicely deep and masculine, surprised me. I had expected a rough, uncouth pushy type – like Schultz. This man was none of that, I knew that immediately.

I offered my hand, amused at the irony of his courtesy, if he sensed my antagonism. He had a fine solid handshake, good looking, too, for a con man, I decided.

Morton remembered his manners and stood, looking ill at ease. Out of the corner of my eye, I saw Philabelle's mouth twitch with amusement and knew I'd hear from her later.

Nourikian pulled out the empty chair to his left, "You'll join us, of course." A man not easily disconcerted, I thought. His smile seemed genuine and I knew right away, he was the type to take control of the situation. A formidable opponent!

As I sat, I gave him my best smile. Morton sat across from me, but he looked slightly nauseated.

Nourikian raised his bushy gray eyebrows at a waiter, "Another menu, please." He turned to me, "We were discussing what we'd have for lunch. I've already ordered a light white wine."

"That sounds good," I said. For a few minutes we read the menu, which impressed me. We had a choice of a meat entrée or a seafood entree, soup and salad, plus three desserts. The quality of food in a residence of this type was essential and this met the test. Covertly, I checked out Mr. Nourikian: well tailored suit, Rolex watch, neatly manicured fingernails — nothing ostentatious, like the décor of his establishment, all in excellent taste.

"Miss Philabelle, have you made a choice?" Nourikian asked, he tilted his head toward her in a gesture of respect, I noted.

"Yes, thank you." And she ordered. Then Nourikian turned those blue eyes on me and I gave him my selection, as did Morton, looking a bit more composed now. Nourikian was a man of excellent manners, inclining me to think 'good breeding'. But manners, which came naturally to gentlemen such as Hugh, could be learned, of course.

The waiter took our orders and the menus and returned promptly with a bottle of wine. We sat silent during the ritual tasting. Nourikian met the waiter's eyes, with a smile, nodded approval and the waiter filled our glasses.

Nourikian's easy acknowledgment of the waiter impressed me. I couldn't stand men so impressed with themselves that people like waiters were invisible to them.

After the waiter left, Philabelle explained, "Mr. Nourikian has some suggestions on how Whitman can be improved and what he can do to help us."

A euphemism for 'hostile takeover', I thought. She sipped her wine and looked at Nourikian, nodding her appreciation.

He cast those clever eyes at me and said, "I'm also hoping that Miss Philabelle ..." he smiled at her. "... will consent to take me on a tour of the Whitman Manse. In the course of business in this area, I've become interested in the Reconstruction Period, especially structures that were damaged and repaired. The few that I've found, which replaced those destroyed in the war, have unique architectural elements."

From that point on Nourikian controlled the conversation, but without lecturing. During the luncheon, he handled the silver gracefully, with ease. In Emily Post fashion, he alternately addressed his remarks to each of us and listened to our comments.

"Those were such difficult days for the residents in this area. Virginia sustained the most extensive devastation. That it recovered is a tribute to the determination of the survivors."

"Were your ancestors living in this area then?" Philabelle asked.

He lifted his hands as if disclaiming an award. "No, I don't pretend to descend from the First Families of Virginia, but I admire their courage." His voice expressed his interest as he continued, "Were you aware of how many of them had ties as close as New Kent? Martha Washington had a home there."

He beamed when he mentioned her and I briefly met Philabelle's eyes. He had done his homework about the historical background, I acknowledged, with some reluctance. He was probably one of the northerners acting like fake southerners.

"LaFayette and Cornwallis both slept in the New Kent Tavern," Morton put in his two cents.

Nourikian nodded, "And they fought more than one battle in the broader area, didn't they? It's a pity so many buildings there were destroyed." Other bits and pieces were introduced by the three of them, while I sat studying our opposition.

I couldn't find fault with any specifics, so I listened and enjoyed myself. The food was delicious, well prepared, and I was pleased that the servings were appropriate for lunch. So often the best restaurants felt obliged to load a plate, as if pandering to the appetites of day-laborers.

Between courses, Nourikian continued his discourse, "In this area, the Manse is the only residence I've seen that is actually a reconstructed ante-bellum home." His enthusiasm undimmed, even I was impressed. "I've found smaller buildings: stables, mills, stores and a number of intact ante-bellum homes. The Manse, however, is an interesting combination of styles, quite unique."

"You've been to Whitman?" I asked, somehow surprised. Before my father died, I had watched him use this same type of pseudo interest, on so-called diplomats, as Nourikian was using on us.

"Absolutely. I visited the town when we were constructing Creek Woods Residence," he gestured at our surroundings. "I noticed several of the stores on Main Street date back to before the turn of the century. They have inspired an urge to ..." he paused, apparently seeking an appropriate word. "... not to *change* the character of the town, but to up-date it in a style which maintains its character. At the same time, it should attract other small businesses."

Philabelle said, "We feel that preservation of the Manse is important to the town historically." She spoke directly to Nourikian, as if Morton and I were not there — which I found amusing and mildly irritating. "You're right that several of the stores across from the Manse were built within the Reconstruction period. To me, it would be a shame for Whitman to go all *modern.*

Nourikian skillfully included Morton in his response, "Morton believes that the town needs a great deal of improvement in existing facilities, such as the fire house." He glanced at Morton, who nodded like a puppet. "At present, the town council meets in a room over the hardware store; am I correct?" All three of us did the puppet thing. "A separate town hall would be an asset. The school athletic field, the doctors' clinic, another restaurant featuring local favorite foods, perhaps some craft stores – these are assets which would invite travelers to stop and spend their cash in Whitman. Additional businesses would increase the town's tax base." He smiled at Morton, who nodded vigorously. Now this cagey charmer was applying the enticement element.

"The Manse property includes that wooded area just north of the house," Morton said. He showed a new restraint and deference in Nourikian's presence, apparently withholding his desire to raze the Manse since it hadn't burned down. A spiteful thought of mine, I suppose, but true nevertheless.

"It's a valuable piece of property and," Nourikian bowed his head, with artful deference, to ask Philabelle, "do I understand correctly that you might donate the Manse to the town?"

"Yes, we have considered that. Minty's son, William, who's an attorney," she tossed a smile at me, "is working on a more specific proposal."

I couldn't hold my tongue a moment longer, "On condition that the

Manse be preserved in perpetuity." I enjoyed using the word 'perpetuity'. It has such a robust sound and it told him bluntly this wasn't a free gift of money for his pocket.

"Very wise. From what I've observed and heard, I suspect that it might qualify for the list of historical houses." He gazed into my eyes with such sincerity that I almost believed him.

The rest of the conversation was an exploration of ways and means. Nourikian encouraged Philabelle and me to ask questions and express our opinions, which we both did in approved lady-like fashion, of course. He used a technique geared to weakening our opposition, which was hard to resist.

Morton put in his two cents, emphasizing that an increased property tax base would be required to pay for these improvements. That confirmed my original expectation of *his* intentions.

"Property taxes are not the only source of revenue. Outside investment could provide the seed money to develop areas that would attract new businesses," Nourikian said. "That's where people, like me, can initiate the process."

Ah ha! I thought. That meant a bunch of outsiders who'd take over the town.

"I don't understand how that works, Mr. Nourikian," Philabelle said.

"Please call me Gus, Miss Philabelle."

He sure could win friends with that smile, I thought. But before he could answer, I took over. "The investors would, essentially, loan the town money to pay for the improvements at a rate of interest which would yield a nice profit for them. Is that right?" I asked.

He nodded, "In a simplified way, yes."

"That sounds great, but the town would have to increase some kind of taxes to pay the interest, plus the principle, which would benefit only the investors." I paused, giving him time to defend his position.

"No, Minty. Let Mr. –eh, let Gus explain how it works," Morton found his tongue.

The obliging "Gus" gestured at the wall surrounding us and continued, "Take Creek Woods Residence as an example. The original investment was mine plus a group of men I do business with often. We speculated on increasing development south of the District of Columbia, when this property was available for an excellent price. That was several years before we began the promotion. Once that process started, the residence was three-quarters subscribed by initial buy-in fee of future residents. This covered the construction costs as well as reasonable amount for reinvestment. Once the residents moved in, their monthly fee provided current operating funds. The 'pay back' to the investors only started gradually. For them, this was a long-term project. They don't expect real returns for some time. Meantime, the corporation is already paying property taxes to Prince Rupert County. This principle would work in downtown Whitman as well."

"Surely the town would need the guidance of someone experienced in arrangements like that," Philabelle said, looking interested, but wary, I was pleased to note.

I was absolutely convinced it was all a scam of some kind — too good to be true – but kept my mouth shut in order to listen and learn.

Gus said, "Of course, you'd need an advocate to handle negotiations. Morton assures me that the council is aware of that and has been discussing it."

I nearly snickered. More money out of tax payers pockets! If Morton was referring to Schultz as town *advocate*, I knew we wanted no part of the deal.

There was more conversation as we proceeded through the entrée, to the dessert and coffee. Philabelle and I had iced tea. Morton had coffee and consequently broke out in sweat. Nourikian - pardon me, our benefactor Gus — had plain water.

When it came time to leave, Nourikian turned to Philabelle and made an appointment to tour the Manse sometime the following week. Probably he wanted to evaluate the cost of demolition and clearing out the arboretum to build one of those popular mylar structures.

It had been an educational lunch and Nourikian was an articulate as well as an entertaining personality. It was easy to enjoy a mature man with gentlemanly manners and easy to miss the trigger of the trap.

I shook Nourikian's hand, when we were saying our good byes, and got a whiff of his pleasantly tangy masculine cologne. This was quite a man, I knew: wealthy, as well bred and as intelligent as Hugh, but he exuded an almost scary aura of power.

I offered to drive Philabelle home. As soon as we were clear of the parking lot, she began.

"Well, Missy, that was very brazen of you to crash Gus's party. Quite contrary to your mother's teaching." Her voice quivered slightly, trying not to laugh, I suspected. "I was glad to see you, however, only because two heads are better than one in assessing such a proposition."

"I'm relieved that I didn't embarrass you, Philabelle. But I agree about two heads. I was glad, also, that Schultz wasn't there, but have no doubt that Morton will tell him everything."

"Possibly. I was impressed with Mr. Nourikian's …"

I interrupted, "Gus. He wants to be our friend, remember?"

Philabelle shook her head at me. "Don't be cynical, Minty. His presentation made a lot of sense. Our infrastructure, I think they call it, does need up-dating and financial help in paying for it would lighten the burden on the tax payers."

"Sure, but don't be deceived, Philabelle. It's basically a money-making scheme for Gus and his associates. I was surprised that he asked to tour the Manse."

"That's a good sign, isn't it? And that he's interested in the period of Reconstruction? It was a significant time for our forbearers and quite unique in the country's history." Philabelle added, "And it may assure the preservation of the Manse."

"Or give Gus ammunition for destroying a local 'fire hazard'."

Philabelle shook her head at me. "Oh, Minty, be a bit charitable. Give the man a chance. Lately, I don't know why you've gotten so ..." she frowned apparently perplexed. "... I don't know what. Is something in your life causing you concern, my dear?" She gazed at me intently, sensing my repressed worry but she didn't know it was about Clay.

We had reached the drive into the Manse and I stopped by the side entrance. "No, hon, the thing that disturbs me is the possibility that these outsiders will slyly take over our town with honeyed words. I don't want Whitman to go the way of New Kent and all the other small towns between here and Richmond." A sigh escaped me as I considered the fact that, between Hugh's pushing matrimony, Clay's involvement and Rachel's wild dancing, I *did* feel harassed. Philabelle, however, didn't need to be troubled by that.

"I understand and sympathize, dear, but a certain amount of change is inevitable. I have a strong sense that Mr ... Gus doesn't want Whitman to lose its character either. He's interested in providing better facilities for the towns-people without ruining our environment." Philabelle inhaled, put her hand on my arm and said, "Let's give him a chance, dear. Next week, when he experiences the atmosphere of the Manse, I think he'll agree that it must remain part of Whitman."

She shifted to open the door, and I jumped out to help her, of course. Despite being filled with doubt and foreboding, I didn't argue. Before she went inside, she clasped my hand in both of hers.

"Are you sure nothing's troubling you, Minty dear? You've ..." she glanced away as if realizing she was home and added, quickly, "You'll join us on the grand tour, of course?"

"I wouldn't miss that for the world," I assured her, wondering if she were going to try to convert me to the Nourikian fan club.

Hugh was on call, so I spent a quiet evening with Buck and, when she deigned to join us, the haughty Cleo. The interaction between those two amused me. Buck was so much bigger than Cleo, but he had learned to respect her claws and teeth. She flaunted her superiority, but more than once I'd found her curled against him in his bed, the pair of them snoozing peacefully.

Only the company of my pets relieved my apprehension about the intervention of a man of Nourikian's caliber.

Tomorrow I'd finish searching the files, so I could make copies of the material that I wanted, before I returned them to Lynn.

Then I remembered: oh crumbs! I still had to face Clay about his role. As Lady MacBeth said, 'If 'twere done, 'tis best 'twere done quickly.'

Chapter 31

The next morning, I rose exhausted from a humid night filled with nightmares about Billy. It was as hot as a two-dollar pistol again. The minute I opened the kitchen door, Buck raced out, across the yard and into the pasture. Cleo acted as lethargic as I felt and refused to leave the kitchen. As soon as I finished setting Edna and Claude up for the day, Buck and I also sought the comfort of indoors. Ceiling fans were adequate, but sometimes I envied Lynn's air-conditioning.

To distract myself from Billy's everlasting hauntings, I would finish searching Elliott's files for more evidence of the conspiracy to get rid of the Manse. For the next hour I browsed through a mass of correspondence, copies of agreements, memos – all dealing with unrelated real estate. I almost dozed off, until the name Schultz caught my eye: it was an informal handwritten note from an attorney in Charlotte, N.C. to Eliott. The section which interested me read:

> "… no further dealings with him because of too many
> questions involving deceptive contractors …avoid any contact
> with Schultz …preventable disasters … lawsuits."

Ah ha! I'm on to something tangible, I thought. But I needed more evidence of Clay's involvement with the fire. This would require further investigation. I still couldn't believe that Clay would try to burn down the Manse. The possibility existed, however, that he knew in advance that they planned arson and had hoped to prevent it. That would explain his presence there at the time. I couldn't put off much longer facing Clay about his dealings with Schultz.

When the phone rang, miffed that I had again neglected to get a second line put in the office, now that I was working there regularly, I rushed into the kitchen.

"Hello!" Too late I realized that I had barked into the phone.

"Mother? What's wrong?" My son William sounded concerned. How pleasant that he cared.

I responded in kind, "Nothing, dear, I've just been working and failing to accomplish much. We all have those days." And procrastinating about Clay, I thought, and asked, "How're all the family?"

"All busy and well. I'll put Myra on later to bring you up to date. Did you receive the information I sent you about Gus Nourikian?" I told him I had and thanked him.

"Also," he continued, "my secretary did some research on the value of property in your area, which I'll forward. She suggested several options that we hadn't discussed which might whet the appetite of prospective buyers. Something for Hugh to consider — and Philabelle, too, of course."

"And me, too, William! As your father's widow, I have a stake in the Manse, you know. In fact, in going through Elliott's files, I feel confident that there is hanky panky going on between Schultz, Nourikian and property owners on the other side of Main Street."

"I hardly think that Gus Nourikian would be involved in any shoddy real estate deals. Don't jump to ill-founded conclusions."

I told him that I was not in the habit of *jumping* to conclusions. This was not the time, however, to aggravate him by sharing my suspicions nor was it productive to mention the possibility of Clay being involved.

"There is one bit of information that I'll pass on to you, verbally, about Al Schultz," William spoke cautiously, as if reluctant to continue. "This is only rumor, not fact, which is why I didn't include it in the data I forwarded. Schultz has the reputation of being involved in questionable deals. Nothing has ever been proven, but a number of men I have connections with have hinted that Schultz operates dangerously close to the edge of the law."

"Ah, ha," I said, jubilantly, feeling justified and about to crow, but William interrupted.

"Please listen to me, Mother. I'm telling you this in confidence, only to caution you. Schultz has never been accused of anything illegal. Lawyers avoid any risk of libel, but they do … well, *gossip* and you know I don't like gossip. So please keep this to yourself."

I assured him that I would, but it felt good to be right in my judgment and curious enough to ask, "What kind of shenanigans was he involved in?"

William sighed before he said, "I don't want to go into specifics based on gossip. Just take my word and you can influence Hugh and Philabelle."

William had spent considerable time in gathering useful information, so I assured him of my sealed lips and thanked him again for his help. Then he put Myra on the phone. As always I enjoyed chatting with my daughter-in-law. She was a lovely woman and too good for my son. I must admit, however, that he was an attentive husband and a good father. And most helpful at the moment.

Cheered a little by my conversation with Myra, I returned to my detecting. There were a number of files still to work through. Immobilized by the weight of my unresolved problems, however, I sat at the desk, staring out the window at the chairs and tables on the side porch.

You think you know all there was to know about people and they turn around and behave totally out of character. Rachel abandoned a career for super-motherhood and now dreamed of dancing competitively. Not the least puzzling was Hugh's sudden need to adhere to convention.

Then there was Clay: actively involved in public service, but how beholden to Schultz was he? I shuddered at the thought of Clay being engaged in any type of deceit and wondered who could give me advice on how to approach him. I wasn't prepared to dump this on Philabelle. Sarah's view of humanity as a New Yorker, however, was realistic, maybe even a bit cynical. She had a wisdom different from us southerners.

I jumped up from the desk, startling Buck who had been sleeping with his head on my foot.

"Sorry, boy. Let's go make a phone call." And we traipsed into the kitchen to call Sarah. I knew she would put me back on track.

*   *   *

An hour later, showered and dressed decently, I was on my way to meet Sarah at the Busy Bee Café. She was already there when I opened the door and I joined her in a booth.

"What are you having?" I asked as I slid across the maroon-colored plastic upholstery. The Busy Bee didn't have much class, but it was clean, smelled of cooking and was the only fast-food place in town.

"Probably a hamburger. Who can ruin hamburger?" she said cheerfully.

"It's possible, but difficult." That was what we ordered, making idle chatter until the waitress set plates and iced tea before us. We both had healthy appetites, but once the edge was off, Sarah began.

"So what in your dirty linen closet needs airing?"

Because Sarah knew as much about Billy and Lynn as I did, I planned to substitute my problems with Lynn as a disguise in asking for suggestions on how to approach Clay.

"I've been questioning my judgment of people's character," I began. "Do we ever really know people in long term relationships as well as we think we do?" I took another bite of hamburger, which was better than usual for the Busy Bee.

"You mean, like a husband?" She looked surprised.

"Well, yes, or a relative or somebody you've known your entire life. I've always felt that I'm pretty good at that. I've learned to accept people as fallible humans and still like them. We all make mistakes and live to regret them, but …" I licked some ketchup off my fingers and said, "I was much more shaken by Lynn's confession at bridge …" I grimaced. "… *that* day than I let on."

Sarah snickered and tilted her head, apparently amused at my admission. But the commiseration in her eyes gave me warm fuzzies. Apparently, she knew me better than I suspected.

"I forgave Lynn during the hurricane and thought she had forgiven me for my harsh words. But every once in a while now, she says or does something that …eh …" I paused, quelling a fleeting memory of anger and to wonder about how far I wanted to go with this … "she'll say something that makes me think that's not totally true. How do you approach somebody to find out if they're being honest with you?"

Sarah leaned back for a minute, chewing steadily with her eyes unfocused, obviously, multi-tasking.

I said, "Maybe I'm being over-sensitive, or too suspicious?"

Sarah inhaled and said, "I think you exaggerate people's actions sometimes, but you're not over-sensitive." She chuckled to take the sting out of her criticism before she added, "I think Lynn is not a very happy person and for years has put on a good face … letting us all think everything was peachy-keen. Maybe, after that confession bit, when you both thought you were going to die, she decided she was tired of *acting* and is letting her *bitchy* side free." Sarah drank some of her iced tea before she added another spoonful of sugar. "You remember when we were talking about Rachel and her new hobby? We touched on Lynn's problems, too."

I nodded as if this was what I wanted. Sarah was so insightful about both Lynn and me, that she didn't bother with generalities. That was one of the things that drew me to Sarah when we were roommates. She was very down-to-earth and had no illusions about our species. In this case, however, I wanted generalities.

Now she presented me with a new idea about my sister, when she suggested, "Possibly, Lynn can't forgive herself until you have forgiven her."

"That's why I drove over to be with her during the hurricane. I said then that I forgave her." Irritation, that our discussion had taken a different course than I intended made me sound crosser than I meant.

"What she did was an awfully hard thing to forgive, Minty. Deep in your heart, *have* you forgiven her?"

I had wanted help with dealing with Clay, but my best hope was taking me literally. "Sarah ..." I exhaled before I said, "What I want to know is how you can approach someone to ask if they're telling you the truth? You know, the *whole* truth?"

Sarah stared at me with a speculative look before we tossed the subject of people hiding disappointment and self-deception back and forth and reached no conclusions. Except that Sarah did say that we all deceive ourselves at times when we need a defense.

Not totally satisfied when we finished and left the diner, as I drove home I re-evaluated Sarah's comments about self-deceit and applied them to Clay. Maybe he was deceiving himself about his dealings with Schultz. I'd have to find out.

Chapter 32

The following week was a quiet one. Several evenings Hugh had to leave right after dinner to visit Mildred, the last of my mother's good friends, who was hospitalized in New Kent.

Hugh said, "The doctors there do what can be done for Mildred, so my visit is more socially therapeutic than medical."

This was so much a part of Hugh; he really cared for his patients, even when they were old.

After my mother's death, Mildred told me with stories of how the two of them shocked Whitman society. "When y'all came home one fall, your mother brought a Bikini bathing suit." Mildred's eyes had sparkled with amusement as she described the shock of the local women. "Your mother was a perfectly lady, but I loved her frivolous side."

Another time, Mildred had said, "Any reference to sex or open gossip violated the old fashioned social conventions of Methodist Womens Circle." She chuckled and squeezed my hand. "Your mother behaved courteously, of course, but what a relief to talk honestly about such things when we were alone."

In my youth, occasionally, I had caught glimpses of that frivolity in my mother and remembered how close we had felt. With a bit of melancholy, I wondered if my children ever felt that way with me.

At the hospital, Hugh did his medical thing, before I went in Mildred's room. She was pleased to see us, so we visited for awhile. On the way home, as we turned up the drive to my farm, I said, "I'm glad we went; she perked up while we were there."

"I'm sure she's lonely. She's the last of her family and friends now. We're making arrangements for her to go into a nursing home." Hugh yawned.

"It's been a long day for you, hasn't it?" I patted his thigh.

"Don't do that. You put ideas in my head that I don't have the energy to deal with," he glanced briefly at me with a grin.

"That's okay. If you want, I'll go with you again tomorrow night to visit Mildred." He walked me up to the porch and I said, "You don't have to stay, if you're too tired."

Hugh left me with a kiss that reminded me how much I had come to depend on him.

"Ummmm!" he whispered against my lips. "I hate to leave, shug."

I agreed, but knew he had an early morning and sent him home. I watched the taillights as he left, grateful that he hadn't mentioned marriage. I was also sharply aware that his being what he was made my dilemma of avoiding marriage more difficult.

*   *   *

On Wednesday, I joined Philabelle and Nourikian for the tour of the Manse. When I arrived, Philabelle said, "I've asked Morton, as chairman of the Council, to join us, also."

"Of course," I nodded and went into the lady parlor. To my surprise, Lynn was already there with Gus Nourikian.

"It's good to see you again, Minty," he said and held up a photo album. "Lynn has been identifying the family members for me."

"That's nice." I smiled at them. Lynn smirked rather than smiled and I swallowed a jolt of annoyance. Her frequent snits were trying my patience. Nourikian asked Philabelle for a brief summary of pre-war Whitman residents until Morton arrived. We greeted him and Nourikian repeated his query about pre-war history.

"There's not much left pre-war," Philabelle said.

"There used to be several large plantations along this road before the war," Morton said and turned to Nourikian. "You should have seen Twin Oaks, the Trueblood Mansion. The longest surviving example of ante-bellum architecture, it was a large white frame home with stately columns on the verandah." Nourikian looked a question at Morton, who hastily added, "Unfortunately it burned down twenty-five or thirty years ago."

"What a pity. There are still a number of pre-war homes, fortunately,"

194

Nourikian said. "I've become interested, however, in the rare Reconstruction structures."

I didn't dare look at either Philabelle or Lynn, but sensed their amusement at Nourikian's subtle put-down. Poor Morton tried so hard to make sure the Truebloods were recognized as one of the First Families of Virginia.

Nourikian turned to Philabelle, "Are you ready, Miss Tour Guide." Philabelle actually giggled.

"Let's start with the early residents of the Manse immediately post-war," she said and led us to the dining room. Nourikian glanced at Lynn, apparently to be sure she followed.

Lynn smiled at him and said, "They're a bunch of grumpy looking ancestors."

Philabelle stood at the foot of the table and said, "The grumpy look was the fashion of the day." And gestured at the portraits on the wall. "*This* is the first lady of the house." She turned to Lynn. "How many greats is it?" Lynn, grinned like an elf and held up two pink-tipped fingers. Philabelle continued, "This, Morton, is your great, great aunt Jenny Trueblood, who married my great, great grandfather Ezra Whitman when he returned from the war." Philabelle gazed at the portrait and announced, "Jenny Trueblood Whitman."

Morton's mouth fell open and he squinted up at the painting; he seemed to struggle to accept that the Manse — the structure he planned to demolish — was a part of his heritage.

"The Manse was her home, Morton. Which means we're kissing kin," Philabelle crowed. I pressed my lips together to contain my laugher and watched Morton's face.

He blinked two or three times, closed his mouth and swallowed, his Adam's apple bobbing, before he stammered, "We're kissing kin? You and me?" You and I, I mentally corrected him.

Philabelle nodded, maintaining that sweet insincere smile.

"Well, gee, Miss Philabelle," he swallowed again and added as if in disbelief, "Are you sure it was one of my ancestors that married a Whitman?"

Her blue eyes mischievous, she said, as if in justification, "Times were very hard after The War, Morton. Jenny Trueblood probably had no other choice in order to survive."

The back of Morton's neck turned red first and the flush crept up his face. He stuttered, "Well, now, I … I mean, eh, oh Miss Philabelle, you didn't think I meant she married beneath her, I hope." He shook his head vigorously and I saw perspiration on his upper lip.

Nourikian, who had been listening, courteously broke the tension by asking Morton, "You're just now learning this? That's fascinating." He smiled at Philabelle and I suspected that Morton's flub had amused him. "How did you come by this information, Miss Philabelle?" She explained about the Trueblood Journal and the light it threw on post-war life. Nourikian was delighted and said, "If you wouldn't consider it an intrusion, I'd appreciate the opportunity to peruse it myself."

"I think Minty's taking notes on the computer, aren't you?" Philabelle turned to me.

"Yes, it's a good idea to transcribe it as I read more. I didn't anticipate this much interest," I said modestly.

Nourikian turned to Morton, "You must be pleased to learn this part of your background."

Morton nodded, "Oh, absolutely. You said it's written by a Trueblood? How did *you* get it?" Did he think she stole it, I wondered?

"I announced at the town meeting that I'd found it in the Whitman library." Philabelle maintained her courteous tone, but I could tell she was quivering with amusement.

"And all these ... " Nourikian gestured at the portraits. "... are family members? This dining table, the buffet and cupboard – they all look antique, as well as those in the lady parlor." Nourikian was visibly excited, and genuinely so, I had to admit. "I'm so honored that you've opened your home to me, Miss Philabelle. It's like a museum."

We women chuckled mildly and agreed. I realized that Philabelle and Lynn believed that Nourikian might, after all, be an ally in preserving the Manse. I'd give him that, but still doubted his larger plan for Whitman.

So the tour had begun on an up-beat note. From the dining room, Philabelle led us upstairs, stopping first in what had been the nursery. I noticed that Nourikian, with good manners, gestured for Lynn and me to enter the room after Philabelle.

"My brothers Billy, Hugh and I used this as a nursery and later as a play room when we were children." Philabelle glanced at me and, behind her smile, I could hear her thinking 'if only you would marry Hugh, all this could be yours'. Everybody but me seems to know how I should live my life, I thought as we moved on.

"This is the only bathroom. It's been modernized. The last time in the 1940s, I think," Philabelle pointed out. "It's adequate for my needs, but should be up-dated. I've considered doing that and adding another downstairs, but since I hope to move into the Creek Woods Residence some day, I haven't bothered."

Oh Philabelle, I pled silently, don't give him justification for tearing it down.

Nourikian said, "If the town accepts your donation, it would be necessary, but would add to the cost of any renovation."

Morton, who had essentially turned up his nose at Philabelle's suggestion, frowned at Nourikian's comment.

"A tremendous amount of expensive renovation! For instance that stairway we came up is awfully narrow, a real hazard for use by the public. Not at all safe in the event of a fire," Morton said. It *was* arson, I thought immediately.

We advanced into the master bedroom — site of the old sleigh bed. I caught Lynn's eyes to see if she remembered how we laughed at the thought of Jenny and Ezra having sex in that bed. She rolled her eyes, making me cough to disguise my snicker. Philabelle, mercifully, didn't tease Morton with that bit of information.

Nourikian stood as if entranced and gazed around at the old furniture: a portable commode cabinet, the dressing table with the clouded mirror, a man's chiffonier.

"What a marvel this is, Miss Philabelle," he said. "You must treasure these family artifacts."

To my amazement, Philabelle and Nourikian discussed the different woods and styles as we progressed from room to room. All the rooms were furnished with a mixture of antique and modern pieces; Philabelle had replaced old drapes and curtains in the same style and colors.

Listening to their talk renewed my affection and respect for the furnishings, for the art, some done by known artists and others of doubtful value. I don't know whether that revived my interest or whether it was their enthusiasm and their knowledge that confirmed my determination to save the Manse.

We returned downstairs to complete the tour.

"The kitchen, the back porch and pantry are not very interesting, most of it added later," Philabelle said. "The stove, refrigerator and microwave are modern, as is the laundry room."

Morton, who had been fairly silent, took that moment to remind us. "It was badly damaged by a fire last month, but I can hardly smell the smoke now."

Irritated beyond bearing, I said, "There wasn't that much damage and none of the older parts of the structure were involved," I sniffed obviously. "… even by smoke. You can check it out for yourselves, if you want." I aimed my comment mostly at Nourikian, who was looking at Lynn. She's done it again, I thought, but at least it's not Hugh.

Nourikian withdrew his gaze and answered me, "Actually, I'm more interested in the original grand parlor. I caught a glimpse as we came in. That intrigued me."

Philabelle picked up the conversation. "Yes, let's go there. It is the most authentic room. Since my parents' death, with both Billy and Hugh in their own homes, I haven't used it much. Leona cleans it routinely, but mostly I keep dust covers on the furniture and the doors closed."

When Nourikian opened the impressive arched double doors into the living room, he inhaled audibly and said, "This could have been a set for Tara, where Scarlet threw her first tantrum at Rhett. Extrordinary."

Philabelle explained that some of the furnishings dated back to after the war, a few of the earlier pieces had survived and had pride of place. She added, "Over the years, various lady mistresses located antiques dating back to colonial times." The original marble fireplace had survived and all evidence of damage repaired. Heavy dark green velvet drapes with gold fringe and cord ties graced the white scrim curtains.

"I don't believe this," Nourikian stood by the door as if enraptured, gazing around in awe. Slowly he moved further into the room, examining a table, a piece of porcelain on the mantel. Engrossed in the accoutrements from the past, momentarily he had forgotten Lynn. Like the rest of us, she watched as he reached out to touch a finger to the carved back of a chair and silently ambled around the room as if memorizing it. Or, more likely, pricing the value of its contents, I told myself.

"These are Chippendale." Philabelle stroked the wine satin upholstered seats on a pair of dainty lady chairs that graced the fireplace. "The sofa is newer, but the same style."

"And the side tables are the Queen Anne," Nourikian pointed out. "Oh! I'm so glad you haven't electrified these Victorian kerosene lamps or those antique wall sconces. They suit the décor."

He certainly was impressed. Like Philabelle I was tempted to stroke the lustrous wood or diddle with the gold tassels on the drapes. I had forgotten the grandeur of that period. No! I chided myself: not even Nourikian nor Morton could stand in that room and say 'trash it.' I blinked, hardly breathing. Dammit, I thought, I don't care what anybody else thinks, I'll do everything I can to keep the Manse intact and to prevent outsiders from changing Whitman.

Nourikian said, "This is more than I hoped to see, Miss Philabelle." She smiled and they commenced another journey around the room, this time talking like appraisers on the Antiques Road Show.

Finally, as Nourikian and Philabelle explored the contents of a document box, Morton and Lynn began fidgeting a bit. I was certainly ready to call it quits.

"Shall we go and wait in the lady parlor?" I asked. Morton and Lynn agreed and we did that. Conversation was desultory and I was relieved when Philabelle and Nourikian joined us.

Philabelle served tea and delicious cakes with her formal elegance.

When it came time to leave, Nourikian took Philabelle's hand and said, "I don't know when I've enjoyed an afternoon as much as this one, Miss Philabelle. You have a lovely home and are a gracious hostess. I look forward to our future working together for the benefit of Whitman."

Lynn said she had to leave and Nourikian offered to escort her home. Of course, he would. She looked dazzling and smiled sweetly, aware that she had charmed him. Actually, as they left, I acknowledged that they made a striking couple — both refined and sophisticated people.

Morton left, but I stayed with Philabelle for awhile because I could see that she wanted to talk. She had bought Nourikian's words, hook, line and sinker. While she babbled on about her relief and confidence in his plans, I listened, tried to look pleasant and let her talk. I was too fond of Philabelle to trample on her hopes.

"He really was impressed with the big parlor, wasn't he?" she said and I cringed inwardly, but nodded. "He's very knowledgeable about furniture."

"It would appear so," I agreed. "Which reminds me: many of the antiques are really valuable. Surely you don't intend to donate them, too?"

"No, no. I thought I'd give each of the family a choice of a few pieces that they would like. What would I do with the rest? Sell them?" Philabelle asked, suddenly sounding weary.

"You must be exhausted, hon, and you don't have to make any decisions right now. You and Hugh can discuss those things at a better time." I rose. "Is there anything I can do to help you with dinner?"

"No thank you, dear. I have something easy all ready. I'm much happier in my mind about Gus's plans for Whitman. He inspires trust and confidence."

"Yes, he surely does that," I said and headed for the door.

"You're still dubious, aren't you?" Philabelle put her hand on my arm and I wanted badly to say what she wanted to hear, but I could not do it at that moment.

Instead, I hugged her and said, "Have your quick dinner and get some rest."

She waved as I got in the car and drove off with a heavy heart.

I did have a lot to mull over. Gus Nourikian was an impressive man. I had tried to trust him, but my apprehension about his intentions for Whitman remained strong. I couldn't disregard his association with Schultz. Him I trusted not at all.

There was still the issue of whether Schultz had corrupted Clay. That confrontation lay ahead. I pushed it from my mind and remembered that Hugh and I planned to visit Mildred again. Hugh was such a good man. Why was I so ... tsk! This was annoying. I felt like crying.

Chapter 33

The next day I planned day to deliver the church ladies' supply of layettes to the hospital in New Kent. While I changed into a cool outfit, melancholy thoughts occupied my mind. Hugh, Rachel, the Manse and now Clay. Feeling a need to talk to Clay, I decided to stop there on my way to take the measure of his friendship, aware that I had insufficient evidence to reveal my suspicions.

In any case, I wanted to remind him that Labor Day was coming up and I'd have a big list for him the next week. When I opened the market door, Clay's plump yellow cat darted out.

"Oh my! The cat got out, Clay," I called.

"It's okay." He came out from the back. "She's spayed and streetwise enough to take care of herself. How's my favorite girlfriend, today?" He gave me a half hug.

"Busy, busy, busy, working on Elliott's files." I hadn't meant to tell him that, but since I had, I might as well ask, "Did you ever meet that developer, Nourikian, that Schultz mentioned?" Fools rush in, as the saying goes, but I needed to see Clay's reaction.

He had turned to go behind the counter, unfortunately, so I was thwarted. Compounding the situation, the bell over the door announced the presence of Schultz himself. Ugh! I thought.

He sort of saluted Clay and smiled at me. "It's a pleasure to see you again."

I pulled my lips into a smile and turned back to Clay. "All I need is a loaf of dill rye bread."

While I stood by the counter, Schultz sidled so close that I could smell his garlicky breath. I surreptitiously eased away to examine nearby boxes of, appropriately, chewing tobacco. Clay had gone to the bread shelf, leaving me to cope with Schultz and his halitosis.

"You're looking mighty pretty today, Minty," Schultz said. When I merely produced a false smile, he continued, "That was an interesting meeting last month. I'm surprised that, at her age, Miss Philabelle is so determined to stay in that big ole house." As he spoke, he oozed toward me again. I pulled my purse in front of me as a shield, fumbled in it wishing I had Mace or Binaca, and blessed Clay silently for returning with my bread.

"That all for today, Minty?" Clay asked and I nodded. He knew to put it on my account and he turned to bag it.

"Thanks, Clay. I have work to do. See you later."

"Don't spend all afternoon studying those files, you hear?" Clay cautioned as I turned to leave.

That must have caught Schultz's attention because he put his hand on my arm. I flinched.

"What files you studying, Minty? Legal procedures concerning donations of real estate?" he asked, not quite sneering.

Sarah would call his query pure chutzpah! Before I could think of a suitable retort, Clay stunned me.

"No, she's sorting Elliott's files for Lynn." He glanced briefly at Schultz before he turned back to the cash register. So I couldn't see his face? Shocked mute I stood with my mouth hanging open.

Schultz raised his eyebrows, as if surprised. "You going to bury yourself in dusty old papers on a nice day like today?"

Too dumbfounded at Clay's divulging my project to do more than mutter the truth, I said, "No, I'm picking up new baby clothes from the ladies circle at our church for the hospital."

I wanted to leave quickly, anxious to get away from them, but Schultz asked, "You driving clear to the hospital in New Kent?"

I was tempted to ask if there was another available hospital or snap that I was taking an ox cart, but eager to get away, I nodded and left.

Disgusted at Schultz's presumption and angry at Clay's blabbing, I drove to the church. My irritation, at Schultz's arrogance simmered all the way. The entire Manse situation was getting out of control. Not only was it involving people dear to me, but I sensed that my efforts sometimes irritated those same folks.

The familiar sight of the old-fashioned white frame church improved my mood. While I parked, I tried to stifle feelings of hostility as inappropriate.

The quiet of the sanctuary, as I strolled between the aisles, calmed me. I inhaled the scent of candles, wishing that, like Catholics, we also used incense to enhance the spiritual feeling. When I opened the door into the social hall downstairs, the murmur of voices, the welcome of the sewing ladies cancelled out much of Schultz's effect

Not one under seventy, the white-haired brigade of women regularly created layettes, nightgowns, booties and little quilted throws for all our newborn babies.

"Hey there, Minty. Sit down and have some cookies and sweet tea or a Coke," Audrey offered.

"Don't have time, I sorry to say. I have to pick up the layettes and get going."

Madge came in from the storeroom and heard me. "Oh, Minty, I told E.J. I'd take Janet for a ride today and I might as well deliver them for you." This was typical of Madge; she was generous with her time, but I wished she'd let me know beforehand.

"So you can stay after all," Audrey chuckled.

I left within fifteen minutes, because Hugh was coming to dinner and I wanted time to change into something prettier.

$$* \qquad * \qquad *$$

At home, when I pulled the car around back, I was surprised to see Buck come loping towards me.

"Did I leave you out all this time?" Making a strange sound, he pushed himself against my legs as if to block my move toward the stoop. "Are you mad at Momma, Sweetie?" I bent down to his level, looked into his eyes and, stoking his head, pondered what had excited him. When he seemed calm again, I headed toward the house, but the dog shoved in front of me. He nipped at my skirt, making unusual noises in his throat. The hair on the back of my neck rose as if stirred by a cool breeze. Hand on Buck's head to restrain him, I entered the kitchen quietly and stood for a minute. Rustling noises came from the hall and I remembered that no cars were parked out front. An intruder or a raccoon? I glanced around for a broom or a weapon and settled on a can of room freshener, my heart pounding.

Leaning my head close to Buck's ears, I whispered the command, "Stay. Stay." He cocked his head, clearly not happy, but obeyed.

I eased off my sandals and barefoot, tip-toed into the hall. Almost at the door to the computer room, I recognized Al Schultz slinking toward the front door. I gasped and quickly barked, "What are you doing here?"

He turned and raised both hands. "Oh, good! Minty, you're back!" he stuttered. "I was about to leave …" He stared like a deer caught in headlights and added, hastily, "I just stopped by for a visit."

"What kind of a visit involves breaking and entering?" I demanded, apprehensive, but mad as a hornet, too. "You thought I was going to New Kent."

Eyes almost bulging with false denial, he shook his head. "There was no breaking and entering." He forced a chuckle of amusement. "The door was unlocked and I just opened it a little and called in. Then I heard your car and –"

"You did a whole lot more than open it a little and call in," I tried to sound threatening. "I'm not stupid, *Mr. Schultz*. And don't call me Minty." His phony southern accent *bugged* me.

"Now come on, Mi…" He hesitated and glanced toward the front door. "…everybody around here just knocks and, if the door's unlocked, sticks their head in and calls."

"As an outsider in Whitman, Mr. Schultz, you may not realize that only *friends* of long standing do that." My hands felt sweaty and I wished that the phone were within reach. Instead, I stuck my head in the computer room; one of file cabinet drawers was open, several folders dumped on my desk.

In fury, I turned to face him. "You had the gall to go through my files! That's some kind of criminal offense." Relieved when he backed away.

"Oh, well. I … eh … Clay Marshall said you were looking through Mr. Elliott's file for evidence of wrong-doing with regard to the Manse." He nodded as if to confirm himself.

He was quick with phony excuses, but he cut his eyes to the side, as if looking to escape. I snapped, "You're lying. I didn't tell Clay what I was looking for in the files."

Slippery Schultz stammered a hasty response, "Aware of my dealings with Mr. Elliott on the subject, I was disturbed that my lawyer-client privilege might be violated. That, also, is a criminal offense."

I tried to laugh in his face and moved toward him. "Are you implying that Mr. Elliott was representing you in some business? That you were his client?" I paused to swallow. "I don't buy that at all. In case you don't know — not being a native here — Randolph Elliott was my brother-in-law and Lynn as his widow has legal custody of his records. It was *she* who offered the files to me."

That caught him off guard for a minute, but he summoned up an argument.

"A release of information concerning me is an invasion of privacy," he lifted his chin intending to defy me, I thought, and added, "... and don't think I won't seek legal advice."

"Fine," I snarled, "You will probably need it. I'm instigating an investigation into the attempt to burn down the Manse." I had hoped to shock him into revealing his complicity.

Instead, he laughed. "You're going to prove arson, are you?"

"Yes. The Fire Chief hasn't totally ruled it out." I knew that wasn't true, but I wanted to shake him up.

"You want to know who set fire to the Manse?" He sneered at me. "Look at your friends and family, not me."

Standing my ground, I shook my head at him. "I know and trust my family and friends."

"Even Clay Marshall? He wanted to sell his property but the Whitman place was part of the deal, so the Manse had to go. He was even caught at the scene." He nodded his head, a sick grin on his face.

He'd struck home, but I wasn't about to let him know that. Besides, I'd had enough by then and, concerned at having heard muffled woofs from Buck in protest at the stay command, I wanted Schultz out of my house.

"That's enough of your scurrilous hints, Schultz." I advanced toward him. "You'd better leave before I decide to call the Sheriff's office with a charge of breaking and entering, plus malicious mischief."

Eyes narrowed and a scowl on his face, he muttered, "I'll go, all right, but I know you're out to sabotage a strong movement toward the development of Whitman." He backed away. "Just because the town is named after your family, you're not the power you think you are," he spat the words and, for a second, succeeded in intimidating me.

But not for long. From the kitchen, Buck let out a long mournful whine, sensing a threat to his mistress. By the way his eyes opened, Schultz heard it, too.

"Go, Mr. Schultz, before my dog roars in here to protect me from your spite."

I thought his face blanched a bit, but he wanted the last word, presumably. "I consider that a threat of bodily harm and don't think for a minute you've heard the last of this."

As he turned to leave, I had a thought. "Where's your car, Mr. Schultz? I didn't see it parked out front." I suspected that he'd hidden it on the old back road, invisible behind the trees. "I hope you didn't walk all the way out here in this heat." I succeeded in laughing, but held my trembling hands behind my back.

He threw me a dirty look and stalked through the hall toward the front door.

In a fit of spite myself, I called, "Come, Buck. Come, boy. Come …"

At the clatter of Buck's nails as he raced into the hall, Schultz broke into a run out the front door. Buck stopped his chase on my command.

I steadied myself, hand on Buck's head, until my internal quaking quieted, lips dried tight. Had Clay lied to me? Fear combined with disbelief rattled me. Buck's wet nose on my hand brought me back to reality. I gave him the praise he deserved for scaring Schultz and a dog cookie as well. He gazed up with the skinned teeth we had decided was his smile.

"Oh you're a brave boy, an excellent boy." Then I rushed into the kitchen to dial Hugh's cell phone. He didn't answer, so I had to leave a message: "Just checking, hon, to be sure you're coming for dinner tonight." I stood, consciously slowing my breathing and convincing myself that Schultz was gone, too scared to face Buck.

Chapter 34

Upstairs, I laid out a mauve and pink voile dress. Pink is kind to an aging complexion, I thought, and headed for the shower. As the cool water massaged the back of my neck, I vacillated over telling Hugh about Schultz. The tepid liquid sluicing over my body calmed me until I reached the conclusion that Schultz was too much a coward to use direct violence. I did suspect he'd malign me verbally behind my back. In my eagerness to be ready for Hugh, I convinced myself that Schultz, a newcomer, was too insignificant to allow him to ruin my time with Hugh.

Successfully sloughing off my apprehension, I was checking my appearance in the living room mirror when Buck woofed and raced toward the front door.

Hugh called, "Hey, anybody home?" and I sang back, "In here, hon."

Buck preceded Hugh, who tossed his jacket on a chair, and kissed me enthusiastically. Then he filled our glasses, before we settled on the couch.

Buck sat on his haunches near Hugh displaying good manners and Cleo, dragging her shoestring, wandered into the room to join us. Haughty queen that she considered herself, she had been given to unprovoked hissing at folks. Fortunately, she had always fancied Hugh and now settled on his other side. When he scratched Buck's ears, Cleo rose, put her paws on his thigh, abandoning the shoestring. Obligingly, he stroked her head, too.

"Pretty girl," he crooned. Buck looked put out, so I patted my lap and he moved over within reach of my hand. While Hugh stroked Cleo, she expressed her pleasure vocally. Abruptly, she rolled on her back and presented her tummy to him. She purred loudly as he petted, until she emitted a loud drawn out yowl and squirmed sensuously on the floor.

Hugh sat upright and laughed like a loon. "That's an orgasmic cry if I ever heard one."

Pretending disagreement, I shook my head and said, "Impossible. She's been neutered, silly."

"That doesn't mean she can't have an orgasm if she wants." He held up both hands.

"There's power in these, woman. Beware!" He grabbed me around the waist and pulled me into his lap.

"Unhand me, villain," I protested faintly. "Buck should go out." Hugh let me stand up and, still holding me, we moved to open the door. He bumped into me several times, with increasingly intimate overtures. Amused, I pretended to ignore his liberties.

While we waited for Buck to come in, Hugh nuzzled up to me and whispered, "Aren't you tired, shug?"

As eager as Cleo had been to let him play with me, I shrugged, opened my eyes wide, and said, "No, not at all." His expression of surprise mixed with chagrin provoked my sense of silliness. Pretending concern, I asked, "Did *you* have a hard day?"

Like lightning, he riposted, "No, my *day* was not hard." And with both arms, he pulled me against him. I didn't resist.

"You're a wicked man, making indecent advances," I tried to say, laughing as I snuggled against him, giddy at our loving foolishness.

After a bit, Hugh released me, strode to the door, opened it and shouted, "Buck, come in, boy."

Blessing Buck's amiability as he trotted in, I let the Schultz encounter, Rachel's marriage, all my worries float away in the bliss of the moment and let Hugh take my hand and lead me up to the bedroom.

*   *   *

Upstairs, I wondered what instinct had influenced my choice of color when I redecorated after Billy's death. The décor reflected a subtle defiance of convention, I thought. Whatever had inspired me had created an appropriate and exciting environment for my affair with Hugh. Tonight, it was filled with the fragrance of sweet peas and honeysuckle and romance.

Despite my reluctance to exhibit my sixty-three year old body to Hugh, over time I had turned the process of undressing each other into a frolicsome strip tease, languidly discarding neatness in the process.

Hugh was a happy lover; he hummed and breathed on the back of my neck as he unhooked my bra. He called a jolly, "Good bye, pink bra," as he cast it aside.

"Delicious," he murmured as if this were his first experience with my breasts. Once naked on the bed, he took his time, whispering his concern for my pleasure as if my satisfaction was more important than his own. So different from Billy's Wham, Bam, Thank you, Ma'am. Hugh's hands instinctively found the places on my body that craved his touch and elicited my own purrs of delight.

At first, lacking confidence, I had needed Hugh to guide my hands. Now, familiar with the contours of his body, my hands lingered over the landscape of the muscles in his back, savoring the taut strength of his thighs and buttocks. I was conscious of the movement of his shoulder blades as he swept his hand across my belly. Did it feel flabby, old to him? A wave of self-consciousness rose and passed, dispelled by my physical need for Hugh's body, a desire to *be* Hugh, to devour him.

Hugh playfully compared me to Cleo as we moved together in the same rhythm, mumbling and mouthing meaningless sounds of desire and gratification. As our ardor intensified, so did my feelings for Hugh.

As the sensuous slip and slide of hands and feet over bare skin, lips nibbling, thigh pressing belly, amid sighs and moans, I ceased to exist separate from Hugh. I was strong and powerful, joyful at the fusion of our bodies, our spirits. The level of our passion increased and, like a gate, I opened to him. Joined physically and in psyche, we rose to our climax, incandescent, merged into a single entity. A communion of mind and flesh, which enveloped both of us; Hugh and I bound together in an ephemeral limbo of time.

When Hugh fell back, panting and grinning, he breathed, "Wow!" I felt his belly quiver with laughter as he added, "My own wild Cleo." I tightened my arms around him.

Jubilant that I knew that I had satisfied him, but still in the throes of our passion, unwilling to let go, I clenched myself around him, until soft and moist, he slid out. I mourned the loss of that connection, that sense of being one, the total union, fearful that it would fade and leave me empty and cold.

As we lay entwined, warm with contentment, he breathed against my cheek, "If I had the energy, I'd climb a mountain and howl at the moon."

We laughed together at that vision, silently acknowledging the bond between us, delicate as a spider web. Not the bondage I had felt with Billy.

Damn Billy's intrusion on this private moment! It reminded me that Hugh and my emotional connection was too fragile to survive. I pressed my cheek against his neck, unwilling to lose the feeling we shared at that moment.

At the same time, I experienced a terrible fear that *I* would be compelled to break the tie.

Hugh's voice was gentle, when he asked, "What, sweetheart? Did I hurt you?" and rubbed his lips across my shoulder. His hand brushed at my wet face.

Touched by his concern, I whimpered, "No, no. I'm crying because we're perfect together. It was beautiful." When had 'frendship with privileges' turned to love?

Hugh cuddled me in his arms, stroking my back as if I were sick. I did feel sick – sick with a guilt and a fear that I didn't understand.

Without warning, Hugh said, "You must know that I love you, shug. Long before I understood the word or the nature of love, I dreamed of this moment with you."

His words struck with almost physical force. I no longer doubted that I loved Hugh, more deeply and more profoundly than I had ever loved before. With that affirmation came the anxieties that had plagued me ever since Billy's death. I believed that Hugh loved me. He had proven that subtly and often since that day. But I was still too scared to commit. The difference in our age, the wound of confidence and self-image caused by Billy – were they the cause of my fear, my sword of Damocles?

Hugh's sympathetic hand on my back slowed until he drowsed off. My tears quit and I reflected on our future. Like a dirge running round and round in my brain, I picked at that fear and guilt, convinced that the source lay in Billy's persistent trespass into my life.

I don't know how long we lay there before the liquid consequences of our loving felt uncomfortable. I slipped out of bed into the bathroom. Washed and clean, I doused myself with bath powder. Armed with a warm, damp washcloth, I returned to clean Hugh, amused at recalled maternal habits.

"Wha …?" Hugh roused, opened an eye and smiled, touching my bare shoulder. He moved his legs to accommodate me and chuckled when I dusted him with Very Irresistible.

"Hmmm, that's sexy." He pulled me down and we kissed, as if sealing a secret pact.

Snuggled together again, I had a tentative, but lovely feeling that we would work it all out together.

Chapter 35

The next morning, I woke alone in bed. A breeze blew the curtains in as well as the scent of nature – elements of farmland, mixed flowers and, seeping through the door from the hall, the aroma of coffee. I stretched with the luxury of comfort, feeling loved and cherished and wondered mildly how long Hugh would wait before rousting me out of our nest.

Farm-woman that I was at heart, once thoroughly awake, I couldn't linger. Instead of my usual terry cloth bathrobe with its pulled strings, I opened the drawer to deck myself in a pink flowered mantle that draped smoothly around me. As I washed my face and combed my hair, something reminded me of Schultz and I considered making a joke of it with Hugh. On second thought, he might not think it amusing and I refused to let it mar our lovely night or day.

After a light spritz of Very Irresistible, I trotted downstairs to join the group.

Hugh was making pancakes, while Buck and Cleo gobbled their own breakfasts.

"Good morning, sweetheart," I caroled brightly, gliding up behind him.

"'Bout time you got your lazy self down here." Hugh turned from the counter to toss that twitchy smile at me. "I even went out to pick fresh blueberries for you."

"Well, that was silly of you." I leaned my head on his shoulder, arms around his middle. "There's a whole container full in the fridge."

"Smart ass," he muttered. "Pour yourself a cup of coffee. These'll be ready momentarily."

I did as I was told and checked the table. It was all set, complete with butter, maple syrup and the blackberry syrup that Hugh preferred, even on blueberry pancakes.

Buck, who had emptied his food bowl, came over for his morning greeting and I scratched all his favorite spots, while Hugh turned off the griddle and brought over a plate of fragrant, hot pancakes. Without hesitation, we both fixed our plates to our individual tastes and ate silently, our eyes occasionally meeting and heads nodding with mutual approval and satisfaction.

When pleasantly stuffed, I pushed back my plate and gave him his due. "That was absolutely perfect. My compliments to the chef."

"Thank you, m'am. You deserve the best." Hugh bowed in acknowledgement.

"Ready for more coffee?" I stood and retrieved the pot. He nodded; I refilled both our cups and put the pot back.

Underneath the humor, my mind raced with a mixture of emotions. I wanted to tell Hugh how much I loved him, how foolish I had been to pretend that I didn't. But a new and unexpected shyness restrained me. I felt childish and frightened. Thrilled at this unfamiliar and wonderful feeling, I wanted to tickle and tease Hugh, to share this magic with him. At the same time, I felt a darkness inside that frightened me.

When I first entered the kitchen, I could sense this new connection. It shimmered like a light around us in every silly word we exchanged, between every touch and meeting of our eyes. I knew, as surely as I knew that I loved Hugh, that he was experiencing the same under-current of love.

So when I sat down again and Hugh leaned close enough to hold my hands, I knew what he was going to say.

His voice vibrated with intensity as he said, "Minty, you know that this isn't just 'friendship with privileges' anymore. This is ... " he searched for words, gripping my hands, "... it's a powerful love added to our solid friendship — this is forever. It's so obvious that we're already married in spirit." With his eyes so focused on mine, I nearly stopped breathing in panic, when he added, "All we have to do now is set a date to make it legal."

Involuntarily, my hands flew to cover my mouth as, holding my breath, I stared at him. The teasing mood had changed too abruptly. Gently, Hugh reached to retrieve my hands, the warmth calming me enough that I could say, "I do love you and I believe you love me, too. Truly, I do, but ..." I licked my lips, frantic to find words.

"But what? You've never told me why you're so reluctant ..." He stopped, holding my eyes so intently that I imagined his brown eyes melting into blue, his nose, lips, his entire face changing into Billy's dying face.

In panic, I pulled my hands from Hugh's, covered my face again, willing the guilty image to disappear. My hands were sweaty against my cheeks, when Hugh eased them away, his voice urgent with concern.

"Minty? What's wrong?"

I felt like screaming, 'I don't know!' But I couldn't scream at Hugh, I couldn't even give him an intelligent reason why the idea of marriage repelled me. At the same time, I feared losing him. Now more than ever, I needed him to love me. Feeling like a temperamental fool, I forced myself to take slow deep breaths, my brain a useless blank, I repeated the same stupid mantra, "I just need more time."

"Time for what? You say you love me and I believe that." His forehead furrowed, he shook his head, obviously bewildered and, I knew, annoyed — disappointed, at least.

"I'm sorry, Hugh," I focused all my mind on making him understand. "I do love you. I'm overwhelmed with this new, all encompassing kind of love."

For a painful moment we sat looking at each other in silence. Finally, he rose. He stacked the soiled plates, balanced his mug on top and took them over to the dishwasher. I slumped in my chair, scared, wretched. All my energy focused on quelling the image of Billy's dying face.

Hugh cleared the remainder of stuff from the table, going back and forth, loading the dishwasher, while I sat with my head hanging, weak with shame and guilt. Embarrassed, inarticulate, I had nothing I could say except the useless, "I just need more time, I guess."

He let Buck out again and sat down across from me, his face unrevealing, and said, "How long do you expect me to wait?" I could see the anger in his eyes. His voice shook slightly with an effort to contain it.

"Please, don't be mad at me," I stammered, panting with anxiety. "Please, just a little more time to …" A sob broke through my control. "Please," I begged.

"For God's sake, quit crying. I can't …" Hugh shook his head, breathing heavily. "He turned away and muttered, "We've been over this, three, four times?"

Hastily I wiped at my eyes, contemptuous of my inadequacy, but terrified and shaking in the silence until he spoke again, his voice heavy with patience.

"If time is that you need, I guess I can wait for …" he gestured with a hand. "… a couple of weeks? It's August already, dammit." His expression invited a response from me.

I was hugging myself so hard that I felt my nails digging through my robe. Mutely, I nodded and stammered, "I *do* love you, Hugh. Please believe me that I just *don't know* …" Short of breath again, despising my inadequacy, I added, "I appreciate your patience."

He sat back, his gaze off in the distance, then he took inhaled deeply and said, "Sooner or later, Minty, you're going to have to face whatever …" he shook his head as if helpless, "… the hang-up that's interfering with your getting on with your life. You seem to be waiting for something. Biding your time until …" he looked at me. "… what?"

Buck scratched at the kitchen door. Hugh got up to let him in and stood beside me to say, "I've filed a couple of applications for work abroad." My shocked expression must have prompted him to add, "I told you several times that I won't stay in Whitman without you as my wife."

This conversation was over as far as he was concerned, I could tell. Too exhausted to speak, I nodded, knowing that it was now my responsibility to either fish or cut bait.

Chapter 36

The next day, I'd just come in from exercising my fur friends in the back yard when I heard the front doorbell. With Buck leading the way, I called, "I'm coming," and heard the door open.

"It's me, sweetheart," Clay answered and we met in the hall. "I'm on my way to New Kent and thought I'd stop by on my way."

On impulse, I thought: *tell him what Schultz said and get it over with.* "Got time for a coke and a visit?" I gestured toward the living room.

"Always for you." He put a large brown grocery bag on the floor, lifted out a white box and offered it to me.

By its odor, redolent of fresh pastry, I knew it was my favorite cream puffs. "How thoughtful, you dear man."

"Fresh from Ola's oven." He stooped to scratch Buck's ears before he sat in one of the comfy chairs that flanked the fire place. "What's on your mind?"

"Unpleasant business first, okay? Then we can chat." I sat facing him. He raised his eyebrows with curiosity, those blue eyes wide with interest. "You know I've been going through Elliott's files?" I asked and he nodded. "Looking for evidence that Morton and Schultz have skullduggery in mind concerning the Manse?" He nodded again and shifted in the chair, a wary look on his face. "Well, I've found evidence that Schultz and one of the landowners across Main Street were involved in some kind of scheme to cheat Philabelle out of the Manse."

Having sort of blurted this out, I paused to take a breath. Clay tilted his head, looking puzzled.

"Where'd you get that idea?" he asked.

"Clay, you own most of that land, so, of course, I had to wonder. That's why I wanted to talk to you before …"

"What land are you talking about? I don't …," his face was guarded.

I interrupted, "The property directly across from the Manse — the market, the dry cleaners, the diner — that whole block." I tried to sound reassuring. To let him know I wasn't angry, I added, "I wondered if somehow maybe Schultz had duped you into …" The expression on his face changed, told me this wasn't going the way I expected. I gnawed at my lip as I waited for him to deny the whole thing.

Clay squinted his eyes and nodded his head slightly. "Duped me into what?"

Disconcerted at his reaction, I spoke hesitantly, "I heard that you're anxious to sell and, at the town meeting, Morton said a lot of business men were interested."

"In what? You're not making sense. What are you trying to say?" His mouth looked tight and he rubbed his palms on his thighs.

"It's a complicated and confusing coincidence that Schultz told Elliott that developers wanted to buy that property if the Manse was part of the deal."

Clay, frown lines between his eyes, and, no longer relaxing back in the chair, he sat upright, his back rigid, and stared at me, "Come on, Minty. Do you seriously think that I'm involved in some scheme to force Miss Philabelle to sell the Manse?" His face was flushed and his voice harsh, not the laid-back Clay I had known forever.

Unprepared for his reaction, I stammered, "Not really, but it's just that these real estate deals are awfully complicated and you could get involved … you know … without realizing … and, eh, be finagled into their deal." He hadn't denied it, as I'd hoped he would

He leaned forward, elbows out, hands on his thighs and growled, "You think I'm either an idiot or a crook?"

"No!" I barked. "I'm just saying — I found evidence in Elliott's file —."

He interrupted me, his voice rough, and said, "All this time, as far back as high school, I just about worshipped the ground you walked on. I believed you really cared for me, dreaming that some day you and I … '" He jumped up and I had to tilt my head back to see his face. I felt Buck, who had been lounging near him, suddenly in front of me, pressing against my legs.

"I *did*. I *do* care about you, Clay. That's why I'm asking …" a feeling of betrayal washed over me again.

"Condescending to *ask* me before you turn me over to the cops?" He marched back and forth in front of the fireplace, obviously making an effort to control himself.

I sat trembling convinced now that he *couldn't* deny being involved. Grieved that it had come to this, I said, "I told you there's evidence in Elliott's handwriting that Schultz planned …" I tried to explain, but he ranted on.

"All my life, I imagined you as a great lady: strong, but feminine; intelligent, full of life and vitality. You were my ideal woman." He leaned down and stared at me as if he didn't recognize me.

Stunned, I sat like a dummy looking up at Clay as he raged on.

"I trusted you, Minty. Gave my heart to you." He stood, breathing heavily. Then moved away. Abruptly he faced me again. "And you've played the fine southern lady, befriending the po' white trash, football jock. Kissing me as if you meant it."

I sat, mesmerized as if charmed by a snake, while Clay berated me. Too astonished to speak, I realized that, despite all our lives as friends, Clay had harbored the same feelings as the die-hard Southerners who wanted to hang the Confederate flag on the capitol and re-enact the Battle of Shiloh. Then I remembered his bitter remark last spring about the South rising again.

He stood, leaning against the mantelpiece, and said, in a softer tone, "And then you dumped me for Billy."

He stood, head hanging, turned so I couldn't see his face. Frantic to convince him that my intention had been only to find out the truth, I stood up. He lifted his head and looked at me with hurt spaniel eyes and I realized that his anger was spent.

He swallowed and said, "I understood that. It was appropriate for you, in your position, to marry Billy, a Whitman in your own class." He paused, his mouth tight, shaking his head. When he spoke, his voice sounded raw and he coughed. His throat must be dry, I thought, and despite my anxiety at his reaction, I needed to convince him that I had been sincere in my affection for him. I did love him and still did, as I love all my friends.

"Let me explain," I was begging him now. "First, sit down and I'll get us some Coke."

As if deflated emotionally, he obeyed. I hurried into the kitchen, almost tripping over the attentive Buck.

Trembling, ashamed and distraught, I was frightened. Not that Clay would harm me — but that I had failed to handle this more effectively. My heart was racing and I leaned against the counter for a minute. Buck nudged me with his nose, but I was too upset to assure him.

Clumsily I had miscalculated Clay's reaction. I hadn't realized how strongly he still felt about me. Maybe he exaggerated: he tended to sweet-talk all the girls. I felt like a total fool. I'd have to make amends.

I grabbed two bottles from the fridge and two glasses and hurried back to the living room.

With two cold Cokes clutched against my chest and a glass in each hand, I returned. Clay, to my shock was examining a gun in his hands.

A glass slipped from my sweaty hand onto the hearth where it shattered with a bang.

"Minty!" I heard Hugh's shout before he rushed into the room – the three of us motionless, like a tableau. Hugh blinked and stared at me. I stood with my mouth open with surprise.

He glanced at Clay's angry expression and back to me and asked, brusquely, "What's going on here?"

Clay stood up, face now bland as white bread, he said, "Hey, Hugh. I stopped by to bring Minty a box of pastry. Then, out of nowhere, she ..." he indicated me with his head. "... accused me of being part of a conspiracy to cheat Miss Philabelle out of the Manse property." He glowered at me unpleasantly.

Beyond patience now, I blurted, "I didn't *accuse* you. I just ..."

Clay turned on me, raised his voice and said, "What do the words 'I have evidence of you conspiring with Schultz to defraud Philabelle' mean?" He frowned at me and added in a sorrowful voice, "You toyed with me. Let me think you were my girl friend. Now I find out that you were condescending to your inferior." He thrust out his chin, like when he played football, in a challenge mode.

Furious, I moved toward him, bumping against the dog, "Mother of Pearl, Clay!" So offended at his words that I shook my fist in his face.

Hugh stepped between us. "Stop it, Minty." He glared briefly at Clay. "Calm down, both of you."

"I'm not going to calm down," I said. "You never denied it and what about burning down the Manse?" I pointed at Clay. "Schultz said you did it. You were the first one there. What was I to believe when I read Elliott's notes? It all made sense that you'd ..."

"Minty," Hugh barked, "Don't be silly. It wasn't ..."

Clay's face got red with shame, I assumed. I thought, ha, I'm right, but was not happy about it.

Then as I watched, Clay closed his eyes and breathed heavily through his open mouth before he almost whispered, "You believe I'd endanger Miss Philabelle's life by setting the Manse on fire?" I'd never heard that weird tone in Clay's voice as if he were choking. "You're cruel as well as a cheat, Araminta Burgess Whitman."

That was too much! I raised my hand to slap his face, but Hugh grabbed it and growled, "Stop it! What are you saying? You can't accuse somebody of arson without evidence. That's slander."

"He accused me of patronizing him," I said self-righteously, threw a fierce glance at Clay. "That's purely stupid. Your ancestors saved Whitman girls during the War and even married one. We're all kissin' kin: the Marshalls, the Trueblood, the Whitmans. My family's *beholden* to yours. Why would I …?"

Clay gasped and looked surprised, but I ignored him and continued: "That's right. It's all documented in the Trueblood Journal." I stopped to take a breath. I felt contrite. I blinked rapidly, determined not to cry in front of these men.

Hesitantly, I said, "Clay, I really was crazy about you." Both men looked at me as if I'd gone mad, but I persisted, "And I never, *never* thought of you as anything except the handsomest jock in school."

With a bitter voice, Clay said, "Until Billy came along."

I felt sweat on my upper lip and said, "That's true. Billy came home and when he chose me, I …" A sudden wave of regret made me shake my head in amazement, "… like all the girls, I fell for Billy."

I looked down and saw Buck sitting on his haunches, his eyes flicking back and forth from me to Clay. I glanced up and both the men were staring at me, as if they expected something more. Looking at Clay, I said, "I had to wonder, Clay. The notes, in Elliott's handwriting and Schultz saying …"

Hugh took control and said, "I'm lost here? What's all this about Elliott's notes?"

"If *she* can keep her mouth shut for a few minutes, I'll tell you the whole slanderous story," Clay said. Buck woofed and I touched his head.

Hugh gestured and said, "How about we all sit down …" He stepped on the broken glass, which crunched, breaking the silence. He glanced down and then up at me with a question in his eyes.

"I dropped a glass," I said. "That was the bang." Clay stood with an arm on the mantelpiece, quivering like an angry bull. Too emotionally exhausted to continue, I murmured, "I'll get another Coke." I left the two men to deal with each other. Buck padded along behind me out of the room.

In the kitchen, I leaned against the counter and closed my eyes, trying to compose myself. I had managed the discussion with Clay very poorly and never anticipated that he'd get so upset. My God! I shivered. I had gotten angry and accused him of trying to burn down The Manse. I had *believed* that liar Schultz. Shame washed over me like a hot flash. Worse, I had lost my temper, something a Southern lady never does.

I was totally bewildered and frightened at how I had mangled what should have been a simple discussion between friends. I pressed my hand against my forehead, trying to calm my heavy breathing, sick to my stomach with the torrent of emotion. Buck nudged me with his nose, but I was too disturbed to respond. Was Sarah right that I was full of anger? Maybe. But at what?

$*$ $*$ $*$

Hugh stuck his head in the door. "What's the matter? We're waiting for …" He came over and must have realized that I was trembling. "It's all right, shug. Clay's hurt, but he'll settle down in time." I nodded and leaned against Hugh, who had put his arms around me. For a minute, I drew strength from his embrace, as I have done often during the past three years. I blinked away tears. No way would I let them see me cry. I sniffed and straightened up, withdrawing from the warmth of his comfort.

"I have to sweep up the glass," I said and walked over to the broom closet. "Can you take the Coke and glasses for me, please?" I got out the dust-pan and brush. Hugh carried the Coke and glasses. I must have looked more composed than I felt and we went back to face Clay.

In the dark hall, we bumped into him. Hugh almost tripped over Buck, who had stayed under foot ever since the gun appeared. This added a touch of wry humor, which threatened to tip me into hysterics.

"I'm leaving now, Hugh," Clay said abruptly and turned back into the living room.

Hugh caught his arm. "No, please. Wait a minute. I need to know what's going on." Without looking at me, Clay stopped and listened to Hugh, who said, "Let's talk about this."

In an atmosphere reeking of tension, the three of us sat at the kitchen table. I sat in my usual chair with Hugh on my left. Over bottles of coke and a bowl of pretzels, Hugh took control.

"Clay, tell me your side of this whole magillah."

Without a glance at me, Clay hitched his chair closer to him, as if I'd been doused with essence of skunk. Then he addressed himself exclusively to Hugh.

"The fact is that Schultz did approach me with the story much as …" Still without looking at me Clay nodded in my direction. "… *she* imagined it."

She was pouring Coke into her glass and *she* kept her eyes on what *she* was doing. I didn't challenge him despite his use of the pejorative 'imagined'.

Clay continued, "Morton was supposed to persuade Miss Philabelle to sell the Manse property to the town at a lower than market price. Schultz said Nourikian had connections who would buy the Manse at a higher price. The town would receive the lower amount." He paused and drank some Coke.

I couldn't keep my mouth shut. "So I was right. There was a conspiracy."

"Oh, yes, you were right about that, but nothing else. *Nothing* else." Clay banged the Coke bottle down on the table. "I was never a part of it."

Quickly, Hugh asked, "What happened next? Was Nourikian in on the deal?"

"No." Clay shook his head. "No. He's a straight arrow. When he was here, I asked him about Schultz and he said when they were working on the Creek Woods job, he'd discovered Schultz had a bad reputation. Plus he works with disreputable sub-contractors. Nourikian won't deal with him any more."

There was a pause and Hugh looked at me expectantly. He smiled an invitation to my joining the conversation, which I was disinclined to do, still too upset. With Hugh's eye on me, I reached down to the reassurance of Buck's rough coat.

Hugh exhaled with exaggerated patience before he asked Clay, "So you were supposed to go along with Schultz on the Manse deal?"

"Yeah. We were all to get a cut," he answered and, although I was looking away, now I could feel *his* eyes boring holes in me. "But I told Schultz to fuck off."

I got Clay's message loud and clear. He knew how offensive I found that kind of language and expected me to react. I felt my face getting hot, and, I suppose, red with embarrassment and anger, but I maintained a dignified silence. Then he pushed back his chair.

Having made me the bad guy, he planned to leave now? "Wait just one minute, Clay. I was told that you wanted to sell the market and retire. That's what …"

He jumped up and interrupted me, "Yeah. I do, but not at that price." His voice had an edge I hadn't heard before and I realized, with a pang how seriously I had wounded him. "That's it, Hugh, so I'll go about my business." He turned, stumbled over the bag of guns before he picked it up and stalked away down the hall.

I jumped up, scaring a yelp out of Buck, and called, "Clay, wait. I want to …" miffed that he wouldn't give me a chance to justify my action.

Hugh held me back, shook his head and, closer to the hall door than I, followed Clay. I could hear them talking but not what they said.

Muddled with embarrassment, regret and shreds of resentment, I plopped down in a chair astounded at the emotion of Clay's reaction. I sat, feeling limp and discouraged. I couldn't make sense of how it had fallen apart.

I felt Buck's chin on my knee. I was not surprised that Buck stayed with me. More than once I swore that he could sense my need for comfort and now he pushed his entire snout into my lap. Idly I stroked the dark curls, and decided that *Clay* had over-reacted, but *I* had messed up.

Chapter 37

Hugh came back, sat down and finished his Coke without saying anything. I looked at him, but he seemed engrossed in the contents of the bottle. The tension around his eyes, the tightness of his lips indicated that he was perturbed. Mad at me probably because I handled the situation with Clay so crudely.

Being a fool, I rushed in and said, "You appeared at a propitious time this afternoon. I hadn't expected you so early."

His eyes on the bottle, which he rotated between his hands without looking at me, he said, "No."

No explanation; just 'no'.

Frustrated and still smarting from my blunder with Clay, I asked, "Shoot, Hugh. How was I to know Clay would take on so? All I did was to tell him what I found and …" I stopped, trying to remember my exact words. Uncomfortable because I was wrong, I admitted, out loud, "Okay. I did word it badly, but …" I rubbed my forehead to erase the throbbing which had commenced and sighed, "I fouled up, didn't I?" Buck whined softly, chin on my knee.

Hugh lifted the bottle and drank it empty, then rose and took it to the sink.

He turned back to me and said, "You can apologize to Clay later. He needs time to recover." Hugh, the peace maker, like everybody else, expected me to do all the apologizing, naturally.

Emotionally, I felt as if I'd been beaten with a stick. Even if I had handled it poorly, the fact remained that if Clay had told me right away what happened with Schultz, we could have avoided all the rest.

I watched as Hugh rinsed the Coke bottle and set it on the counter to dry. I noticed lines between his eyebrows, his shoulders sagged, as if he were totally weary.

Worried now, I yielded, "I'll apologize to Clay for my lack of tact, for sure, the next time I'm in town."

He leaned back against the counter nodded and said, "That would be good, the right thing to do. But it was more than tactless. It was cold and insensitive." Heartless words from the man to whom I'd recently given my heart. They hurt as well as compounded my shame.

Eyes riveted on me, he continued, "You could have *asked* whether he was involved with Schultz. Instead, you accused him of trying to burn down The Manse."

He had never spoken to me so sharply in his entire life. I already felt chastened, but I wasn't entirely to blame. Clay had scoured me thoroughly and unfairly, so I defended myself.

"That's a low blow," I said and confessed, "I merely quoted Schultz." I paused and admitted, "I'm not feeling pleased with myself right now. What I'd like here is a bit of warm fuzzy."

Hugh's eyes pierced too deeply into me. I felt vulnerable and emotionally naked. He walked back towards where I sat at the table and sat down, facing me.

"Would it work if I reminded you that I love you and came to ask you again to marry me?" he said, but there was no doubt that, under his tender words, he was scolding me.

That remark plus the tone of voice undid me. I couldn't switch from his severe criticism so abruptly. I gasped, too surprised to answer. I'd forgotten that Hugh was waiting for me to decide.

"Minty?" he asked again, his tone so gentle now I could have wept.

My hands flew up to cover my mouth. "I ... eh," I stammered, "I don't ... I'm confused ..." I couldn't look at him, but answered truthfully, "I don't know what to say." Dropping my hands to the table.

His attention fully on me now, he spoke quietly, "You could just say 'Yes'." He paused, eyes soft, his head inclined toward me before he asked, "Shug?" He covered my hands with his.

My hands were cold with tension, my mind a maelstrom of emotion.

"You've had three full months to *think*." Although he had not raised his voice, it held a chill that disturbed me. I wanted to tell him how much I loved him, but, after a minute, he, released my hands, rose and announced, "We've run out of time now." He glanced down at me. "How long did you expect me to wait?" The lines in his forehead made him look despondent as he continued staring.

I felt numb and licked my lips as fear enveloped me.

Then Hugh said, "I left the clinic early to tell you that I've been accepted to work with the International Medical Mission. I have to leave for Kosovo in January."

As if punched in the stomach, I yelped in surprise, "What? You never said …" Had I heard right? "I can't believe you didn't tell me …" Panic rose in my throat like nausea and I began to shake.

Hugh stood staring at me and said, "I told you, quite a while ago, that I was considering several jobs out of the country. I *told* you that I couldn't stay here in Whitman, if you wouldn't marry me."

I nodded, but still couldn't comprehend what he meant. "You're actually leaving Whitman?" I stammered, "But why so soon?" In disbelief, I curled my hands into fists, hugging myself.

He took an audible breath and explained, "They need me to replace someone who's leaving in January, but I have a three month orientation and language program first." I glanced up. His eyes, steady on my face, gave me no clue to his expectations.

Too stunned to protest, I sat, dismay probably showing on my face, as I tried to make sense of what he was saying.

Calmly, Hugh continued, "I asked if I could bring my wife and described your management skills, your energy and experiences abroad. They would be delighted to have you, too. There are a variety of jobs that need your help." He paused and his eyes narrowed with humor as he coaxed me, "Come on, shug. How about taking the plunge and joining me on this adventure? The chance of a lifetime — two years in romantic Kosovo."

My bones turned to jelly and my thoughts were scrambled eggs with annoyance at his attempt at humor. I was trembling and my heart fluttered within my chest. I swallowed, still not believing that he'd just leave me. I glanced at him and knew that, beneath the surface smile, he was serious. This was too much for me to digest.

Then I remembered: "You don't have to go until January? That gives me more time …" I was desperate for something to cling to. I braced myself against the table and burst out, "Mother of pearl, I can't just up and leave. What about Buck and Cleo? The goats? Philabelle? I can't just … "

"They can all be provided for," he said. I shook my head violently and he countered, "Jesse and Mike would love to have Buck." He paused before speaking. "None of those are insoluble problems."

I closed my eyes, clasping my hands in front of me, gestured as if pleading.

Abruptly Hugh sat down and took both my hands again, holding them close to his chest and said, "We don't have time to quibble, Minty. There's a lot of paper work, physical exam to get you vetted — passport, stuff like that to get in the mail. Stat!"

I couldn't believe how calmly he told me that he was leaving me in January. By now my heart raced so fast I felt suffocated. My lips were dry down to my tonsils.

Using all his power to sway me, he coaxed, "Come on, shug. It's a novel place for a honeymoon," and smiled at me.

"Stop that twitchy smile; you know it annoys me," I said, still not fully grasping what he was proposing.

"I wasn't conscious of a variation in my smile. It doesn't mean much." Hugh squeezed my hands and wiggled his chair closer, apparently, to win me with a display of affection.

"I've known you long enough to …" I started to speak.

He leaned over and murmured in my ear, "It's better when we know each other in the Biblical sense, darlin'."

His frivolity when I felt coerced caused a sudden fury. I pushed at him and said, "You're being unfair. Why is it fair for men to accuse women of using sex maliciously but it's all right for them." I felt faint, close to tears, but refused to cry. Women who used tears as an offensive weapon were contemptuous. I was not some easy twit.

Hugh leaned away, shoved back his chair and said, "You're right. My apologies. I was taking advantage." He looked abashed, all humor absent, his voice serious and added, "Nevertheless, Minty, as I said, it is yes or no time now. It would be a wonderful adventure for us together as husband and wife." His eyes on me held that cocker spaniel look — Billy's dying face pleading … I blinked frantically, trying to concentrate and heard Hugh saying something "… me. We have to act fast."

Hugh rose, leaned down to kiss the top of my head and left me, confused and wondering what had taken place.

Chapter 38

Another sleepless night after Hugh dropped his medical mission on me. Fortunately, I thought, he wasn't leaving until January. Too busy to give voice to my situation, I never got around to telling him about Schultz's threat and now it seemed inconsequential.

To say that the next few days were miserable was like saying a tsunami was a big wave. I felt so discouraged with my life that only will power enabled me to function. As a last gasp of summer, the week reverted to hot and humid. Compounding my dismay at Hugh's departure, I realized that Labor Day was less than a week away.

Until Billy's death, we had held a backyard party every Labor Day. For our circle of friends, this had become a tradition — the last big outdoor event of the year. Personal disappointment was insufficient cause to break such a tradition, so I had revived it the previous September.

Preparations for that took precedence over everything else and I sat at the computer to make lists of priorities and of groceries: that presented a problem. Dutifully, I printed them off and considered my position. Hugh's admonition that I should apologize to Clay echoed in my head.

All righty, I thought. I'd go do my shopping and apologize to Clay, too. While in town, I could return Elliott's files to Lynn. There was no point in continuing *that* project — if Clay was right — and I believed his explanation despite his hurtful attitude. Without Nourikian's support, Schultz's conspiracy collapsed, along with my momentum for pursuing it. At least temporarily, I believed the Manse was safe.

Because of the heat, I wore the flamboyant muumuu, smiling at the irony that Clay always commented on its colors.

Then gathering up all the files, I lugged the boxes out to the old Volvo and drove into town. On the way, I rehearsed my apology to Clay. By the time I parked in front of the market, I was confident and almost eager to speak my piece.

The bell tinkled cheerily as I opened the door and stepped inside. Fortunately the place was empty. Clay was probably in the back so I helloed to let him know I was there. When he came in, I smiled my best smile and greeted him.

"Hey, Clay. I'm glad to see you."

Poker faced, he said, "What do you want?" his voice chilled me, but I plunged ahead.

"I've come to apologize for my poorly worded anxiety about your involvement with Schultz et al." I schooled my voice to sound remorseful.

Without changing expression, he said, "At no time have I been *involved* with Schultz. I thought I had made that quite clear." He displayed no emotion whatsoever in either his voice or his face, which shook me.

"Well, yes, and I believe your explanation. I just wish you had told me right away. We've been friends all our …"

"Don't give me that crap. I was *your* friend, but I don't know what you think you were," he growled. This was not going the way I expected. I still hadn't had a chance to really apologize.

Quickly, I said again, "You're right. I didn't act like a …"

"If you have a grocery list, leave it and I'll have it delivered." He wasn't going to give an inch, but I'd try again.

Truly frazzled, I said, "Clay, I'm sincerely trying to apologize for my sus…"

"I'm not in the mood to ease your conscience. If you need groceries, please conduct your business. I have work to do."

"But I want to …" This was not fair. I'd made the effort, admitted my fault and he wouldn't listen.

Clay leaned towards me with both hands on the counter. He stared into my eyes and said forcefully, "Don't even ask me to forgive you for believing I'd *ever* put Miss Philabelle's life in jeopardy." He straightened up and added, "Now, either conduct business or leave me in peace." He turned away, as if to go in the back, but the bell tinkled again and Joe Russo came in.

"Hey there, Minty, Clay." He looked at each of us and added, "Something wrong? I've never seen a gloomier pair of faces. War been declared or something?"

As calmly as possible, I said, "I came in to apologize to Clay, but he …"

"What can I do for you, Joe?" Clay was still frowning, his voice tense.

Joe backed off, holding up both hands. "I don't want to get between you two if you're at war." He looked embarrassed, but I was the one blushing red hot with equal parts bewilderment and anger.

"She's just leaving. Aren't you?" Clay said and stared at me with venom in his eyes. Totally discomposed, I stood there, blinking, not knowing what to do.

"Good bye, *Minty*," Clay said coldly, and without conscious thought, I opened the door and, like a beaten dog, left. Back in my car, I sat for several minutes. I'm not a weepy woman and part of me wanted to cry with hurt feelings and sorrow. The other half wanted to go back and punch Clay in the nose and make him listen.

Wishing I had brought Buck, I sat trying to bring coherence to my muddled feelings. I wiped my eyes, aware that they had been watering a lot lately. Clay's reaction was so unexpected that I figured I must have approached him badly — again. My mind was blank. Lately, it seemed like lots of things weren't working well for me. I had planned to drop off the files at Lynn's, but then, hot, sweaty and dizzy, I gathered what wits I had left, I started the car and drove for home.

Chapter 39

The temperature continued hot that week and Clay's obstinacy left me feeling lonely. When I remembered that my car was full of Elliott's files, I decided to return them. I needed new bulbs for the Chinese lanterns anyway. Before I got in the car, I realized that, although I had fed, watered the goats and cleaned their run, I had not taken the time to play with them. Most of their run was in the sun, and it occurred to me that Edna might enjoy being tethered out in a shady plot full of tasty weeds. I tied her rope securely to a strong stake in the pasture. It was long enough that she could cover a large area. She pranced along cheerfully as I led her away from the pen. Meantime, Claude commenced a pitiful bleating, which he continued until I returned.

"Are you telling me that you want to go browse in the brush, too? You think you're old enough now?" I scratched his head, tugged on his ears, all of which he enjoyed. When I stood up, I looked at him differently and decided that he had grown enough in the past two months. Why not give him an outing, too? So I tied him to the same stake so he was within talking distance of Edna. Buck had assisted me by running back and forth with us and, knowing his propensity to tease, I brought him back into the kitchen.

"I know you, my lad. You'd drive Edna and Claude crazy if I left you out doors with them."

He sat on his haunches meeting my eyes, trying to convince me that I had hurt his feelings by my callous admonitions. Animals!

Twenty minutes later, at Lynn's she greeted me cordially and offered me iced tea, I accepted it as therapeutic — until I saw Hugh sitting out on the sun porch. His presence usually warmed my heart. Today, however, a strange uneasiness swept over me.

"I'm returning Elliott's files," I managed to tell Lynn. "Where do you want the boxes?"

"Oh. Just dump them down there." Lynn flipped a hand of indifference toward the bottom of the stairs. "We're taking a break. I have martini makings, too, and the sun's over the yard arm, whatever that means." She sounded cheerful.

"The sun's not over the yard arm. But you've already had one, obviously." I had sniffed alcohol on her breath, which annoyed me.

"A mid afternoon aperitif then. Do you object?" She tilted her head and smiled sweetly.

"It's not my place to object, Lynn. I was just making an observation." I tried to keep my voice neutral. I'd had enough anger directed at me lately. I didn't want any more. I just put down the boxes and said, "The files have been very helpful. I found evidence of hanky panky on Schultz's part, which probably involved Morton. It confirms my contention that there was a conspiracy to burn down the Manse." With Hugh so near, I couldn't bear to mention Clay. Besides, at that point, I was no longer sure that I understood what was going on.

Lynn gestured toward the sun-room and said, "Go sit. I'll get you a drink." And went into the kitchen.

Hugh rose, of course, when I entered the sun-room. The closed plantation blinds kept out the sun fortunately. The steamy jungle-like ambiance, created by the enormous banana tree in one corner plus all the other house plants, felt appropriate for my mood.

As soon as we sat down, Hugh asked, "Have you apologized to Clay yet?"

I said, "Yes." I resented being put on the defensive, so I refused to say more.

"Good. I'm sure you feel better." Hugh was hard to endure when he was sanctimonious. Based on his tone of voice, he had expected me to report back to him, like a chastened child having done its duty. But, I gave him the benefit of my doubt and decided he was in a doctor/patient mode.

Lynn returned just then with my iced tea and her martini. Hugh stood up and said he'd see us later and Lynn walked him out.

As soon as Lynn sat down, she introduced the Manse situation into the conversation. "I think you're making a fool of yourself with this wild talk of a conspiracy. Nobody tried to burn down the Manse. The arson people said it was an accident — something about oily rags under the back steps or something." I blinked at what felt like an attack, but Lynn was on a roll.

"Philabelle was delighted with Gus's reaction at the tour. He knows antiques and will do more than you can to preserve it."

"That's a mean thing to say," I had no intention of telling her that I'd abandoned the project nor about the situation with Clay.

"I wasn't being mean." she shrugged. "Just making an observation," sarcastically tossing my earlier words back at me. There were times when the flame of my anger at Lynn's perfidy flared up, despite my having forgiven her. Nevertheless, I stifled it successfully.

"It doesn't change the fact that Morton and Schultz described it as a fire hazard." After Clay's reaction to my apology, my patience with dramatics was exhausted.

"And that proves what? Casual words prove that they set it on fire?" Lynn laughed. "Considering your superior intelligence, you're totally wrong on who did what." She laughed again and took a drink of her martini. "Gus was surely impressed with what he saw on the tour. I can't see him involved in burning it down."

"I agree with that, but he certainly coveted some of the antiques." I preferred staying off the subject of the Manse.

The phone rang then and I sipped the iced tea while Lynn went to answer it. It was disconcerting that even Philabelle and Sarah, although they said they supported my efforts, both gave credence to Nourikian's plans for regenerating Whitman. If Lynn had given it any thought, I supposed she did, too. Based on Clay's explanation, it was possible that I was off-base about Nourikian. But not about Schultz; William had made it clear that he was a liar if not a criminal. But I had *believed* Schultz! I lamented my foolishness, but privately.

Lynn returned, sat down and said, "Hugh's coming back." She looked me in the eyes, a calculating glitter in hers. "Are you going to marry him or do you hope to just continue your affair?"

Shocked at her bluntness, I opened my mouth, but before I could think of what to say, she added, "Because if you're not, I may consider it myself. I like Hugh. He's the only real *gentleman* I know and he's lonely." She put her glass on the side table and laughed, "Don't look so surprised. I know he asked you to go to Kosovo with him." She leaned forward, a smile on her face – a smile that wrinkled her nose and that I believed genuine. "Come on, sister." She tilted her head, smiling enigmatically. "Talk to me."

My hands were cold and my throat felt fluttery with fear. To my dismay, I floundered like a defenseless schoolgirl, but with my dander up, I said, "I don't think my relationship with Hugh is any of your business." Quaking inside, I added, trying to shock her, "Unless you are seriously considering marrying him? Then, as a good sister, I'd back off, of course." Lying seemed to be coming easier to me lately.

Lynn laughed again in genuine amusement and said, "That rattled you a bit, didn't it?"

I didn't answer, because she *had* rattled me. Unlike me, Lynn, with no responsibilities, was capable of dropping everything and whirling off to Kosovo. Anxiety about Hugh's opinion of me was a new worry. I had definitely angered him by my tactlessness with Clay. My hands were so sweaty that I had to put the glass down and swallow back my fear.

Lynn leaned towards me, her eyes narrowed as she stared into mine, and said, "Listen, Minty, Hugh's too good to let him get away." She sounded serious, but then she sat upright and added flippantly. "He's very attractive and he might find some appealing Central European girl eager to latch on to him. Who knows?"

Really angry now, I made some non-committal remark, but internally I was trembling. Hugh was coming here *again* and I hated the idea of leaving Lynn alone with him. Weak and sick with insecurity, compounded by Clay's rejection of my apology, I couldn't cope with watching Hugh react to my sister's seductive charm. Reminding myself that I trusted him, that he was not like Billy, didn't help. Hastily, I took my leave with Lynn's words about another woman runnning like a broken record in my head.

Too upset to drive, again I had to sit in my car to regain my composure.

At first I thought Lynn had been teasing about marrying Hugh; then she seemed serious about letting him get away. From me or from her? Immediately after that, she joked again. I didn't know how to react to her rapid mood changes. But I had refused to give her the satisfaction of observing my distress. The truth was that I had panicked at the thought of witnessing Hugh falling under her spell.

Quelling the urge to cry like a baby, I automatically thought of my old friend, Sarah, and headed for her house instead of home.

Chapter 40

As I pulled into Sarah's driveway, I had a moment of anxiety that she might not be home. When I rang the bell, tried the door, and called, "Hey, Girl, it's me." her answering "Come in, hon," almost brought tears to my eyes.

We met in her hall and I opened my arms for a hug and said, "You are an angel from heaven, Sarah. I need your support."

"You down in the dumps, Minty? Life full of shmutz?" Her Brooklyn Yiddish, so wonderfully Sarah, sounded like music.

An ironic spurt of laughter escaped me and I said, "It's more a situation of nothing going right."

She interrupted, "You want I should help you with something?"

I snorted and said, "You have an extra shoulder I could weep on?" Of all my friends, at the moment, Sarah was the only one I could trust to listen objectively. When she asked if I wanted something to drink, I said, "You're a true blessing, which justifies a drink — symbolically a spiritual drink of spirits." My attempts at humor struck me as weird, but so did my life at that moment.

"How about a glass of white wine or something more robust? Does the occasion warrant a beer?" She rallied to my need. "Let's sit in the kitchen. It always feels so down-home and comfy."

In the brighter light of the kitchen, I did a double take at my friend. "You've cut your hair!" Sarah had a lovely heavy head of dark hair, naturally sprayed with silver just above each ear.

Sarah fluffed up what was left of it. "A Lynn wannabe!" she added, laughing. "I got tired of washing and drying all that long hair." She produced two bottles of beer. "Mel'll gripe for an hour when he gets home," she shrugged. "The things we do for men."

"Yes. Billy carried on the first time I cut mine short, too. Anyway, it's very becoming." I picked up my glass and gulped some, chagrined that, like everybody else, Sarah mimicked the Lovely Lynn. "You look very chic," I said. Nobody ever copied my hairstyles.

Sarah smiled and dipped her head. Then, being the direct person she is, said, "So, who's been giving you trouble?"

I took a deep breath and exhaled before I spoke, "First, last week I inadvertently hurt Clay's feelings." Sarah made a face of disbelief. "Actually, it's worse than that." Having decided to tell her the worst, I took another gulp of the strengthening beer and began explaining, as briefly as possible, how I came to believe Clay had been involved with Schultz and ended up admitting, "Based on Schultz's information, I gave Clay the impression that I was accusing him of setting the Manse fire." My throat dry now, I paused to sip my drink.

Sarah, who had listened attentively as always, nodded as she got the picture, grimaced and said, "That must have gone over like a lead balloon."

I nodded and continued on about Hugh's entry, the argument Clay and I had and how he stormed out. "He was really, really mad and Hugh rightly told me to apologize to him. That was just before he dropped his bomb of leaving in January for Kosovo." Distressed still about that, I stopped, unsure how to continue.

"Maybe it would have been better not to get involved in whatever Schultz is up to," Sarah said. My face must have expressed my distress because she quickly added, "I mean, if Philabelle's going to donate the Manse –." She shrugged her shoulders. "You tend to jump into things too quickly. You don't want to become a yenta. Not that you ..."

"Are you implying that what happens to the Manse is not my business? You think I'm an interfering busybody?" I couldn't believe *Sarah* misunderstand my intentions.

"Gosh, Minty, I'm sorry if I hurt your feelings. I'm concerned that your worry hurts *you* and accomplishes nothing." When she softened her voice that way, I relaxed. After all, she had eagerly offered her shoulder for me to cry on.

Relying on our long friendship, I said, "Tell me the truth, Sarah. Do you think I'm bossy? Lynn said I was. Do you think I interfere in people's lives? I *do* care about them, you know, and it's hard to just sit by and let ..."

"Of course you care. That's why the temptation is to be ... I'd call it too ... too helpful." The affection in her eyes soothed my hurt feelings. I nodded permission for her to continue. "You have a real talent for managing things, for getting things done. You're the force that makes things work for all the Whitman celebrations and activities." Sarah finished her beer, her eyes holding my attention. "Maybe, with all the projects that Gus talked about for Whitman, you could work *with* him." An wicked grin creased her face, "That way you could keep him in line if he went too far."

Surprised and amused at her cleverness, I could only say, "Wow! You're suggesting that if I can't beat 'em, I should join 'em?" Sarah never bored me. She was so creative in her thinking and her wild ideas were often as sensible as they were wild.

"Nothing ventured, nothing gained," she chuckled. "Speaking of Gus, I saw him and Lynn having dinner in the Diner the other evening." She wiggled her eyebrows, snickering.

"That's my sister all right. Any single man in the county is fair game for her. Would you believe that she threatened to marry Hugh, if I didn't?" I laughed in an effort to assuage my apprehension. "What really bothers me is that Clay's so mad he wouldn't accept my apology. And Hugh's going to Kosovo is a blow," I shrugged with helplessness.

My buddy leaned towards me, her eyes full of sympathy and said, "I hope you're going with him." Sarah's very appealing when she fosters romance.

Fidgeting with my glass, to avoid an answer, I said, "I've got the animals, the farm to think of. Besides, it's cold there in the winter." I tried not to sound whiney and not put out when I rebutted by asking her, "Aren't you being a yenta now?"

I apparently failed, because Sarah laughed and said, "No. I'm being a matchmaker." Then she put her hand on my arm. "The Keens would take care of the animals and the farm and you can buy warm clothes."

She squinted her eyes and leaned closer. A frown puckered her forehead and her voice was serious when she said, "He's a good man, attractive and he adores you, Minty." She looked at me out of the corners of her eyes, head tilted. "You're afraid to marry him, aren't you?"

"Why does everybody keep urging me to get married, to defer to other people? Philabelle made me apologize to Lynn; Hugh told me to apologize to Clay, who cut me off and told me to clear out of his market." I heard myself ranting and saw the hurt surprise on my friend's face.

"Oh, Sarah. I'm didn't mean to dump all that on you, but I get so frustrated." I shook my head, staring down into my empty glass, ashamed and blinking to keep back tears.

Sarah's voice was gentle when she asked, "What's really scaring you?" She paused, as I struggled to regain my composure. I disliked temperamental displays of emotion. Uneasy, I shifted in the chair and gazed out the window.

Sarah continued. "Lately, I get the feeling that you're angry, suspicious, as if something's ..."

"I'm *not* angry or suspicious. It just seems as if everybody finds fault with me. Even Philabelle, who's usually the soul of kindness, was irritated because I refuse to pander to Gus Nourikian, like the rest of you. Then the disaster with Clay." Surprised and ashamed of my annoyance with Sarah, of all people, I modified my tone of voice, when I added, "Then Hugh comes all over like a crusader and he expects me to uproot my whole life to go with him."

Sarah spoke, softly, "Minty, we've been buddies all our adult lives and that friendship is too important to me to take offense." She paused before she met my eyes and said, "I just don't understand *what* keeps you from marrying Hugh. Something you're afraid to talk about?" She almost sounded teary.

I felt like crying, too, because her voice quivered with tenderness and concern. Then she said, "You do know that I'm totally on your side, don't you?"

She had touched something that triggered my recurring nightmare: Billy's death. Feeling as if I might collapse into a puddle of misery, I wiped my eyes surreptitiously and said, "I'm sorry, Sarah, I don't know ..."

"I feel that your hurting and I don't know how to help you," Sarah's concern nearly tipped me over into the weeps, but I sniffled and blinked rapidly.

I patted her hand. "Your friendship always helps me, Sarah. What I need to do now is concentrate on my big end-of-the-season bash." I tried to smile and rose to leave. Sarah rose, too, and we shocked ourselves by an unaccustomed hug.

On the drive home, my heart was heavy because I had come close to yelling like a harridan at my dear friend. Trying to squelch self-pity, and think positively, I had the crazy idea of calling up Billy's ghost. I didn't have to worry about hurting his feelings.

Chapter 41

Still not liking myself much, I heard the phone ringing as I neared the kitchen door. I rushed inside, picked up the phone and held the door open for Buck to go out.

It was Howard. Full of my problems, I asked, "What's wrong?"

"Nothing's wrong, Minty. I'm sorry if I startled you."

I tried to laugh. "It's been a busy and troubling day. I guess that was a nervous reaction." Breathing slowly and regularly to induce composure, I swallowed and asked, "How's everything with the Nesbitt family?"

"Couldn't be better. Adrienne loves her pre-school and she's actually learning to read. Last night she was sitting in the big chair with me and asked me if I knew that one hundred apples was a gazillion more than four apples. She's not yet five. I was surprised."

We both chuckled. "I'm not. She's a smart little girl. All she needs is exposure to knowledge and like a little sponge she absorbs it. What's Hammie doing?"

Howard said his day-care was working out very well. He, too, was learning to recognize letters and numbers and sing songs in Spanish. We discussed the advantage of teaching a second language to youngsters – how much more quickly they learn. It was a pleasure to talk about something fun for a change.

Then Howard said, "I had a purpose in calling you. We'd like you to be our guest for a few days around September fourteenth. That's a Saturday and the important occasion is Rachel's first public performance with Tony at a dance recital."

My mouth dropped open, stunned that, apparently, Howard approved of Rachel's fantasy of a dance career. I didn't know which of several questions I should ask first.

"Minty? Are you still there?"

"Oh yes. Yes, I'm just sort of taken aback. A dance recital so soon? It's only been a couple of months." I was flabbergasted and a bit annoyed that my daughter hadn't called.

"It is, but Rachel has a genuine talent for ballroom dancing. She started on the tango, already, and picked it up in no time. When Tony realized that, he added the waltz, foxtrot and a couple more Latin dances." Howard sounded pleased.

Almost speechless, I had to ask, "Why didn't Rachel invite me herself?"

He hesitated a bit, but answered, "I suspect that she's afraid you'd disapprove, but I know she wants you there for her premier performance."

"Yes, I guess so, but I never knew …" I frowned thinking back. "She never showed any interest in dancing as a child. She was always the scholar in the family: got top grades, took A.P. courses and you know how successful she was as an attorney."

"Yeah, I know. But this has opened an entirely new vista for her. She's so happy and so graceful. I know you'll be as proud as I am." He sounded delighted, which is good, I guess — but the strain this would place on their marriage concerned me.

I heard Buck 'Woof' and scratch at the kitchen door. I let him in, where he rushed to snuffle up water from his bowl.

I still couldn't adjust to this change in my daughter, but I stifled the feeling of resentment. "I wonder why she never showed any interest in it before. Dancing is such a … not wild, but so different from law." I leaned against the wall and tried to understand how Rachel could conceal this urge to dance from me all these years.

Meantime, Howard continued. "She's more like your father than any of us expected, I think. He was very extroverted and …"

"He was a diplomat, a very serious and responsible man. Dancing to him was part of his duty at social functions. I never saw anything flighty like that in him." I was dazed and tired.

"Flighty's not the word I'd use for dancing. It has elements of freedom, of movement, of flowing. I think it releases the constraints that are characteristic of much of society." I nodded at his perspective on dance, which boggled my mind. Distracting me, Buck bumped his nose against my thigh, his muzzle sopping wet.

"What do you think, Minty?" Howard asked.

"About what?" I made a face; I hadn't been listening as I attempted to brush water off my slacks.

"About my theory that your father joined the State Department to escape the limitations of small town life. It was your mother who insisted on returning to Whitman. As a young man, your father worked hard to escape into a broader world and I think there is that spirit, that urge toward physical release of limitations, that inspires Rachel."

For over half an hour we hashed over this desire to fly rather than walk. Meantime, I had managed to pull over a chair and admitted to myself that I understood, reminded immediately and, with heart burn, of Hugh and his mission. Was he looking to fly, too? I knew that this time I had to make a decision. Hugh wouldn't wait forever, but at least I have until January, I thought.

When Howard and I hung up, I sagged in the chair and recalled the Rachel that I knew: serious, determined and focused, almost sedate. Then I realized that my son-in-law had just gently, but positively, informed me that I didn't know my daughter at all.

He had been diplomatic and I hadn't taken offense. I respected and liked Howard too much for pettiness. It did, however, confirm my suspicion of unplumbed depths in him. How could I have miscalculated both of them so badly.

The sting that wounded me was that I'd been mistaken about so many things lately. Philabelle said that I lacked insight into Lynn's problems. When I had told Hugh, he agreed.

Maybe, I should have trusted Clay's loyalty, not assumed guilt. I found it hard to believe that I was so wrong about people that I knew so well. Everybody had always admired my good judgment, my acuity. Now I was even hearing ghosts and talking to them.

*   *   *

I sat in the kitchen trying to remember what I needed to do next. This was Friday. The barbecue three days away! My mind felt soggy with conflicting emotions: Clay, Hugh, Lynn and now Howard all jumping on me with both feet!

In the middle of my debauch of self-pity, the phone rang again. I was tempted to let it ring forever. Fortunately, my curiosity wouldn't let me. It was Jesse, the comfort of my life.

"How are things with y'all, sweetie?" I asked.

"We're just fine, but I could tell something is bothering you when you answered," he said, inviting me to dump my burden on him. There was only one that I was inclined to talk about.

"Jesse, y'all see Rachel and Howard now and then don't you?"

"Yes, as a matter of fact I watched Rachel and Tony rehearsing the other day. She's good. You'd be proud."

"I don't know about that," I said, needing reassurance.

"Why? You afraid she's not good enough for competition?" Sometimes he's clairvoyant and I yielded to weakness.

"It's that Tony I'm worried about. According to Rachel, he walks – or should I say 'dances' on water."

"Come on, Mom. You're not worried about Rachel falling in love with Tony, are you?" he laughed and added, "We've known him for years. He's one of us."

Surprised, my mouth fell open wide enough to let flies in. Highly amused, Jesse assured me that the only thing Rachel and Tony were interested in was dancing. Mightily relieved and feeling foolish, I managed to continue our conversation. Jesse had called to see if I needed help with the party. They could come earlier as Philabelle had invited them to stay at the Manse again.

I thanked him, but declined. I couldn't cope with company and we hung up. His news gave me the boost I needed to complete my list.

Buck, however, normally a quiet fellow, barked at the door as if the hounds of the Baskervilles were after him. Impatiently, I opened it.

"What's the matter with you? Come in and hush that noise." I turned to check his water bowl. Half in the kitchen and half on the stoop, the dog stood in the doorway, alternating woofs with staccato barks. Not in the mood for temperament, nevertheless, I felt uneasy.

"Either come in or go out, Buck."

On second thought, his unusual behavior disturbed me. "What?" I asked, staring into his dark eyes. The intensity of his voice riveted my attention. "Is something wrong?" He woofed and backed out, turned to look at me and woofed again.

Oh God! More trouble. Buck grabbed my shirttail in his teeth and pulled with such strength that I was really frightened. Not Schultz again, was my first thought. I hastened off the stoop, down the steps before I remembered the goats.

They were gone! I gasped with dismay. Buck sat on his haunches as if looking to me for direction. "Come on," I shouted and I ran across the yard to where I had staked them out. The rope was gone and the stake pulled loose from the ground. My heart racing with anxiety and annoyance at my carelessness, I panicked.

Maybe Buck could track them. "We've got to find them, Buck." I looked around for something with their scent and dragged Buck by the collar back to the run. I pushed his nose into the hay.

"Sniff up their scent, Buck. Sniff, boy!" I knelt down in front of him, sniffing a handful of hay to show him. "Smell them? We've got to find them, Buck.

With Buck close by, I stalked out into the open to check the entire area. Calling their names, I hiked out further and scanned the empty meadow, hoping that Edna's head would be visible over the foliage.

Buck headed towards the pasture Billy had been plowing. Don't go there, I silently willed. Buck, however, checked it out and returned to where I stood paralyzed with guilt.

As far as I could see, in all directions, from the Keene's place on the north to my other neighbor behind my property, no sign of the goats. Buck sniffed here and there, but not on a specific scent.

Frantic now, I didn't know what to do. Fear and anger at myself rose in the back of my throat. Neither Edna nor Claude had any notion of cars or what happened outside their circumscribed little world.

I trotted back to the house, into the kitchen, nearly letting the door slam in Buck's face, and dialed the Keene's number.

"Hey, Pat. It's Minty. My goats have gotten out …" I was panting. "… run away somewhere and …" I took a breath. "I wondered if y'all had seen them?"

I wiped my palms on my skirt while I waited, trying to stay calm. I heard her asking John and his response that he'd check and call me back.

I thanked her and hung up. Feeling helpless and stupid, I gazed out beyond the garden and tried to conjure the goats up and back safely in their run. Buck finished swilling down the water in his bowl and hovered around, obviously as nervous as I was, until the phone rang again.

It was John. "I can't see them around here. It's too dark now, but first light tomorrow, I'll get in the truck and look around for them and check all the neighbors."

I nodded and stammered, "Okay." I was grateful for his help. He added that I should call the sheriff's office to check on any reports of stray goats, which I did. No reports and nothing to buffer my anxiety about Billy's silly animals, I flogged myself. I should have used a stronger stake, something more secure. My brain felt shredded, unable to function. The loss of the goats was the perfect end to a thoroughly rotten day.

I didn't look forward to tomorrow. The way things were going, we'd have an earthquake!

Chapter 42

The heat finally broke and Sunday's weather dawned pleasant. I attended to the needs of Buck and Cleo, trying not to fret about Edna and Claude.

The next was Labor Day, however, and I was too distraught to go to church. Besides, I hadn't finished preparing for the barbecue. True to his word, Clay had already delivered the groceries, not personally as he usually did, but via his current delivery boy. Another painful blow to my tattered psyche, but that was a big job finished. I took up my list of things still to do and commenced checking on paper napkins and table clothes, silver — all the mundane chores required of an efficient hostess.

As I moved from dining room to pantry, however, my mind circled like a merry-go-round: why didn't things work for me anymore? Usually confident in my judgment in assessing people, their problems and providing solutions, now, according to Sarah, I gave off vibrations of anger and suspicion or worse.

I was not worried about Rachel any longer and Howard had implied that I misjudged her. Earlier in the week, Philabelle had insisted that I had also misjudged Gus Nourikian. Even Hugh seemed to believe that I had disrespected Clay in my effort to clarify his relationship with Schultz. I did admit to occasional bursts of anger at Lynn; her betrayal was harder to forgive than I expected. Nevertheless, my intentions always had been to support my family and friends by sharing my experiences in life in the hope that they could benefit from them.

Weary of this recycling of misery, I braced myself and refocused on preparing for the barbeque.

Several people had volunteered to bring a dish: Sarah, her mother's German potato salad, Philabelle petit fours, others desserts. I checked the fridge for the perishable items that I was providing. In the process, the phone rang. I bumped my head in my haste to answer. Rubbing the sore spot, I grabbed the phone, "Hello?"

"I'm just calling to be sure you have things under control for tomorrow." It was Lynn.

"Of course, I do. I always prepare as much ahead as feasible." I probably spoke with some irritation.

"Fine!" she barked. "I just called to see if you wanted help," and she hung up.

Great, I thought. It was not enough that she called me a fool and threatened to marry Hugh. Now she got miffed because I admitted that I'm efficient.

That entire line of thought threatened to interfere with the tasks at hand. I stalked into the dining room and inventoried the items arranged on the table ready to take out the next day. From the utility room, I dragged the tray-tables and stacked them on the stoop. Sarah and Mel had volunteered to come early to help with them and to hang the Chinese lanterns. Despite my silly temper tantrum, I knew Sarah would not fail me.

When I returned to the kitchen, I heard Lynn calling from the front door.

"Where are you, Minty?"

"In the kitchen," I yelled and wiped the sweat off my forehead. "If you'd been here ten minutes ago you could have helped with the tray-tables."

"You're certainly in a grumpy mood today. Determined to do all the hard work yourself as usual," she snapped and grabbed the folding chairs from my hand.

"I've got plenty of cause, so don't give me a hard time," I said and told her about the missing goats. I could hardly believe that she laughed.

"It isn't funny. They don't know anything about cars on the road and could get killed."

"It's funny because you're so proud of being more efficient than anybody else and you can't manage to pen in a pair of goats adequately," Lynn retorted and, before I could respond, she added, seriously, "I'm really sorry. I know you're worried. Would it help if I drove around and looked for them?"

"No." Touched by her reversal, I shook my head. "John did that yesterday, and the sheriff's on the look out, but thanks." Mollified, I asked, "How come you hang up on me then drive out here?"

"I genuinely wanted to see if you needed help for tomorrow. Also, can we sit down for a minute and talk?" She pulled out a chair and sat as if she had no intention of leaving.

I sighed, feeling pressured from all directions plus distressed over Hugh's Kosovo plans. "Would you like a Coke or something?" Manners forced me to offer.

"No, thanks. Please sit down, Minty." She patted the chair to her left. "I need to say something to you and I would like you to hear me out before you smack me up'side the head. Can you be that patient?"

This was yet another Lynn. She sounded sincere and friendly and I felt too emotionally drained to continue our sibling spat, so I sat.

"First, I want to repeat that you're a damn fool if you don't marry Hugh and go to wherever with him." I opened my mouth to protest, but she held up a hand and shook her head. "You're so busy minding other people's business, because you think you're smarter than the rest of us, that you won't admit *you* can make a mistake; not marrying Hugh would be your biggest mistake."

That knocked the breath out of me and released a torrent of anger. "Damn it! I am sick and tired of people telling me what to do and what's wrong with me. I don't go around telling ..."

"Shut up and listen to me," Lynn interrupted, frowning. I thought there were tears in her eyes, despite the sharp edge to her voice. "Believe me, Minty, telling the truth to the sister I've always admired and looked up to is not easy. But you *are* my sister and I need to say this because I want you to wise up." She softened her tone and reached a hand toward me. But I was too far away to touch. "You're loosing your credibility with all the people who mean so much to you. You're obviously impervious to the truth that you've been wrong about a lot of things."

That was too much. I started to jump up, but Lynn half rose and grabbed my arm, pushing me back in my chair. Leaning close she stared into my eyes, still clutching my arm. "It's okay to be wrong. We all are, but learn to accept it. Admit that you're wrong and leave other people free to make their own mistakes. You have to get down off your high horse and revert to the Minty we're used to, the one we love."

I'd never seen this Lynn before and I felt half way between tears of sentiment and rage, I pushed back my chair, intending to rise to my full stature and stated, "That's enough! I ..."

Lynn tightened her grip on my arm, kept me seated and barked, "Sit down and shut up. I haven't finished. About Hugh: I think you're afraid to take the risk of a second marriage. Despite having a disappointing marriage and a painful divorce, he's eager to face the future with you." She shook her finger at me. "Quit being blind to your own faults. Marry him and return to what you do best: being the perfect wife." She released my arm, her eyes and mouth opened wide as if surprise, and she said , "But you're scared. For shame, Minty! I never figured you for a coward."

With that final blow, Lynn stood up and marched out of the kitchen, leaving me sitting with *my* mouth hanging open in shock. I heard the front door slam.

Seething, I rose, shaking my fists. Then I realized that Sarah was right: I *was* angry. I was furious at my sister and had been ever since I found about that she had seduced Billy. And my friends were not much comfort.

I paced back and forth, trying to dissipate the adrenaline raging through my veins. If they found me so full of faults, maybe I'd cancel the entire barbeque on the grounds that they wouldn't want to waste their time with someone so difficult. Why should I knock myself out lugging lawn furniture around, cooking and baking, when I'm exhausted physically from shopping and cleaning, I wondered?

I stomped around the kitchen, into the hall and the living room. I couldn't stand looking at the couch where Hugh and I had yielded to our passion three days ago. Tears welled up as I remembered how much I had enjoyed our lust! Like his brother, Hugh charmed me into falling in love with him and then he came over all conservative. Now he planned to abandon me.

Abruptly, I returned to the kitchen, and nearly tripped over Buck who was following me around, the ever faithful friend. I sniffled, brushed my eyes and plopped down at the table.

Tomorrow morning, I'd call Lynn and tell her that the party was cancelled and she'd have to let everybody know.

Then I burst into tears.

Chapter 43

I spent another sleepless night, wrestling with the auguries of terror. *Tangled in the bed sheet, I was drenched in sweat despite the chill of breaking day. As the sun shot streaks of red into the last of the night sky, I found myself slogging through the weeds and brambles of the pasture, searching for Billy. The horizon melted into shades of rose, then into pink as the indigo of night faded gradually into blue. Why, when Billy's death had turned me into an emotional wreck, would I risk an encounter with his ghost? Reluctantly, my mouth formed his name. I called, "Billy, Billy, Billy."*

"I'm here to help you, Minty.".

"How can you help me? I can't seem to help myself," I whispered as if someone might overhear me talking to a ghost.

Startling me, Billy's voice had an echo-chamber sound, and I half expected him to appear before my eyes.

"You have to accept the fact that my death was a fortunate accident for you," the voice said matter of factly.

"That's a horrible thing to say. It was a ghastly experience— nothing fortunate about it!" Flushed and hot with anger despite the persistent chill, I cried out, "What haunts me is holding you in my arms while you lay dying." I rubbed my hands together as if Billy's blood still stained them.

"Face it, Minty. You were glad to be free of me — of what had become a tedious marriage."

Furious, I lashed out at him, "You can't use our marriage, however <u>tedious</u> for you, as an excuse for your disgusting behavior. You not only cheated on me, *but your whole life was a lie. You said you loved me. We had the perfect marriage, you said, and I believed every lying word. How dare you use our marriage as an excuse for your tom-catting."*

I detected anguish in his voice, *"I do love you, only you, and I meant that* you *found our marriage tedious after ..."* he made a choking sound. *"I'm trying to say that it's all right what you felt. Your being glad didn't hurt me. Don't let it torment you."*

He couldn't know how I felt and, no longer afraid of a specter, I taunted him, *"You have psychic powers or something now that you're merely a spirit?"*

"I am a spirit. But, yes, I do have an insight that, to my sorrow, I lacked when I was alive."

"Even dead, you're still lying when you accuse me of being glad that you died. What kind of a woman do you think ..." I was so enraged that I wanted to hit something – with nothing to strike. Impotently, I yelled, *"You wounded me deeply, Billy."* My jaw tightened with rage as I searched for words that would hurt him.

"You were a perfect wife for me and I know, like Johnny, I done you wrong."

"And Frankie killed Johnny," I faltered. *"But I can't kill ..."* I blinked back tears of frustration.

His voice sounded amused as it said, *"Yeah. I'm already dead. But* you *didn't kill me. Don't waste your energy feeling guilty."*

"I'm not guilty, but I am damned angry," I bellowed.

"That's guilt disguised as anger, Minty girl, because you were glad I died."

"I was not *glad,"* I stated, too hoarse to shout now.

"Hush and listen to me, please. This is not easy. I don't have time ..." His voice began to waver. *"Try to understand,"* he pleaded. I strained to hear his fading words. *"Forgive yourself, Minty. You're alive, so liiiivvvveeee ..."*

"Billy, don't go," I called. I had questions. His words, however, echoed in my ears.: *"Forgive yourself."* Then softer than swan's down, that long drawn out *"live"*.

Confused and disturbed by his accusation as much as by my own ambivalent feelings, I heard myself whimpering. I moved my legs. Shivering and wiping my damp hands on the sheet, I struggled back to awareness — until I realized that I was still in bed.

Although still shaken to the marrow in my bones, I recalled that Billy had said that I should forgive myself. I shuddered at the thought that being glad that he died was acceptable. Contemptible, I thought, sitting up. Of course, it was: Billy was Hugh's brother. I rubbed my forehead aware of an impending headache. Hugh would be disgusted if he knew.

Vaguely, I became aware of Buck pressing his body against my legs. I reached to touch his head, drew a quivering breath and exhaled, fully returned to consciousness.

"Did I wake you up?" I asked, still trembling. Buck whined softly. I was grateful to hear a normal sound, to see Cleo stretch her hind legs and yawn. She walked up within reach and, for a long time, I lay stroking them, grounding myself in reality.

When I rose, I noted that it was not quite full daylight. Clouds in a cobalt blue sky were edged with pale pink. 'Red sky in morning, sailors take warning,' I recited. My dominant recollection was that I somehow failed Billy – everybody.

Like an automaton, I followed the routine of letting Buck out, fixing breakfast for my fur friends, and filling Mr. Coffee. All the while, fragments of Billy's words returned to me: "forgive yourself." And that long drawn-out "L-i-v-*e*". From habit, when the buzzer sounded, I poured myself a cup of coffee and sat at the table to bring order to the chaos in my brain.

My encounter with Billy weighed like a burden on my shoulders, casting doubt on the validity of my emotion. Why had Billy's death always made me feel guilty. Because I felt *glad?* I shuddered at the thought.

Bewildered, I began to examine who I was. Maybe not, as I had believed, a successful, respected, hard working and beloved leader of my family and Whitman society. The words: meddlesome, interfering, lacking insight into my frailties and in judging character, given to hallucinations. The list of my sins against society – the worst being glad that Billy died – came to mind. No, *not* glad. I argued with myself.

A slight irritation rose in me. Since my family and friends found me inadequate, I *would* cancel the damned party. I'd call Lynn and tell her to do it. Let her dis-invite them! At that inopportune moment, the phone rang. Not in the mood to talk, but remembering my call to the sheriff about the goats, I answered cautiously.

"Good morning, Minty, this is Sam Warner. I'm calling to tell you that my neighbor brought Edna and Claude to our place last night! He heard them bleating out in his pasture."

I gasped, "Oh Sam." Relief washed over me like a spring breeze. "They're okay?"

"They're fine and well fed," he reassured me. "You sure must have been worried."

"I couldn't sleep last night. Thank heaven they're safe. And thank you for rescuing them."

My mood lightened. I remembered that I had too much to do before the — I stopped. Was I canceling the barbeque or not? Sam interrupted my internal debate.

"My whole family's excited about the barbeque this evening. It's the final social event until Christmas — a Whitman tradition now. So I wondered, since you're busy as a bee today, would you like me to keep Edna and Claude here for a few days? Give you a chance to catch your breath again on Tuesday? You'll have a mess to clean up and with Hugh leaving so soon and all ..." His voice wavered.

I hesitated, too discombobulated to absorb all that he said. The goats were safe and Sam and his family were enthusiastic! "Yes. Yes." I stuttered, "That would help. Thanks again, Sam. You're a true friend."

After we hung up, I exhaled with relief. A Whitman tradition, he said. I probably shouldn't cancel — and what did he say about Hugh leaving so soon?

I plopped down on a kitchen chair again and stared vacantly as I vacillated, until Buck nudged my knee with his nose. I ran my fingers through the fur on his head. Buck's affection plus the good will in Sam's voice reminded me that he and his family had indeed been friends to me for years. I sighed. As had Philabelle and Hugh. And all the others who were expecting a good time tonight.

Despite their lack of sympathy, I'd rise above my melancholy. True friends were too important to disappoint because I was in a blue funk. I'd always led our social group and I'd do it even if I died in the attempt.

"Okay, old boy, " I leaned down to rub my cheek against Buck's ragged top knot. "the party's on again." Buck made a wiffling sound. "I guess you agree." What a joy he was. I said, "We've got work to do."

Then I burst into tears again! Mother of Pearl! What was the matter with me?

Legs wobbly, I sank back down on a chair, closing my eyes and letting myself relax,

I tried to bring order out of my warring thoughts. Buck lay with his head on my foot.

First, I needed to clarify my latest encounter with Billy: ghost, hallucination, psychic anomaly, whatever it was, I had to come to terms with my feeling about his death.

Would Hugh continue to love me if he knew? Lynn had called me a coward. I needed to prove her wrong. I jumped up and began to pace the floor, Buck's eyes following me.

Visualizing the field where Billy died, I walked the length of the hall from kitchen to front door and back, dragging my feelings up from the swamp of denial. Finally, I faced the ugly truth: I *had* felt freed from the burden of Billy.

Back in the kitchen I fixed a cup of chamomile tea and sat out on the side porch. Swinging back and forth eased the process of acceptance. It also allowed the pleasures of the past – and recalled that hilarious sprawl amid the peanuts and whiskey sours. That happy time convinced me that I would have to reveal my shame to Hugh.

"Buck, I've prided myself on following the edict of old Polonius: 'this above all to thine own self be true.' I couldn't disregard the opinion of others, however, gently or cruelly expressed. My friends were admonishing me to be true to myself, to get off my high horse."

Buck woofed, in agreement, I decided. Closing my eyes, I forced myself to recollect a series of my meanness toward people – the people who were my treasured friends.

I had hurt Clay when I failed to trust our friendship. Although I was courteous to Philabelle, secretly I assumed that she was incapable of judging Gus Nourikian's character. I vowed to work at acknowledging her wisdom. I might just learn something from her.

Practical and faithful Sarah suggested that I work with Gus. That idea presented a possibility for the future. That left my sister Lynn: she'd made foolish decisions in her life – like sleeping with my husband. But my hasty judgments and my lack of trust were not the wisest choices I'd made, either. I saw now that they were *choices,* as was my interference with Rachel's life. I sagged in the swing and leaned back my head, heavy with the weight of my shortcomings.

Sadder but calmer, I remembered reading and loving Cervantes' Don Quixote. Now I realized that I, too, had been tilting at windmills. Also like the good Don, my logic had been faulty but my intentions were noble!

I looked at the clock, startled by how late it had gotten. Energized, I pushed myself out of the chair, I began to prepare the end of summer celebration and a welcome to autumn! I had responsibilities and I would be ready to welcome my guests that evening.

That would be the perfect time for me to tell Hugh that I was free to marry him now.

Chapter 44

About three thirty that afternoon, Mel and Sarah, with two bowls of her grandmother's potato salad, arrived. Her smile was as warm and sincere as if I had never yelled at her. We cheek kissed and I whispered, "Thank you for being my dear forgiving friend."

We put the bowls in the fridge and then Sarah and I carried out the boxes of Chinese lanterns to the side yard, while Mel strung up the electric cords which we used every year and attached the lanterns. Once they were all in place, Mel turned them on to be sure all the bulbs worked.

"Ah, isn't that lovely! Even in the day light, they're romantic," Sarah warbled. I agreed and I really did feel better. Optimistically, I convinced myself that everything would turn out all right.

Close to five o'clock, John and Pat Keene came over, bringing loaves of Pat's homemade breads for our ham sandwiches. Between the five of us, we got the chairs, a dozen tables, linens, silver, plates and bowls in order on the side lawn.

Mel set up the bar, with the help of the Keenes and Sarah, and it was ready for Joe Russo, the genial teetotaler, to take over. Lynn always prepared clues and prizes for a treasure hunt in the backyard and around the outbuildings. I had hired a high school senior, with aspirations of becoming a clown, to organize games for the youngsters.

Daylight was fading and, when Mel turned on the Chinese lanterns, nostalgia, tinged with sorrow at sullied memories, touched my heart fleetingly.

Mel had brought their grill to supplement mine, loaded them both with charcoal and started them burning. He and Hugh would be chefs.

Like lightning, flashes of previous barbeques, before Billy's death, crossed my mind. Billy had been Number One Chef with Hugh his aide. An image of Billy's ghost hanging over the night's proceedings both amused and made me shiver. Either I believed in ghosts or my mind had come unhinged — neither appealing, but I *would* live, I assured myself.

Tucking random distractions into the back of my brain, I focused on the barbeque site.

The three buffet tables, the stacks of plates and the silver caught the glow from the lanterns. A copper bowl of chrysanthemums decorated the middle of each table. The background music of the fifties and sixties from the CD player and the fragrance from the grill set the stage for the festivities.

∗   ∗   ∗

The next guests arrived and the party began. Surrounded by the chatter and laughter of all my family and friends, I felt myself healing and any fears I had about my past or my future, whatever it would be, faded in the atmosphere of good fellowship.

I welcomed each arriving group and indicated the buffet where people gathered briefly and filled their plates before separating into smaller groups. I directed the kids to the back-yard.

Then I began the rounds of clusters of friends. Lynn, devastatingly charming in a flared denim skirt, red and white checked shirt, posed gracefully beside Gus, her date for the evening They had brought Philabelle and were chatting with the Warners. Hugh wasn't with them and, glancing at the grill, I saw that he had joined Mel. I didn't have to worry about Hugh doing 'his job'.

I planned to wrangle a few private minutes alone with him sometime during the evening and, I hoped, we would clarify our situation. The direction the conversation would take, however, was shadowy.

The Warners had wandered off, so I joined Lynn's group. Philabelle greeted me with a hug and said, "I'm quite excited this evening. This afternoon, Lynn and Gus drove me out to Creek Woods to show me several apartment lay-outs. There's a lovely one with a creek view that is perfect."

"Don't commit yourself to leaving the Manse too hastily, Philabelle," I said panicky.

"Don't worry, dear. Nothing is definite. I'm just exploring." She looked happy — because she was with Lynn and Gus? And not me?

As if to counter my concern, Gus said, "Philabelle will stay in the Manse

251

until she's ready to leave. That won't be until all the red-tape of donation legalities finalize." He glanced at Lynn, who smiled her sweet smile.

Also, observant as ever, I was not surprised at the way they looked at each other. Clearly Gus was smitten with my sister and she reciprocated the feeling. I refrained from showing any resentment. As if I were jealous!

The Reverend Leon and Shirley Clover joined the group and, as I eased away, Lynn said, "I almost forgot; Clay asked me to tell you that he and Marge aren't coming. They're spending this holiday with one of their sons and family this year." This was a slap in my face that caused a nasty clinching of my stomach!

"That's a shame," Philabelle said. "They're so much a part of our group; it's not the same without them." Obviously she didn't know that I was persona non grata with Clay.

I inched away. As hostess, I wanted to greet every guest. I gazed around at the scene. Some folks sat at the tray tables scattered across the lawn and others stood while they ate. More lingered around the grill and the buffet tables dining and socializing.

I had seen William and Myra arrive and scanned the crowd to locate them. I spotted them, standing with Jesse and Mike, which alerted me. I couldn't see William's face and, to forestall trouble, I headed in that direction. Gus put his hand on my arm, however.

"Minty," he said as I met his eyes, "I wonder if, sometime in the near future, we could get together. I'd appreciate your insight into what facilities in Whitman need priority."

Gus's invitation caught me completely off guard. Still apprehensive about William with Jesse and Mike, I kept my eye on them, while I managed to thank Gus and said I'd be glad to help. When he turned to greet the Wrights, I wove my way toward my sons.

When I got closer, I saw that the back of William's neck was pink and feared the worst. That's all I need, I thought, feeling the urge to kill or at least throw something. As I approached them, Myra said something and put her hand on Mike's arm. Then all four of them burst into laughter.

I stopped in my tracks, nearly backing into Joe Russo who was talking with Rachel and Howard. The three greeted me with enthusiasm and with compliments on the set-up. I congratulated Rachel on her approaching recital. She seemed genuinely pleased with my comments.

"I'll call you next week and we'll set a date for you to visit. I hope you'll make plans to stay for a few days, Mom. It's been a long time since Fourth of July," she said. She looked especially lovely tonight, in a rose slack suit, a new hairdo and different makeup. Apparently, she had forgiven my interference.

I silently vowed to believe that this dance hobby would be good for her and the family.

I scanned the various coveys, all enjoying themselves in the reddish glow from the Chinese lanterns. The fragrance of barbecuing beef and pork, the conglomerate of cheerful voices and the rainbow colors of the women's dresses assured me that everything was going splendidly.

Now I needed to find Hugh. For the first time I dreaded that encounter. I stiffened my spine and surveyed the crowd. He stood talking with the Warners and, surprisingly, Morton and Hazel Trueblood. I wanted to make it up to Morton, I thought. He was really no more pompous than William and they're Southern gentlemen.

I concentrated on staring at Hugh and ambled in that direction, greeting other friends along the way. Finally, he glanced up and saw me. I gestured with my hand toward the kitchen and headed in that direction. In a minute, he followed.

He looked very much at home as he leaned against the counter, arms crossed on his chest and so handsome I almost cried.

"Another successful end of the season for Whitman's elite," he said.

That took the wind out of my sails; Hugh was not usually sarcastic.

"We don't consider ourselves *elite*," I said, trying to collect my thoughts, to organize what I wanted to say.

"But we *are* the elite. And you're the queen reigning over our social life," he smiled that twisted smile that I disliked. It put me on defense.

We stood without speaking for an uncomfortable second, before I said, "I've had a very difficult couple of weeks, Hugh, and have things I'd like to say to you. First, I must tell you that I've spent a lot of time coming to terms with … eh … mistakes in judgment that I might have made recently — the one obvious to you, probably, was my rudeness to Clay." I paused, intent on his reaction, but he leaned there, his face expressionless, except for that half smile.

I continued, "Various family members and friends have made me realize that, what I intended as concerned helpfulness, was taken as interference." My hands were so wet, I reached behind him for a tissue on the counter.

Then I took a deep breathe and said boldly, "More importantly, I've realized that I love you too much to let you go to Kosovo alone." My chest felt tight. I inhaled quickly and said, "I'd be honored to marry you and go … wherever." I stared at his face, seeking his eyes, but he looked down at the floor briefly. He uncrossed his arms and then looked up, licking his lips. My heart lurched.

"It's too late now, Minty." He met my eyes, but I couldn't decipher what I saw.

Surprised and dismayed, I stuttered, "But you're not going 'til January. I thought we could get married and I could go," I was pleading, — a thing I never do!

He interrupted, shaking his head, "The deadline for filing your application was last Monday." I heard anger in his voice as I tried to assimilate what his words meant.

Like a fool, I said, "*Last* Monday? I don't understand. I thought ..." I swallowed and feeling annoyed said, "Well! You didn't give me much time after dropping the bomb shell on me," I spoke abruptly, but I couldn't think straight. Panic threatened.

"For three months I've tried to persuade you to marry me. Two weeks ago, I told you that I needed an answer by Monday," Hugh pronounced, clearly blaming me for my uncertainty.

"I didn't know ... Eh ..." Desperation tightened my throat so my voice cracked. "You could have called and reminded me."

"When you didn't call Monday, I ..." he closed his eyes for a second, shook his head and speaking fast, said, "I realized that I'd put too much pressure on you. I didn't mean to coerce you into marriage. That's not ..."

Reason in full flight, I reached out to touch him, but he shifted away slightly. "You're not coercing me. I told you that I'm willing to marry you. All I want is to be with you." I couldn't believe this was happening. I gulped, trying to think how to persuade him to ... But he looked away from me.

Then he said carefully, "Your failure to make a decision that weekend — and now, your words '*willing* to marry' – convince me that you really don't *want* to." His voice was unsteady. He stared over my head before saying, "It's probably better that I go alone." And as he moved away, he whispered, "I need to get away."

I stepped toward him and stretched out my arm to stop him. "You can't just go like ..."

But he walked into the hall and left.

I heard the front screened door close and knew that the world had come to an end for me.

My lips, my entire mouth felt dry and my fingers numb with cold. This wasn't real. I couldn't believe Hugh would just walk out of my life. He didn't even say good-bye.

Truly frightened, I swallowed an urge to scream, to bellow like a wounded animal. Wildly, I rushed to front door and stood, watched him drive away, red taillights disappearing as he turned onto the main road.

"Minty?" Sarah's voice broke my trance and I heard her footsteps in the hall. "Oh, there you are. Come on outside, girl. We have a surprise!"

Stunned speechless, I let Sarah tug my hand and lead me out to where the Chinese lanterns glowed over the crowd circling one of the tables.

"Come on, Minty, your birthday's next week. Come blow out the candles on your cake and make a wish!"

Chapter 45

September again, and I had survived two years without Hugh. The morning Philabelle expected him to return from Kosovo, I woke tired and grumpy despite blue skies and sunshine. When I opened the door to let Buck out, I inhaled a lungful of crisp fresh autumn air. Fall usually invigorated me and I held onto that expectation as I prepared breakfast. I concentrated on the moment, not the afternoon ahead when he would come to see me.

Brave words, but it was a long, tense morning of waiting. Lunch tasted like paste and cardboard and I gulped two cups of coffee. After showering and vacillating over what to wear, I choose a black and white hounds' tooth checked skirt, a white silk shirt and a flaming red cardigan — which I could discard if I started sweating. For courage, I added a flamboyant pair of red and black dangling earrings.

Two years older, I wondered what Hugh would see in me. I remembered my mother, old at sixty-six, but illness had led her to debility and discomfort. For me, I was healthy – as if age had not begun its destructive process — but during the past two years, I had struggled to rout the hollowness inside me in Hugh's absence.

Buck sensed my nervousness and stuck as close to me as possible. Finally his nuzzling demanded my attention and I leaned down to run my fingers through his scraggly top-knot. Suddenly, he drew away, listened intently and I, too, heard a car driving in.

Taking a deep breath, I walked through the front hall. I trembled internally as I opened the door and remembered Lynn's warning that Hugh might find some younger woman overseas. I watched him park and get out of the car.

I stepped out, holding on to the porch railing to steady myself.

Hugh stared up at me as he walked toward the steps.

My heart beat painfully fast. I had to blink to prevent tears. Handsomer than I remembered, he met my eyes.

"May I come in?" he said.

His voice vibrated through every nerve in my body. I wondered what he saw as I looked down at him. My hand went to my neck as if I were choking. I twisted my mouth into a smile, nodded like an idiot, managed to say, "Please." And gestured a welcome.

As he started up the stairs his eyes never left my face. From the top, I could see more gray in his hair.

"Come inside," I said and stepped back. My heart bounced around in my chest like a rubber ball. At least he's alone, I thought, whatever that portends.

"I made whiskey sours to celebrate your return." I forced another smile, my voice steady.

He asked, "And whole peanuts?"

I fumbled opening the fridge for the pitcher. I wondered if Hugh would get out the glasses as he used to.

No. His hands rested on the back of a chair, his face expressionless. Oh God, I thought, he's going to tell me he's married someone else.

"There's peanuts in the bowl over there," I pointed and set the pitcher on the counter. Perspiration trickled down between my breasts as I reached up to get the glasses. Maybe it was time to shed the sweater, I thought, concentrating on each action.

Fortunately Buck had followed us and distracted Hugh, who leaned down to fondle him.

Behind me, he asked, "We have a lot of news to catch up on, don't we?"

I nodded, took two cocktail napkins out of a drawer and, with the glasses, walked over to the table, saying, "Uh huh. A lot of changes." My mouth was so dry I licked my lips and swallowed trying to moisten my throat. Nervousness blanked my mind.

Hugh brought the bowl and the pitcher over, put them on the table and pulled out a chair for me.

"Philabelle says you've been busy running the new Whitman Revitalization Committee," he said, as we sat down at the table.

I shook my head, "No. I've taken pains to avoid 'running' it." I filled our old fashioned glasses, relieved that he introduced that subject. "Gus, William and Joe all have the final say." I pushed his glass toward him, sneaking a quick look at his face. He was smiling that quirky superior smile.

"I can't believe you don't contribute a lot, keeping the others on track. You're an excellent organizer, Minty." The smile relaxed a bit before he lifted the glass to his lips. "What about the demons Morton and Schultz?"

I shrugged and said, "Morton's one of us. Fortunately, Schultz moved to Texas. I suspect Gus's involvement was a threat." I sipped my drink and decided that although Hugh appeared controlled, his shifting eyes indicated his nervousness. There was something on his mind.

I reached for the peanut bowl. "Oh!" I jumped up, nearly tripping over Buck, who had lain down under the table between us. "I forgot something for the shells. We can't ..." I stopped, my face flushed as I almost said 'dump them on the porch floor'. I pretended to fumble for an appropriate dish, glad that he couldn't see my face.

"It was also *Philabelle* who told me that Jesse and Mike bought Clay's Market and have settled into Whitman without any noticeable waves in society's boat," he said, emphasizing who had kept him informed. "Where are they living?"

I put the dish on the table, aware that Hugh had not helped himself or started to shell the peanuts. He doesn't remember; he's forgotten all our silly rituals, I thought. My insides quivered as a torrent of apprehension washed over me. Hugh diddled with his University ring, no longer looking at me. If he's married someone else, I'll just die!

I took a quick breath and said, "They're in The Manse until they finish the apartment over the Market." I faked a light laugh, conscious that my e-mails *had* been impersonal. "Gus often comes down from Alexandria to stay there, too."

I took another sip from my glass telling myself the rosary of what I'd learned in self-reflection: to acknowledge my feelings, however distasteful; decide when to relinquish control and when to exert it.

"It must be nice for you to have Jesse closer," he said. He leaned down and wiggled his fingers at Buck, who moved away from me, closer to Hugh.

I grabbed the peanut bowl and hastily shelled nuts. "Yes. They took over, after Philabelle moved to Creek Woods. Are you comfortable there with her?" I held out some nuts for Buck and he returned to me.

Hugh said, "Yes, but it felt odd. I miss my old house."

I offered him some nuts. His hand brushed mine when he took them. I squelched a spurt of desire. Hugh hadn't said whether he had found some one new and until he did ...

"You've accepted Gus Nourikian into your social world, I take it," he said grinning.

"What else could I do after he paid such a good price for the Manse?" Then added, "Rachel, Howard and the kids visit me regularly, too. She's quite successful in ballroom dance competition, you know." I kept busy shelling nuts. "After Clay and Marge sold the Market, they spent last winter in Florida. They'll go again in January, I expect."

I was babbling, my nerves as tight as violin strings. I wondered how to finesse Hugh into saying whatever he had to say. If he didn't say something soon, I'd come right out and ask.

"You on good terms with Clay again?" Hugh drummed his fingers on the table. Reluctant to break the bad news to me, probably.

Aware that I was crumbling a peanut shell to powder, I relaxed and nodded, "Finally! I coerced him into talking to me and we agreed we'd been friends too long to sustain hard feelings." I smiled, recalling the circumstance and said, "I used Jesse's interest in buying the Market as an opener and reminded him that Marshalls, Truebloods and Whitmans are all kissin' kin." Hugh smiled at me like old times. My heart skipped a beat.

Then he asked, "How's Lynn doing? You wrote that she saw a lot of Gus." I refilled his glass and he took a gulp.

I babbled, "Yes, they've become an item. Philabelle and I have a bet on the date that Lynn becomes the Lady of the Manse." The bowl was full of shells and I rose to dispose of them, reflecting that once I had acknowledged to myself my ambivalence toward Billy, I'd been able to forgive Lynn. Then Lynn had forgiven herself — the first step toward her accepting our renewed friendship.

I rejoined Hugh and sat across from him. I felt a smile on my lips thinking of Lynn. Apparently, that encouraged Hugh who returned it fully.

"I enjoyed your e-mails and could imagine the sights you saw," I said. That was true, but I had resented that they sounded more like a travel log than personal communication – as apparently mine had felt to him. Then I remembered Lynn's comment, like itchy poison ivy, regarding his social life in Kosovo. Rather more tartly than intended, I asked, "Did you come home alone?"

Hugh frowned with surprise and said, "On a plane with a couple hundred other people? What do you mean?"

Having hoist myself on my own petard, I decided to say precisely what I meant, "Lynn said she wouldn't be surprised if you found an attractive young Kosonovian woman and ..."

"Kosonovian?" He chortled at my pronunciation and for the first time sounded and looked like himself. "There were lots of them around, but I didn't bring one home with me." He leaned back and stared at me grinning broadly.

"You're teasing me now, Hugh, and I'm not in a playful mood." I released a trace of anger into my voice. "I'm having a hard time here."

Impatiently, he leaned closer, his face serious, both arms on the table, "What is it you're asking?"

Feeling as if I were sinking into quicksand, I asked bluntly, "Do you still want me to … eh, marry you?" During the two years, I discovered that for me Whitman was a wasteland: a vacuum without him.

His annoyed expression faded to cold and, dead serious, he said, "Isn't the question more whether *you* want to marry *me*? You made it abundantly clear, two years ago, that it was not marriage with me that you wanted." Abruptly he rose and moved around the room to stare out the window at the field.

Mentally I traced his silhouette, the angle of his head, the way he planted his feet on the floor – shapes all so familiar that my hands could feel them. Realization of the depth of my love for Hugh overwhelmed me and I knew that I'd have to reveal the worst of my frailties.

I'd seldom seen Hugh angry, but I recognized it in his eyes when he looked at me and said, "I was tempted to take care of business here and leave without seeing you. So tell me, Minty, what do you *want* from me?"

Too stricken to think of anything but the truth, I said, "I want you to love me, to marry me."

Hugh grunted with exasperation and said, "You thought it wouldn't work before. What makes you think it would now?" He turned his back to me.

I spluttered, "I've changed."

Looking at me again, but, as if I hadn't spoken, he said, "Your rejection was very painful. I'm not prepared to go through that again."

Breathing deeply to relax, I called on my determination to live with the flawed, but truthful person, I knew myself to be. Painfully in touch with the intensity of my love for Hugh, I answered, "I never meant it as rejection. But I need to tell you *how* I've changed." As so often now, tears rose close to the surface. I squeezed my eyes tightly and stammered, "Regardless of what you decide."

"It certainly felt like rejection," he spoke less harshly, but paused. I opened my eyes and saw him, still standing and rubbing the back of his neck. "We've been best of friends for a long time," he hesitated. "I'm still prepared to be friends, but …" His voice trailed off into silence and he stared just over my head.

As if uncomfortable in our presence, Buck stood at the door and woofed. Hugh let him out.

'Best of friends' wasn't good enough for me — for us, I knew. My fingers felt cold and it was essential that I be absolutely honest with Hugh. For a second I faltered, but with him here before me, I knew the moment was now or lose him forever. I licked my lips and began, "I, eh … " I gulped and blurted it out, feeling myself blush from the neck up, "I have a confession …"

When I hesitated, breathing shallowly, he turned and asked softly, "What is it, Minty?" as if I were his patient.

"It wasn't until after Billy died … and I tasted independence again that I realized how … I had let him dominate me." I searched for the precise words. "In retrospect, I'd walked a tightrope during our marriage. I submitted as Southern ladies are taught to do. Yet, at the same time I thoroughly enjoyed the life *he* designed for us." I glanced down and saw my fingers twisted together painfully. I released them and reached for my glass.

My voice rose in pitch, but I couldn't stop. "When I discovered the extent of Billy's infidelities, I let anger consume me. You remember my *generous* act of allowing Billy to continue living in our home?" I met his eyes, shamed at my duplicity, "That was my Janus face, Hugh. I refused to release him from the yoke of marriage. Then for three years, I ruled the roost." He sat down facing me.

Suddenly weary of Billy's intrusion, I rested my head on my hand. "Until Billy inadvertently engineered his own death," I shuddered with shame and added, "and I was … relieved," I used the gentler word. "Until the guilt set in."

I held my breath and looked at Hugh. Arms on the table, he stared at his clasped hands.

"I understand that," he said softly. "I watched you learn to appreciate your freedom after he died. I saw how you took charge of your life."

I groaned. He's horrified at what I said and no wonder, I thought. What kind of woman felt relief when her husband died? Despite Billy's absolution, I feared Hugh's reaction. I had ruined any chance of our being more than friends. How could we even be friends, if he understood fully? I had revealed too much. I started crying openly.

He sat up straight, but still avoided my eyes, and said, "So you assumed that if you married me, I'd control you, take away your independence — like Billy did?"

"No." I ran a napkin carefully under my eyes, blew my nose and shook my head. "Well, yes. Partly that, but when Lynn told me she had — you know – with Billy, I grew very resentful. I wanted revenge, sort of." I paused, "I had always been jealous of Lynn: she was petite and pretty and I was big and *smart*. I got tired of being smart and efficient, but I did want to be in control."

"Oh, come on, you've loved being smart your whole life and …" he snorted, "being efficient."

"Dammit! I can't help it, but I *am* smart and …" I defended myself until

I remembered my misreadings of Rachel, Clay, Lynn, and Gus. That made me hesitate, and I added quietly, "And usually efficient."

"Okay," he held up his hand, looking at me now. "Don't fuss. I'm sorry you felt controlled in your marriage and that Lynn cheated on you with Billy. You went through a rough time. So you rejected me because you were afraid of my cheating on you? Or being controlling?"

"I didn't reject you. Dadgummit!" I'd lost my train of thought and restarted. "I'm not very skillful at explaining how all that affected me. But I wasn't strong — like you — and not as in touch with my feelings. But I've changed over two years."

He shook his head and mumbled something which I didn't catch.

I continued, "I love you enough that I'm not afraid of marriage now." I disliked the desperate tone in my voice, but allowed my weakness to show anyway. Irritated at his lack of response, I barked, "Why can't you understand?" He jumped up and strode across the room and back again as if too angry to sit. I demanded, "Don't you believe that I've changed?" I was surprised when he sat down again.

"I've changed too, Minty." Wary, I watched as he pressed both hands against his forehead, his mouth taut and grim.

Apprehensive, accepting that he was reluctant to hurt me, I clasped my hands, holding on to my composure. But my fingertips were icy cold and I told myself to take rejection courageously, like a lady.

Finally, he said, "You think I don't understand." He was breathing heavily and his voice quivered, as if uncertain. "I almost lost my son because of an unsuccessful marriage." He shook his head as if to discard the memory. "So I'm not unaware of the risks of remarriage."

I held my breath and closed my eyes, until he said, "I courted you, patiently, until I believed that you and I – with the strong foundation of our friendship – that we loved each other enough to make it worth the risk, the effort to keep it good." I opened my eyes when he muttered, "Then without explanation, I thought you dumped me."

Confused by two questions in mind, I wondered: had he quit loving me? Self-centered, I had forgotten his divorce and his struggle to keep in contact with Smith. I'd forgotten how painful that must have been. How could he think I had rejected him? Overcome with remorse, tears of regret ran down my cheeks. All I could say was, "I'm sorry, Hugh. I'm so sorry that I failed …"

I fumbled for Kleenex. He rose, got the box from the counter and handed me a tissue.

"For God's sake, quit crying," he growled, almost gently.

Buck woofed at the door and Hugh went to let him in and stood staring out side. During the silence, I heard Buck slurping up water. Without turning around, Hugh asked, "Where are the goats?"

Caught off guard, I played it his way. "You knew Edna had pulled out the tether? Well, she got pregnant and the Warners took care of her for me. I gave them the kid and — Oh! Did you know that John and Peg Keene have a little daughter? I gave Edna and Claude to them." Nattering again, as if we were still friends.

When he didn't speak, I added, "They keep Edna fresh and make goat cheese." As Billy had planned to do, I remembered. "It's good, too."

He turned around, looking at me as if I were stark raving mad.

Totally discomposed now, I rose, returned the tissue box and realized how much time had passed with nothing resolved between us. We'd both go crazy if we didn't settle the issue of marriage.

"Hugh," I met his eyes and said firmly, "We need to talk this through."

"Yes, at least finish what we started." He walked away from the door and said, "I do understand why you were angry, resentful. I was observant enough to see how Billy used people. But he did love you. You can't doubt that?" he asked.

I nodded, as Billy's last words echoed in my head. Automatically, I reached to touch Hugh's hand, briefly. Hugh felt it; his lips twitched a slight smile and he followed me to sit again.

Then he continued, "Minty, you were the perfect wife for Billy: intelligent, vibrant, a society leader and an extremely attractive woman." I smiled and shook my head.

He paused, ran his fingers through his hair. "And, like all the rest of us, you loved Billy and were blind to his flaws. I understand perfectly the pain of your disillusion, because I loved you, too." His laugh seemed touched with irony and he added, "I dreamed that someday you and I would marry."

I must have made a noise, because Hugh lifted a hand and, his tone serious again, continued, "I accepted your marriage to Billy, made an unsuitable one myself and when Billy died, I …" he drew in his breathe. "I had a moment of pure joy."

"Agh, …" I gasped, like me! "You did?"

Hugh nodded his head. I thought he looked tired. His shoulders sagged and he leaned an arm on the table. I recognized his pain. He straightened up, nodded and said, "I felt guilty, off and on for months, before I rationalized guilt into neutrality."

For a bit, we were silent. Probably, both digesting this common experience. Hugh had surprised me. I felt a new kinship; it was a dreadful experience feeling relief at someone's death. And the shame, the inability to do penance were intolerable.

Oblivious to that, Hugh looked at me, his face anxious. "Can you see how your rejection …?"

"I *didn't* reject you." I interrupted," I understand how you felt, but I never for a minute didn't love you."

Hugh laughed harshly, closed his eyes for a minute, opened them and said, "I was a fool not to realize that you might have felt relieved when Billy died and the guilt that it precipitated." He shook his head. "Too intent on giving you time before I declared my love, I forgot to be a doctor. I should have realized." His forehead furrowed with lines of such dismay that I reached towards him and he took my hand, holding it firmly.

"Can you forgive how clumsy, how inept I was, in my arrogance?" I hesitated, but determined to make it perfectly clear, I added, "Both Lynn and Sarah, in their different ways, told me to get off my high horse and I've done that."

"That's more appropriate than arrogance." Hugh laughed. I wondered how he could be amused.

Nevertheless, I insisted, "But can you forgive me? I really have changed."

"Not drastically, I hope. I liked the original Minty, quite a bit." He chuckled and squeezed my hand.

I rather liked the new me, too and felt hopeful.

He, however, had more to say. "Unfortunately, like you, I've changed, too."

I gasped, convinced that my confession had come too late! I clenched my teeth, trying to avoid hearing him say he no longer loved me.

Instead he continued, "In Kosovo, I discovered how desperately doctors are needed in other parts of the world. While I'm still capable of it, that's what I want to do. What I *have* to do is use my skill, my knowledge in some of those places." His eyebrows drew together and his eyes confirmed his determination. "I can't settle down in Whitman."

He's going to leave me again and maybe for good, I thought. The song, 'How you gonna keep 'em down on the farm now that they've seen Paree?' ran through my dazed brain.

He interrupted my thoughts. "You think that I'm strong. Maybe so, but I was the younger brother to a brilliant and handsome older son." He met my eyes and smiled and said, "Ironic, isn't it? But it explains why your reluctance hurt so much. Now *I* need reassurance …"

I could see his vulnerability by the expression on his face and blushed with shame that I had wounded him so deeply. I knew that the new me would never hurt him and hoped it wasn't too late.

Trembling, I said, "You're telling me that you don't love me anymore, aren't you?" The bottom fell out of my world.

Hugh made a noise, a sort of angry chuckle, and said, "Apparently, *nothing* can change the way I love you. Best of friends doesn't describe all that I feel for you."

"Hugh," I looked at him, my eyes blurry with tears, and played my ace. "If you love me and want to go to Africa, South America — even Afghanistan — there's nothing in Whitman I can't leave."

He tilted his head, smiled his skeptical smile, and said, "Leave your family? Buck? All the work you're doing for the town — all the things that you're so good at, that make you happy?" He shook his head. "It's asking a lot."

In desperation, a Bible quote came to mind: "'Entreat me not to leave thee, nor from following after thee. Whither thou goest, I will go...'" I said.

He looked startled, as if I didn't know what I was saying. Miffed that he put me on the defensive, I declared positively, "I love you. Do I have to *beg* you to marry me?"

"All that you have going for you? You'd go with me?" He looked really surprised.

"Dammit, Hugh! Do you want to marry me or not?" I slapped my hand on the table, startling him. Even Buck, who had been snoozing there, yelped and jumped, bumping his head. "My children are adults and Buck would be happy with Jesse and Mike. I'd miss watching my grandkids grow and develop, but I can send them Flat Stanleys from strange places." I sighed, "My children don't *need* me anymore." I smiled at myself.

I watched his face change with pleasure, from plain to handsome. My knees felt weak, but my heart began to sing. He picked up my hand and held it to his cheek.

"*I* need you, shug," he said. His smile thrilled me through and through.

"But the world needs you, too; you're a true healer, my dear."

Still holding my hand, he rose, pulled me up from the chair, and, with a lascivious grin, said, "Yeah, I am a good doctor. But more important, I'm a more manly man when I'm with you." He put both arms around me and we both burst out laughing – a laugh of understanding, forgiveness, friendship, love and passion.

*   *   *

In the warmth of our bed, Hugh sleeping soundly beside me again, I woke in the serene darkness.

A strange compulsion drew me to stand by the window. Naked and chilly,

I gazed out, past the backyard to the meadow where Billy had died. In that moment I realized that his ghost wouldn't haunt me any more. Did I believe in ghosts after all? Were his visits only a form of neurotic hysteria? I sighed, because I didn't know. I rather liked believing that Billy's ghost had visited me in order to heal my wounds.

I shivered in the cold and returned to the bed where my heart's husband slept and slid in gently beside him, perfectly content.

Fini

In 1938, circumstances took me, a recent college graduate from Blue Mountain College, Mississippi, from my home in the Deep South to seek my fortune in the wide world. On subsequent visits down south, now neither a true Southerner nor a Damned Yankee, I was proud and intrigued by the way small town southerners have adapted to the social changes since my youth, while maintaining their ties to their antebellum heritage. This inspired Rough Ride on a High Horse; the story of a mature Southern Lady, with world experience, dealing with romance in this transitioning environment. Early in life, I formed the habit of dreaming stories that merged into writing. Some poems and excerpts from travel journals have appeared in various literary magazines. Retirement provided the time to graduate to novels. The first, THE WISE CHILD was awarded first place by the Washington Press Association and honorable mention by the Federal Press Womens Association. After a career of forty years and world travels, I retired to write, take art classes and socialize with family and friends. Now I make my home near my daughter-in-law, Irene, son, Kim, grandson, David and the cat, Ajax, in Bellevue, WA.